1

Those open spaces outside the sub-district town, where the tents of the Great Kanchana Circus were pitched. Seen from a distance, the big top looked like the summit of a mountain range. The flag atop it fluttered in the wind. Enjoying this pleasant evening breeze at the ticket counter stood the owner of the circus—Sarang Daaji Shinde.

On either side of the circus tent were freshly furrowed fields, on which were gathered hundreds of bullock carts. The bullocks, freed from their yoke, were eagerly chewing the dry jowar stalks placed before them. The horses were dipping their muzzles into their own share of fodder. The Great Kanchana Circus was an event which the assembled crowds had awaited for months together—such was the reputation it had earned. Now that it had arrived in their neighbourhood, the villagers wouldn't miss it for anything.

At the entrance to the big top, two tea plantation companies had set up big kiosks. These companies had lately taken to promoting the favourite drink of the White sahibs: tea. These kiosks would be put up in village bazaars. Palates accustomed to buttermilk and jaggery syrup were now being lured towards this foreign drink served free and piping hot.

As on other days, today, too, huge crowds had gathered round the circus grounds, ogling at the painted cut-outs of the great feats of courage and adventure they would soon witness inside the tent. Right in front of the big top was a hoarding that had been framed in a rectangle of bright little lamps. It showed the picture of a ferocious tigress with its jaws wide open, its red tongue leaping out from behind menacing teeth. Holding the jaws firmly in her hands was a young girl. The kids gathered around this hoarding pointed at the girl and excitedly called, 'Kanchana! Kanchana!'

Another cut-out on the other side showed a herd of gallivanting elephants. The elephant in the lead had curved its trunk nicely in the middle, creating a crescent seat. On this couch sat Kanchana, sporting a bright smile and waving to the audience assembled there.

There was plenty else on display on these hoardings and cut-outs that promised the spectator a magnificent visual feast. There was the trapeze with its high-slung swings, smart young girls with impossibly flexible bodies caught midway between one swing and another; acrobats and jugglers in the middle of acts that defied all laws of gravity; monkeys on mono-cycles, button-eyed chimpanzees, nightingales from different parts of the world, rainbow-hued parrots and, among them, the cockatoo with its resplendent plumage and sharply bent beak. These displays were designed to fire the imagination and stoke the appetite, and they were doing exactly that.

Sarang Daaji had worked as a Subedar with the British Indian Army for a few years. He was by instinct an army person, hence extremely disciplined. The journey of his life—starting as a cowherd in a small village and ending up as the proprietor of one of the biggest circuses in Asia—was inspiring.

Satisfied with the size of the crowd assembled at the ticket counter, Daaji began to walk back towards his tent when Kanchana emerged from it, dressed in a muslin shirt over breeches and knee-length leather boots. She possessed a strong, supple, five-foot-nine-inch-tall body that combined the best elements of Maratha and Punjabi blood. Her lithe

THE GREAT KANCHANA CIRCUS

Vishwas Patil is one of the most acclaimed Marathi writers today. He has written iconic novels like *Mahanayak, Chandramukhi, Pangira, Zhadazdati, Panipat, Sambhaji, Nagkeshar* and *Lust for Mumbai*. He has also written a literary biography of Anna Bhau Sathe, the founding father of Dalit Literature in Maharashtra, titled *Annabhauchi Dardbhari Dastaan* (Anna Bhau: The Upholder of Dalit and Women's Literature; published by Sahitya Akademi), which is considered an outstanding work by literary critics. He has received the Priyadarshini National Award, the Bharatiya Bhasha Parishad Award (Kolkata) and the Sahitya Akademi Award for *Zhadazdati* and the Gadkari Award for *Mahanayak*. *Panipat* has received thirty-eight awards since its publication in 1988. *Panipat, Mahanayak* and *Sambhaji* have been published in English by Westland Books. In 2020, he was awarded the prestigious Dr Indira Goswami (Mamoni Raisom Goswami) National Literature Award. His latest published works include three novels in the ongoing Shivaji Mahasamrat quartet on the Maratha Empire.

Nadeem Khan has been a teacher of English since 1973. He retired as Head of the Department of Languages, Shivaji Science College, Amravati in 2010. In 2011, he became the founding director of the Western Regional Centre of the Indian Institute of Mass Communication run by the Ministry of Information and Broadcasting, at which post he remained till 2018. Other than translating four other novels by Vishwas Patil, he has also brought into English the novels of the young Marathi writer Avadhoot Dongare, as also the works of celebrated writers like Bhau Padhye, Rangnath Pathare and Anant Deshmukh.

THE GREAT KANCHANA CIRCUS

VISHWAS PATIL

TRANSLATED BY
NADEEM KHAN

ekadā

ekadā

First published in Marathi as *The Great Kanchana Circus* in 2025 by Majestic Publishing House

Published in English in 2026 by Ekadā an imprint of Westland Books, a division of Nasadiya Technologies Private Limited

No. 269/2B, First Floor, 'Irai Arul', Vimalraj Street, Nethaji Nagar, Alapakkam Main Road, Maduravoyal, Chennai 600095

Westland, the Westland logo, Ekadā and the Ekadā logo are the trademarks of Nasadiya Technologies Private Limited, or its affiliates.

ISBN: 9789371974561

10 9 8 7 6 5 4 3 2 1

Typeset by Jojy Philip

Printed at Parksons Graphics Pvt. Ltd

frame, tapering waistline, limpid eyes and pearly set of teeth made her striking to look at.

Seeing her father, she first hugged him tight and then bent down to touch his feet. Patting her back in the style of a wrestler, admiration ringing in his voice, he asked, '*Pori*, is everything in order? Have you checked out the elephants and horses?'

'Yes, Baba. I just took a round. The men have readied them for the ring.'

'And your Lakshmi? Has she been fed?'

'Of course, Baba! Why do you have to ask every day?'

'We are in a dangerous trade, pori. Double-checking is paramount. You thrust your head into a tigress's jaws, and our other artistes stake their lives around animals that are inherently wild—no amount of caution is enough.'

'But is it necessary to do it every day?'

'Yes, absolutely. I've done it as a part of my army training, but I want this meticulous checking to become your second nature too!'

'Okay, Baba, point taken.'

'I know that your heart is altogether with our two hundred animals and the three hundred people who work with us; but without the head coming in, you can jeopardise everyone and everything!'

'Understood, Baba, understood!'

'And stop being frivolous, or I'll be cross.'

'Ah, really, you'll be cross with me?' shrieked Kanchana in delight. 'Try it, Baba, try it!' With that, she swung her arms round her father's shoulder, gave him a sloppy kiss on his cheek and ran away laughing. Daaji looked at the receding figure with a mixture of mock anger, joy and pride.

The sky was turning dark. The first strains of bandmaster Charlie's musical instruments began wafting out of the tent. For a few days now, Charlie had been getting a whiff of something burning somewhere within his company and was on the alert. The Great Kanchana Circus had earned for itself a place among the top circuses in all of Asia. With its fame spreading far and wide, Daaji wouldn't be surprised if this rapid rise upset someone somewhere. In any case, historically, the circus world had been a notoriously fertile ground for subversions and seditions—tents suddenly caught fire mid-show, poisonous meat was fed to crowd-pulling carnivores, top artistes were lured away overnight with higher pay packages; in effect, anything was possible.

In the last fifteen years, tying wheels to their feet, Sarang Daaji Shinde had taken his circus troupe across the length and breadth of India: from Karachi–Lahore in the west to Calcutta–Dhaka in the east; from Rameshwar down south to Pushkar, Kashmir, Gudmukteshwar up north; and to Assam, the home of Goddess Kamakhya, in the north-east. They had trodden over the soil of East Asia too: Burma, Jakarta, Malaya, Thailand, right down to Ceylon.

'After all this adventure,' Daaji would often tell his daughter, 'the heartless world has taught me a one-point lesson.'

'What's that, Baba?'

'It doesn't take much intelligence or skill to handle these so-called wild animals, but what's truly challenging is to find a remedy for the violence of the animal that hides within a human being.'

The closeness between Sarang Daaji's beloved daughter Kanchana and the flame-striped Bengal tigress Lakshmi was a subject of intense discussion among the company employees. The affection they shared was astounding. Could they actually be breathing through the same pair of nostrils? It was a good thing that at least, up until now, Kanchana slept in her own tent and not in the tigress's cage.

Altogether, Kanchana's close relationship with the birds and animals of the circus was quite puzzling, to the extent that many considered it unnatural; some even considered it supernatural! Some conjectured that Kanchana Kagwadkar knew the language of animals, which was why the dumb creatures thought of her as one of their own. One call, and a ferocious creature like the lion would turn straight as a thread before her! Some others hazarded that the tigress was the ride of goddesses Durga and Mahakali, and it was quite possible that Sarang Shinde's family had the personal blessings of these goddesses, particularly his daughter. That would explain the meteoric rise of the father–daughter duo.

2

Outside the circus tent, it was pitch dark. Inside, however, the central ring was bathed in a flood of light. All around were small, coloured bulbs, glittering like flowers woven into a young woman's hair. Up there on the bandstand, Charlie's thirty-piece orchestra had warmed up. Pleasant notes of the violin, slow dance beats and the soft entry of the saxophones, Portuguese style, could be now heard outside the tent.

The 7,000-seater tent was full to capacity, and ticket sale had stopped. With such a big circus in the vicinity, spectators had arrived from many neighbouring villages on horseback and in bullock carts to experience a grand visual treat. They had unyoked their animals in the fields on either side, laid out fodder before them and polished off their bhakris out in the open before the show began.

The large crowd of female spectators was marvelling at the image of womanhood that Kanchana presented. A woman in India was yet nothing more than a slave. Even the city girls were required to observe purdah. There was prohibition on their roaming with uncovered heads and faces in the bazaars and in other social circles.

Being a widow was a sin. Whatever the reason for the husband's death, she was branded as being responsible for it. 'She's eaten up her husband,' would be the common refrain. A widow was at the very root of everything inauspicious.

Going to school was a sin, too; in fact, worse than a sin, it was a rebellion against society, an impudence not to be tolerated. Villagers had lately begun to hear of the people of Pune and Bombay, and the dissolute lives they had begun to lead. They had even come to hear the shocking news of some city dwellers, particularly the Parsees, sending their girls to school. And now, here was Kanchana, this chit of a girl, dressing up in shirt and trousers like an English memsahib and wrestling with tigers in full public view! It was a scenario that these poor, innocent women couldn't have imagined in their wildest dreams!

An interesting event of a similar nature, however, had unfolded some ten or fifteen years ago. In the village of Khadaklat in the state of Kapshi near Kolhapur, a girl called Tarabai, the daughter of Gulab Shinde, had sprung into public attention. She too had begun to wrestle with tigers as if she were a boy! She was the first woman wrestler who had had the guts to slap her thighs and jump into an arena that was the exclusive preserve of men. The small circus run by her had become a topic of discussion in the states of Miraj, Sangli and Kolhapur. Another Tarabai had later taken birth in a Jaat household in the Karnal-Sonepat region on the other side of Delhi. She too had turned into a sandow, a wrestler, and ran a circus.

3

After the show inside the tent had commenced, Sarang Seth came out and stood next to the ticket counter. His six-foot-tall wrestler's body was the kind that commanded immediate attention. On his head he wore a Kolhapuri pheta. His Jodhpuri coat reached up to his knees, below which could be seen a crisp, muslin dhoti. He was shod in brown Puneri shoes that curled up and back stylishly at the toe.

The air inside the tent was thick with excitement. The ball was set rolling with ten young girls marching in with flags, breaking into dance as they proceeded. Along with them arrived other performers somersaulting backwards and forwards. Then came the horses—Arab, Turk and some of the snow-white Russian stock—proud animals strutting about arrogantly. Some among the spectators whispered, 'This Sarang Seth has always had a fetish for horses, you know! Even before he went into the army.'

These foreign horses of multiple colours—roan, brown, black and milky-white—were given the best possible feed; as a result, they looked handsome, strong and agile. People hadn't seen such a majestic bunch even in the stables of kings and nobles.

The tent was lit up with thousands of colourful bulbs. Faces coated lime-white and painted over with red stripes, some eight or ten clowns loitered into the centre ring. This electrified the kids and set off peals of laughter and clapping. The midgets could be seen among them. They got between others' feet and tripped them, much to the merriment of the spectators.

Next came wagons carrying chimpanzees inside them. Five camels followed with their peculiar hopping, swaying stride. Bears came dancing in to the tune of Charlie's band. And suddenly, from nowhere, a covey of forty–fifty parrots in multiple hues flew in and out like a swarm of bees. Right after them rolled in twenty-two wagons carrying tigers and leopards. Charlie changed his tune. Drum-sticks caressed the taut leather ever so lightly to go with the waltz music that had begun to weave its magical web. Twenty-one wagons made their way towards the centre ring, carrying inside them the kings of the jungle, the awe-inspiring, majestic lions. Their thick, lustrous manes were enough to mesmerise the spectators.

The music changed again. Trumpets began to blare a martial tattoo, as if calling soldiers to arms, carrying the spectators back into the times of the Puranas at the gates of ancient Ayodhya or Hastinapur. Accompanying this music rumbled in a herd of thirty-two elephants, nodding their massive heads to the rhythm of their walk towards the ring. Even the wedding procession of kings and emperors wouldn't have seen elephants decorated in such splendour. They were caparisoned with red, yellow and orange brocade, which was studded with beads and had tassels woven in silk, gold and silver threads.

The trunks and legs of the elephants were painted with floral and geometric patterns. On their backs danced beautiful young women, swaying and twisting and twirling as if they had India-rubber spines. Exuding the innocence of youth, these seventy-odd damsels created the illusion of butterflies swarming around flower-laden vines and bushes. An equal number of girls arrived dancing, bouncing, jogging and somersaulting, throwing broad smiles at the spectators. Some more came riding in on bikes and began circling the inner ring.

The tempo of the music rose. When it reached a crescendo, the spectators were treated to a sight that was straight out of a fairy tale. With a loud trumpet and its trunk raised high, in strode an elephant the size of a hillock. He couldn't have been an inch less than eighteen feet. The knowledgeable among the spectators cried out, 'Gajaratna! That's Gajaratna!' Gajaratna had become as much of a household name all across the countryside as the most famous singers and stage artistes of those times. Sarang Daaji had got special, jewel-encrusted gold sheets hammered out to fit the curvature of the elephant's beautiful tusks. As the two strode in—the elephant and its muscularly built master Sarang Shinde—it was difficult to decide who walked with a lordlier gait.

When they had arrived at the centre of the ring, Sarang threw in the elephant's direction a thick, five-foot long garland of roses, which the animal dexterously caught on its trunk. It then lifted the trunk in the manner of a trumpeter, loosened the muscles of its giant limbs with a vigorous shake and took a round of the central ring. It came to a halt in the centre of the ring and turned to face a four-foot statue of Lord Shiva placed on a high pedestal at the edge of the ring. Gajaratna stepped forward with the greatest deference, garlanded the statue, took four steps back and lowered its front body by folding its fore legs under itself. This done, it brought its head down, flapped its ears, large as winnowing-baskets, then stood up and walked back. The spectators broke into deafening applause.

Gajaratna was back in the centre of the ring. The lights went dim, very dim, and then slowly began gathering strength in the entire spectrum of colours, making it appear like a peacock unfurling its feathers in the soft morning sunlight. Something stirred on Gajaratna's massive back and straightened up in the form of a shapely human being sitting astride. That was Kanchana, the superstar of the circus. She stood up with delicate grace and performed four dance numbers on the elephant's back, swirling and swaying and somersaulting like a bird from heaven flapping its multi-coloured wings. The dance over, Gajaratna lifted its trunk backwards and picked the young woman up as if it were plucking a fruit. It held her delicately in the fold of its trunk and trumpeted in delight. The spectators clapped as if under a spell.

The band struck a slow drum roll to signal the retreat. In the lead was Gajaratna, with Kanchana sitting on its trunk curved in the shape of a seat. The rainbow-coloured lights fused into each other and cast an ethereal glow inside the tent. Kanchana smiled warmly at the mesmerised spectators, waving and then folding hands to acknowledge their love and appreciation.

As the night advanced, the enchantment of this stupendous show began firming its grip on the dazzled spectators.

The band picked up a new tune. Kanchana returned from the wing, dressed in a high-collared shirt and breeches that ballooned at her thighs, a leather whip in her hand. Charlie's band began gathering speed. Just then a tigress started to make her way through a barbed-wire tunnel that led her right into the ring.

A roar went up among the children seated in the gallery. 'That's Lakshmi, the tigress!' The beast stood up against Kanchana and licked her cheeks with her large red tongue. Then she feigned biting her wrists. Kanchana tapped her on the nostrils and the tigress growled, jumped and opened her jaws wide. The sight of that wide-open mouth and those murderous teeth brought knots in the stomachs of the children as they watched in awe.

Kanchana then marched up to the tigress and Lakshmi leapt on her shoulder. Kanchana held Lakshmi round her neck like a stole and took a round of the ring. She then got the tigress to slide off her shoulder and the two frolicked with each other, Kanchana laughing as she ran in front and Lakshmi growling and giving her a mock chase. The audience broke into loud hurrays. Their clapping could be heard a good distance away from the tent.

Once they had taken a round of the ring, Kanchana pulled Lakshmi's cheeks and the tigress opened her jaws. This was followed by the climactic piece. When Kanchana thrust her head into the cavernous maw of the tigress, even the most stronghearted adults sitting on the ring-side seats felt a thrill of fear run through them. Children clung to their mothers, and the more timid ones wet their pants. Kanchana pulled her head out of the jaws and took a bow, the tigress's saliva glistening on her face. She had won the field within minutes.

4

Kanchana woke up early that morning. She had a job to do. A new horse had been added to the circus—a gift from one of her father's friends. Its intractability was becoming a source of worry for her horse-trainers. It would either have to be broken in or kept out of the ring altogether.

She arrived with a long leather whip in her hand and stood by the ring. The lean five-foot horse stood there insolently, while a bunch of helper boys and a couple of ringmasters stood like convicts in the death row waiting for their name to be called. The Arab steed stood calm while the ringmaster next to it nursed the swollen jaw it had given him the previous night. Next to the ringmaster stood five injured sub-trainers and helper boys, with either an arm or a leg swathed in bandages. One of them had a heavy bandage on his shoulder, the result of a chewing delivered by the horse. The animal seemed to have derived a perverse pleasure out of destroying Kanchana's men one after the other.

The company owned as many as sixty-one horses of various breeds, countries and hues, but this sixty-second beast had turned out to be a particularly sadistic rogue. It lured its victim into believing that it was the most sweet-tempered animal ever. It would go and sniff him, allow itself to be petted, shrink coyly and allow the rider to seat himself on its back. It would even walk a few dainty steps to completely disarm the rider. Then, suddenly, it would throw its back so violently that the unsuspecting rider would go flying in the air and come crashing down at a distance.

Kanchana cracked her whip hard and screamed at her men, 'Come on, bring that demon into the ring. Let's see how to put it right. And what a fancy name—Phakkadrao!"

Phakkadrao refused to be tamed. It bit anyone who came from the front and kicked the unfortunate who approached from behind. The rare ones who managed to perch themselves on its back were thrown into the air in no time. Others got their feet caught in the stirrup and were dragged some distance, elbows skinned, knee-caps scraped.

It was now nine o'clock, and bandmaster Charlie was busy with his musicians hammering out some new tunes on the bandstand above the ring. Some friends had come visiting him, and they were all enjoying hot coffee. Observing the mayhem below, Charlie turned to a tall, lean, dusky young man and said, 'See that, Raghav? The state to which this new beast has reduced our mistress? D'you think you can do some magic here?'

When the girls on the swing heard this, they broke into giggles. What could this novice do when better people had failed? A loud roar of 'Jai Kaalamma Devi!' resonated in the air. Raghav leapt down the bandstand ladder like an expert swimmer jumping into a river and landed straight on Phakkadrao's back. The startled horse stiffened for a moment and then went berserk.

Horse and rider shot off like an antelope being chased by a cheetah. As they circled round the ring, Raghav gripped the horse's back between his thighs and kept shifting his balance rapidly as he cried 'Hiyya! Hiyya!' like a soldier off to war. But for all his riding skills, Phakkadrao got the better of him: it threw its forelegs into a slant and suddenly took a sharp, semi-circular swerve, throwing the rider up into the air. Raghav fell to the ground like a sack of grains tossed out of a truck. But even as he was falling, Raghav made sure that he fell well.

As he got up and dusted his clothes, he heard laughter from the swings on top. A few of the girls threw piteous glances at him. Kanchana stood wondering what was going on. Raghav collected himself and once again leapt towards the horse. Phakkadrao folded its legs deep into its stomach as it galloped full tilt. The two were speeding like bullets shot out of a gun, frothing at the mouth in unison. The horse refused to be caught and the man refused to relent. The contest had everybody hypnotised. The action got so hot that the spectators broke involuntarily into shouting and clapping.

Finally, Raghav took a frenzied leap upwards and landed straight on the horse's back. The next moment, so much dust got kicked up into the air that it became impossible for the spectators to see anything. They heard the sound of a heavy object falling. A crushing fear gripped the spectators' bellies: had the horse squashed the poor man underfoot like a banana-skin?

They heard a loud, agitated neigh as the dust began to settle. The horse lay on its side, like a bullock felled for castration; Raghav was astride its body, his hands still pulling the reins.

Phakkadrao sprang back to its legs again, and Raghav sprang up with it, his thighs still holding its back in a tight grip. Raghav gave the reins a hard tug, which sent sharp needles of pain racing through Phakkadrao's muzzle. The agony impelled it to leap out of the ring, leaving the ring behind; the horse galloped out of the circus camp and into the woods nearby, with Raghav still astride it.

The afternoon went by and the shadows began to lengthen, but there was no sign of either the horse or its tormentor. Kanchana's eyes were fixed in the direction of the woods. 'I don't care whether that rogue horse lives or dies, but that unknown rider must come back alive.'

It was evening now. The circus girls stood watching the horizon with anxious eyes. Suddenly a distant image of a horse and rider shot into view. As it neared, they recognised Phakkadrao. Its body was covered with wild thorns, brambles and caked earth, as if it had been rolling in the mud. Its dense tail too was coated in slime. However, its gait betrayed no hint of injury or distress. On the contrary, it came swaying and frolicking like a young woman returning to her once-estranged husband.

Of far greater concern was the man who had gone riding on it. Was he returning with all limbs broken and shattered? But there he sat, proudly astride Phakkadrao, throwing mischievous glances at the circus girls. His eyes finally came to rest on one and asked, 'Hullo madam, are you Kanchana Kagwadkar, the proprietor of this company?' Charlie had joined the gathering by now.

'Yes, and it appears to me that you are Uncle Charlie's friend.'

'That's right. My name is Raghav Bhosale and I've known Charlie since before he joined your company. He's been telling me amazing things about you. Putting your head in the mouth of a tigress and all that!'

'Well, yes, one has to stay a step ahead of the competition, you know. But my god! What a horserider you are! And what have you done to this beast? It's suddenly become a docile kitten.'

'Well, ma'am,' Raghav said with a mischievous smile, 'one has to stay one step ahead of the competition, don't you know?'

The three burst out laughing. 'Uncle,' Kanchana addressed Charlie, 'why don't you ask Raghav-ji to stay back tonight? He'll see for himself everything that you have told him about us.'

'Well,' said Charlie, nodding at Raghav, 'he knows a few things about circuses too. He's staying back for a couple of days—we'll ask him what he thinks of our circus.'

'Charlie, Kanchana-ji,' Raghav spoke with modesty, 'Sarang Daaji is a phenomenon among circus owners and I'm simply too small to be passing opinions on what has already been acknowledged as the queen among circuses. But yes, I'll be honoured to enjoy the hospitality of your company for a couple of days.'

'Oh, that's great. We'll be seeing each other then.'

The manner in which Raghav had brought a rogue horse like Phakkadrao into line had taken everybody by surprise. The people at the circus, and more particularly the girls, were thrilled at Raghav's victory. Gulbakshi went up to Daaji and said, 'Don't look at the young man merely as a prospective trainer or ringmaster, Daaji sahib.'

Daaji looked at him quizzically.

'If you take my advice, God has actually sent in his form your future son-in-law.'

'Hmm, that's a good thought, Gulbakshi. 'Daaji sahib, he has come here as Charlie's friend, hasn't he? Maybe he can give you a lead.'

Sarang Daaji wasn't the kind of father who made decisions on his daughter's behalf. He thought it imperative to take Kanchana's opinion before speaking to Charlie. Evenings were no time for private talks in a circus artiste's life. Whatever conversation needed to be done would have to be done now, before everybody got busy preparing for the evening show. Time thus being in short supply, he walked with firm strides towards Kanchana's tent.

Kanchana's head had been in a whirl since the horserider had returned to camp with a tamed Phakkadrao. Even as she had walked into the ring that evening, she had felt a strange excitement at seeing him sitting in the second row, scrubbed and neatly dressed and eager eyed. She was so used to having dignitaries sitting in the ringside seats that it didn't make her nervous. This young man wasn't even a dignitary, so why should she be jumpy or excited like a little girl? But each time she did her piece, her eyes involuntarily travelled to that young man sitting in the audience, and each time she felt an unusual surge of joy when he tensed up or dropped his jaws or clapped with what seemed to her like genuine appreciation.

At night, too, stretched out on her bed, she had lain wondering what kind of impression she had left on this stranger. Well, one way to find out would be Charlie. But what a stupid thought! She had never taken feedback from him or anyone else—wouldn't he consider it strange if she began quizzing him on what his friend thought of her performance? *Absurd! Get hold of yourself. Yes, he's a good man by the looks of him, all right—an attractive man too. But he's here today and gone tomorrow! So, stop being a fool and go to sleep!*

It was around a quarter past seven in the morning. In another fifteen minutes she would set off for a round of the menagerie, as was her routine, to say hello to the animals. She was a little surprised when she heard a discreet knock at her door. Charlie stood there, with his friend standing behind him, shuffling his feet.

'Sorry, Kanchu,' began Charlie with a smile, 'I hope you weren't busy.'

'Of course not, uncle. Good morning, Raghav-ji, how are you today? Why don't you come in?'

'No, we won't come in. I knew you'll be heading for the menagerie anytime now. Raghav thought he would take a round with you.'

'If it's no problem for you, Kanchana-ji,' said Raghav with a sheepish smile.

'Why would it be a problem? I love showing off my menagerie to animal lovers.' When they began their tour, Raghav instantly praised Kanchana's show from the previous evening. The performances of many artistes in the circus were of the highest caliber. In skill, he found Kanchana equal to the best of them, but the grace she had brought to every one of her items was of another order altogether. Kanchana blushed at this compliment. She knew she was failing miserably at masking her glee. She put in a few shy 'Thank you's', looking at her toes.

There were more surprises coming. She was bowled over by the knowledge Raghav possessed on circus animals. In the menagerie, he instinctively connected with them; the animals responded to his overtures with surprising ease, especially the elephants and horses—and most particularly of all, Phakkadrao. The horse simply could not contain its joy when Raghav ruffled its mane.

An entire hour gone, and it appeared to Kanchana that they had been walking for fifteen minutes at the most. Raghav was in awe of the excellent state of the animals. Another ten minutes, and they split up to get ready for breakfast.

It was around eleven o'clock, and Kanchana had been sitting musing on the events of the morning when she heard her father's heavy footsteps approaching her tent.

'Kanchu, busy?' asked Sarang Daaji as he walked in.

'Well, no, not really. I was thinking about this friend of Uncle Charlie's. What a magician he is with animals!'

'All kinds of animals, it seems,' he said with a mischievous grin. 'You two talked of nothing else at the breakfast table, and the way you were hanging on to his every word, it was an interesting exercise observing you.'

'What do you mean, Baba?' Kanchana responded, going red.

'Pori, I have brought you up as father and also as a mother, haven't I? I know you better than you know yourself. You know very well how concerned I am about you settling down. While I couldn't be happier about the way you have grown up to be an independent person—'

'Well, it's you who made me that, didn't you, Baba?'

'Yes, but I'll be even happier if we can find a life partner for you.'

'Well … '

'So, straight to the point. What do you think of Raghav?'

'What do you mean, Baba?' Kanchana turned scarlet red and refused to meet Daaji's eyes. 'I don't think anything!'

'Stop playing games with me, pori, and tell me—should we try to find out a little more about him?'

'Well … well, there's no harm getting to know a person, is there?'

'That's my girl! I'll immediately call Charlie into my office. I want you to be there too.'

'Why do you need me there?'

'Told you, girl, stop playing games with me. Come over in ten minutes' time, you hear me?' With that, Sarang Daaji delivered a thump on her back and walked away laughing.

'Well, Daaji,' began Charlie, 'I've known him for a decade now, and he's a gem, of that I can assure you. You knew his uncle, Daaji: Shripati Sali.'

'I never knew him personally, Charlie, but I knew of him,' said Daaji. 'An honourable man, he owned a successful circus company. He died a few years back, didn't he? So, how's this boy related to him?'

'Yes, old man Sali died five years ago and since then Raghav has been running his circus for Sali's widow, two sons who are wastrels and a daughter. He is Sali's sister's son.'

'Oh, I see. But how did he finish up with his uncle?' Daaji wondered.

'Well, he is a little reluctant to share that story freely. What I know is that his own mother died when he was barely four or five and his step-mother didn't treat him well. Shripatirao was very close to his sister. His wife also liked the boy. And so, the couple brought him over at a very young age.'

'But what about the father?' asked Kanchana. 'He didn't mind the son going away?'

'The father was the head-groom and horse-trainer in the stable of the Maharaja of Kurundwad. A hugely talented man, but addicted to the bottle. He took a much younger woman as his second wife and turned into a thoroughly henpecked husband. He would have been relieved to see his son settle into a more loving environment.'

'So, then, he grew up as Shripati Sali's adopted son, is it?' queried Kanchana.

'No, I don't think he was ever officially adopted. But they certainly brought him up well. I've seen his interaction with the old couple. There was a lot of mutual love and respect there. Raghav grew up to be a gifted acrobat and a wizard with animals. In due course, he became an important pillar of the circus. Before Shripatirao passed away, he granted Raghav a twenty per cent partnership in his company.'

'That doesn't matter one bit,' said Daaji.

'But what about his father, then?' asked Kanchana. 'What happened to him?'

'He doesn't talk much about his father, but he might not have forgiven him for abandoning him the way he did. He died before I made Raghav's acquaintance. I guess that chapter's closed for him. The drinking got him relatively young, from what I could gather.'

'Charlie, he looks like he's on the wrong side of thirty,' said Daaji, 'so, most importantly, does he have a woman in his life?'

Charlie laughed and said, 'Most certainly not, Daaji. I am a close enough friend to know. And yes, he's just crossed thirty.'

'Your opinion, Charlie. Would you recommend him as a match for my daughter?'

'Daaji, I would, wholeheartedly. I can't think of two people more suited to each other than these two.'

'Very well, then. Kanchu, do we take the next step forward in this matter?'

'What can I say, Baba? You and Uncle Charlie know what is best for me.'

'You clever, clever girl! As if you haven't understood a thing. All right, so be it. Charlie, can you, this young man and I sit for a drink after the last show is over?'

They were already an hour into their sitting. It was for the first time that Charlie sat drinking with his boss. Once the first few sips of Chivas Regal began circulating inside them, words came out trippingly. Sarang Daaji told stories of his father Bajappa, his older brother Kashinath and him labouring on the farms, of the friendly rivalry between the two brothers, of how despite being the younger brother, Sarang was the more robust and the more adventurous one. While Kashinath was the timid kind, Sarang was forever getting into scraps with other boys his age, sometimes even older ones. As he poured some more Chivas Regal into the three glasses, he talked about his gang that would go swinging on trees, hunting for wild fruits and birds' eggs in the jungles. They would hold swimming contests in the Krishna river. A few episodes from his life in the army, a few from his early struggles while establishing his circus and Sarang was now ready to steer the talk into more delicate areas.

'So, Raghavrao,' Sarang refilled the glasses as he made his gambit, 'it turns out that you are a circus man yourself, Shripati Sali's nephew. Never met your uncle, but I've heard great things about him.'

'He was a good man, Daaji sahib, a good administrator too, but he wasn't driven by the same vision as you were.'

'Why do you say that?'

'Well, sir, the two of you would have started off at the same time, but while his continued to remain a local circus, look at the distance your own company has travelled.'

'So, what was missing? You say he lacked the vision. How?'

'Daaji sahib, he wasn't as enterprising as you. I guess he also didn't have the same kind of passion for animals as you. I tried my best to get him interested in investing more in animals and their training, but I could not push him beyond a certain point.'

'Why? Why couldn't you?'

'Daaji sahib, although he loved me and gave me free rein to express myself as a performer, I suppose he couldn't escape the dampening influence that his sons had on him. They looked on the circus only as a business and not as a passion. They do so even now. It's always been about the returns they can get on their investment, and whether money can be better invested elsewhere.'

'It's so different in our company, Daaji, isn't it?' said Charlie. 'The energy you bring to your men, your animals, the pride you take in this circus, all that shows. They love you, Daaji—your staff and your animals. And then you have Kanchana who replicates your dedication in every way.'

'Yes of course, Daaji,' chimed in Raghav, 'that's the other critical difference—the indifference of my uncle's sons against Kanchana-ji's zeal.'

Daaji's face lit up. A door had been opened. 'So you think this daughter of mine has made all the difference?'

'Well, Daaji, your own commitment has been extraordinary, who can doubt that? But would you not say that it has been greatly reinforced by your daughter's enthusiasm?' argued Charlie.

'That's quite true. How about one more drink?'

'No, sir, not for me. You go ahead. But it's the talk of the circus world, sir, that Kanchana-ji is the star of your company. And now that I have seen her in action with my own eyes, I can say that they are not mere rumours.'

'Well, then,' Daaji took a deep breath, the Scotch helping him in no small measure to get the required impetus, 'we have been picking Charlie's brains regarding you. What he's told us is heartening. To me as well as to Kanchana. You agree, Charlie? From what you've said now, Raghavrao, I understand that you also hold us in good esteem. You think highly of our Kanchu too. So, Raghavrao, would you consider marrying our Kanchana? Charlie, tell him.'

'He's heard you, Daaji. So, Raghav, what do you think?'

'Daaji sahib, I am overwhelmed. You and Kanchana-ji belong to another orbit. I'm an orphan living in the reflected glory of my late uncle. So—'

'I know all that, son, but Charlie has known you for so long, and I trust Charlie's judgment. I find you a perfect match for my Kanchu. So, your background, and even your current status is good enough for us. Tell him, Charlie.'

'You've already told him, Daaji.'

'Yes, of course, I have. So, Raghavrao, is the proposal worth thinking about? Of course, I don't want an immediate yes or no.'

'Daaji sahib, I can only see this proposal as an honour. I am so fortunate. But—'

'Why but?'

'I'm telling you, Daaji. My uncle's sons are useless for the circus, so I'm the one running it. There's an unmarried daughter too. My uncle and aunt brought me up with great love and affection, so I continue to remain beholden to my aunt. And now, she has a problem.'

'What problem?'

'Sir, her daughter Neelima has a slight limp. Nothing serious, but even so, it has marred her marriage prospects. In the Sali community, Daaji, marrying the maternal uncle's daughter is the done thing. In fact, it is often the first choice. So, my aunt has often hinted that I should marry her. But, Daaji, we've grown up as brother and sister, and for both of us, the idea of marrying each other is unthinkable. My aunt remains unconvinced by my argument, so she still keeps hoping I will comply.'

'I see. That's a problem, then.'

'Yes, Daaji, the first hurdle is that I cannot abandon my uncle's circus and jump ship. The other is Neelu's marriage. Since I cannot reject my aunt's wish outright, I can only bide time till a match is found for her.'

'Yes, I see that you are in a moral bind. For your circus, we may be able to find a solution, perhaps. But do you think either Charlie or I could talk to your aunt?'

'I don't think that'll work, Daaji. This will only hurt her. I can only wait. Neelu is only twenty, so I hope someone will come along.'

'Raghavrao, I appreciate your sense of duty and your values. But, obviously, we cannot wait indefinitely. We will continue looking for a prospective groom, but certainly hope that you find your freedom before the next match comes along. What do you say, Charlie?'

'Daaji, this is the sensible course of action,' replied Charlie.

Kanchana, who had been listening to the conversation from behind the tent flaps, walked away quietly.

When Raghav got ready to depart the next afternoon, Charlie sent a message to Kanchana. In a little while, he saw two grooms coming, leading Phakkadrao by its reins. Kanchana followed close behind.

Raghav couldn't take his eyes off the horse. Silhouetted against the setting sun, it's glossy chestnut body looked beautiful. Even as he stood admiring the magnificent beast, Kanchana held it by the reins and said, 'Here, please take this darling horse of yours. I'm giving it to you complete with saddle, reins, stirrup and tassels.'

'How much will it cost?'

Kanchana laughed sweetly. Bending over slightly, she said in an affectionate tone, 'Our guest is big as a mountain. The cost of the horse is nothing in comparison.'

'But Kanchana-ji, how can I take this magnificent animal away from you without paying you for it?'

'Well, Raghav-ji, yes, it's a beautiful looking beast, but it's too temperamental for our people to handle. Also, it has clearly fallen in love with you, so, you have no choice but to take it with you.'

'How do you mean "no choice"? This is outright tyranny!'

'No, tyranny it is not, and that's what our Daaji sahib's instructions are. This priceless horse had best stay with the person who knows its moods well.'

'This rascal and priceless?' said Raghav with a big laugh. 'Whatever virtues your horse may possess, it is naughty beyond compare. I don't think you should pass this bundle of mischief over to anyone else.'

'Well, if you don't want to take it with you, you may discard it anywhere on the road. Once Daaji gifts something to a guest, we snap all ties with it,' Kanchana said, arching her eyebrows.

Raghav held the horse's muzzle against his chest and sent his fingers combing through its mane. 'Watch out, Kanchana-ji,' he said, 'you are going to regret this one day.'

'What for?'

'For having gifted away a God-sent horse like this one.'

'God-sent? It is more like a beast sprung out of hellfire!' Kanchana looked at Raghav and giggled.

The moment for Raghav to say his goodbyes had arrived, but her feet refused to turn around. She wished to continue this pleasant banter with Raghav. When she giggled again, Raghav felt snubbed and asked in annoyance, 'What is it that you find so amusing?'

'Oh, I'm not amused, I'm simply worried for you?'

'Why?'

'Well, you're taking this mutinous horse of ours with you, so you'd better take care.'

'What about?'

'That your limbs continue to remain intact.'

Raghav looked up at the sky in mock despair and then brought his eyes to rest on Kanchana's face. 'Let's lay a bet, madam,' he said with supreme self-confidence. 'I can state with absolute certainty that both of us are going to be fit and fighting. As a matter of fact, I am going to return to your doorstep not only with this horse, but also with a brass band to announce our arrival.'

'Why would you do that?'

'To dance in your wedding procession!'

'Mine?' As she stared at Raghav, her eyes incontinently filled up with tears.

'Of course, madam! A day will arrive when you stand next to someone at the altar. Won't you then need a horse as magnificent as Phakkadrao to add grace to the wedding procession?'

Raghav laughed out loud at his joke, not noticing that Kanchana's eyes had turned moist. Deeply upset, she responded in a raised voice, 'Enough of your fun. How do you even manage it?'

'Manage what?'

'Burying the knife in someone's heart and then letting out such a crude laughter?'

Kanchana turned around and hurriedly walked away towards her tent.

5

Kaagwad was at the border of the Bombay Presidency and the state of Mysore, a fairly affluent town in the principality of Kurundwad. Nobody from Kaagwad went too far adrift of its old, fortified walls. It had a large population of Marathas, Lingayats, Brahmins and traders. The Brahmins and the Marathas regarded themselves as belonging to a higher status. The oppressed and the nomads lived outside the town walls. They were miserably poor. The Mahamangs were considered untouchable and were treated with the greatest contempt. Their very touch was regarded as inauspicious. It was out of this tradition-bound town that Bajappa Shinde's younger son, Sarang, had ventured out, and ventured out big. He had gone all the way to the Frontier Province, right next to Kabul and Kandahar, and established a name for himself and his native land and the river Krishna.

It was the masculine pride in Bajappa Shinde's Sarang that pushed him into joining the army. He rose to be a Subedar in the British Indian Army and carried three bright yellow medals on his puffed-up chest with a panache amounting to arrogance. Sarang was the premier sportsperson of his regiment. In his veins coursed a wrestler's blood after all. His favourite activity was riding. He enjoyed grooming and training horses. In shot-putting and archery, too, he was well ahead of others.

Life was moving along merrily. The next item on his agenda was to apply for leave and go home and tie the wedding tassels round his brow. Many a father of eligible girls in Kaagwad had been making the rounds of Bajappa Shinde's house for bagging the boy. That was when war broke out in the Kabul-Kandahar region and his leave got cancelled. Skirmishes began with some rebel groups on the India–Afghanistan border.

Then happened the incident that stuck in his head and refused to dislodge itself from there. There were those two huge sand dunes between which lay a dry riverbed. Beyond, on the other bank, were half a dozen or so wretched houses—huts, actually, made of grass and mud.

Gangs of rebels would often be seen roaming on the other side of the dunes. Their squads would suddenly come racing down like a desert storm. Units of the British Indian Army posted on the hillock on this side of the riverbed would mount guard too and give bitter battle to the rebels. Sarang belonged to one such unit. If the attack was violent, these units would sometimes withdraw a furlong or so; but when they noticed laxness on the other side, they would push the rebels further behind a couple of furlongs. The white commander of the army got disgusted with this tug-of-war one day and glared at the little settlement beyond the dunes. He decided that if they had to move forward, that bunch of huts should first be razed.

The army was in dominance that day and as dawn broke, Sarang's small unit stood in front of the settlement like the angels of death. The sand and dust blowing this way and that with every gust of wind round those half a dozen huts, the date palms withering due to lack of water, that dismal poverty and helplessness and the screaming loneliness made a deep impression on Sarang's mind. The gunfire coming from both sides had either caused the mud walls to collapse or at least punched a number of holes in them. This little world was painted over with soot in no time.

When Sarang's unit closed in on the hutments, there was pin-drop silence everywhere, with not a soul in sight. Except for those structures, even the butterflies seemed to have fled away in fear. The soldiers then noticed a few lambs playing about close by. They jumped upon them and broke their necks. Their dinner that evening would be sumptuous.

The commander, however, was unhappy. How could this have happened? How could every person in the settlement have just vanished into thin air? Could this be a ruse to catch them unawares? As he began walking round the houses to take an assessment, he felt the sandy earth give out a hollow sound at a spot. He got on his knees and knocked the earth again. He then scratched the earth with his baton and hit upon a plank of wood just an inch or two below. From there to uncovering the plank and tearing it out took him just a few minutes. He was now peeping into a dark, tunnel-like structure quite like a tiger's cave. He couldn't suppress a sadistic grin at his discovery and he growled, 'All right, bastards, I'm going to get you!' He yanked out a hand-grenade attached to his belt, pulled the pin out with his teeth, tossed it into the hole and ran. Within seconds there was a dull explosion, spewing up a mushroom cloud-burst of sand and dust from below.

Immediately followed a cacophony of agonised cries in Pashtu from the other side of the huts. Within minutes emerged a bedraggled bunch of dust-laden ghosts, some fifteen or sixteen of them, thin, gaunt, emasculated with years of warfare, shivering at the sight of death, searching against hope for a reprieve. There were women among them, with children clinging to their legs. There were two girls, barely sixteen or seventeen, new mothers, both, holding their suckling infants wrapped in flimsy cloth like kittens, tight against their chest.

An old man, seemingly their patriarch, stood behind. When he saw the sten-gun wielding soldiers on the other side, he panicked and tried to run away. 'Stop, you bloody old crow!'

screamed the commander and then signalled to his men. A burst of fire and the old man fell forward and lay sprawled out on the dusty earth. The earth below his body rapidly turned red.

As the commander closed in upon the rest with his unit, the shiver among the hunted increased, their teeth chattering as if hit by a blast of cold wind. One of the infants clinging to its mother's chest began whimpering.

'You, Sarang Shende! Fire! Kill them!' the commander barked his order.

Sarang was petrified. He felt as if someone had lifted him up by his hair and held him dangling on top of a blazing cauldron. 'Sarang Shende, fire!' But Shinde's entire consciousness was snared in the terrified stares of those kids in front, in their state of helplessness, in the trembling of their knees. From nowhere at all, a strong smell of mother's milk came and flooded his nostrils. His hands stayed jammed on his gun.

As Sarang Shinde stood thus paralysed, a rat-tat-tat of gunfire broke out from behind him, exploding his heart and mind into a thousand pieces. As he saw those scarecrows standing in front collapsing like ninepins—men, women and children—he had the delusion that the bullets had shot out of his own gun. For a moment he teetered on his heels, but by sheer force of will he managed to keep standing.

'You insubordinate piece of Indian shit!' The inflamed roar from behind brought Sarang back to his senses. He turned around to see the gun of the soldier standing next to the commander still smoking from the shooting. 'You have disobeyed my orders! The orders of your superior! You shall suffer for it, do you hear?'

Sarang lifted his eyes to look at the Military Inquiry Commission seated in front of him in a semi-circle. The matter had been taken up that very evening and their judgement was ready for delivery too.

He had been dismissed from service with immediate effect. Somewhere at the lower end of the incriminating papers was a sub-note that read: Top-class sportsman of the army. Those five words—along with the predicament in which he had been placed—saved him from the firing squad. Although he was declared ineligible for any kind of retirement benefit and asked to walk out in disgrace, his life had been spared.

As far as Sarang was concerned, the disgrace was only on paper. He set out of his barracks with his trunk, feeling a sense of immense relief.

However, he could not bring himself to return to his village and decided to settle down close to his friend Beant Singh in the town of Ambala in Punjab. The road from the Afghanistan border passed through Ambala on its way further down to Delhi. It was alongside this road that Sarang Shinde put up a tea-stall. The White sahibs had only lately popularised this beverage and got the natives hooked to it. The young men in those parts loved chatting over cups of steaming hot tea.

One of Beant Singh's wife's brothers had been martyred on the Afghan front. His sister Shaira had also been widowed at the young age of eighteen. When she had received news that her husband had been admitted to the Army hospital at Patiala, she had hastened to meet the mortally injured man. The poor man's body had been roasted like a mouse thrown on a burning log. Even as he was breathing his last, he had patted his wife on the cheek and admonished in a failing voice, 'Don't waste your life mourning me. Fill it with joy.'

Shaira would stay home all day. Sarang used to love the chholey-bhaturey she cooked. Tall, big-boned and well-built, she was a particularly beautiful girl. Like her husband, she was also fond of horse-riding. With Sarang himself being a horse lover, it was natural that they should seek each other's company. They would often go riding till as far away as Kurukshetra and back. Sarang's company brought joy back into Shaira's empty eyes. Sarang, on his part, felt a thrill of excitement in her presence. He fell head over heels in love with Shaira.

Sarang didn't take much time to come to a decision and the two of them got married. They had a daughter whom they named Kanchana. One day, they took her to a renowned ascetic in Sonepath. The ascetic looked deep into the future. 'This valorous girl will attract the attention of a great king very early in her childhood. She is destined to earn glory for her father as well as for her own self.'

Ten delirious months of joy and cheer slipped by. Kanchana could now get to her feet with the support of a wall and toddle along. That was when calamity struck. An epidemic of smallpox broke out in Punjab and claimed Shaira, leaving a frightening, disorienting hole in Sarang's life.

Shaira's memories chased Sarang from all directions. He was drowning in misery. One day, he decided to return to his village on the bank of the Krishna, carrying on his shoulder the only thing that gave meaning to his life: his little daughter, Kanchana.

Smart, well-built Sarang was still great husband material, and many proposals came his way, some from the best families of the region, but Sarang would have none of it. 'No more talk of marriage,' he responded with folded hands. 'From here on, my world shall have only me and my daughter.'

Little Kanchana became the darling of the village of Kaagwad. The genes of her Punjabi mother shone through her soft, glowing, fair skin. She was a bundle of energy, prattled endlessly and was quite easy to befriend. In no time she had everyone dancing to her tune. Everyone—from the young to the grave and elderly—became clowns to get a giggle out of her. Sarja *vahini*, however, was one person whose hackles she raised. 'Jinxed brat,' she would mutter. 'Ate up her mother within days of taking birth!'

The same village, the same hangouts, the same routine, all those old, dilapidated temples and the unending stretch of cacti along the riverbank—Sarang was soon bored of the monotony of his directionless existence.

A new wind had begun to blow in this region that stretched from Kaagwad, across Miraj–Mhaisal, right up to Tasgaon. For those who had a fondness for wrestling, a passion for animals like dogs and horses, and for those who were willing to invite risks and live life on the edge, a new profession had begun to open up. Circuses had started attracting crowds and there was dire need for dauntless, swashbuckling young boys and girls who would find thrill in riding elephants and swinging on a trapeze strung eighty feet above the ground.

This wave had been triggered by the arrival of a gentleman named William Harmston, who had brought his circus to India in the winter of 1875. There was this big open ground in front of the Bori Bunder station in the Fort area of Bombay where the Harmston Circus had pitched tent. The circus boasted of a rich menagerie of around 400 animals, including elephants, horses, tigers and lions. The staff comprised 800 performers, acrobats, jugglers and other workers.

The big top had been erected on four main steel poles 100-feet high, with hundreds of subsidiary poles around the circus ring. The tent could easily accommodate 10,000 spectators at one go. There were hundreds of young boys in the circus and a band that boasted of the latest musical instruments. Over 150 young boys and girls would come dancing into the ring with the band playing a lively lilt. This novel mode of entertainment, though stationed in Bombay, had become the talk of the entire country, and people from all corners of India came in hordes to witness the amazing show almost as an act of worship.

Among those who made this pilgrimage to Bori Bunder were Dhundirajrao Patwardhan of the Sangli royal family, the Rajasahib of Budhgaon and a young Chitpawan Brahmin named Vishnupant Chhatre. Vishnupant was a police officer in the court of the Sangli royalty. Besides being an ace rider, he was an expert in all matters relating to horses, including health care. The citizens of Bombay were thrilled to the core at witnessing the amazing dance items that the circus horses performed, along with many other feats of great daring and dexterity.

The resounding ovation that the performances received went to William sahib's head and he bragged, 'Do you Indians have even a trace of the skills and the audacity to put up a show as grand as this one? You people of the East are all weak and wimpish!'

Vishnupant Chhatre felt deeply insulted. He sprang up from his seat and replied, 'Mr. William, sir, I will make you eat your words. I give you my word: if I don't bring into existence a flawless circus like yours within a year's time, I shall shave off my moustache!'

Chhatre was as good as his word. A number of his princely friends gifted him horses and elephants from their own stables. Before the year was out, he opened a circus company that brought the hauteur of the Europeans down a few notches.

6

'Look, Sarang, running a circus is no joke.' This was Parshuram Mali at the Jejuri camp of his renowned circus, dispensing wisdom to a boy he had begun to like. 'It needs the chest of a lion, the strength of a hippo and the intelligence of an elephant.'

Sarang always looked at Parshuram's giant body, his barrel chest and his luxuriant moustache with envy and admiration. Only recently had Lokmanya Tilak conferred upon him the title of 'Lion of the Indian Circus' at a function held in Bombay. From then on, his circus was recognised as 'Parshuram Lion Circus'.

The circus had recently finished a tour of East Asian countries such as Burma, Thailand and Singapore. Parshuram Mali had hired a special cargo boat for the purpose and tasted the salt of many a harbour. His shows in Ceylon and in the southern regions of India had been wildly successful. Just a few days ago he had returned from a successful tour of the tea gardens of Coorg district in Karnataka.

Wrestling had always been an obsession with the youth in Tasgaon, but lately it was circus that had captured their imagination. So much so that within the small sub-district, as many as thirty-two big and small circuses had come up, with fourteen of them commanding a country-wide presence. Around the time when the youngsters from the banks of the Krishna–Koyna–Varna were migrating to Bombay to earn their livelihoods in the cloth mills, the residents of Tasgaon and Mhaisal were getting hooked on the circus in a big way. Even auxiliary professionals like blacksmiths, carpenters, perfumers and tent-makers and people of all castes and creeds were busy establishing circus companies. The joke doing the rounds of the region was, 'How have the Marwadi youth of Tasgaon not launched their own circus yet?'

Sarang went to Jejuri to pay his respects to the presiding deity, Khandoba Raya. It was with the same devotion that he went to Parshuram next, and fell at his feet. He implored, 'Master, please accept me as your disciple!' Parshuram took him in a warm embrace. Sarang had already earned a name for himself as an ace wrestler in the tournaments organised on either bank of the river Krishna. Parshuram also knew of the man's equestrian skills.

Sarang felt a strange sense of contentment when he saw Parshuram's huge tent. Then he met the great artistes and acrobats of the circus and his cup of contentment overflowed. There was Chhabu tai who played around with wild animals, Master Bidwe, who was recognised as the best trapeze artiste in the business and acrobat Rakhumabai from Telangana, who made tigers and lions dance at the crack of her whip.

In the office of Parshuram Mali, he met the company's general manager, Ramchandrarao, a Deccani Brahman. Commenting on the efficiency of this man, an employee informed Sarang, 'Take a good look at that man. He's done his Master's in Management, or whatever you call it, from the University of Cambridge.'

'Are you joking? Why would a *Vilaayat*-returned sahib want to come here and sniff at elephants and horses?'

'That's the fun. This circus was running at Bangalore four years back when Ramchandrarao came over to meet Parshuram Baba after a show. "Such a huge setup, hundreds of men and animals under a single umbrella, their boarding, lodging, healthcare, where else can I get this kind of an opportunity to practise my management skills?" he said. "Please hire me, sir." Parshuram immediately decided to give him the opportunity. He's been working with us since then.'

The Parshuram Lion Circus became a veritable school for Sarang Daaji for the next two years. The scale was huge: 350 people and 200 animals. Food and fodder had to be arranged for so many: 100 kilos of meat for the carnivores, carts upon carts of dry fodder for the elephants, thousands of litres of water to be fetched every day from the river. The erecting of temporary toilet arrangements every time they hit a new place. Ten sanitation workers to keep the toilets clean and working. Another fifteen men and women for the kitchen. The dismantling of the camp late in the night, its re-erection in a new place; the transfer from one region to another across the length and breadth of India—Sarang was soaking it all in.

As soon as his item was over, Sarang would return to his tent to look after his daughter. Little Kanchana would sleep on his chest. 'Kanchey, little one,' he would whisper softly, 'I'm not going to spend my life playing the drum in somebody else's wedding party. I will put together my own circus.'

Sarang would enter the ring for rehearsals with his little daughter in tow. Even before she began to walk, she had learnt to ride on the back of a tiger, holding its furry back firmly in her little fists.

Sarang would often sit down with Ramchandrarao, picking his brain about the intricacies of managing a circus company. Sarang was driven by a single dream: come what may, he would create a circus company of his own some day.

He slogged night and day at the circus. Alongside this, he exploited every opportunity to make a quick dash to his village Kaagwad. He would assemble his wrestler and athlete friends at the temple ground of Kugutraya and Kalammadevi. They would practise through the night. Fencing and sword-fighting, horse-jumping, javelin throwing, shot putting, lifting iron bars and swinging on ropes tied to the branches of tall trees—these activities carried on through the night till the hens began to cluck in their coops, announcing the arrival of a new day.

Blacksmith Dagdoba and carpenter Taaranath of Kaagwad were Sarang's childhood buddies. Both of them had landed jobs in the new factory that the Kirloskars had set up in Belgaum. But eventually, both of them decided to turn down the opportunity, and joined Sarang in dreaming about their own circus company. Sarang became the target of considerable abuse for luring the young men with fanciful, unrealisable dreams.

Sarang was busy working one evening when he felt someone nudge him from behind. He turned around in the dark. A friend of his had come with a message. 'There's trouble brewing. Mahaling sends word that you should drop everything and see him immediately.'

'Now? To Belgaum? So far away?'

'No, he's lying right here, on the other bank of the stream.'

'What do you mean lying?'

'He got shot at. There are two bullets lodged in his thigh.' Sarang jumped on to a colt and galloped across the stream. They examined Mahaling's wounds in the light of a flambeau. They didn't look more than twenty-four hours old. 'What have you done to yourself, Mahaling?' Sarang asked in a worried tone. 'And why are you here instead of the armoury in Belgaum?'

'I have revolted,' groaned Mahaling.

'Against whom? The White sahibs?'

'Yes. In any case, this was bound to happen some day!'

'But why have you acted so recklessly? The underground revolutionaries of the south need you there in the factory.'

Mahaling had been working in the British armaments factory in Belgaum for the past four years as a technician. After having slogged as a mere orderly for two years, he had moved up to work in the foundry. He was among the few skilled workmen who poured melted steel for manufacturing guns. His expertise in this field, his connections with the army people and his knowledge of the movements in and around the factory were invaluable information to the revolutionaries.

Sarang and his friend immediately got busy tending to Mahaling. 'You should have been a little more circumspect, Mahaling,' Sarang remonstrated. 'What was the need for you to go revolting in such a hurry?'

'I couldn't help it, Sarang. The circumstances had left me with no choice.'

'What did you actually do?'

'There is a military post in the Belgaum fort. Three of the White officers had a personal grievance against me because I had walked in on them indulging in something that was neither legally nor morally defensible. They cooked up a fictitious complaint, accusing me of being an insubordinate rebel, and dumped me in a dark cell. A court martial inquiry was soon to begin against me.'

'So, shouldn't you have faced the inquiry?'

'Are you mad, Sarang? The inquiry was just a ruse. They just had to keep the show going till the next evening; they had already decided to shoot me dead!'

Sarang looked at his wounds and asked the pertinent question: 'How did you manage to escape from the fortress?'

'They had dumped me in a barrack located on top of a high wall. Because of its height, they had not bothered to keep the window overlooking the moat shut. It was impossible for anyone to climb down that wall, but in my obstinacy, I ripped the pagdi on my head into strips, knotted them together and began climbing down. The sentries posted on the ramparts noticed my movement and blew the siren. I just about managed to leap to the ground, and ran into the bushes, with the sentries in hot pursuit. I somehow managed to jump on to a horse and rode away. But just as I was about to exit Belgaum, their bullets found me. Fortunately, the horse wasn't hit. I rode non-stop for two days before getting here.'

'Good you came over. I needed you anyway.'

Mahaling was taken to a farm house near the mountains and treatment of his wounds began in earnest.

To fulfill the dream of building his own circus, Sarang needed a friend like Mahaling by his side. He advised Mahaling to grow a beard so that he could pass off as a Muslim.

7

Sarang woke up, startled out of his dreams of Shaira. The stars had flooded the entire sky with a smoky white light. He wanted to reach for a few stars, but an unbridgeable distance separated the sky from the edge of his terrace. His hopes crashed.

As the darkness began to fade, Sarang looked at the peaceful face of the precious girl sleeping beside him, and smiled to himself. He suddenly remembered the prophecy that the holy man of Sonepath had made about her future. 'Your little one will catch the eye of a king. Through her luck, you will accrue a lot of wealth.'

It occurred to him that it was Dussera the next day. The images of Shahu Maharaj's town Karveer, its horses and elephants and its grand processions rose in his mind's eye. The very same afternoon, Sarang tied little Kanchana to his back with a length of cloth and galloped out of his village. Father and daughter reached Miraj early in the evening. Sarang had many friends there.

Word quickly went around and soon a bunch of them assembled to greet him. They began making plans to visit Kolhapur to enjoy the royal Dussehra procession of Shahu Maharaj. They set off early in the morning, hit Hatkanangali before noon and were in Kolhapur before evening had set in.

At the Dussehra Chowk in Kolhapur, the palanquins of the local elite had begun to arrive. These included high dignitaries, chieftains and businessmen. Sarang noticed a herd of forty elephants walking into the square. Never in his life had he encountered a city that had so many horses neighing and elephants trumpeting. As soon as the sun set, the rich and famous of the city began driving in, announcing their arrival with the rattle of their four-wheeled carriages. The animals that preened themselves most in that massive procession were the horses of Shahu Maharaj's stable. They were handsome, healthy and bubbling with energy. Their riders were dressed in red livery. Their shiny leather riding-boots reached up to their knees, and on their heads they wore jaunty Kolhapuri turbans. Every one of them carried a fluttering flag atop a sharp-tipped spear.

There were more than fifty bullock carts in the procession loaded with cannons. Behind them followed cages with leopards growling inside them. Accompanying the cavalry were the foot soldiers walking on either side of the road, guns on their shoulders and shiny swords slung from their belts. The bullocks were draped in mirror-work caparisons, complete with tassels bobbing at the borders; their horns were painted in bright colours. The caparisons on the backs of the elephants, with intricate patterns sewn along their borders were a lot grander.

Suddenly, a loud, resonating sound of musical instruments invaded the air: drums, horns, Western bands, lezims, trumpets, as also the swish of thin-bladed swords cutting through the air, and their clang as they hit one another. Red gulaal tossed by the fistfuls into the air, the loud hubbub of excited conversation, the overflowing pride of the townsmen—it was a sight to beat all sights. From the front entered a herd of elephants, led by an animal that looked like a mountain walking on legs. The frills of its caparison were made with gold and silver threads, with silk tassels bobbing and swinging on the edges. On its back rested a howdah covered with silver filigree work, and in the howdah sat Shahu Maharaj. Broad face, thick whiskers, sharp but limpid eyes, fancifully fluffed out turban on the head and a smile that reminded one of the soft early morning rays. Maharaj made his entry into the square to the sound of countless trumpets and other musical instruments.

As soon as the worship of the shaami tree was over, the ritual of plucking 'gold'—the leaves of the shaami tree—would begin. An electric current ran through the assembled religious scholars, priests and dignitaries. The musical instruments began playing again at a higher decibel and the pyrotechnics began. The king had invited the renowned pyrotechnics specialists of Tasgaon to the celebrations. Fire-crackers exploded, Catherine wheels spun, rockets went whizzing up and colourful sparks resembling pearls, emeralds and rubies shot into the air. Eleven cannons boomed in unison to salute Shahu Maharaj.

A huge elephant stood in the back rows. A carelessly positioned rocket, instead of shooting straight up, described a parabola and descended to hurt the elephant's eye. The animal screamed in a fit of pain. Believing that it was under assault, it began stamping its massive legs, lifted its trunk high and swung it wildly in all directions, injuring the people who stood in the vicinity.

A panicked cry went up in the crowd: 'Run, run! The elephant's gone mad! Run!' This flustered the guards and a bunch of them picked up their spears and began jabbing at the elephant. The already enraged animal became even wilder and began running amok. A minor stampede ensued.

Some officials rushed up to the king and said, 'Please grant us permission to shoot the elephant down.'

Shahu Maharaj frowned and responded, 'This king loves his mute animals, he doesn't go after them with guns.'

'But, Maharaj, what else do we do?'

'Isn't there a real man among you? No one who can tame an animal without killing it?'

Two dark-skinned mahauts with stubbly beards stepped forward and made what they thought were cunning movements towards the dumb animal, but the elephant settled the matter with two swings of its massive trunk. That put paid to whatever courage some others had begun to gather; they tried their best to disappear into themselves. Sarang watched this pantomime for as long as he could and suddenly his patience snapped. He handed over his little girl to one of his friends, and patting his horse Sikandar's back, tugged the reins and applied the spur. Horse and horseman shot straight at the elephant. The surprise assault gave the horse the opportunity to land a few hard kicks on the elephant's back and stomach. When the elephant recovered from the shock, it was infuriated that an ordinary animal should show such cheek and swung its trunk mightily which, if it had landed, would have sent the horse flying. But Sikandar deftly swung out of harm's way and came back from the other side to kick the elephant.

Sarang pressed his horse forward towards the elephant and began teasing it all over again. The agitated elephant could think of nothing better than chasing the horse down and trampling it under its mighty feet. As it leapt forward, Sarang knew that his ploy had worked. He swiftly turned the horse's head around and galloped away, with the elephant giving chase. Hunter and hunted had soon left the crowd far behind and were out in the wide open spaces. They came to a stream with a dense overgrowth of bamboos and thorny brambles on both its banks. The horse and rider managed to maneuver through it, crossing the stream and negotiating the shrubbery on the other side. The riled-up elephant let the momentum of its chase take it through the nearer bank and into the water, but its thick skin took a horrible scouring when Sarang and his horse provoked it to climb up the other bank, pushing itself deep into the murderous trap of bamboo and brambles there.

The agile horse got into the bushes from another angle and harassed it from there, whipping the elephant into a frenzy of kicking and flailing and swinging of trunk, injuring itself each time and tiring itself out with each wild display of passion. In due course it was so exhausted that it broke into a sweat and could hardly groan, leave alone scream.

Back in the square, the evening had deepened. The Dussehra rituals were over and Shahu Maharaj returned to his palace. He kept thinking about the audacious man who had lured the rogue elephant away from the crowd. He was keen to meet this miracle worker. Just then, the bells round an elephant's neck tinkled in front of the palace and the heads of the assembled courtiers turned towards the door. They rubbed their eyes in disbelief: the enraged elephant from a few hours ago now walked in, meek and docile as a lamb, while Sarang strode alongside as if he and the two animals had known each other since childhood.

Holding little Kanchana, Sarang dismounted and bowed before the king with deep reverence. The king laughed and asked in typical Kolhapuri style, 'Yes, *pora*, tell me what you want as your reward, a thick gold necklace or something else?'

'Why a gold necklace, Maharaj? I am an ordinary farmer's son. I am worth nothing at all, yet I dream big.'

'What's your name? And tell me about your dreams.'

'I am Sarang Shinde. I come from Kaagwad. The dream of starting a circus is driving me crazy. I was a subedar in the army of the White sahibs earlier. Now I work in a circus.'

'So, whose ring do you perform in these days?'

'Maharaj, Parshuram Mali has taken me as his pupil.'

'*Waah*, son of a farmer, you've dodged the plough and now dream of the circus world! Wonderful!'

The king called Sarang over to his side, placed an arm round his shoulder and took him to the stables behind the palace. Pointing towards his herd of forty elephants, he said, 'Go on, boy, pick any one of them, and I will give you one of my choosing.'

Sarang went round the stable, examined the elephants on display and came back empty handed. He then looked at his little daughter and asked, 'Yes, Kanchu, which elephant would you like to own?'

Kanchana ran up to the elephant standing outside the stable and put her tiny arms around its trunk.

Shahu Maharaj broke into laughter and said, 'Wonderful! I can tell you, Sarang, your daughter is a few steps ahead of you. Taking a fancy to an animal that was hell-bent on crushing you only a few hours ago!'

'Maharaj, the fault was not the animal's at all. It was the burning rocket going into its eye that made it flare up like that.'

'You've stolen my heart, young man. Do you know what we call this highly gifted elephant? It's a jewel among my jewels, and I have named it Gajaratna. I give it to you today with the blessing that this elephant shall soon have other extraordinary animals for company.'

The king hadn't exhausted his generosity yet. He added to the big elephant a calf of his choice and seven strong, broad-backed horses from his stable.

Sarang and little Kanchana set off for their village in the manner of having won a war and reached their village three days later.

Soon, Sarang announced the establishment of his small circus company and cracked open a coconut to complete the ritual. The chests of the residents of Kaagwad swelled with pride. They were feeling dizzy at the honour that the great Shahu Maharaj had bestowed upon their boy Sarang. The parents of both Dagdoba and Taranath walked up to Sarang's house and said with admiration, 'You can hypnotise big kings and princes. Lakshmi, the goddess of wealth, has marked you out as her favourite. Take our sons with you. We are certain that you will hoist the flag of victory wherever you go.'

Sarang already had his sports companions with him. Three or four circus troupes that worked with larger circuses in the border areas of Karnataka came over and joined Sarang's firm. The king of Kurundwad, Maharaja Patwardhan, got news of the munificence of Shahu Maharaj; this honour bestowed upon his subject by such a great king inspired him to immediately gift two of his best camels to Sarang. Before a year had passed, Sarang's menagerie had expanded considerably with the arrival of new elephants and horses, even tigers, lions and a host of other animals.

Young and athletic artistes from the nearby regions began joining the company. The small circus grew rapidly in size. Sarang found the time right to form a proper company. He had it registered under the name of 'The Great Kanchana Circus'.

The young men from the nomadic tribes and the untouchable communities who stayed outside the village walls were extremely keen to join Sarang's circus. Ordinarily they would go about sweeping dust-laden municipality lanes. Many of them were tasked with dragging dead animals out of the village to the bank of a stream or the bramble woods nearby. They felt humiliated by the compulsion to undertake these demeaning tasks and the contemptuous behaviour of the upper castes.

The treatment meted out to these poor boys in the village was deplorable. Their utter destitution would be visible from the clothes they wore. Their shirts reached up to their knees. They were either discards of some landlord or bought at throw-away prices in the flea market. They yearned to step out of their filthy clothes and debilitating poverty, and Sarang's circus provided them with the opportunity. The circus company dressed them in shirts, T-shirts and trousers worn by the English sahib and often gave them sola hats and jackets too in which they could strut around with pride. Sarang was very affectionate towards everyone. He addressed everyone with respect. When these untouchable boys were addressed in English terms like ring-boys, cage-boys and kitchen-assistants, they took it as a mark of honour and appreciation. .

The circus began to travel to new towns and districts. A few Brahmin and Maratha troupe members approached Sarang and complained, 'Your circus has people from all castes and religions, like Mahars, Maangs, Ramoshis, Christians and Muslims.'

'So? What's your problem?'

'We get polluted by their contact. Shouldn't you make some special allowances for us upper-castes?'

'What allowances do you want?'

'You compel us to sit and have our meals with these impure, low-caste people. The least you can do is to provide us with a separate kitchen. Give us our meals separately. Otherwise, our religion will be destroyed completely.

'I will not allow any such thing in my company. There will be a single ring, a single company for disbursement of salary, and in the same manner, a single kitchen-tent for everybody. Those who are not okay with it can leave.'

Around this time, ten European couples were appointed by the Great Kanchana Circus on three-year contracts. When the native girls saw the energetic White girls leaping on the trapeze, riding the mono-cycle and riding robust horses like sprites of the forest, their hesitancy left them and they felt encouraged to emulate them.

When these native girls somersaulted on the swing, their long hair would often get tangled in the swing's rods, causing them discomfort. As a remedy, Sarang called over the company barber and got their hair cut. The girls were delighted at wearing their hair short like the White women. Soon their saris were abandoned too, replaced by shorts and a strip of cloth round their chests.

At a time when women were not permitted to move freely even in a temple, when going to school was considered a sin, the Indian circus companies sprouting up on the banks of river Krishna provided these girls with personal liberty, and the Kanchana International Circus was no exception. Sarang's company was particularly keen on recruiting deserving young girls and giving them a place in the sun.

The circus was camping at Miraj, from where they were to travel to Bangalore by train. Two days had been set aside for making the preparations. Since the shows had been happening back to back, without a break, it had become necessary for the bigger animals like horses and elephants to be given a good scrub. Sarang's stables and menagerie had plenty of mahouts and helper boys, but experience had taught him some important lessons, one of them being that employees worked best when the master was present to supervise them.

It was still very dark on the banks of the Krishna. The moonless night was getting over, but there was still some time left before the sun rose. Sparrows had begun to twitter here and there. A rare owl also flitted past. Sarang's mahouts had lowered fifteen elephants into a pool in the Krishna's waters. At the very sight of the water, the elephants had rushed in, lifting their trunks and letting out trumpets of delight. The mothers had pulled in their little calves and were bouncing in and out of the water.

After the elephants had had their fill of fun, Sarang rolled up his sleeves and got into the water along with the team of mahouts. They held the elephants by their trunks, caught them by their ears the size of winnowing baskets, went round their pillar-sized legs, and scraped off the cakes of dried mud and dung, using coconut husks as scrubbers.

The sky began to turn lighter. A tinge of orange shone on the horizon. Birds began to clamour on trees. Suddenly someone came running from the direction of the fields and, in the blink of an eye, leapt into the water from a high end of the bank.

People who set off to commit suicide are very often driven by an uncontrolled surge of emotion. They jump into the jaws of death in a fit of passion, but when the teeth begin to bury themselves into their flesh, they suddenly realise the value of life. A woman screamed frantically as she flailed about. One end of her sari could be seen floating along the disturbed waters.

At the very first shriek, Sarang stirred into action. Screaming, '*Arrey*! Some woman has jumped in,' he began swimming rapidly towards the spot. The water would have been a good four-men deep there. He took a deep breath and dived under. He located the woman, caught her by the hair and brought her up. Then he towed her to the other bank and dragged her out of the water.

The woman lost consciousness. Sarang stretched her out on her stomach and forced the water out by pumping her back. As she began regaining consciousness, the woman groaned and coughed violently. When she turned round, Sarang was astounded. 'Vahini Sahib? You?'

He remembered that his maternal cousin Kurundwadkar Sawant Sarkar lived on the other side of the river, and this woman, Hirabai, was his wife.

He took Hirabai to his tent in the camp and put her in Kanchana's charge. Hirabai kept saying, 'Why did you save me, Daaji Sahib? I would have been much better off dead.'

Hirabai began telling stories of her philandering husband Sawant Sarkar. 'Daaji Sahib, the cheap harlots of the marketplace have him wrapped around their finger. His debauchery, vulgarity, gambling—I can't bear the misfortunes he's heaped upon me ... Why did you save me?'

Sarang looked quizzically at Hirabai.

'It's now three years since my husband has so much as touched me. How long can I continue in this manner? This man gets all the dancing girls of the town and has them walk all over me. Why should I continue suffering all this?'

'Please don't say such things,' Sarang said. 'You are a sister to me. Look, committing suicide is a sin. Looking pointedly at her, he asked, 'Now tell me, when do you want me to take you back to your husband's home?'

'There's so much more merit in surrendering myself to the Krishna than looking at the face of that snake. Please don't try to save me. Let me die in peace.'

Sarang thought it wiser to give Hirabai time to cool down. Later, in the afternoon, when he thought that she was relatively less agitated, he made her the offer: 'Vahini, why don't you stay with us, then, in our company?'

'Here? In this circus?'

'Yes. Look, there are a good 300 people who live here, so a person from my family is going to be no burden at all. Also, Kanchana, who has never known her mother, will benefit from your protection and care.'

'Yes, but—'

'The outside world need never know that you are living here with us. I'll take care of everything else little by little.'

Hirabai mulled over the offer for a few days and then told Sarang, 'I'll stay in your circus. I'll also participate in the running of your company to the extent I can.'

'That's excellent!'

'But I will live the life of a widow here.'

'Why?'

'My husband is as good as dead for me.'

The first year of the Great Kanchana Circus went by like a breeze. The tours of Gujarat and Malwa set the tills overflowing. On its return journey, the company took the Warhad route, crossed Aurangabad of the Razakars and finally reached the Sangli area via Daund. The crowds that had gathered for the Uroos—the Muslim religious fairs—on the way had so flooded the tents that the boys would get tired counting the currency notes and coins. They would often stuff the cash in sacks and put them aside for counting the next day.

Sarang Daaji's proud march to prosperity had barely gone on for eighteen months when it was halted by the plague that hit the Sangli, Miraj, Kaagwad and Belgaum belt. There was mayhem everywhere.

It began with people detecting dead mice in their houses and then they found that knots had developed in their armpits. Within a couple of days, they would be dead. They began dying in their hundreds. Cremetoria began running out of wood for the funeral pyres. A time came when ten bodies had to be loaded on to a single pyre for cremation.

A person of Sarang Daaji's fortitude began shivering with fear. Suddenly, nothing was going right. He began to feel that the circus was going to sink.

Towns and villages started emptying out. Fearing that the Goddess's curse had descended upon them, people had started abandoning their houses and built makeshift huts outside the village precincts. When Yama, the God of Death, came riding on his bull and knocked on each door, people fled in all directions. There was bedlam everywhere. Such being the state of the world, who would want to step out for a night of entertainment?

The weekly markets stopped, religious fairs disappeared, even the gods were required to pass their days without a bath. Their worshippers had vanished and their palanquins lay gathering dust in a corner.

Sarang Daaji was on the horns of a big dilemma. Eighteen months had gone by since he had started his circus with the support of Shahu Maharaj and a few other princes. He had worked hard and set up some great items, and in order to do so, he had signed three-year contracts with foreign troupes and brought them over. Looking at the wonderful prospects of the circus, a number of traders of the town had given him large amounts of money as loan.

But the epidemic had now brought the circus to a grinding halt. How was he to provide food and shelter to 200 animals and 300 native and foreign employees? The carnivores alone needed a 100 kilos of meat every day. How was he to meet every-day expenses?

His greater worry was: what if plague-infected mice entered the circus? In less than a week's time, his entire team of men and animals would be wiped out. The remedy to keep the circus going and escaping the epidemic, therefore, was to move over to a region where the fatal disease had not reached. He could keep the show going and prevent the disintegration of the company.

He got news that the southern part of India was plague-free, including the districts of Coorg and Shimoga in the state of Mysore. Even as preparations were set afoot for an early departure, little Kanchana fell ill. She was barely ten. Panic-stricken Sarang took his little girl to the British hospital. He was relieved to know that it wasn't the plague. The fever, however, was refusing to come down. Taking her on the long journey south would be too taxing for the sick child. Besides, Sarang Daaji had immense faith in Dr Brook.

In sheer desperation, Sarang went to Kaagwad and explained to his brother's wife Sarja the state of his daughter's health. When the villagers saw him approaching, they were terrified. Right since his army days, Sarang had supported his brother's family. But Sarja refused to take responsibility of the girl. 'How can I take such a risk? What if she catches the plague? Where would I go carrying her corpse?'

Sarang returned to the hospital in Miraj and broke down before Dr Brook. That's when Martha, who worked as a nurse with Dr Brook, stepped forward and offered to look after Kanchana in her father's absence. She arranged for Kanchana to stay in her quarters in the hospital complex. It was on Dr Brook's reassurance that Sarang Daaji left with his circus for the south. Although his heart was heavy at leaving behind Kanchana, he took his circus from town to town. He immersed himself in serving his audience and looking after his troupe. The six months spent in the south proved to be fruitful. The circus was saved, his men and animals were saved, and plenty of profit was made too. After the season was over, Sarang returned to Miraj to be reunited with his daughter, who had been nursed back to health by Martha.

The company's tours spanned from Assam and Bihar in the east to Lahore–Karachi in the west and to Madurai–Rameshwar in the south. With the passage of years, Kanchana had grown into a child artiste.

Performing in the circus, she met people from different places and saw how multi-dimensional the world was. Her mind and values were shaped by her extensive travels. She resented the conservatism and narrow-mindedness of her family in the village. You are a girl; being born as a woman in this society is a sin, so whether you like it or not, you will necessarily have to settle for the shorter end of the stick … Her blood boiled when this kind of sagacity was dished out to her. She once told her father, 'I am never going to accept this rubbish. I'm telling you this straight, Baba: I will always be in the circus, performing. And I want to see who can stop me.'

These rebellious words would thrill Sarang Daaji no end; he would often pat himself on the back for having succeeded in instilling the right values in his little girl.

He would often declare before Hirabai and the others, 'Our circus will be travelling all across the country and to foreign parts too, and so I want Kanchana to learn to be able to speak well.'

'What do you mean?'

'Look, we train dumb animals and make them smart; in the same manner, if humans are given knowledge, they too automatically sprout eagle-like wings.'

'So, what do you want to do?' asked Hirabai.

'I think Kanchana should be admitted to school. I want to send her to this girls' school called Huzoor Pagey in Pune.' Maharaja Patwardhan of Sangli had given the land on which the Huzoor Pagey School had been built. He advised Sarang to get Kanchana admitted to the school and got his administrative officer to draft a recommendation letter with the royal logo and stamp.

Sarang began to make preparations for sending ten-year-old Kanchana to school. New clothes were bought, pickles and ghee made from cow's milk were packed in jars, and a whole lot of other things were packed in neat little bundles.

The train left Sangli station and carried father and daughter out of the Krishna valley, leaving green mountains and rills behind. Kanchana was sad at having to part with her father and all the animals and people of the circus who had been her constant companions. As the train gathered speed, she couldn't hold herself back. 'Baba,' she began to wail, 'I cannot live without you and without the birds and animals of the circus. Please don't drop me off like this!' The fellow passengers were flabbergasted. The women, particularly, were so incensed that they looked at Sarang Daaji as if he were a lunatic. How could a father do such injustice to his daughter? Kanchana's howling brought matters to such a pass that it became impossible for Sarang Daaji to continue the journey. When the train stopped at Karhad, for the first time in his life he yelled at Kanchana, 'All right, let's get down, you spoilt brat, we're going back to the company.'

When they returned to the circus, Kanchana said, 'I promise you, Baba, that I shall find a way to educate myself.'

As it happened, remedy was close at hand. When Lilian heard of Sarang Daaji's failed attempt at admitting Kanchana to a school, she hurried up to meet him. 'Uncle, don't worry,' she told him. 'It is your desire to give a good education to Kanchana. Why should you worry when you have standing before you this teacher who studied at a school in Dehradun?'

Sarang simply stood staring at Lilian.

8

One day, Sarang Daaji came to Kanchana with news from Maharaja Patwardhan, the ruler of Sangli. He had, on his own initiative, suggested to Ramsingh Mane, the chieftain of Budhgaon, Kanchana's name as a prospective wife for his elder son Naubatrao. The boy was modern in his outlook and had recently returned after spending five years in England and America.

'So, pori, what do you suggest we do? Although I would have loved for Raghav to be your groom, he has indicated clearly that we can't count on him as a certainty. I've never had a good feeling about feudal families, though. Their women may carry tons of gold on their person, but they are nothing more than appendages to their husbands.'

'Well, Baba, what I suggest is this. Since this message has come from Maharaja Sahib, we should honour his word and go and see him. Accepting or rejecting the prospect is in our hands.'

It was decided that the meeting would happen in the historical mansion of the Budhgaonkars. As Hirabai climbed into the car along with Kanchana, the girl laughed and said, 'Well, let's go and see. If this sugar-candy fife blows, well and good; if it doesn't, we can always eat it!'

'How can an intelligent girl like you call your husband-to-be a sugar-candy fife, Kanchu?' growled Sarang Daaji.

The party set off in the station wagon. Kanchana was dressed in the upper-class Maratha style. Two or three women had battled to drape a dark green nine-yard sari round Kanchana's lithe figure. By the time they reached the mansion, Kanchana was ready to kill. She was unaccustomed to wearing such heavy clothing and was melting in perspiration.

The mansion was big enough to be called a fortress. On the other side of the stone-paved courtyard was the massive hall, decked in sandalwood pillars, covered with silver plating. The sitting area was littered with tiger-skin spread everywhere, while from the walls stared down deer-heads out of the trophies into which they had been affixed.

From his conversation, Naubatrao appeared to be a relaxed and uninhibited person. His father Ramsingrao also sat in the company, and from the manner in which the two interacted, it was obvious that they were in an easy relationship, more friends than father and son.

Naubatrao was delighted by Kanchana's impressive personality. He turned towards the assembled relatives with a smile and nodded his head, indicating that he had passed the girl. All that was left to do was the formal draping of the traditional wedding saree. He turned towards his father and said in a facetious tone, 'I'm thrilled, Dad, to enter into a marriage with a girl who plays with lions and tigers every day.'

Turning his gaze towards Sarang Daaji, he went on, in English, this time, 'But, father-in-law, I first want to talk to your daughter about everything.'

The prospective pair came together. Kanchana stood before Naubatrao, trying very hard to look coy. Naubatrao again addressed Daaji in English, 'Look, Daaji sahib, I want to have a free and frank conversation with your daughter.'

'Go ahead. Speak whatever you have in your heart,' responded Sarang Daaji.

'Very well. Daaji sahib, we are the offspring of chieftains; when in the jungle, we cannot be expected to be satisfied with just one hunt.'

'What does that mean?'

'Look, after marrying your daughter, I should be free to marry again. It's good to be candid right at the beginning. I don't want any emotional drama later. There should be no obstruction from your side.'

Sarang Daaji was nonplussed for a little while. But even before he could frame an answer, Kanchana spoke, 'Please hold on, Baba. Let me handle this. Yes, so, gentleman, you were saying something?'

'Look, Miss Kanchana, let me speak openly with you. I want to be free to enter into a couple more marriages when I desire to do so. When the British law does not object to sons of the nobility marrying more than once, why should anybody stand in the way?'

'I have no problem with your proposal,' responded Kanchana, tucking the end of her sari in her waistband. Her eyes swept over the entire assembly, and she said, 'If, like you, I too take a fancy to two or three men, then do I also take them as husbands?'

The nobility gathered there was shocked into silence at this cutting remark. Both Ramsingrao and Naubatrao were enraged. Naubatrao strode forward with the intention of delivering a resounding slap on Kanchana's face, but before the hand could reach her cheek, she caught hold of his wrist and twisted it. This steely counter-attack from a delicate looking woman stunned Naubatrao. In the push and pull that followed, Kanchana shoved him with such force that he went flying into a wall and withdrew with a big lump rapidly emerging on his forehead. That done, Kanchana took her father by the hand and the entire party trooped out with a smile on their lips and their heads held high.

Naubatrao and family were publicly humiliated. They badly wanted to teach the father and daughter a lesson, but finally fear and discretion prevailed. Besides, what would they tell the world? That a circus girl had given Naubatrao a thrashing he would never forget?'

It was, however, impossible for such a juicy story to stay within the bounds of the mansion. People everywhere began to whisper to each other: 'That circus girl, Kanchana, beat that stupid son of Sardar Ramsingh Mane within an inch of his life!' Another outcome of this event was that the few young men who had been toying with the hope of marrying into Sarang Daaji's riches snuffed out their thoughts instantly.

9

The Great Kanchana Circus was playing in Belgaum. A car pulled up at the circus gate one afternoon, and four young men got out of it, dressed in stiffly ironed, white clothes. Sarang Daaji welcomed them effusively and sent for Kanchana.

One among these men was particularly striking, straight-nosed, with a frank, open face, a soft flowing beard reaching down to his chest. He could so easily be a painter. It turned out that he was not only that, but also a famous producer who owned a big cinema company.

When Kanchana entered her father's tent, all eyes turned towards her, taking in her tall, athletic, slender form. 'This is my daughter,' he informed the gathering. 'Pori, meet Baburao Painter, the director of the famous Maharashtra Film Company.'

Baburao Painter came straight to the point: 'Maharashtra Film Company has decided to make a film on Maharani Tarabai, the wife of Shivaji's son Rajaram and the founder of Karveer State. We believe you will be a perfect fit for the role of Tarabai.'

Getting into his stride, Daaji came in enthusiastically, 'Avo Painter sahib, my Kanchana will not only get astride a horse like your Tarabai, but she can ride a tiger too!'

'That's exactly what I'm saying, Daaji sahib, we are utterly convinced. It's your Kanchana alone who can play the warrior queen Tara Rani.' Baburao Painter said, 'I've been observing her demeanour, the way she carries herself … She will breathe life into the character of Tarabai, of that I am certain.'

The excitement on the faces of Baburao Painter and his colleagues made Daaji catch his breath. He wanted an important question answered, 'But, sir, how is your cinema going to fit in with our circus?'

'You just have to say yes.'

'Yes, but how many months will it take for the shooting to get over?'

'Well, it'll take a year, at least.'

'One year? How are we going to manage that?' Daaji was in a quandary. 'We could bring the tents down for that period, but how are 500 men and animals going to survive without work?'

Shutting the circus down for an entire year was an impossible ask. Finally, the film company had to leave disappointed and empty-handed.

Kanchana too felt disappointed at this opportunity slipping away. Although Daaji had bid the film people goodbye, he kept wondering whether he had made an error of judgment. A number of people came and told him, 'Daaji sahib, why did you let this chance go? This profession has a great future.'

Hirabai too chipped in, 'She would have reached great heights! Why did you have to stand in the way of her road to fame?'

Such criticism stung Daaji to the quick. He called Kanchana over to his tent and said, 'Look, pori, this cinema business wasn't a bad idea at all. But if a lead artiste like you were to be absent for one full year, we would have to shut the company down for the entire period.'

'That's quite true, Baba.' But for all her brave words, Kanchana could not keep her disappointment from showing.

'Pori, if a circus as huge as ours were to stay shut for a full year, the company would never be able to rise to its feet again.'

'Let's just forget it, Baba. The survival of 500 men and animals is far more important than chasing personal glory. Besides, why shouldn't I be the heroine of my own world?'

10

The Great Kanchana Circus had just finished shows in Mangalore and Udupi and was now heading towards Hubli—bullock carts, the cages of lions and tigers, the entire caravan.

The plains were now behind them and the dense forests of the Ellapur hills had begun. They had started their journey at the break of dawn, and when they came upon the Kaalu river with its banks lined with dense mango groves, the animals instinctively lost all traction. The exhausted elephants and horses made a beeline for the cool, inviting water. The elephant calves also made a dash for the river and began spraying water over themselves with their little trunks. The bullocks too had had a hard day pulling their heavy carts and the attraction of cooling their over-heated bodies sent them scrambling in with their tongues hanging out.

Just as they had begun to settle down, a bunch of twenty-five odd horsemen emerged from the bushes and surrounded the circus company. Their khaki shirts, shorts and head-gear announced that they were from the Mysore State police force. Sarang wondered why the police would want to mount a raid on his troupe in the middle of the jungle.

By nature, Sarang was a discipline-loving man and he kept his entire operation clean and on a tight leash; but who could say whether some of his men hadn't got a few bottles of country liquor secreted somewhere? A packet or two of marijuana tucked in the fold of a shirt, perhaps? The policemen were in an aggressive mood. They got the steel trunks and wooden boxes emptied out and went through the spread with a fine toothcomb. They demanded to see the licenses of the four guns and two revolvers that the company carried for self-defence and took a close count of the bullets and cartridges left with them. After they had shaken out every piece of cloth and every file and folder, the policemen relaxed. Then, without uttering a word by way of explanation, they rode away.

A couple of the policemen, though, continued to hang on. When the troupe had finished stretching their limbs and resumed their march, they trailed behind them at a little distance. The jungle track was an arduous one, and it took the company two days to plod through it before the Bombay State border came into view. Two days of travelling together had put the two parties at reasonable ease with each other. When Sarang Daaji softly queried the two policemen about the reason for the raid, Police Sergeant Basappa smiled and said, 'Tell us now, at least, what secret exchanges have been going on between your company and that hot-headed Lokmanya Tilak of the Congress.'

'I'm sorry, I don't think I've understood your question.'

'All right, who is Kashinath?'

'Oh Kashinath! He is the younger brother of Vishnupant Chhatre, the greatest among our circus men.'

'About fifteen years ago, this Chhatre's circus was playing in Kathmandu in Nepal. That was when a subversive group of young men that included your Damu Joshi, Banda Ruikar and Bhagwandas Gangadhardas of Solapur had quietly sneaked into Nepal. They had made plans to cause explosions and instigate people to revolt against our *huzoor* British government.'

'Meaning?'

'These rebels had stayed in Chhatre's circus camp on entering Nepal. While there, they had called over some German officials or agents to discuss the setting up of a factory.'

'What factory?'

'For making guns and rifles.'

'*Baap re!*' said Sarang as he swallowed hard and turned a frightened eye towards Kanchana. 'Such audacity?'

'Yes, and it was your Tilak who was egging on these hot-headed revolutionaries. They were trying to set up a secret gun factory there.'

As the border of Bombay State came nearer, one of the policemen couldn't hold himself back any longer. 'The British government has passed a secret order that companies like circuses which are always on the move should be kept under close surveillance. They always have a legitimate excuse for moving in and out of the country.'

As they neared Hubli, the Mysore police withdrew. As they were leaving, they asked Mahaling for some tobacco. Mahaling not only gave them tobacco, but he served them properly folded paans too, which pleased the policemen.

The Great Kanchana Circus was an instant hit in Hubli, running houseful for seven days at a stretch.

The day was about to dawn. Daaji was in a deep slumber when Dagdoba the blacksmith and Taranath the carpenter woke him up. Two men from Satara, who looked quite conspiratorial, if not altogether secretive, stood outside. These men were dressed in coarse khadi clothes typical of Congress volunteers. They had a confidential message to deliver to Daaji: You are in danger. White vultures have been circling round you and your company. Wind up your operations here and clear out from these southern parts. Travel to the northern towns—Ratlam, Gadmukteshvar, Lakhnau, anywhere. The winds of the south are harmful for your health.

The seasons were changing. The wheels of the circus caravan, meanwhile, moved on from this land to that, from this state to the next one. The years were flying by swiftly.

One day Sarang Daaji called Hirabai to his office. She arrived and, as always, sat before him respectfully at a distance of a few arms. Daaji cast a look at her white sari, her bare wrists and the blank parting of her hair and felt sad at the role of widowhood into which Hirabai had cast herself. He said, 'Look Hirabai, I consider you my sister. I want you to think about—'

'What, Dada?'

'The wise men have said that we humans are given just one life, and once gone, it will never return.'

'What do you mean?'

'Why have you decided to spend your life draped in a white sari?'

Hirabai was startled at this sudden question, but she composed herself quickly and replied, 'Look, Sarang dada, no matter how much you try to persuade me, I will never again see the face of that debauch who calls himself my husband.'

Daaji laughed out loud and said, '*Aga Akka*, why do you think he's desperately waiting for you? He's not. Why should *you* so pointlessly burn yourself out like a piece of camphor?'

'What do you suggest I do, Dada?'

'Akka, I have got everything ready: dark-green sari, a box of *kunku*, jewellery—'

'*Ago bai!*'

'You must remarry.'

'Why do you want to lead me back into that world of delusion, Dada?' Hirabai's eyes were wet.

'I'm saying this after careful consideration.'

Daaji made his next move. 'He too has been pining away for you, poor chap!' he put in slyly.

Hirabai heaved another sigh and shot a question straight as an arrow: 'And who could this person be? Don't name just any man on the street.'

'Oh, he's a good man.'

'Name him only if he's someone whose mention fills your heart with pride.'

'He's valiant and patriotic.'

'Patriotic?'

'Both your lives will light up from here on.'

As Hirabai continued to stare with curiosity, Daaji smiled and said, 'Akka, I'm talking about Mahaling Jaitapkar.'

Hirabai's eyes lit up. She could hardly believe her ears.

11

The circus was the school of life for young Kanchana. What she was learning there about the world was not bookish knowledge; she was taking lessons from direct exposure to new regions, new towns and their people, new cultures and traditions and a wide range of climates. These experiences were inculcating in her discernment and wisdom. Some of the greatest experiences she had had were on her visit to Burma, particularly Rangoon, as an eleven-year-old.

Whenever the topic of Burma came up, she would get carried away on the breeze of memories to Rangoon or the bank of the Irrawaddy river. If she happened to have her friend Champa by her side, she would break into a never-ending narration. 'There are so many things to describe, Champa tai, I don't even know where to begin! The buildings there all look like palaces, the kind you see in the Fort area of Bombay. There are trams that run like elephants on the streets. Those slim, slender natives in their lungis and shirts! Their eyes forever blinking, their teeth turned dark brown from chewing all that tobacco, and the hukkaas!'

'Oh, Kanchu, How do you remember so much? You were barely eleven when you went there.'

'True, but I can't get those people out of my mind's eye. The Burmese women with their colourful umbrellas, they looked like butterflies! Those cheroot-smoking aunties and grannies, they would dip their buckets and pull water out from a couple of feet below the ground ... the wells in the hinterlands always overflowed.'

'They have many different ways of using colour,' Kanchana went on. 'The girls there apply delicate strokes of wet turmeric on their cheeks. They call it tenkha.'

'You sound as if you just came back from Burma!'

'And the rivers there, tai—they're as huge as oceans. The Irrawaddy is so vast, you can't see the other bank. There are big and small row- and motor-boats plying across it all the time.'

'What about the temples in Burma? What are they like?'

'They're called pagodas there. Just imagine a huge bell placed on the ground, that's how these pagodas look placed upon hilltops in unending rows. You also see *sadhus* moving around in large groups in the marketplace. Their hair is all matted up. The Bauddha *bhikkus*, on the other hand, shave their heads, and wear saffron shirts and lungis. Often, two or three elephants lead their groups.'

'Is Rangoon your grandmother's home, Kanchana, which you go visiting every summer?'

'My grandmother's home is up north in Punjab, silly; it's in Ambala. But where my heart really goes flying at every opportunity is Rangoon. It wants to go bathing in the soft golden sunrays that spread around the Shwedagon pagoda. I've been telling Baba that we should make another tour of Burma.'

'Do circuses make good money there?'

'You know what they say these days? In Europe it's Paris and in Asia it's Rangoon. How will you understand the prosperity that reigns there unless you witness it yourself? Rivers flowing over a thousand miles and more, the quantity of teak that gets transported down them, the scale of the commerce happening there ... Add to them those oil wells and refineries. Then, also think of the emerald and ruby industry! Does it end anywhere at all?'

'So, another tour of Rangoon, then, is that what your heart is set on?'

'Why not? Baba is convinced that there is no richer place to perform in than Rangoon. Truth be told, the manner in which the circus comes into its own on the Mandalay maidans … that glitter and the grandeur and income can never be attained anywhere else.'

When Kanchana brought up Burma with her father, she was surprised to find him more worried than excited. 'You remember the police raid in the hills the other day, pori?' he asked in a grave tone. 'The name of Lokmanya Tilak kept cropping up there too?'

'What does that mean, Baba?'

'The British goverment has marked circuses for heavy surveillance. They believe circuses are secretly helping freedom fighters.'

Kanchana broke into laughter, which was not how Sarang Daaji had wanted her to react. 'Why this unnecessary laughter?' he snapped in annoyance.

'You think these Sahibs are mistaken in their suspicions, Baba?'

'What are you trying to say?'

'Well, just see what happened four days ago. Lawyer Soman from Satara, Limaye from Pune and our Nana Patil and Babuji Patankar paid a quiet visit to our camp and swiftly disappeared at dawn. You stayed up with them through the night, didn't you? And our Mahaling uncle repairs guns for these revolutionaries, doesn't he—?

Daaji looked right and left in alarm, leapt forward and clamped his hand over Kanchana's mouth. 'Are you mad, girl? Don't ever say such things out loud!'

That night, memories of Rangoon, Ziawaddy and the Mandalay of nine years ago swarmed around their heads like butterflies in a dense forest.

Much before Sarang Daaji ventured into Burma, circus stalwarts from Maharashtra like Parshuram Mali, Shankarrao Karlekar and Yashvantrao Morey had already earned a name for themselves in East Asia. Sarang went on to entertain the audience they had created, using the goodwill they had garnered. In the company of Kanchana, he had raised the bar higher in providing thrill and entertainment to the viewers. The District Collector of Rangoon as well as the Deputy Commissioner had honoured Sarang and Kanchana by throwing lunch parties for them in their bungalows. For a good month, the horses and elephants from the banks of the Krishna and the Koyna had tasted the sweet water of the Irrawaddy that came flowing down from China.

During that stay in Rangoon, an extremely rich and influential man had paid a visit to the circus camp. Rao Bahadur Sinha belonged to Ziawaddy in the district of Tamu, where, twenty-five years earlier, the British government had granted over 22,000 acres of land to him. Determined to make it a farming enterprise, Sinha Sahib had brought over thousands of farm labourers from Bihar to work on his lands, resulting in sixty-four separate settlements of these Indian labourers in Tamu district. Sinha's venture had paid off and Ziawaddy had now been acknowledged as the front-rank agriculture centre in all of Burma.

Sinha Sahib had then gone on to grow sugarcane, and information had reached Sarang Daaji that he had started setting up a sugar factory that would be named the Ziawaddy Sugar Works. On his visit, Sinha Sahib was so pleased with the quality of the show that he had immediately invited Daaji to bring his troupe over to Ziawaddy for a few days.

The eight-day camp of the circus in Ziawaddy turned out to be a runaway success. Sinha organised a grand dinner for Sarang and his daughter at his palatial bungalow, to which he invited his closest relatives and friends. The children assembled there were delighted to shake hands with the 'Didi' who was the 'Friend of the Tigress'. They proudly lined up to be photographed with her.

As the elephants were putting into place the tall poles on which the big top would be erected on the Mandalay ground, Sarang stood with his hands on his hips. In the glow of the setting sun, his eyes took in the hillock in front called the Mandalay Hill. On the lower side of Mandalay Hill, partly concealed by vines and trees, stood some tile-roofed buildings that looked like government offices. It was now a small British Army cantonment. A little below, on the plains was a walled area of some fifteen to twenty acres; the old but well-kept buildings inside the walls suggested that it was a palace complex. The battlement walls were manned by army guards. Sarang told his daughter that this was the famous Mandalay Jail. In its heydays, it was the palace of the king of Burma, King Thibwa. The cunning British had arrived and made King Thibwa a prisoner for life, banishing him to Ratnagiri in India.

The first performance of the circus in Rangoon that evening went off like a dream. Among the other dignitaries present at the show were the jailor of the Mandalay Jail, Mr Flaubert, and his family. During the break, the White sahib paid a visit to the wing in the company of other jail officials and some police officers.

It had become a tradition for British officials in South Asia to go and watch Indian circuses. They guaranteed first-rate entertainment. The items with ferocious wild animals made their eyes pop out and the trapeze shows of supple athletes performing somersaults eighty feet above the ground sent them into a swoon. Chhatre, Dewal, Karlekar, Shelar, Parshuram the Lion and now the Great Kanchana and the G.A. Circus of Bombay, not one of them had allowed the standard to slip.

When Flaubert visited the wing a second time after the show got over, Sarang hastened forward, held his extended hand and said, 'Jailor Sahib, my daughter and I are very keen to visit the jail one of these days.'

'Visit us by all means. Do so as my honoured guests!'

Sarang Daaji and his daughter were received at the jail with a lot of fanfare. Garlands of fresh flowers made by the inmates were put round their necks. Mr Flaubert himself sat down with his guests for tea and biscuits. 'I shall take you round the jail myself,' he announced warmly. 'Tell me if you have any special requests here.'

'Sir, there is one barrack that I particularly want to see, the one where you British had incarcerated our Lokmanya Tilak. I shall consider myself blessed if I got the chance to touch my forehead to that hallowed ground.'

'Who's this?'

The senior sergeant whispered into his boss's ear, 'He's talking about that extremist Tilak.'

Flaubert's face underwent a complete transformation. His face darkened as he said, 'Look, I cannot possibly overlook the impertinence of your request. You will get into trouble. However, since you are only an artiste, let me inform you that Tilak is seen as an enemy of Her Highness's government.'

The glow on Flaubert's face had disappeared. He abandoned his offer to accompany Sarang round the premises, suddenly remembering he had urgent work to attend to and walked away with quick steps.

The sergeant took over the responsibility of giving Sarang and Kanchana the tour. When he pointed towards an old, damp-looking barrack, Sarang's eyes became wet with tears. He prostrated himself on the ground and touched his forehead to the floor in front of the barrack, as he would before the image of God Khanderaya in Jejuri. Seeing his daughter similarly stretched out beside him, he said, 'Okay, Kaanchu, say it out loud, 'Tilak Maharaj ki Jai!'

12

'Forgive me, Daaji sahib,' said Saibu one morning as he peeped inside Sarang Daaji's tent, 'I apologise for stepping beyond my station, but may I say something?'

'What?' said Daaji, putting aside the morning edition of *Kesari* that he had been reading. 'All right, go ahead.'

'Daaji sahib, why are you getting entangled with these *Congresswallahs*? These Gandhi cap-wearing volunteers sneak into our tents late in the night and disappear early in the morning. Their movements arouse a lot of suspicion.'

Daaji was a little surprised. He looked at Saibu with displeasure, but Saibu continued talking, 'I went to the Collector's office in Belgaum a couple of months ago. The sub-district magistrate told me in no uncertain terms that I should ask my master to be careful. He asked me to tell you that you should focus on your circus and not get into secretly supplying revolutionaries with funds. He said that they are in the process of preparing a history sheet—or whatever it's called—of your company.'

'But what crime have we committed?'

'Daaji, what he was saying was that they still haven't got hold of any strong written evidence against you.'

'What does that mean?'

'He said that the day they landed some evidence that could hold in court, they would break the spine of our circus and send you and Kanchana to break stones in Yerawada Jail.'

Daaji laughed it off in front of Saibu, but deep inside he was worried. The atmosphere in the Satara district of Bombay had become exceptionally volatile and rebellious. The Civil Disobedience movement against the government had turned particularly strong in places like Karad, Kundal, Tasgaon, Waduj, Ashta and Charan.

'The sub-district magistrate also said that the British Collectors and DSPs of many places hold you and Kanchana in high esteem for being artistes and circus owners of the highest calibre,' Saibu went on, 'and they want you to retain this respect.'

Gajaratna was Sarang Daaji's favourite elephant. Lakshmi, the Goddess of wealth, had stepped into his house the day he had brought Shahu Maharaj's gift to his village. Daaji would sit down for breakfast only after his animals had been fed. He would take a walk around the menagerie every morning, carrying nine kilos of *sheera,* sweets made of flour and ghee, shape them into balls and feed them to his darling Gajaratna.

It made for a heartwarming sight—Daaji holding the tray of hot, sweet, aromatic sheera in one hand, while caressing Gajaratna's trunk with the other, and then Gajaratna sliding his trunk round Daaji's waist. This had become an indespensable part of their routine. Without this ritual, neither would touch any other food.

One day, Gajaratna took the first ball in his mouth and spat it out. After that, no amount of coaxing would persuade him to accept the second ball. After a few such balls had been tossed away, Daaji got suspicious and took a bite of the sweet himself. It tasted all right to him the first time round, but after letting the sheera roll around his tongue, he called cook Akaram Jogta and mumbled something into his ear. The sweet was prepared fresh and brought over again.

This time, the very aroma floating towards Gajaratna got him excited. He polished off the entire nine kilos. Quite a crowd had gathered around by this time, with everybody egging the two on. When the tray was cleaned out, Kanchana went up to her father and asked, 'Baba, what's this secret between the two of you?'

Daaji looked around at everybody and laughed. 'It's such a small thing,' he said. 'That idiot Akaram had forgotten to add cardamom to the dish. The slightest difference in taste, and our mighty Baburao got upset!'

Daaji often addressed Gajaratna as 'Baburao'. Gajaratna would instantly respond by lifting his trunk and trumpeting.

13

It was late afternoon. The frenetic activity on the Calcutta docks had slackened. One could see barges floating on the Hoogly like little paper boats. Raghav sat on the desolate bank with a long face and disheveled hair. He had landed in Calcutta three days ago with the barest of bare remnants of his uncle's circus, and since then he had just been drifting around scratching the stubble on his distraught face.

It was from this very harbour that he had departed six months earlier for a tour of Jakarta, Malaya and Singapore with his late uncle's Great Sali International Circus. It had a number of artistes of European and African descent. It was a strong company that Raghav had taken to Singapore, but what he had brought back was four eighty-foot long teak poles, eight surviving artistes, ten horses and an elephant named Rajmangala. All the friends and well-wishers of those prosperous times had immediately distanced themselves from a ship that had sunk. Misfortunes had beaten the stuffing out of Raghav and there was nowhere left for him to go.

This was his state when his eyes fell on a poster that caused his heart to leap. Snarling down from the poster was the face of a tiger, and below it was a name that brought memories flooding back into his head: The Great Kanchana Circus. It had now been four years since that visit to his friend Charlie at Sarang Daaji's circus. He recalled his first encounter with the irrepressible Phakkadrao, the banter with Kanchana ... the images came rushing back to him, and he grabbed at them like a drowning man clings to a floating log.

The circus had set up camp on the bank of the Hoogly; at a little distance, another circus by the name of Lotus India had erected it tents. There was an unwritten courtesy that circus companies observed across the world: not to compete with each other in the same town. This convention was based upon sound business sense: it would cause serious damage to both companies. Often, even procuring enough fodder in the town to feed the animals of both the camps would pose a challenge. Despite the evident dangers of getting into competition at such close quarters, the fact was that two circuses—the Great Kanchana Circus and Lotus India—were now locked in a contest that had frayed tempers on both sides. It was around this time that Raghav stood arguing with the doorman. 'Please do me this favour,' he was pleading. 'Just tell madam that Raghav is here, I'm her friend.'

The doorman, however, refused to relent. 'There is a lot of tension inside,' was his repeated response. It took endless pleading before the doorman was persuaded to carry Raghav's name inside. At the pronouncement of the name Raghav, Kanchana looked at Daaji in disbelief. Daaji, however, couldn't keep the joy out of his face. 'You had to come back, hadn't you?' the expression on his face read. 'There was nowhere else you could have gone.'

Looking at Kanchana's flushed face, Daaji snapped, 'Why are you keeping the poor chap waiting outside? He must be roasting in the heat.' He rushed to the door and brought the bedraggled Raghav inside.

'Hello, Kanchana-ji,' he said, 'I apologise for the state in which I am presenting myself before you.'

'What happened to you?' Daaji's voice was full of concern.

'It's a long story, Daaji, and it will need a long time to tell. In brief, I had carried a flourishing circus across the waters to Singapore and I came back to Calcutta three days ago with the few pieces I could save: some tent material, eight of my men, ten horses and an elephant. I have left my animals at the farm of a well-wisher on the outskirts of the city. I was trying to work out how to carry my surviving team back home when I saw your poster, and so here I am.'

Daaji asked, 'Where are you and your men staying, then?'

'We have rented a room in Shalimar Lodge near the harbour.'

'Raghav-ji, in what state are your animals on this farm you talked about?' asked Kanchana.

'Well, they have been in dire straits since calamity struck, but we've been somehow managing to feed them.'

'Raghav,' said Daaji, 'my suggestion is that you bring your men and animals here. Come stay with us.'

'Daaji,' responded an overwhelmed Raghav, 'this was the hope with which I came running to you. I don't care so much for myself or for my men, but I want to keep my animals safe.'

'We are glad that you thought of reaching out to us,' Kanchana spoke this time. 'We will make the necessary arrangements.'

It was time for the evening show. The air had suddenly turned cold, and a strong wind began to blow, dislodging leaves and stems from the trees around the camp and the riverbank. The owner of the land on which the circus had set up camp, Saukitra Sen Babu, came to meet Daaji and Kanchana. Casting a worried look at the overcast sky, he said, 'You should call off the evening show and save yourself huge losses.'

Kanchana was surprised. 'Why do you say that, Babu Moshai?'

'Look, you have no idea how fierce these sudden storms rising from the Bay of Bengal can be.'

'Our tent is already filled to capacity with people, Dada. How can we sustain such a loss?' She then turned to her manager and instructed, 'I don't think I can afford to call the show off. This show must go on.'

Kanchana looked at her father from the corner of her eye. He said nothing, but clearly he was restlessness too. Kanchana was simply being true to her father's motto: The Show Must Go On! Her father, however, took her to a side and said, 'Look, pori, these locals are sure to know the circumstances better than us. I have seen big programmes being washed out. It's never safe to challenge the forces of nature.'

'But, Baba, if the storm doesn't strike and the ticket holders do in their thousands, how will we handle them?'

'Well, yes, that could happen. In any case, it is impossible to take down our entire tent and raise it all over again. I guess we will have to take our chances. If the storm passes, we have our show, if it hangs on, our audience won't arrive anyway.'

The evening lights were lit. The female artistes were swinging on the trapeze, the elephants were trumpeting. Charlie's band had got into its rhythm too. That was when the wind started building up rapidly and lifted the tent-roof. The cloth began to rip, and its pieces flew away like dry leaves. The tent filled up with so much dust that visibility sank to zero.

Kanchana was in a tizzy. It was clear to her that her expensive tent-material, costing hundreds of thousands of rupees, would now be ripped to rags. An intense fear gripped her. She called out to the girls on the trapeze, but when the fierce winds weren't allowing elephant trumpets right of passage, how far could her voice have travelled?

She thought of getting the tent dismantled, but with the steel frame of the trapeze still hanging up there, how was that possible?

By a stroke of luck, the audience had all emptied out of the tent. The wind caused the steel wires radiating out of the central pole to snap. A number of secondary poles were uprooted and the stout ropes broke and dangled like noodles.

There was fear of violent animals breaking free. Daaji took a platoon of boys and roped the cages to the earth with additional stakes. Experienced horse-riders and ring-masters ran up to the panicked elephants and horses, got them under control and corralled them in stables and outhouses.

The scene of the shredded tents, twisted and splintered posts and the devastated camp the next morning was enough to make the spine tingle. It looked like a dinosaur that had been ripped clean of all skin and flesh by violent vultures, and all that was left was the skeleton. Kanchana's face, however, presented a still more pitiable sight.

The night was pitch dark, the river flowed, making a loud sound almost amounting to a roar. What had begun with squally winds soon turned into a downpour. Raghav and his friends watched the fury of nature from the window of their seedy room. As they wrapped the thin blankets supplied by the lodge round them and stretched out for the night, there were two things that were uppermost in Raghav's mind: the safety of his animals on the farm and the state of the Great Kanchana Circus.

Morning finally arrived, however reluctantly. The sun unexpectedly secured a temporary victory and peeped out from between the coconut palms. Raghav creaked up into a standing position and looked at the haze that had spread outside the window. He suddenly noticed a midget of a man getting down from a tonga. He was Kanchana's manager. Soon enough he was at Raghav's door. 'Babuji, you?' he asked in surprise. 'So early in the morning! Anything urgent?'

'What a stormy night it was! It ripped up our expensive tent to ribbons. The mistress wants you over immediately.'

Raghav reached the circus camp to find Kanchana standing in the midst of her tattered tents. Her embarrassed laugh suggested that she had accepted her folly of the previous evening. She said, 'Raghav-ji, our local agent had warned us and I paid no heed. Look what has become of our tents.'

'The damage caused to you seems immense, but try to put it aside, madam.'

'Daaji told me to call off the show, but I didn't.'

'Did Daaji really say that?'

'Yes, he did.' Kanchana's voice turned hoarse. 'The only consolation I can draw from this—and that's a mean one—is that the Lotus India Circus people have suffered heavy damages too. They are better off, though, because they have another tent in reserve. Raghav-ji, the reason why I sent my man to you was to ask if you could help us in any way. Yesterday you had said that you had some tent material with you.'

'That's just what I was about to say. As luck would have it, we do have one tent left over from my uncle's circus; it's in excellent condition too. And I shall not only lend it to you, my men and I will also help your men erect it. I'm sure I will have brought the top flaps together before dusk.'

True to his word, Raghav had the tent erected.

Finishing the work on time, Raghav went over to Kanchana's tent and sat hesitantly, as if he wanted to say something but didn't know how. Kanchana helped him out by asking, 'Something on your mind, Raghav-ji?'

'Well, Kaachana-ji, yes. Do you think you could create space in your circus for a small item with my horses?'

It was now Kanchana's turn to hesitate. She had seen Raghav's skill with horses four years ago, still, she couldn't allow an untested item such easy entry into a circus of her level. But on the other hand, it was only because of Raghav's generosity and help that she would now be able to hold her shows.

'Well, Raghav-ji,' Kanchana took a long shot at getting out of the bind, 'what I worry about is that your horses might all be weak and tired after the ordeal they have been through. They should take some time to recover, shouldn't they, before they are ready for the ring again?'

'Kanchana-ji, I am a circus man myself, and I wouldn't have made this request without knowing my animals well enough.'

Kanchana thought for a few moments and then let out a sigh. Smiling as brightly as she could, she said, 'All right, then, Raghav-ji. Actually, this combat between us and Lotus India is going to leave one of us mortally wounded. So I can squeeze out for you just about twenty minutes in tomorrow afternoon's show. I'm doing this as a special gesture for you alone.'

14

The time for his entry arrived. Noticing Kanchana's absence, Raghav went up to her tent and called in an ardent voice, 'Madam, it will be very gratifying if you came to the tent and watched our show, if only for a few minutes.'

Kanchana looked up from the account books and said, 'Of course, Raghav-ji, I'll be there in a few minutes.' Raghav walked away, a little disappointed at her lack of enthusiasm.

She had again immersed herself in her account books when she was startled by roars of laughter reaching up to her tent, followed by the sound of loud clapping. She then remembered Raghav's invitation, shut the books and hurried towards the main tent. The booming laughter and the clapping emerging from the big tent accompanied her all the way. What met her eyes when she entered the tent made her gape in astonishment.

Two horses were galloping round and round the ring and a man was dancing on the backs of these two racing animals, hopping like a monkey from one back to another. And, oh dear lord! He was now doing somersaults too. How could he possibly leap off those horses on to the ground and then leap back upon them without losing his balance? Did he not have any bones inside him? Was he made of rubber?

It was only when he sped past Kanchana's bewildered eyes that she realised this artiste was Raghav.. The horses were now running alongside each other and Raghav had planted one foot each on their bouncing backs with indefinable grace. Double riding was known all over as a sure invitation to a miserable death. The slightest error from rider or either of the horses and the rider would finish off with a smashed skull.

The viewers couldn't shut their eyes for fear of missing the miracle happening, yet they couldn't keep them open for the horror of its calamitous potential. Never had they seen such daredevilry in a circus ring. This man was beating the monkeys at their game of leaping from one rooftop to the other! The monkeys, at least, didn't have to negotiate roofs galloping at forty miles an hour. This utter disregard for death had converted Raghav into an instant hero, and the spectators were going berserk rooting for him.

Standing next to Lilian as she watched this jaw-dropping show, Kanchana thumped her back and shouted in excitement, 'Don't shut your eyes, Lilu Didi! You'll never see this feat again!'

'No, I can't! My head begins to swim. Is this Raghav a phantom or a demon?'

Once the item was over, the entire audience stood up and began clapping and whistling as one man. The thunderous applause refused to die down. Up on the bandstand, Charlie decided to intervene and started off a galloping tune. As the spectators were getting into the groove, Raghav and his men strapped bells round their horses' ankles. The violinists joined in at the appropriate moment and Charlie brought the saxophone to his lips and seamlessly insinuated himself into the flow. A nod of his head and the drums and flutes came in. As the folk music from the forests of Aarag–Bedak gathered strength, the musicians broke into a song. A shiver ran through the horses; Raghav and his men stepped in and the horses began dancing to the beat of the music as if they were peacocks in the wild. The singing went on:

Rangu nighaali naandaaila, hai naandaaila

Maazhi Rangu nighaali naandaaila!
Aambe-mohor bhaat raandhaayla,
Rangit maadiche ghar baandhaaila
Hai Rangu nighaali naandaaila!

(Rangu is setting up her new household, a new household
My Rangu is setting up a new household
She'll cook fragrant Aambe-mohor right
And she'll paint her balconies bright
Hey, Rangu is setting up a new household)

Rainbow-coloured lights threw their beams into the ring and over the mesmerised audience. The mellifluous notes of Charlie's Goan-Portuguese melody changed the mood inside the tent. It wasn't just the horses and the band, the viewers were so enraptured that they left their seats and began dancing as well.

As Kanchana watched the horses dance, she was particularly struck by the one in the lead. 'Lilu Didi,' she said, '"look at that horse! It surely belongs to a royal stable. Look at its glittering coat!'

'Kanchu, stupid girl, can't you recognise your own horse? That's your Phakkadrao!'

15

There was talk everywhere of Raghav's riding skills and of his magical show with the horses. Despite all the accolades showered upon him, he didn't allow himself to get carried away. He thought of his uncle's circus where he had learnt his skills.

It was just last month, when they were on a tour of Singapore, that the unexpected calamity had struck his company.

A strong wind was blowing from the sea that morning. The mahauts had spread fodder before the elephants, mountains of hay stood all around them. The motorman was oiling the giant generators and switching them on and off to ensure that the oil was reaching inside. It was during one such exercise that a spark had flown out of one of the generators and fallen straight on a heap of hay, setting it aflame. With the wind as an eager accomplice, the flames travelled fast and within no time, took the tents, the menagerie and the stables into their murderous embrace.

Some men had rushed to the stables, untethered as many horses as they could from their stakes, removed the chains on the elephants' legs and driven them out. For all their alertness, they could only save three elephants; six had fallen prey to the flames. Over seventy percent of the circus had turned to coal and ash within two hours. Everyone had fallen upon what was left after the fire. They wanted the circus to be dismantled and sold. There were also the kitchen manager and the foreign artistes demanding to be paid. Raghav, however, did not know how he could settle with them till he reached India.

'But why should we wait till then?' complained a few.

A few said, 'The French circus Cirque Amar as well a German circus are playing here these days. They will readily buy off the animals and equipment our circus is left with. Settle the matter right here.'

Like rats abandoning a sinking ship, several workers from Raghav's company began negotiating with foreign circuses to sell the remaining animals.

With nobody to lean on in the foreign land, Raghav was left with no choice but to find buyers for the animals and equipment. But he refused to part with his best-trained horses and his favourite elephant Rajmangala. When she was a calf, he had bought her from a temple in the jungles of Udgiri.

As the boat sailed away, Raghav sat watching the Singapore coast recede. After the proceeds of the sale had been distributed to various claimants, all that was left with him was a 100 pounds. That would cover the travel expenses of ten horses, an elephant and a handful of colleagues.

The immediate question now was, what temporary arrangement could he make for his animals on reaching the Calcutta harbour? And what about the journey thereafter? By a stroke of fortune, there were a few sadhus sailing with them along with a few animals and pupils. The head of this group was a radiant-looking young man called Swami Anandji Maharaj.

As they got talking, Swamiji gave Raghav word that his animals would be looked afterby his friend Mishra who lived near the harbour and owned a big mango orchard with a stable in it. The swami looked closely at Rajmangala and said, 'Son, you don't know how fortunate you are. Elephants that rock sideways from right to left and left to right are countless in number, but not even emperors own the kind that rocks forward and backward from head to tail and back. This Rajmagala will bring you luck and serve you till its last breath. Take good care of it.'

16

Within days of Raghav's performance in the matinee show, he moved in with his men and animals into the circus camp.

The item with Phakkadrao and the other horses had created a veritable storm. The viewers would cheer and whistle right through the item. Kanchana was so taken with Raghav's presentation and the unprecedented response he was receiving that she immediately billed him as a star and put him into the evening show. Posters and handbills inviting people to 'Come and enjoy the magical horses of Prince Raghav' and 'Come and see Mad Raghav and His Dancing Horses!' were printed immediately.

However, Sarang Daaji continued to carry furrows on his brow. He confided to his daughter, 'Kanchu, there's one thought that keeps niggling me: in spite of Raghav's daredevilry in the ring, why has our circus not taken off as it should? Why haven't we reached the same heights as a foreign circus?'

Father and daughter arrived at a decision. The manager of the circus drove out in the jeep and went knocking at the doors of every English and vernacular newspaper in town, inviting them all to an evening show. The pressmen arrived in hordes, they marvelled at Raghav's amazing skills, ate a grand dinner and left. Three days went by, but there wasn't a single column mentioning the circus in any newspaper. The stress over this mystery showed on every face.

The next evening's show was about to begin. Charlie had struck up his notes with a song in his heart. The crowd was distinctly bigger than before. Sarang Daaji's darling Gajaratna entered the ring.

In that very instant, there was a commotion outside, a few feet away from the entry gate. Loud hurrays could be heard from the spectators gathered there. The guards and the ring-boys ran in that direction. In the open space out there, a couple of patromax lanterns were hissing, their glow inviting wasps and other insects of the night in large numbers. A huge crowd had gathered around a twenty-foot-long nylon rope that had been strung thirty-five feet into the air on a pair of crossed bamboo posts on either side. Leaping off this rope was a circus artiste.

Holding it between his toes and dancing upon it, he had turned the rope into a spring. Pressing down on this spring and then jumping up, he went swinging into the darkness above. This artiste was none other than Raghav, known until now only as a horseman.

He now clasped his knees and rolled himself into a ball. Touching the rope with his feet, he bounced higher up in the air. While the spectators' hearts leapt into their mouths, this bouncing ball began doing somersaults on the rope ... one ... two ... three ... four! Oh dear god! If he were to miss a step, he would come hurtling down forty feet and explode like a pumpkin. Not many had the steel to watch the sight, and they shut their eyes tight. Only when they squinted them open, they saw the monster still bouncing. Higher and faster than before. The crowd broke into a deafening applause.

This ovation was so loud that it reached the Lotus India Circus's tent camped not too far away. The loiterers outside the tent first came racing in, then a few others from inside the tent peeped out curiously and then rushed over. What had begun as a trickle now grew into a wave! Masses of viewers from the Lotus India camp were now heading towards that patch of light in the sky in which they could see a silhouette getting into impossible contortions.

For the benefit of the steadily growing crowd, Raghav went through his unprecedented performance five times over. He now stood on the rope with his toes wrapped tightly round it. Drenched in perspiration, he looked down at the sea of humanity looking up at him wide-eyed. Among them he noticed Kanchana, Sarang Daaji and Taranath, with their arms raised up to the sky, swaying in a trance as pilgrims do when moving in a procession.

Raghav took a bow and climbed down the rope. He was immediately pulled into Lilian's embrace. 'What a dare-devil you are, Raghav!' she burst out. 'If you fall, you idiot, who is going to collect your bones?'

As Lilian released Raghav, Kanchana gathered him in a tight hug and rained kisses on both his cheeks. 'What are you, Raghav,' she screamed in excitement, 'man or demon? Do you at all know what fear is? I am a circus acrobat, yet I was shivering. One misstep, and you were done for!'

Raghav was lapping up this adulation greedily. 'My game is always in my hands,' he said with pride. "This is what I truly am, this is what I do. I perform best under the open sky.'

When Sarang and Kanchana saw the crowds gathering around the box office, their eyes twinkled with joy. It took no time at all for the ticket counter clerk to shout, 'No tickets left.'

'What? How can that be? Okay, what about advance tickets for tomorrow?'

The lucky ones who managed to get the tickets for that night's show were still starry-eyed from watching the magical act in open air. Even before they settled into their seats inside the big top, they were yelling, 'All other items—later. We want Raghav's Bouncing Rope act first!'

Raghav's act became the main attraction of the Great Kanchana Circus. Wherever one went—the Calcutta harbour, Shyam Bazaar, Howrah, the Hoogly banks or Alipore—one heard only two names: that of the Great Kanchana Circus and its star performer Raghav. Crowds came in massive waves. Special permission was procured from the magistrate to hold four shows a day, and yet there was no damming the flood.

17

Following Raghav's rope act, Lotus India thought it prudent to pull up its tents and create as much distance as possible between itself and the Great Kanchana Circus.

The day after Raghav's flying rope item became a sensation, Daaji asked Charlie to find out where matters stood between Raghav and his aunt. By evening Charlie had all the answers: his cousin Neelima had got married a year back, and the aunt had passed away soon after the marriage. And now, after the circus had disintegrated in Singapore, Raghav had come out of the partnership with the tent material, the elephant and ten horses as his share. He was free of all attachments and obligations. Charlie had also gone on to ask him whether he would still be interested in tying the knot with Kanchana. Raghav said, it would be an honour.

Four days later, Kanchana, Raghav and Sarang Daaji sat in conference in the office tent. The barriers between Raghav and Kanchana were rapidly disappearing. There was no yours and mine in Daaji's eyes as he looked at them. But since Raghav had been called with the declared intention of settling Raghav's status in the company, he looked at father and daughter and asked, 'What's my salary going to be?'

'You decide on that.'

'And what about my animals? What about Phakkadrao, my other horses and Rajmangala?'

'That too is going to be your decision.'

Raghav shifted in his seat. 'How will this do?'

'This is exactly what you will have to do, son.' Daaji smiled.

'Why?'

'Because I am giving both my daughter Kanchana and my circus to you. So, naturally, you will have to take your own decisions.'

Raghav received an urgent message early in the morning: 'Kanchana madam wants to meet you immediately at the red tent.'

What was the urgency about? Could someone have gone and queered the pitch for him?

A helper standing outside the red tent informed him, 'Madam is at Lakshmi's cage. That's where she asked you to come.'

As he stood outside the cage, he couldn't see the tigress's head, but her beautiful yellow- and black-striped coat shone. It was inside this beast's jaws that Kanchana would place her head in her celebrated act.

'Good morning, come on in. Watch your head, though, you'll have to bend a little,' came Kanchana's voice from somewhere on the other side of the tigress. There was a slight mischief in her voice as she added, 'Please don't be afraid of Lakshmi. She knows who belongs to the inner circle and who doesn't.'

Raghav bent low and pushed open the door of the cage. The tigress growled, causing Raghav to freeze for a moment.

Kanchana's soft laughter followed, and then the reassuring words, 'Come on in! Push that inner barrier a little bit!'

Raghav stooped, got into the cage and then slid past Lakshmi where there was about four feet of free space; and there, leaning against the steel-meshed wall of the cage sat Kanchana with her legs stretched out. Bent still, for there was no scope for straightening up, Raghav moved forward and sat down in the narrow space beside her. 'Why are we meeting here, madam?' he asked.

'I have my Lakshmi here to guard me. Nobody will dare come anywhere close. Relax, sit comfortably.'

'Yes, but it's rather cramped in here.'

Ignoring Raghav's protests, she once again giggled and said, 'You've grown only in years, haven't you? No sign of wisdom teeth sprouting, it seems.'

She craned her neck up and sent her gaze skimming past the cage bars over Lakshmi's back, just to ensure that they wouldn't be visible from the outside. She then grasped Raghav's hand with her warm hands and placed it on her breast as she said, 'You'll forgive me, won't you?'

'What for?'

'The other night, as I was congratulating you on your splendid performance, in all that excitement I bit into your cheek.'

'Madam,' Raghav said with a smile, 'don't I know the difference between when the teeth bite in error and when they bite with intention?'

'So, you do understand the difference, don't you, my darling?' she said, nuzzling closer, pulling him by the collar and placing her head on his chest. 'Then tell me this,' she continued, now in a petulant voice, 'why did you stay away from me these past four years? Where had you disappeared?' In an effort to pull him closer, Kanchana tugged at his shirt so hard that the buttons gave way. Raghav sent his arms around her. Their breaths turned hot. They felt giddy, drunk on love. That's when Lakshmi growled and cracked her tail like a whip on Kanchana's back. Kanchana winced. 'What's wrong with you, girl? Why are you getting jealous?'

Raghav became an important unit in the circus. It had also become obvious to all that he held an important place in Daaji's heart.

'What kind of magic had you wrought upon me, Raghav, that it survived a separation of four years?'

Kanchana and Raghav were sitting in Daaji's office while he was away on a visit to town. Kanchana's words delighted Raghav. 'You didn't forget me, Kanchana, I am grateful.'

'And, what a change you have wrought in your own self! Where were you then and look at the heights you have scaled now.'

'What do you mean?'

'The bouncing rope act, oh my god! Not a single circus in India will have an artiste like you! Those somersaults in the sky, simply unbelievable! Where did you learn this act?'

Raghav leaned in and said, 'Madam, it's your horse Phakkadrao that turned my life around.'

'Oh my god!' laughed Kanchana.

'It's the truth. Phakkadrao and I created wonderful items together. Our circus manager couldn't keep the crowds out. Surat, Junagadh, Ambala, then further north to Sirhind, Lahore, Peshawar and right up to the border of Afghanistan—wherever we went, Phakkadrao and my team were a huge hit.'

'Where did you go from there?'

'We travelled down south to Malabar, Kerala. Reached a village called Chirakkara nestled among palm and coconut trees. There I made friends with Kaanan, the son of a poor farmer. He taught me the rope act. When the rest of the camp would be fast asleep, he and I would sneak out into a coconut grove at dawn, and stringing a sturdy coir rope across two palms trees, start practising the jumps. We polished the act till it dazzled.'

'Raghav, why don't you call this friend over to our circus, then?'

'He's not alone now. He's married. To a young woman called Philomena.'

'Oh!'

'Yes. Her entire family works in a European circus called Canstrolli. When Kaanan climbed up the rope and began spinning on it like a top, Philomena fell for him. They're in Europe now.'

18

Sarang Daaji had always regarded Gajaratna as the wellspring of his prosperity. This gift from Shahu Maharaj had brought about the establishment of the circus company. That was why he decided that Gajaratna would lead Kanchana's wedding procession. Sarang Daaji had called over from Belgaum the most expensive tailor to prepare Kanchana's wardrobe.

Sarang Daaji handed Kanchana a notebook that had the names of the traders in Belgaum, Pune and Bombay with whom he had invested his disposable money. He told her about the bank lockers where he had stored his promissory notes. He gave her all other important papers, along with bunches of keys. He sat down with her and instructed her on what care she should take as the owner of a big circus such as theirs, its trade secrets.

The Nipani fair was underway at this time. Even if they had held nine shows over the next three days, they would not have exhausted the viewership that was moving about in the fair. The locals too loved Daaji's circus. But it was important to wind up here and start for Kaagwad with the entire retinue the next day. Nothing was more important than Kanchana's marriage.

The last show of the day was on. Just a few numbers remained. The audience was eagerly waiting for Kanchana's item, followed by Raghav's Bouncing Rope act. They had already performed the Roman rings, bending their bodies into circles and spinning around like tops.

When the show finally came to a close, Sarang Daaji took the mike in his hand and expressed his deep gratitude to the circus lovers of Nipani. His voice heavy with emotion, Sarang Daaji said, 'My revered patrons, the gate money we have received this time in your town has broken all previous records. It's one and a half times more than we had expected it to be. I consider this earning a gift from all of you to my beloved daughter. Please come to Kaagwad tomorrow and give her your blessings on her wedding day. Friends, when my circus comes next to your town, I may or may not be there to accompany it. But I expect you to continue showering your love on my daughter as you have on me.'

Sixteen elephants, forty odd horses and cages with lions and tigers entered Kaagwad, heralding the arrival of Sarang Daaji. It seemed as if an emperor had returned to his capital city.

Sarja's face was a sight to see. It was about fifteen years since she had turned down Sarang Daaji's appeal for looking after Kanchana. She carried the twitch of that mean act somewhere in her heart. If only she had feigned sympathy and concern back then, she would have been a partner in this grand celebration. Making her alienation more painful was the hospitality being extended to Martha the nurse. Daaji had sent his car to Miraj to bring the old lady over for the wedding ceremonies.

It was against a background of famine and abject poverty that Daaji had emerged. With no industry or enterprise anywhere in the vicinity, his village had not known much apart from deprivation. Daaji had defied all barriers and lifted his circus to a level of professional efficiency. As an obvious consequence, affluence and grandeur had come flowing in.

This had stirred up deep envy among the idle members of his community. Many found it difficult to digest Daaji's success.

In those days, even sighting a motor car was only a dream for the ordinary villager. Only one or two people in an entire sub-district owned a car; most often they were Marwari traders. Motor cars were a far cry, even an ordinary cycle was a bridge too far for the common person. If ever a rare car roared in, followed by a cloud of dust, children from villages on either side of the road would stand gawping at it in wonder.

News arrived in Kaagwad that Sarang Daaji had purchased the station wagon belonging to the Raja Sahib of Mysore, and it created a commotion. Many of the villagers were bewildered and unsettled, but the relatives were finding it impossible to keep their bile down. 'So, just by buying a king's car, you consider yourself the king's grand-dad, do you? When your tent catches fire and the entire circus is reduced to ashes, that's when you will come crashing down to earth.'

Sarang Daaji, however, had a deep affection for his place of birth. He brought a number of temples in the vicinity into good shape. If there was a wedding in a house, the people of Kaagwad chased him down from Assam to Rameshwar and fleeced him off handsome amounts as a matter of right. It was always transacted as a loan, with both parties knowing that the money would never come back.

As he thought of his daughter getting married, he decided to spare no expense. He wanted the wedding to be a memorable event.

He gathered his friends around him and said, 'Look, I am a circus man, therefore it's natural that horses and elephants will dance in the procession, tigers and lions will go on parade in my daughter's wedding. But how can girls from poor families ever get to experience this joy?'

'Well, what do you want to do then?'

'Let a herald go round the ten or twelve neighbouring villages and inform people that if they have girls of marriagable age, they can bring them over to my Kanchana's mandap. I shall bear the entire expenditure.'

Despite the short notice, twenty-one couples decided to join the communal wedding. In a beautifully decorated mandap, twenty-two couples took the rounds of the holy fire and committed themselves to a lifetime of togetherness. Daaji provided wedding clothes to each couple and their nearest relatives. Each bride was presented with a ten-gram gold mangalsutra. A great procession then did the rounds of the lanes and bylanes of the village, beautifully decorated elephants in front, followed by sixty handsome horses and carefully selected cages of lions and tigers on bullock carts and lorries. The procession was led by the circus band that played in tandem with the English military band that had been called over from Belgaum. The villagers were awestruck. They had never seen such a show before.

Eleven mahouts had got busy since the crack of dawn on the wedding day, sprucing up Gajaratna. Daaji had called tailors from Indore to prepare a special caparison for him. It was made from thick velvet with mirror-work embroidery and silk tassels at the borders. On Gajaratna's back, under a sandalwood canopy replete with engravings, sat the bride and groom. In their brocaded finery enhanced by jewel-embedded gold ornaments, the two looked like a divine couple straight out of an epic. His Highness Patwardhan Maharaj of Sangli as well as the prince of Jamkhandi were in attendance.

Never before had the gathering seen elephants, horses and camels so heavily ornamented. The pyrotechnics that followed, the sparklers, the Catherine-wheels, the fizzing rockets and the deafening crackers, completed the picture of a marriage conceived in heaven and played out on earth.

The leader of the eleven dogs in the circus was a mongrel called Balarao. In honour of this happy occasion, Daaji had also got velvet jackets made for the dogs. Balarao was marching at the head of the pack with great dignity and alacrity.

The eye-popping procession was now nearing the temples of Kaburaya and Kalamma. Along with the fireworks, the thrust and parry of the two bands contesting with each other had electrified the atmosphere. Suddenly, Balarao began to bark frantically. It negotiated its way through the crowd and reached Daaji. It held the loose end of Daaji's silken dhoti and began tugging at it. When Daaji looked at Balarao in confusion, it began rolling on the ground, coating its jacket with thick layers of dust.

When Balarao finally realised it wasn't able to catch its master's attention, it leapt forward. Gajaratna was now quite close to the temple. Balarao shot forward fifteen paces ahead of the elephant and began frantically scratching the earth. It dug out a bag that contained a couple of coconuts and a few other things.

Balarao picked up the bag in its mouth and leapt with it into the bushes on one side of the dirt track. Within a minute or two, a giant flash of light was seen at a distance. There was a massive explosion, immediately followed by a billow of smoke and dust swelling out into the air. Daaji rushed forward to find that Balarao had been blown to bits. Saibu reached the spot on Daaji's heels. Some company boys also rushed in, and they soon began locating splintered pieces of hard, metallic objects, shrapnel scattered by the explosive device. Another boy showed Daaji what looked like the casing of a piece of gelatin. A terrified Saibu found his voice. 'Look, Daaji Sahib,' he said, 'the time had arrived, but destiny hadn't; otherwise one doesn't know what would have happened to the bride and groom.'

Daaji felt faint. 'Oh my God!' he exclaimed, gripping his head with both hands.

'It was Kalamma alone who saved you, Daaji.'

Daaji stood frozen like a statue. Taranath came forward, held Daaji by the hand and said, 'Come, Sarang, go and bow before God. You escaped by a whisker. This entire marriage procession could have transformed into a funeral procession.'

Daaji regained composure. The band was still playing. Many people in the rear were not even aware of what had just happened. They had taken the explosion to be a part of the fireworks. Daaji's shirt, however, had turned wet with perspiration.

Up to this point, Daaji had been consumed with the fear that the wedding of his daughter would remain a dream that would never be realised. But now that he had seen the royal ceremony to a successful conclusion, he was within an inch of touching heaven. He was beside himself with joy.

The next day, all the energy seemed to have drained out of the wedding pandal. The banana trunks that had been planted for decoration now looked dry and listless. Daaji was sitting in the mandap talking to friends. Saibu walked in and sat beside Daaji. 'Why do you continue to take risks?' he murmured.

'What risks?'

'The wretch who planted the time-bomb right under the elephant carrying Raghav and Kanchana, you should start an investigation and find out who it was. Try to get to the root of the conspiracy.'

For a moment or two, Daaji was lost in contemplation. Then he shook his head, patted Saibu on the back and said, 'Let that go, pora. A calamity had come visiting, but with the blessings of Goddess Kalamma, it was blown away. My daughter and son-in-law are safe. In this moment of joy, I forgive that schemer and decide to put the entire episode behind me.'

'Kanchana's voice interrupted them, 'Baba, you might have to pay a heavy price for this forgiveness. Saibu *chachu* is right. We must get to the bottom of this.'

19

Raghav went up to Kanchana one morning and placed a bet: 'Within the next four or five days, I'm going to be friends with your Lakshmi.'

'You're going to lose!' she laughed mischievously. 'She's Lakshmi—no ordinary tigress.'

Raghav began visiting Lakshmi. He would sit in front of the cage and get into a one-sided conversation with her. For the first two days, Lakshmi ignored him altogether, but slowly there was a change in her. Every time she saw him, she would walk over to the bars of the cage and lock eyes with him. In a few more days, she began sitting before him with her forelegs spread out, as if listening to Raghav's prattle.

Sticking chunks of meat to the end of an iron rod, Raghav started feeding Lakshmi. She would gobble up the meat with great relish. After a few days, Raghav took the next daring step forward: instead of extending the flesh at the end of an iron rod, he picked up a biggish lump in his hand and presented himself in front of Lakshmi's cage. The animal trainers were aghast. This foolhardiness could cost Raghav his life. Nobody could be certain how the beast on the other side would behave. Lakshmi, however, simply moved forward and took the meat off Raghav's fingers without any fuss. Raghav then did the next harebrained thing and placed his palm on Lakshmi's head. He was thrilled at the touch of her warm coat.

Kanchana had been watching Raghav's moves with interest. 'Anybody can charm young girls, Raghav-ji,' she said, 'but winning over an obstinate creature like Lakshmi is a different kettle of fish. It's amazing that you have made inroads with her.'

'Nothing amazing about it. My friends Kashinath Thorat and Damu Dhotre taught me a very important lesson: taming them with your eyes and with your heart is far more important than controlling them with sticks and whips. We need to spend more time in their company, we need to understand their innate nature, their individual likes and dislikes.'

'How do you do that?'

'By spending time with them. They should begin to want your company, develop a need for it. Give an elephant a stick of sugarcane when you meet it, it's crazy for sugarcane. Horses love sliced apples and carrots, even bananas sometimes. See how hippos open their jaws when you toss cauliflowers at them. That's how you develop intimacy with animals. They should want to come close to you without any fear.'

'Having grown up in their company since I was a toddler, I guess I have been doing all this unwittingly. Never thought it out this way.'

After a few days, Kanchana finished her act with Lakshmi and stood wiping the tigress's saliva off her face and hands with a napkin. She stood before the audience, bowing in all directions in acceptance of their applause.

When she looked to the left, what she saw stunned her. It was Raghav now, with his head in Lakshmi's wide-open maw. In a little while he pulled his head out and wiped the sweat and saliva off with his handkerchief. Then he began patting Lakshmi's head with affection.

Lakshmi—who was known to growl even at the wind that brought human smell, who swung her foreleg at anybody who dared to come close—now stood before Raghav as tame as a cow. Feigning anger, a delighted Kanchana scolded Lakshmi, 'Such disloyalty, girl? You have broken my heart.'

20

When Daaji had brought Lakshmi from the Sundarbans, she was barely two months old. Now she had grown into a giant Bengal tigress. Her majestic appearance alone established her as the unchallenged empress of the menagerie.

It was Lakshmi's habit to walk into the ring with a stately gait. But on spotting Kanchana, all her ferocity would disappear and she would turn into a pet cat. Their games would then begin. But lately, the tigress did not seem like herself. She began to growl at Kanchana as if she were an enemy. She let out grunts of pain. Kanchana had seen these temper tantrums in almost all the animals in the menagerie. Lakshmi's restlessness, her frequent belching, constant stretching as if to release muscle cramps, her howling triggered by the burning sensation under her tail, all of these were very strong signals that Lakshmi was in heat.

'All right, then,' said Daaji, 'let's get one of those big cages emptied as soon as today's shows are over.'

Rustam the tiger and Lakshmi were placed in the big cage. The two shook up the cage as well as the night. Their grunts and agitated growls could be heard from far away. They grunted, snorted, teased, coaxed and fondled. They swung their paws and snapped their jaws and tried to toss each other away.

The excited male drooled all night while Lakshmi kept him at bay, delivering blows with her paws. With the cool wind of the early dawn, their temperatures came down a little. The two rubbed nostrils and took in each other's scent. Lakshmi, now in red-hot heat, became anxious and twitchy.

After a night-long battle, the alert Rustam noticed the tired tigress shut her eyes for a moment and immediately grabbed the opportunity. Gathering all the strength in his hind legs, he leapt upon the tigress, pulled her underneath him, pressed her down under his belly and rubbed himself on her. The two bodies fused into a single wriggling, thrashing entity, in the manner of two dry logs of wood catching fire together. Rustam caught hold of Lakshmi's nape in his jaws and held her down. It was after a long time of heaving and grunting and twitching that the two animals suddenly began to go limp.

When Kanchana visited the cage in the morning, she saw them lying like two huge bundles of cloth thrown into a corner.

21

On her way back from the kitchen tent, Hirabai told Daaji, 'You look very pleased with yourself these days.'

'It's natural, isn't it? My daughter is going to be a mother soon. As a father, I'm bound to be excited. My lineage is growing.'

By and large, the mood in the company premises was that of jubilation. The grand wedding of Kanchana and Raghav, the substantial earnings made by the circus from their shows in various carnivals and market towns, these had brought a smile on everybody's face. And now the entire troupe eagerly awaited the arrival of Kanchana's baby. Daaji would find out from Lilian and Hirabai about Kanchana's cravings and go hunting in the market for different kinds of food items. He would return every day with his hands full of *soan-papdi, chilli bhajiyas,* corn on the cob, tamarind fruit and what not.

Kanchana, on the other hand, was charged up about Lakshmi's pregnancy. Even though she was in her seventh month, she didn't seem to be concerned about her own pregnancy at all. She would frequently visit Lakshmi's cage and sit there, watching the tigress's distended stomach.

Often she would send the boys to nearby jungles to hunt, particularly rabbits, whose meat Lakshmi loved. When the aroma of the food reached the tigress, she would let out deep growls of joy.

The July rains had been heavy and widespread. The paddy fields were full to the brim, making it impossible to erect circus tents in the villages. Hence they had pitched them in the *taluka* town of Islampur on the open grounds behind the Tahsildar's office.

The field in front of the office had become the favourite meeting ground for slogan-shouting patriots. Loud cries of 'We want *Swaraj*' and '*Vande Mataram*' reached the tents at frequent intervals. The situation had turned volatile in this belt in merely a month's time. The tricolour flag of the Congress party had been hoisted in Islampur and Ashta on thirty-foot tall poles. News kept arriving of farmers defying the British administration everywhere.

This tempestuous scenario had Kanchana worried. The activities of the underground revolutionaries of Satara district were on the rise. Special agents of Nana Patil and G.D. Laad would quietly visit the circus. On the outer side of the camp was the stable for horses, but hidden behind them was Mahaling's foundry, which would be blazing far into the night. Sledge-hammers fell on iron and melted steel was given shape. Mahaling was an expert at making country pistols and guns. The work was very risky, but the man was driven by passion and patriotism.

Till as long as Mahaling's bellows worked the furnace, till as long as the sparks flew red and white, Hirabai's eyes would mount guard like a pair of torches. Her eyes would scan the sky from one end to the other. The drop of a leaf anywhere would prick her ears. Their daughters Shanta and Babita would come up to her, put their heads on their mother's lap, and fall asleep in a state of exhaustion.

Saibu had warned Sarang Daaji about the police, and soon enough, a gentleman came to the camp riding a fancy horse. He had come down from the jungles on the hills and he looked impressive. Tall and well-built, with a wide face and big, alert eyes, he had a cap on his head and wore a loose white jacket with many pockets. He gave the impression of being a landlord and was accompanied by a number of lathi-wielding guards.

Sarang Daaji received him warmly and escorted him into his tent. Turning towards Kanchana, he said, 'Come, pori, meet our guest Ganpatrao Patil of Bilashi village. Patil Sahib, this is my daughter and heiress Kanchana.'

'Ah, so this is the brave Kanchana. She's the one who plays with the tigress.'

'Absolutely right. Ganpatrao, do what you have to, but bring us deliverance from these White monkeys that have been ruling our country.'

Leaning against a bolster, Ganpatrao said, 'Daaji, it's because of their censorship that you don't get to hear what's been happening around the country. The fact is that a massive jungle satyagrah has been underway in Shirala and in my own village, Bilashi. The tricolour has been fluttering atop a thirty-five-foot tall teak pole for a few weeks. We have wiped our village clean of every sign of English administration. An entire cavalcade of Swaraj volunteers has been resident in our village for a month now. We have been celebrating Independence Week in our Mahadev temple from sunrise to sunset. A good 1,000 men and women assemble there every day. We have placed a statue of Mother India right next to that of Mahadev. People from around thirty to thirty-five surrounding villages come dancing in with the tricolour in hand.'

'Haven't the British police got wind of it?'

'How can they not? That Sub-Inspector Bankat Singh had arrived the other day to Bilashi with a posse of his men, but the people there are so fired up with the spirit of non-cooperation that the policemen couldn't get so much as a glass of water to drink, nor did their horses get any fodder. Bankat Singh returned in quite a rage.'

When the secret discussions between Ganpatrao and Daaji began, Kanchana and the others thought it prudent to leave the tent. As per Gandhiji's call, major satyagrah movements had begun at Balia in the north and Bilashi, Baglan and Chirner in the west and south.

As the days went by, the situation in Islampur became more and more turbulent. Two months had rolled by, and the tricolour flying in Bilashi village hadn't yet been brought down. The atmosphere had been turning tenser in every patch of land in the vicinity. All kinds of news was circulating in the town: a British cavalry unit from Pune has been brought over two days ago; seventy high-quality army horses disembarked at the Takari station at dawn today and have now been stationed at the government stable in Islampur. Preparations at this scale by the British Police had sent a wave of anxiety among the common people.

The police sent a serious report to the Tahsildar one day, and the Tahsildar issued a notice to the circus, that in view of the delicate law and order situation in the region, the circus would not be allowed to hold late evening shows. There would just be one show per day, the 5.00 p.m. one.

Kanchana was furious at this injustice. She immediately jumped on to her horse and went riding to Sub-Inspector Bankat Singh's office. 'Why are you being unjust to us?' she demanded. 'How will we feed our men and horses?'

'Is it really about your men and horses?' asked Bankat Singh in a voice dripping with sarcasm. 'Or is it about feeding Gandhi Maharaj's worthless Congresswallahs?'

The late evening show remained suspended. The situation in the town turned grimmer. On 1 September 1930, Islampura was placed under curfew. The soldiers of the British Army kept all-night vigils on the streets. The tricolour was brought down and the Union Jack hoisted in its place. The Great Kanchana Circus was shut down for eight days under government orders.

Despite being under close surveillance, Daaji didn't feel cowed down at all. Volunteers from Miraj, Belgaum and Dharwad continued sneaking into the camp for shelter in the darkness of the night. With well over 500 men and animals milling around, it wasn't difficult for these shelter seekers to melt into this crowd.

One day, it appeared as if the entire police force had disappeared from the streets of Islampur. By afternoon the market was hot with the news that these men had been dispatched urgently to Bilashi; also that Collector Aminuddin had left Satara with a police force of 250 men, and reinforcements had been called in from Pune. An infantry force of 250 men had been rushed from Kolhapur too. These developments rattled Sarang Daaji and Kanchana. Just a couple of nights ago, a few revolutionaries from Karwar had taken five horses from the circus stables and disappeared into the jungle tracks en route to Bilashi.

News arrived late in the night from the Warana valley. Two workers who had fled from there were telling Sarang Daaji, 'The British belaboured 800 women, children and old people. When the tricolour was brought down, the villagers put up a strong resistance against the White sahibs. The soldiers beat up the farmers. Some unlettered women like Rajakka Patlin, Mainabai Dhangar and sixty-year-old Muktabai stood up strongly against the authorities. When the intrepid Mainabai held the flag close to her chest, refusing to let it go, she was literally dragged away. The police opened fire.'

'What?' Kanchana screamed in agitation.

'Two young boys, Dhondi Kumbhar and Shankar Chambhar, fell to the bullets. The British dragged their blood-soaked bodies down the streets. There was panic everywhere.'

Dark shadows of worry settled on Daaji's face. But there was one piece of news that kept his hope alive. In the jungles and heaths of the Sahyadris, on the bank of the Varna river, young peasant boys had decided to rise up in revolt and had given the British bitter resistance.

It was past midnight. The stomping of boots and the clip-clop of horses on the wet earth and slush outside drifted into the camp. Sensing that the sound was headed towards the camp, Kanchana hurriedly got up and peeped out of a gap in the tent wall. A squad of British police along with gun-toting soldiers was coming towards them. Something disturbing was afoot.

Police Sergeant Beloshi's loud call reached them from a distance, 'Arrey, you Sarang Daaji, and that Raghav or whatever his name is, and your dare-devil daughter, come out! You have to come to the police station.'

Daaji, Raghav and Taranath hurried out and stood forming a wall in front of the sergeant. The sergeant looked them up and down. Then, placing a pinch of tobacco in his cheek, the sergeant said, 'All of you are wanted. The boss's order is that you should bring that circus-girl with you. Where is she?'

'Sergeant, sir, she is unwell.'

'Like hell she is! Just last week she came over to the police station and ranted at the officers. Chattering like a mynah!'

'*Aho*, she's in her seventh month of pregnancy. She's been in bed since yesterday.'

'What rot! Come, let me have a look.'

When the sergeant pulled aside the drape drawn across the door of the tent and peeped inside, he saw Kanchana stretched out on a bed, her hair spread all over her pillow. Her face looked tensed up with fever and the kohl in her eyes was smudged. The lamp near the head of her bed was flickering. The air was thick with the smell of asefotida and other herbs. Also visible was her swollen belly as she lay stretched out on her back. Next to her sat Hirabai, looking distressed.

The active men were marched away with a gun barrel poking them from behind. The moment they had disappeared from view, Mahaling and his helpers leapt out of the bushes on the other side of the stream. They had been in the middle of completing the order for six rifles for the revolutionaries. They were to be dispatched for Shenoli and Waḍuj. Nanasahib's revolutionary colleagues were waiting to pick up the consignment in the banyan grove on the heath near Sakhral. Mahaling was due to set off with the rifles as soon as they were ready.

Taranath had already got two wooden boxes ready for the merchandise. The rifles were placed in them after removing the butts. Mahaling was giving the rifles a careful look-over; a defect could well lead to the death of the person firing the rifle. The hurry, therefore was punctuated by the cautionary interruptions of Mahaling when Kanchana rushed in. 'Kaka, you have to hurry up. Tonight seems to be a night of betrayal.'

'You are quite right, pori. The cops rounded up the menfolk, took them away,' said Taranath. 'There could be a raid here any time.'

Mahaling speeded up. The next phase of delivering the weapons was very important. It was a two-hour ride, and the route was infested with danger. Mahaling said, 'Kanchu, give us a robust horse.'

'Take Phakkadrao, he will run like a bullet.'

Taranath took a few ring-boys with him to the stable and brought Phakkadrao out. On both sides of the saddle, they tied up the wooden boxes and secured them with strong coir ropes.

The night wind was strong. From the stream-side came the hoots of owls. A rifle workshop in the middle of a circus was more inflammatory than fire itself. Every second's delay brought the possibility of the gallows closer. Mahaling tied a muffler tight round his waist and put his foot in the stirrup to swing over the horse. Just then, his face twisted in agony, *'Arrey deva!'* he groaned. 'This sudden call of nature at this critical time!' Even in the middle of this grave moment Hirabai couldn't hold back her laughter. She ran in and brought out a can of water and handed it to her husband.

There was a makeshift latrine in a corner of the camp, but Mahaling didn't want to risk going in. Instead, he disappeared into the bushes of the farm on the other side. Within seconds the air was filled with cries of 'Run!' 'Don't let them get away!' accompanied by the clatter of over a dozen horses galloping in towards the camp. Bankat Singh had launched his assault.

Kanchana was stupefied. The fluid around the foetus in her womb sloshed. No catastrophe could be bigger than the one that was now threatening the circus. If the gun workshop and its secret fabrication were to land in the hands of the enemy, the consequences would be utterly disastrous. A couple of dozen at least would be taken to the Yerawada Jail and hanged. The company would be crippled for life. Also, the freedom fighters who had trusted her father and entrusted to him this serious responsibility would roll in the dust. The thought uppermost in her mind was that the company's infamy had to be prevented, whatever the cost.

Kanchana was drenched in sweat. Her hair stood on end and her throat turned dry as sandpaper. She swung her head frantically from right to left to right, not knowing what she was looking for in the darkness that surrounded her. If only the earth could split and the circus camp disappear into it! But Kalamma Devi, this calamity had to be prevented from happening!

As she stood shivering, her feet kept moving backwards and forwards and sideways, her brain trying to snap out of the panic into which it had got jammed. Her eyes then fell on Phakkadrao standing with the two boxes of guns hanging on either side of his saddle. She heard the sound of the raiding party coming closer and also saw a few horses approaching from the direction in which Mahalinga had fled. Mahalinga, therefore, was not likely to appear for some time, which would mean that the rifle-boxes would soon land in the hands of the enemy. Without consciously working it out in her head, forgetting the state she was in, she leapt towards the horse.

'Move, Phakkad,' she rasped as she jumped into the saddle and spurred the horse into a gallop. Her feet had found the stirrup, and she felt she was swinging on a trapeze strung eighty feet high in the big top. She couldn't possibly have heard Hirabai's anguished cry of 'Pori! What are you doing? You are in no condition—'

Now through slimy earth, now through the flowing stream, across the dew-soaked grass, Phakkadrao was zipping past like a ball of fire. Kanchana couldn't hear a thing. All she had for company was the slaty darkness and the wild night wind. Kanchana could as well have been riding astride that wind. Over pits and stones, through slush and rubble, through streams and furrows, Phakkadrao simply kept blazing forward. Its eyes were bulging and its mouth was frothing. Despite the chill in the wind, both the rider and the ridden were bathed in sweat.

Bankat Singh was hopping like a monkey that had been fed a few pegs of rum. He swished his cane at anybody who came within his arm's range. The helper boys and girls, the grooms, the ring boys—they were all receiving liberal doses of his fists and boots. Despite such energetic attacks, his anger showed no signs of ebbing. When he saw Hirabai, he swung his leg to kick her butt. Missing the mark, he rained his cane upon her, yelling, 'Come clean, you old hag. Where's that Kanchana gone?'

'To the hospital, *sarkaar*!'

'What hospital? And what emergency did the bitch have?'

'She's seven months pregnant. She had started having contractions.'

'So, where did she go?'

'To the east—the hospital of Wanles-wadi, towards Miraj.'

Bankat Singh immediately dispatched three horses in that direction.

Once it was daylight, the police went through the camp with a toothcomb. Mahaling's furnace was still hot, with an occasional cinder retaining a trace of pink under the ash. The circus staff told Bankat Singh that the furnace had been lit for making various things that a circus needed for running its show: horse-shoes, bolts for the stables, repairs of chairs and benches and so on.

Bankat Singh sent the entire company premises through the finest of sieves. The haystacks in the stables, the mountains of grass stored for the elephants, the stores of grains in the kitchen tent, everything was examined with a microscope. He came across a temporarily erected tank made of bricks and was struck by the strangeness of the surface of the water stored inside. As he stood gazing at it, he was almost blown off his feet when he noticed the surface go swelling upwards like a balloon. Soon emerged the button-eyed head of Mustafa the hippopotamus which locked Bankat Singh in his beady gaze. Bankat came within an inch of screaming when the hippo opened his prodigious jaw and went on opening it till all that could be seen was a huge mass of pink, bulbous, palpitating flesh.

It was about eight o'clock now and the day had begun to warm up. Bankat Singh was on the point of ordering the departure of his men when he saw at a distance a horse ambling at an easy pace towards the camp, ostensibly with no rider on its back. It was only when it had come sufficiently near that a figure became discernible, bent upon the mane as if sleeping on the horse's neck. As Phakkadrao came closer, exhaling laboured puffs of breath, Hirabai and Lilian rushed towards it.

When Hirabai reached up and turned the limp Kanchana's head towards herself, she was stunned. Kanchana was lying unconscious. It was entirely on account of Phakadrao's instinct that she had reached the camp alive. As Hirabai and the girls began off-loading Kanchana from the horse's back, they noticed that her shirt and trousers were caked in slime and blood. Hirabai also noticed that the swelling around Kanchana's stomach had vanished. The horse's legs were coated in mud and the moss that floats on water bodies. His tail was wet and filthy, with tangles of briars and bristly thorns lodged everywhere.

There was a rank, mouldy smell coming from Kanchana's body. Bankat Singh closed in with his men and immediately took charge of Kanchana's body that lay on the ground. From behind came the loud sob of Hirabai. She had tried to suppress it by stuffing her mouth with the end of her sari, but keeping it down had become impossible. She just went on staring at Kanchana's flattened stomach. There were lumps of dried blood and other gooey substance on her legs and ankles.

'Boys, go and check what's happened to this bitch.'

'Let the girl go, sir,' Hirabai pleaded. 'Can't you see that she had an abortion on her way to the hospital?'

'What kind of fool goes to deliver a child on horseback?' growled Bankat Singh. 'These circus rascals are not as straight as they look. They are devious to the last drop of their blood. Get a motor car ready and take this girl to the Miraj hospital. I want the doctor's report telling me what exactly has happened—whether she really had an abortion or just stabbed her thigh with a knife to stay out of our reach. I can bet my last penny, though, that this troupe has been busy playing a sinister game.'

Hirabai finished her breakfast at the kitchen table and set off for the office tent to meet Daaji. As she walked through the camp, her eyes fell on the cage kept to a side. Her daughters Shanta and Babita stood in front of it, staring at Kanchana and Lakshmi with awe.

Hirabai noticed that Lakshmi's auburn coat had begun to glisten with a new sheen. Her pregnancy was evident now. The animal lay listless on her side, the whiskers on her face twitching now and then. The swelling of her belly had increased the rattle in her throat and her breathing was laboured. Kanchana caressed her distressed body. When she noticed Shanta and Babita outside, she took their little hands and had them stroke the tigress's beautiful coat. They were thrilled.

As they stood clapping their hands in glee, Hirabai called out to them, 'You two, what are you doing there? Go for your practice!'

'Yes, *Aai*,' they shouted in unison and scampered away.

Hirabai peeped into Daaji's tent and said, 'Daaji, your daughter was certainly born to a tigress or a lioness in her previous life.'

'Why do you say that?'

'Her heart is certainly made of stone, and the bones in her body from steel.'

'Well, I've also had the same feeling sometimes.'

'Just look at her! It's been just a few days since she lost her baby, and that too while riding a horse. Another woman in her place would not have left her bed for the next three or four months.'

22

Raghav woke up with a start. Kanchana wasn't by his side. He could hear loud, painful growls coming from the direction of Lakshmi's cage. He jumped out of bed, picked up his flashlight and rushed towards the cage. Many from the troupe had assembled around Lakshmi's cage. In front of it sat Kanchana on a stool. Behind her stood Lilian, her hand on Kanchana's shoulder. Their eyes looked droopy for having spent a sleepless night.

When Raghav threw an angry glance at her, Kanchana pacified him with a smile and said, 'Can't you see that my baby is in distress? The time for her delivery has arrived.'

'Yes, but you should have called the vet over.'

'I sent him advance money a week ago. But he's had to rush to the District headquarters, it seems.'

'But, Kanchu—'

'Take it easy. In the world of circus, living, dying, delivering a baby—there's no difference between them. Everything's an examination. What do you say, Lilu Didi?' Both of them smiled.

Kanchana readied herself to help Lakshmi through her labour. A loud rattle emerged from the tigress's throat and her nostrils quivered. As if an electric current had been sent through her body. She shuddered violently, pressed her rear legs against the cage wall and pushed. She growled loudly and released faeces and warm urine. Tensing up her entire body, she began breathing heavily and stamping her rear legs.

She stood up, grinding her teeth in agony. Nobody had the courage to go anywhere close to her. Kanchana, however, let herself into the cage and placed a reassuring hand on Lakshmi's throbbing back. 'Go, Lakshey, one more push! No relief for you until that balloon bursts inside you.'

Lakshmi went on gurking and eructating loudly. She looked helpless with pain. She was twitching and convulsing. Her contractions picked up speed. The uterine sac had come very close to bursting now. Gathering her entire strength, the tigress splayed all her four legs out, pressed her belly down on the floor and began jerking her body like a woman. The outer sheath of the sac tore open.

As everybody watched dumbstruck, a long, shiny, plastic-looking balloon began emerging from under Lakshmi's tail. 'Go, baby, go!' screamed Kanchana. 'One last push!' A movement could now be detected inside the transparent, bluish film of the emerging balloon. Whitish specks became visible inside it. Lakshmi grunted hard and stamped her legs, and finally the balloon burst. Two tiny legs emerged first, like the pistil in a blooming flower.

Looking at the tiny cub, Kanchana hugged Lilian in joy. The people standing behind clapped in glee. Lakshmi too could feel her stomach going light. She turned her head round to see Kanchana holding the throbbing ball of yellow close to her stomach. Around this time, Sarang Daaji arrived and stood watching the scene. His eyes, however, were hovering over the artless face of his daughter. The joy he saw on it suggested that it wasn't the tigress but she herself who had delivered the baby. He felt a sudden stab of pain in his heart.

Kanchana placed that sticky ball of life in front of Lakshmi, at which the tigress began licking it vigorously with her sandpaper-like tongue. Everything that was sticking to the newborn's coat—blood, mucus, amniotic fluid—she scraped off with her tongue and swallowed it. The little cub was yet to open its eyes; its nostrils seemed to be blocked with a white, sticky substance, preventing it from breathing freely. Lakshmi immediately licked it off and blew her breath into her offspring's tiny nose, thus clearing the passage for air to travel. She licked the little ball clean as a cat would lick clean a bowl of cream.

After an hour had passed, Lakshmi pushed out her second cub, and after some more time, her third one. She then scraped together with her paws all the hay that lay on the cage floor. Gathering it under her stomach, she pushed it round her three little ones for warmth. Then she let out another loud burp and gave birth to her fourth cub. That was when she relaxed her muscles. Kanchana was holding a rag in her hand with which she began to fan Lakshmi's perspiration-soaked body. It would be another nine days before the cubs opened their tiny button eyes.

Animal trainer Ayub and Raghav peeped into the cage. Kanchana's face was blooming at the successful delivery of the cubs. The fourth cub looked extremely weak and emaciated. It was shivering incessantly. Kanchana and Lilian prepared a special cotton mattress for this scrawny cub. They covered it up with yet another piece of cloth, providing for it as much warmth as possible.

Daaji took Kanchana aside, made some enquiry and then left.

Kanchana arranged for some fresh meat and laid it out before the new mother. Lakshmi gobbled it all up immediately. She had now begun to lactate and her teats had swollen up with milk. The first three cubs latched on to the teats and began suckling eagerly. Lakshmi hadn't slept for a long time. A lethargy descended upon her now. Her eyes became heavy and she fell into an exhausted slumber. Her little cubs too, having had their fill, nuzzled into their mother's soft stomach and fell asleep.

When Kanchana returned to the cage, her eyes fell on the fourth cub. It was still shivering and looked exceedingly weak. It didn't appear that it had enough strength to fight on. Kanchana picked up the cub wrapped in cotton-wool and held it to her chest.

It was important to provide the mother and the newborns protection from the cold wind as well as from the swarming mosquitoes. Kanchana arranged for a brazier to be placed in front of the cage in which she sprinkled a fistful of carom seeds. The fumes got into Lakshmi's nostrils and she immediately felt better for it. Mother and cubs were safe now.

It was morning by the time Kanchana stood up to return to her tent. Lilian accompanied her. As Lilian was leaving, Kanchana said, 'Didi, while Lakshmi was in labour, did you notice how my father kept coming to the tent and then going away.'

'Yes, I did.'

'His face was dark as a cloud. He must have been thinking: if only he could have seen the face of his grandchild ...'

'You are right.'

'And I'm sure he still hopes that I will give him a grandchild again.' Kanchana's voice cracked. 'The fact is, Lilu Didi, that I made the doctor swear he would never reveal to my father that I won't be able to conceive again. And I trust that you will keep this to yourself. I'm still gathering the courage to break this to Raghav ... Can I have your handkerchief? My eyes refuse to dry up.'

Kanchana took the handkerchief Lilian had offered. A chill ran up her spine when she turned around. Raghav stood at the entrance of the tent, his eyes unblinking. Walking up to Kanchana, he took her in his arms, and she broke down.

Lilian went running to Kanchana at the break of dawn and dragged her to the ring. They stood in a spot from where they could see the frame of the trapeze. Kanchana had the manager bring it down. She examined the frame closely from all angles. She was alarmed by what she saw. 'How did you find out about this, Didi?' she asked Lilian.

'Completely by accident. I was climbing up the rope to rehearse my act when my eyes fell on this.'

The knots on the ropes that held the trapeze up had been loosened. Who could have hatched this dastardly conspiracy against one's own company? Sarang Daaji too was rattled. 'How can such a thing happen in our circus? Who would dare do this?'

Gajaratna had been showing signs of ill health. Where had the playful, mischievous Gajaratna disappeared? He dragged himself as he walked and looked frail.

If it had been in heat, a trail of sticky discharge should have shown below its ears. It refused to touch food. Daaji went to Gajaratna with a tray full of his favourite sheera, but he refused to eat it.

Just as dawn began to break, Sarang Daaji went to the rear side of his tent. The helper boys had kept a pot of hot water ready for him. Daaji added some cold water to it and began to bathe.

There was a sudden commotion in the menagerie. Four boys came running towards Daaji's tent. The mahaut Kismatbhai shouted from where he stood, 'Daaji! Come over here! Come quickly!'

'What is it?'

'Gajaratna has turned rogue. He rammed into a steel pillar and bent it in the middle. He is bringing the camp down!'

'What?'

Daaji dried himself with a dhoti, wrapped it round his waist like a lungi, slipped on a sleeveless vest and made a dash for the menagerie. Some eight or ten mahauts had gathered there with their helper boys. They had jammed together the elephant's rear legs with strong steel rods. Gajaratna's legs were tightly caught in a scissor-grip. On the inner side of this scissor-grip were blunt nails which, besides causing Gajaratna pain, prevented it from moving forward.

An enraged elephant is the most dangerous animal on earth. A knock from its massive head can bring down trees and turn walls to rubble. It was on account of such potential for destruction that the scissor-grip cross-rods had been used since the time of the Mauryas.

Although the darkness hadn't lifted altogether, there was enough light around to see Gajaratna's limbs. In front of him stood a few mahauts with burning torches in their hands. Daaji took in his beloved Gajaratna's wide forehead, colossal body, legs, big and strong as the pillars of a temple, and button eyes. Looking at the state to which the fortune-maker of his company had been reduced, Daaji felt a heavy weight descend on his heart.

Gajaratna's distraught face stabbed at Daaji's heart. He became deeply anxious. Kanchana too stared at the elephant with frightened eyes. Where had the playful, affectionate Gajaratna disappeared?

Could someone have fed him glass shards, concealing them in his food? That would explain the excruciating pain he was experiencing. Driven out of his mind, Gajaratna refused to recognise Daaji and Kanchana.

Holding Kanchana by the shoulders, Daaji broke down. 'Pori, someone's cast an evil eye on this brother of yours,' he said, sobbing.

'Baba, we won't be able to take him into the ring.'

'Doesn't matter if he rests for an entire month. I want to save him at all costs.'

After some time, Gajaratna calmed down. A vet arrived from Jamkhandi and fed him a herb extract. Gajaratna hadn't eaten for the past two days, hunger alone could have unhinged it.

The cook brought a plate with ten kilos of sheera, Gajaratna lay on his side, looking completely spent. His breath came out with a rattle. His legs were still firmly trapped in the scissor-grip. Daaji and Kanchana went close to him. Daaji couldn't hold back from petting the poor tormented creature. He picked up a lump of the thick sheera and eased it into Gajaratna's mouth. Ten kilos of sheera vanished in no time. There was, however, no sign of recognition in Gajaratna's eyes.

The afternoon show was houseful. All tickets had been sold and the box-office window was shut. Daaji hurried through his prayers.

There was a sudden chaos outside. 'Run! Run for your life!' was the call everywhere. The cage boys thought a carnivore had slipped out and they rushed towards the cages. The noise appeared to travel from the menagerie towards the circus arena. 'The elephant's gone mad!'

Daaji rushed out of his tent to find that Gajaratna had uprooted a tent wall along with the iron poles holding it in place. He was now tearing into the arena.

Daaji was horrified. Gajaratna had uprooted the long stakes to which his leg chains had been secured and was now dragging them behind him. War elephants, before they were taken to the battleground, were often fed marijuana to charge them up. Gajaratna's uncontrollable frenzy was like that of war elephants.

Pulling the stakes behind him, he now entered the empty circus tent and began tossing up the steel chairs and galleries as it moved. The crew members inside ran helter-skelter in panic. Daaji stood firm. He wanted Gajaratna to come to no harm.

There was no stopping Gajaratna now. He was wreaking destruction in all directions with his flailing trunk. An iron-hearted man like Daaji was reduced to tears. He sat on the ground, picked up fistfuls of earth and cried, "Gajaratna, my son, come to me!'

Gajaratna started moving in Daaji's direction. The circus managers, clerks and security men ran towards Daaji. Kanchana rushed alongside them. Every one of them began begging Daaji to move away. Kanchana cried out, 'Baba, turn round! This is not the Gajaratna we know!'

A few mahauts found courage and attacked the elephant's massive legs with rods and spears, forcing Gajaratna to change direction and head out of the circus tent. Even after the massive destruction he had wrought, he was nowhere near cooling down.

There was a big heap of iron poles lying behind the circus tent. Gajaratna started throwing them far and wide as if they were sugarcane sticks.

The situation became particularly hazardous because it was carnival time and large crowds had gathered everywhere. Their inability to control the rogue elephant turned the guts of the circus crew into jelly. Five thousand tickets had been sold for the show and it was due to begin any moment now. Massive queues had formed at the gates, waiting for the entry to begin. Daaji stood looking towards the elephant and bawling in his wretchedness, 'My son! My boy!' His lowing, however, was yielding no results. The crowd outside had begun to turn restless and people had started jostling each other.

Left with no alternative, Saibu began allowing the audience inside. The audience streamed into the tent. Meanwhile, news spread among the revelers on the carnival grounds that a circus elephant had gone mad. The police became alert and headed towards the circus. Instructions were rushed to the circus administration: Get the elephant under control. Shoot it down if you have to. If you cannot do it, we will get in and do whatever is required.

Kanchana saw a police van coming to a halt at the rear gate. It disgorged a squad of armed British soldiers. The police inspector got into a quick consultation with the army commander.

Kanchana ran up to her father, shouting, 'Baba, please do something, please save Gajaratna!'

The soldiers marched forward in their army boots, pushing Kanchana and Daaji out of their way. When Saibu rushed forward from inside the tent, an officer hit him hard and barked, 'Get the show started, you idiot! Who will control the public, otherwise?'

Saibu turned towards Kanchana. She looked at the 5,000 people gathered inside the tent. If they panicked and ran out, there would be a stampede. Inside the ring, Raghav and Taranath had somehow managed to keep the attention of the crowds engaged. They saw Kanchana enter the tent and were greatly relieved. Charlie on his bandstand saw this opportunity and started playing the loudest piece in his repertoire.

The British commander saw that the show had begun. He looked towards the rear and saw that Gajaratna was moving steadily towards the gate. He shouted out a loud order to his squad: 'Attention! Move forward! Get your guns ready! Get on your knee!' When his men had taken position, he barked, 'Fire!' The soldiers who had gone down on a knee aimed their rifles at Gajaratna and released a volley of bullets. Twenty-one bullets pierced the elephant's skin and blood began spurting out of the punctures. Gajaratna screeched in unbearable agony but continued to stand firmly on his feet. Life was refusing to abandon him.

Daaji couldn't bear the sight. It was imperative for Gajaratna to be released from the tussle between life and death. The gunfire stopped and the soldiers looked questioningly at their commander. Gajaratna stood there like a huge tree that had been denuded of all its branches, but refused to topple down.

Uncaring for his own life, Daaji leapt forward and deliberately placed himself in the firing range of the soldiers. His heart shattered at the sight of blood squirting from the bullet holes in Gajaratna's body. The poor elephant was drenched in his own blood. His thrashing trunk and bleeding jaws, his eyes bulging out in pain, his entire body swaying like a massive wall being brought down—the sight set Daaji's insides on fire.

He looked up at the sky helplessly, as if trying to gather strength from the gods in the heavens. Steeling himself, he whipped out the pistol at his waistband and aimed at the centre of Gajaratna's forehead. Steadying his trembling hand with supreme effort, he pulled the trigger twice. The bullets found their mark with unerring precision. Gajaratna shook like a building juddering under the force of an earthquake and collapsed.

He now lay there like a small hillock, sputtering blood that soon began to form a pool around him. Daaji was moving round and round in a small circle like a chicken that had lost its head. He was searching for the revolver that he had let fall from his hand. He was hoping to send one bullet into his own head. Dagdoba and Taranath tried to cool him down, but he was wailing, 'Gajaratna was gifted to me by a king and it lived like one. The sin of a father strangling the son of his own loin, why should that have happened at my hands? Gajaratna, my boy, it was you who brought glory to my company. Now, with you gone, what are we going to be reduced to?'

The police had sent Gajaratna's viscera and blood samples to Belgaum. By the time the troupe reached Mysore, Kanchana had the post-mortem report from the veterinary doctor in hand.

The report said that the elephant had been fed some poisonous herb over a period of time. When Kanchana placed the report before Daaji, he fell into stunned silence for some time. Then, letting out a deep sigh, he said, 'Pori, stay on the alert from here on. The company has enemies.'

Daaji called over Raghav and Kanchana that night and said, 'The person who planted the bomb on your wedding day, the person who loosened the trapeze rope and the enemy who fed my Gajaratna poison, is one and the same. There is envy and hatred in this air.'

'Please, Baba, take some rest. You look completely drained out.'

'I swear on my mother's name, pori—the person who is scheming to destroy our company is not an outsider. He is close to us.'

The sight of the massive gates and palatial houses of Mysore revived Daaji's spirits a little. Maharaja Wodeyar had arranged a grand dinner for the young couple in his palace. Kanchana and Raghav bowed at the king's feet and took his blessings. That evening Daaji, Kanchana and Raghav hiked up to Chamunda Hill and visited an ancient temple of the Mother Goddess. On their way down to the camp, Daaji suddenly started feeling out of breath and began to sweat profusely. His state deteriorated rapidly.

He was taken straight to hospital. As soon as the hospital staff moved out of the room, Daaji called Kanchana and Raghav close to him. He tried very hard to formulate words but failed.

He sputtered and looked helplessly at the two, not knowing how to get his thoughts across. Then he heaved himself up frantically and managed, 'Kanchu, you had tried to warn me. I ignored your warning—'

'Please, Baba, please rest.'

'Our Gajaratna managed to escape that first attempt with the bomb, but was finally done in by poison.' Daaji was bathed in perspiration. Suddenly strength returned to his voice and he spoke out loud: 'I can see our nemesis standing before my eyes. He is no other than—'

Daaji tried to gather the little strength that was left in him, but the sheer effort sent him into a swoon. He fell back on his bed never to rise again.

23

'Raghav, there's a letter from Devika Rani.'

'Devika Rani?' Raghav said in a startled voice.That was a big name. She was India's biggest, most loved actress. She had come to India after learning acting in England. Raghav was curious: 'What does madam have to say?'

'She wants to make a movie about the circus world.'

'That's great!'

'It's the story of two sisters. She will play the role of the elder sister and the younger sister's role has been written specifically for me, she says.'

Raghav smiled. When the Great Kanchana Circus had been playing on the municipality grounds of Bandra in Mumbai, Devika Rani had made three consequent trips from Malad to watch the show. The renowned singer Sundara Bai, who was a close friend of Devika Rani, had accompanied her on the first day to do the introductions. After watching the show, Devika Rani had patted Kanchana on the back and said, 'You are amazing. Your art is unique.'

'Kanchana had squeezed time out and gone and watched Devika Rani's *Achhoot Kanya*. She had immediately fallen in love with her. Raghav asked, 'So, will you accept the offer?'

'Raghav, nothing has changed since the time Baburao Painter offered me the role of Tara Rani. We can't afford to shut the company down for me to shoot a film.'

'Yes, we can't afford that.'

'Besides, the invitation from Burma has been lying pending for so many years.'

24

It was the time before lunch when most of the circus staff would be pottering around in their tents doing their own things. Kanchana was rearranging their wardrobe while Raghav played her assistant when Dinu, the cage-boy, appeared at their door looking very flushed. 'Kanchu tai, Raghav dada,' he said, panting, 'You are wanted immediately in the kitchen tent. Taranath *kaka* and the others are waiting for you.' The kitchen tent was often used as a conference room when the gathering was likely to be large.

The boy ran away without waiting for an answer. Kanchana looked at Raghav. She thought she saw a trace of excitement on his face. A perplexing sight met her eyes when they reached the tent. The expressions on the faces of the assembly displayed a wide range of emotions. While Taranath, who seemed to be leading the meeting, had a triumphant gleam in his eyes, Dagdu, Mahaling and Hirabai looked scandalised, as if they had just come back from a vulgar play. The head cook Akaram Jogta, Lilian and a few senior animal trainers including Sulaiman Chacha sat there looking stunned; Shekhar Paranjape, their manager, kept a poker face; but what surprised Kanchana was the presence of their electrician Bablu Quraishi who, only ten days ago, had been dismissed by Raghav in a humiliating manner after he was caught trying to secretly sell off circus equipment. The smirk on his face suggested that he was immensely enjoying some private joke. However, Saibu couldn't decide whether he should look terrified, offended, ashamed, defiant or resigned. He looked disheveled. His hands were tied behind his back. Next to him stood another man, about forty years old, also with his hands tied.

'What's going on here?' Kanchana asked.

'Maybe Taranath kaka can tell us about it,' said Raghav.

Looking at Raghav, Taranath said, 'Raghavrao, your hunch turned out to be correct. We've managed to catch the culprit red-handed and we've got his accomplice too.'

'Look, this is getting to be too much,' snapped a bewildered Kanchana. 'Raghav, you obviously know a lot more than I do, so will someone begin explaining?'

Raghav said, 'I can begin by giving you the background, and then maybe Taranath kaka can take over. Is that okay, kaka?'

When Taranath nodded his consent, Raghav began, 'If you remember, the very last words that Daaji had said were that an insider was trying to destroy us. Unfortunately, he couldn't name the suspect. From that moment on, I was determined to find the mischief-maker before he managed to succeed in his mission. Taranath kaka and I hatched a plan. We created a mole who would be able to sniff out the villain. Not many know that this Bablu here is the son of Taranath kaka's childhood friend Rehman Quraishi.'

Bablu's grin widened as all eyes turned on him, with Taranath casting a particularly benevolent look on his protégé.

'So, Kanchu,' Raghav continued, 'we arranged the drama of catching Bablu trying to sell off some electrical equipment to an outsider, so that I could humiliate him in public and dismiss him. That would give him license to hate me and want to do me harm. If you remember, I gave him just a few hours to collect his belongings and clear out of our camp. From this point on, Taranath kaka, would you like to take over?'

'Why me?' Taranath laughed. 'Let's hear some of it from the hero's mouth. Bablu, tell them what you just told me.'

For all the thrill he felt at becoming the centre of attention, Bablu was not the natural raconteur. He hummed and hawed and began, 'So, Raghav dada, you told me to sell the generator parts. I did that, and you caught me. Then you started abusing me and pretended you wanted to hit me. I then went all over the camp abusing you. Sorry, Kanchu Didi, I bad-mouthed you, and I ranted against Daaji as well. Even as I packed up my things, I went around shouting that I had always hated all of you and I would exact my revenge. I said all kinds of things. I would poison the animals, burn the tents down with a short circuit, drug or injure the horses so that Raghav dada would fall during his act. I acted as if I wouldn't rest until I had avenged my public humiliation. As I left, saying goodbye to everyone, I casually dropped the address of my friend's house where I could be found.'

'*Baap re*, Bablu!' Dagdu broke in, 'I really bought into your threats. In fact, I wanted to meet and reason it out with you. Later, I thought I would wait and watch.'

'Dagdu kaka,' Bablu smirked, 'I did get a visitor the next day, and it was our Saibu chachu!' Raghav and Taranath exchanged knowing looks. 'He tried to calm me down, but when he realised that I wasn't backing off, and that I was a naturally crooked person, a bad character, he went away. But then he came back the next day. He looked different this time. He began by telling me that Raghav dada was a demon. He had cast a magic spell on Kanchu Didi and Daaji, and so it was important to snuff him out. He said that he would give me a full 100 rupees if I helped him.'

'So, how were you supposed to help him?' Kanchana's voice turned cold as steel.

'Didi, he knew someone who would make a bomb that worked on a time-piece. My job would be to sneak into the camp and plant the bomb. Saibu chachu knew that Raghav dada visited Phakkadrao's stable from six in the morning for at least an hour every day. So I was to time the bomb to blow up at 6.30, hide it in the horse's manger at 5.30 and disappear.'

'You have something to say, Chachu?' hissed Kanchana.

'Kanchu, this man is lying. I have known you as a child!' Saibu said in a panicked voice.

'You aren't older to me by more than five years, Chachu!' Kanchana snubbed him.

'Anyway,' said Taranath, 'let's continue with the story. We'll soon know who is lying. A couple of days ago, Bablu reported to me his conversation with Saibu. Saibu and he went to a man named Satyanarayan at nine this morning to fetch the time bomb. I was waiting outside his house with four of my stoutest boys. We counted exactly up to five minutes after Bablu and Saibu entered the house, pounced upon them and caught them red-handed.'

'Some fisticuffs, Taranath?' asked Mahaling.

'Oh, plenty,' replied Taranath. 'But counting Bablu and me, we were six against two, so they stood no chance. We tied them up and brought them here.'

'I'll talk to you later, Saibu chacha,' Raghav said as he got up from his chair and walked towards the stranger. 'So, you are Satyanarayan?'

'Yes, my name is Satyanarayan,' said the man, not knowing whether he should act defiant or submissive.

'Bablu, untie Satyanarayan's hands and give him a chair to sit on,' said Raghav. 'Akaram dada, bring tea for all of us, except for our Chachu here. And a special tea for Satyanarayanji, please.'

'Now, my friend,' Raghav addressed Satyanarayan, 'we have no enmity between us, so I don't want to harm you. Do you understand?' Satyanarayan's face relaxed a little and he nodded. 'Therefore,' continued Raghav, 'if you satisfy us, we will let you go. But if you decide to be uncooperative, I shall hand you over to the police. You very well know what a serious crime bomb-making is in these riotous times. They may very well hang you. You know this, don't you?' Satyanarayan looked down. 'Don't you?' Raghav said in a sharper tone.

'I want to cooperate.'

'Good man. So, did you make a bomb for Saibu?'

Satyanarayan lowered his head and remained silent. Taranath walked up from behind, slapped him hard on the head and said, 'Come on, Satya babu, we caught you with the bomb, didn't we? We've got it here with us.'

'So you did make the bomb. You've known Saibu for long?'

'Yes, since childhood.'

'Ah, childhood buddies! So have you lent him your toys before?' Satyanarayan bowed his head again. Taranath slapped him hard on the nape, almost causing him to fall off his chair. 'Answer!' he snarled.

'Ye ... yes, yes. I had made another bomb for him about seventeen or eighteen months ago.'

'That was when we had gotten married, Kanchu,' Raghav said. Turning back towards Satyanarayan, he continued, 'Was that also a time bomb?'

'No, it was a simple device, with an electric circuit that would close with the press of a switch.'

'Who pressed the switch then?' Kanchana asked.

'I don't know, tai. My job was to assemble the bomb and hand it over to Saibu.'

'Chachu,' Kanchana turned to Saibu, 'who pressed the switch? You? No, it couldn't have been you—you were walking with the main procession.'

Saibu remained sullenly silent.

'Look, Chachu,' Raghav said, 'you are a clever man. You know that your game is up. So think up lies that we may swallow. If your lies are believable, we may be kinder to you.

If not, you will first be beaten up for a full week, then chopped up and fed to our animals. So gather your thoughts while I talk to your friend here.' He turned to Satyanarayan: 'How else did you help Saibu?'

'I can swear on the heads of my children that I haven't been involved with anything else that Saibu might have done.'

'How many children do you have?' Kanchana asked.

'Tai, I have five girls and a boy.'

Raghav and Kanchana exchanged looks before Raghav turned to the man and continued, 'All right, Satyanarayan, as of now we are taking your word for it. For the sake of your children, we are letting you go. Any further mischief from you, and you will suffer. That's a promise ... Kanchana, you want to say something?'

'Yes, Raghav-ji. Satyanarayan, you say you have five daughters. Before I forgive you, I want to know if you treat them well. Do you promise to provide them with the same opportunities as your son?'

'I already do, tai. My children are the light of my life. You can visit me some day and see for yourself.'

'All right. You must meet me before you go. I must send a gift for your girls.'

Satyanarayan was overwhelmed by this sudden change in circumstances. His eyes became wet and he bowed his head to hide them. Then he looked up and said in a hoarse voice, 'Tai, Dada, I had heard about Sarang Daaji's big heart. Now I see it in the two of you. I feel miserable for having caused you hurt. I shall always remain your servant. Please summon me if I can be of any help to you.'

'Good. Meet me before you leave,' Kanchana replied. 'And now for my favourite Saibu chachu. Bablu, pick up that cane and hit this man very hard on his calves.'

At this, Saibu's head jerked up and he looked in the direction of the cane and then towards Bablu. Fear began mounting in his eyes and he broke into a whimper. His eyes widened as Bablu gleefully picked up the cane, gave it a wide swing and brought it down on Saibu's calves. Saibu collapsed on his buttocks with a loud cry of '*arey baap reyyy!*' and sat there snivelling.

'Now, chachu dear,' Kanchana continued, 'I am making an offer to you. We can begin with Bablu flailing you first like cotton is flailed for carding, or you promise that you will answer my questions honestly and we finish this with the least amount of fuss. You have ten seconds to decide. I'm counting.'

Even before Kanchana had counted up to three, Saibu grovelled before her and begged, 'I'll answer all your questions, Kanchu!'

'Don't you dare call me Kanchu, you ungrateful, back-stabbing wretch!' Kanchana screamed in rage. 'All right, you gutter-worm, who was given charge of the switch on the day of my wedding?'

'It was just a boy from the village. I had told him that pressing the switch would set off fireworks. I had got him to hide behind a bush for the purpose.'

'Spill out the rest of it!'

' I … I had buried the explosives on the path along which the procession would pass. Then I joined the device to some electric wire concealed under the earth that led right up to the bush where the boy would hide. The boy was to press the switch as soon as Gajaratna crossed a line I had drawn on the road.'

'If your plan had succeeded, the boy would likely have squealed. Anyway, what happened after that?'

'You saw that. Much before Gajaratna reached the spot, that dog of yours smelt the explosives, dug them out and ran away with the bag. He ran in the direction of the bush the boy was hiding behind.'

'Why did the device blow up?'

'My guess is that the dog's wrench would have broken the connection of the device with the lead wires. And as the dog ran, the two ends would have touched, causing the device to blow up.'

'All right, so, the boy was never required to turn on the switch. Sounds reasonable. As for loosening the ropes on the trapeze, I won't even ask you. You would have done it yourself. Right?'

Saibu just kept staring at the floor.

'Just a minute, Kanchana, I have a question,' Raghav cut in. 'I want to know where Saibu got the money for funding his nefarious activities.'

'No mystery there,' chimed in Mahaling. 'He did so many of the purchases for our company, didn't he? Even if he were to save five rupees for himself every day, that would give him a 150 per month. Enough to buy three tolas of gold every month.'

'That makes complete sense,' Raghav said. 'All right, Kanchu, Go on.'

'I understood that you did all this out of hatred for us,' Kanchana continued, 'but the loose knots on the trapeze got noticed before a tragedy could occur. Your second conspiracy also failed. The third one of blowing up Raghav and Phakkadrao also never ran the entire course. But your wicked design of killing Gajaratna worked. Tell me about it.'

'Honestly, Kan ... madam, I had nothing to do with that.'

'Bablu!,' Kanchana called out, and the boy brought the cane swinging down on Saibu's back. He had been waiting for this opportunity.

'*Arey baaaap reyyyy!*' yelled Saibu. He recovered his balance and said, 'Please believe me—'

'No, Kanchu, don't believe him!' The shout rose from an unexpected corner. Sulaiman stood up shivering. Tears were streaming down his eyes.

'Chacha? What's the matter? You know something, don't you?' Kanchana's face was a mass of confusion.

'Yes, I do, and you can hold me guilty of having caused Gajaratna's death, even if unknowingly.'

'What do you mean, chacha? Please don't talk in riddles.'

'Kanchana beti,' Sulaiman stuttered, 'this rogue had got some *kusumba* kind of herb ground with opium, made a decoction of it and given it to me. I was a fool to have trusted him and fed it to Gajaratna for fifteen days. Those jungle herbs turned a friendly, loyal animal into a monster. They destroyed his brain.'

'But, chacha, how could you have possibly done this?' Kanchana's voice was distressed.

'Completely my fault, *beti,* for having let myself fall victim to his sweet talk. He told me that some exalted sadhu had given him the healing powder. It would double the elephant's power, he said. And why would I not want my beautiful Gajaratna to become stronger?'

'Oh, chacha, how could you have done it? But how can I blame you alone? This fiend fooled my father too, fooled all of you, my father's friends, and would have gone on fooling us till he had sent us to our graves. Saibu, you scoundrel, you sinner—killed my elephant, and that killed my father, the person you should have worshipped. I want to skin you alive. Why did you do it?'

Saibu sat on his haunches with his head down.

'Bablu!' screamed Kanchana and the boy took the opportunity of landing two blows instead of one.

'No! Please stop! I'll tell you! Please stop!' Saibu refused to lift his eyes off the ground. 'I did it … because … I hated this man, Raghav.'

'Raghav?'

'Because … he stole your and Daaji's heart … and got to marry you … and became the owner of the company …'

'So? Why hate him for that?'

Saibu remained frozen. 'Bablu—' Kanchana ordered.

'No, wait!' Saibu trembled. 'Because … I wanted to marry you.'

'What?' Kanchana moved towards Bablu in wild rage. 'Give me that cane!' She snatched the cane and began raining blows upon a writhing Saibu. When Raghav saw gashes opening up in Saibu's body, he wrapped his arms round Kanchana and pulled her away.'

'You will kill him, Kanchu,' he said, patting her back. 'We don't want that hassle on our heads.'

Saibu lay groaning, blood oozing out of his many wounds. In a little while, Kanchana began cooling down. She said, 'Raghav, will you please arrange to give 500 rupees to this man … what's his name … Satyapal? It's for your daughters. Take good care of them.'

'Sure,' said Raghav. 'And, Satyanarayan, I'm giving you another 100 rupees. It's your responsibility to carry this filthy worm away and get his wounds dressed … No, Kanchu, don't interfere. I know what I am doing. All right, boys,' he addressed the circus boys standing around, 'go to Saibu's tent, bring out his belongings and send him packing with Satyanarayan. Is that clear? And Saibu, you are never to darken our doorstep after this. We leave you to be consumed by your sins. This is how our Daaji would have wanted it.'

BURMA

25

The wheels of time were turning full steam ahead.

The conflagration of the Second World War had engulfed humanity. Hitler and Mussolini held the puppet strings of big European powers like England and France. Fired up with the desire for revenge, German tanks had begun rolling towards Russia. Alarm bells were jangling everywhere. The atmosphere in India had turned extremely tense too. The British Armed Forces had mounted a huge campaign for recruiting young men to become their cannon-fodder in the theatre of war.

The air had turned incendiary. The freedom struggle had now gathered a critical mass. Guns were being loaded on both sides. The question that had been nagging Kanchana, however, was whether her circus should tour Burma or stay in India. On the one side was the sea and on the other was a volcano waiting to erupt.

She had reached a tentative agreement with Nirmal Roy, the circus contractor for Arakan, Burma and Malaya, who was by no means a small personality to displease. Not a leaf moved in Bengal Province, Assam or Burma without a nod from him. He controlled all the circus grounds of the east and was on back-slapping terms with British, Indian and Burmese officials. Falling foul of him would be like pulling at a lion's whiskers in its own den.

There was also a fourth and an extremely insistent letter from Devika Rani. She had written that the shooting of her movie *Anjaan* had begun in the Bombay Talkies studio at Malad, and she was very keen to start shooting for the circus movie too. She wanted Kanchana to wind up her Bengal tour and come over to Bombay. The circus could pitch its tent in the open space in front of Bandra Municipality or in Malad.

'Kanchana,' Raghav advised, 'it may not be right to turn down an important actor like Devika Rani.'

'But what does one do about this World War? Will it be wise to step into a territory like Bombay at such a volatile time?'

'Why not?'

'Have you forgotten the police raids on our camps at Walva, Nipani and Daund? It's been years since Mahaling kaka went underground. The White sahibs have already declared a prize of 50,000 on his head. How can we forget that the British always have our circus in their sight? Drifting in that direction during these stormy times will be unwise.'

'Weigh it against the opportunity to work alongside an internationally renowned actor like Devika Rani. This movie will create history.'

'You think I don't want the glory? What can I do if the times are so uncertain?'

Lilian's husband who had worked in the British Army had died suddenly, leaving behind very small children. She had been a famous sportsperson, but to raise her children on her own, she had joined the circus.

Her children, a boy and a girl, had now finished their school education in Delhi and had shifted to Simla to attend college. She had received a frantic letter from the daughter, saying that her brother was turning a little wayward. He had fallen into questionable company and begun smoking marijuana. The only remedy Lilian could think of was to take a break from the circus and go live with her children.

'Yes, I understand, Lilu Didi. Your first priority has to be your children. But do you think, after having settled matters satisfactorily, you may want to come back to us?'

'What a question to ask, Kanchu? If only it had been possible, I would have got the children to settle down closer to me, but we never have any permanent address. We are ininerant workers, travelling across the length and breadth of the country, and now we are planning this Burma tour.'

'Yes, things are always in too much of a flux. Your absence will leave a huge hole not only in the company, but in my life too.'

'Kanchu, no one is indispensable. We somehow learn to live around people's absence.'

'Yes, that's true. Look at me, I am living around the absence of my father.'

'That's the only way to handle life, Kanchu. Right now it's necessary to take this break from the circus. We'll see how things pan out in the days to come. But this much is certain: if you go to Burma, I won't be able to accompany you.'

26

The Great Kanchana Circus people were not sending out good signals. When Nirmal Roy's manager informed him that they still hadn't made up their mind about going to Rangoon, he flared up. He immediately had the assistant manager of the circus, Shekhar Paranjape, called over.

The tall, handsome, willowy Shekhar Bhau Paranjape had an arresting personality. The red, jaunty Kolhapuri turban on his head, his Karvati dhoti and his long knee-length coat suggested not a circus accountant but an official of the Peshwa's court. But he had retained his native Konkani flair.

Nirmal Roy was aware that Paranjape enjoyed his masters' confidence, which made him an important person to persuade. 'What's this, Paranjape,' he began, 'does your mistress have any understanding of profit and loss? Literally hundreds of tons of American goods get offloaded every single day at the Rangoon airport and harbour. Goods ranging from food supplies to ordnance like gun and gunpowder are loaded on thousands of trucks and sent up north to the border of China. These Americans have spent millions of dollars and built a highway for this purpose; they call it the Burma Road.'

'From Rangoon to China?'

'Absolutely! The highway is regarded as a marvel of modern engineering technology. Mountains had to be cut through, and bridges a couple of miles long had to be erected across Burma's massive rivers.'

'But why are the Americans so much in love with China?'

'They have jumped into the East Asian power games to checkmate Japan. They are pouring money and resources here for their new-found love for Chiang Kaishek.'

But why should we bother about their power politics?'

'You should be bothered about the profit and loss of your business, shouldn't you?' Nirmal Roy's voice rose a few decibels. 'Paranjape, with so much American money flooding into Burma, do you have any idea how trade there has multiplied?'

Paranjape shook his head dumbly.

'Well, this year alone, the season has been so good in Rangoon that people's earnings have jumped up three-fold. Go, explain all this to your ignorant boss. I'm concerned because she is the daughter of Sarang Daaji, whom I considered a good friend. Tell her that the Irrawaddy is much larger and much more profitable than the Ganga.'

Paranjape staggered back to his camp greatly impressed. He saw that Dr Ghosh of the Veterinary College of Calcutta had come visiting and everyone was in the menagerie. When Kanchana set her eyes on Lakshmi's emaciated state, she felt a sob rise up her chest. Lakshmi looked more like an ailing deer than the awe-inspiring tigress she had once been. Her piteous eyes stabbed at Kanchana's heart and she walked away, her eyes moist with tears.

Lakshmi's fever subsided by afternoon. However, if she were taken along on the tour, she would certainly die on the way; she would not survive to see the Burmese coast. So it was decided that she would be kept temporarily in a zoo called Deer Nature Park in Calcutta.

As she was bidding goodbye to Lakshmi, Kanchana held her head against her chest. Finally she kissed her fevered cheek.

Lakshmi's paw and nails had got entangled in Kanchana's sari, and it broke her heart to disentangle them.

The tall, heavily built Mr Roy arrived at the camp that evening. Running his hand over his drum-sized belly, he tried to instil confidence in Kanchana, 'Why are you getting so worried? You are the daughter of a very dear friend of mine.'

'I'm finding it difficult to muster up the courage to step out the country, Roy sahib. The blaze set off by this war terrifies me. My animals too look unwell, unconfident.'

'It's now eighteen months since the war began. In which parts do you see life rolling along as it did earlier? You simply have to gather your courage in your hands, Kanchana. See, there's already an Indian circus there in Burma that's been playing successfully.'

'Which circus??'

'Rakhumabai Circus is doing roaring business in Mandalay.'

'Arey waah, that's wonderful!'

'I hear a second circus is on its way there.'

'Whose company is it?'

'Karlekar's.'

'Uncle, can you give me another night to decide?'

'Well, all right. What difference will one night make?'

Around ten o'clock that night, two boys came running to Kanchana to inform her that Tambat kaka had arrived.

The man slipped into Kanchana's tent after ensuring that there was nobody loitering around there.

'Pori, I had gone to Howrah Station this afternoon to catch a train to Bombay. That's when my eyes fell on Bandya Joshi and I turned cold.'

'Who's this Joshi?'

'He is a Jamadar in the DSP's office at Satara. I called out to him and he began to probe me. I bluffed that I had come to visit the Kali temple nearby. I probed him too, but couldn't get a word out of him. Just as he was leaving, he let slip an important piece of information.'

'What was that?'

'He said that he had come on some urgent work that had come up in the Police Commissioner's office here.'

'And what does that mean, kaka?'

'That there's danger looming, for sure.'

'Why would the British administration suddenly decide to come after my company?'

'All right, then, here it is. I met Baburao of Kiwal the other day. According to him, someone from the village has turned against you and become an informer. He has got hold of documents relating to the company and has been visiting government offices. Moves around in tattered clothes on a half-starved stomach, they say, but keeps the offices well supplied. He's clearly hell-bent on destroying the company.'

Tambat kaka left after giving Kanchana this information. A short while later, a group of people from Calcutta Cinetone came to visit Kanchana. They had received a letter from Devika Rani, requesting them to meet Kanchana and intercede on her behalf. But with the wind changing every minute in these times of war, Kanchana wasn't left with the luxury of looking this way and that. She was not at all inclined to risk going down south. She folded her hands before the visitors and excused herself.

In fact, she did not feel safe anywhere. Neither in the Deccan nor in Bengal.

27

The evening sun had turned the waves a glittering red. The workmen at the Koyla Ghat harbour had been busy since morning, loading the boat with huge animal cages and steel chairs meant for the audience. When the cages were lifted up by the cranes, the ferocious tigers and lions sitting inside shut their eyes in fear.

The circus staff were upset at the inoculation exercise being conducted at the harbour. British doctors were compulsorily giving injections to the passengers setting off for Rangoon to prevent the spread of the plague. The circus troupe was lined up shirtless since morning for the jab on their forearms.

When the menagerie was being loaded on to the ship, the elephants presented a comical sight. Since they couldn't be contained in cages, their legs were chained to rafts with a protective railing of iron pipes around them. When the rafts were lifted, the giant animals began screeching and trumpeting and turned their terrified eyes towards the unbounded waves. However, when Rajmangala was being lifted, she seemed to have made a prestige issue of not creating a ruckus. Frightened she certainly was, but she decided to suffer it in silence and stood in dignity right through the transfer.

The sirens were sounded, and the ship moved out of the Calcutta dock at around nine in the evening and set sail for Rangoon. The cooks had already taken charge of the lower floor in the afternoon and set their stoves going; at nine o'clock the tables had been laid for dinner. It had been a tradition since Sarang Daaji's time to begin such a journey with a grand feast. Everyone was served chicken and mutton curry followed by some spicy biryani. The next three days meant nothing but relaxation; the circus staff stuffed themselves to the gills and went off to sleep. Outside, it was the sound of the breaking waves, and inside the humid, cool sea breeze. Nobody had any idea when exactly they fell asleep.

They had for company now the sound of the crashing breakers and the sticky sea wind. Kanchana's heart was rolling on the waves of joy and sorrow. In earlier times, she at least had the company of her father, but in the recent months, everything had turned topsy-turvy. The British had made it impossible for Kanchana to live peacefully in her motherland. If they were to apply some archaic law and dump her in jail, her circus would have to close down.

The crimson rays of twilight had begun playing upon the vast waters. Swarms of sea-birds were circling the sky above. The darkness on the waters was uninterrupted, the air thick with the sound of the sea-birds, lashing waves and perhaps the fish jumping above the waves and diving back into the sea. The ambience was heady. Kanchana took Raghav into a tight embrace and went on holding him tighter. 'I feel so safe when I'm in your arms,' she heaved a deep sigh. 'You've already left me once, Raghav. Promise that you won't ever leave me again.'

'When did I ever leave you?'

'When you came to our company for the first time, you strutted around, broke Phakkadrao and disappeared for the next two years.'

'Well, Kanchu, you were stupid in thinking that I would make a good life partner just because I was good at breaking horses. Also, if I had committed myself to you without even knowing what the future held for me, I would have been the meanest rascal alive.'

Kanchana turned silent for a while. She then spoke in a hoarse, unsteady tone, 'I may be foolish, I may be mad, I may be worthless, but remember this, Raghav, that I am yours and yours alone. You are the very air I breathe. I still look back on that two-year separation with dread; if you try to go away from me another time, I'll simply die.'

Raghav laughed, kissed her lovingly and said, 'What did you say? Say that again.'

'You are not to go away a second time.'

'Why not?'

'Because I'll die from the pain of living apart.'

'How will it do for you to die, Kanchana?'

'Meaning?'

'I live because you live!'

They both laughed out loud.

They could see the wet atmosphere outside the cabin window. The stars had turned dim. The good and bad experiences of her life were racing through Kanchana's mind. A strange fear, a nagging sense of forboding had lately been overwhelming her. She placed her hand on Raghav's chest and said, 'Raghav, I haven't had a good night's sleep in a long time.'

'Why is that?'

'I barely doze off when I'm jolted awake again.'

'But why does that happen?'

'I have this strange premonition that evil things are afoot. It seems to me that the animals in our menagerie are lowing and whining and growling because they can sense something ominous.'

'For all your strength of mind and character, you surprise me with your talk of premonitions and superstitions. Life is what we witness during our waking hours, not what we dream about in the night. It's the stress of undertaking this journey that's giving you these nightmares. Trust me, we will go through the ups and downs of life together, with grit if not always with a smile.'

28

The circus camp had been pitched at the Padaang Maidan in Rangoon. The big top was large enough to accommodate over 10,000 spectators. Decorated with beautiful frills, it stood proudly, as if preening itself .

Nirmal Roy made a personal visit to Padaang with his staff in tow. He came swaying like an elephant, spraying liberal quantities of paan spittle in all directions. Some seventy or eighty helpers and labourers immediately got busy. Using elephant trunks as cranes, they erected six tall poles on which they strung up a tent that looked like the silhouette of a mountain. Once her staff, animals and equipment had been set up and settled, Kanchana felt as if a huge burden had slipped off her shoulders.

The next day, as Kanchana sat sipping piping hot *peyheen* from a china bowl, Sushi came running, crying 'Didi! Didi!' and the two instantly hugged. They were meeting after a gap of eighteen years, but time hadn't left its mark on that small-built Burmese girl. The same sweetness of demeanour, the same laugh that reminded one of blooming flowers, the same bright spirit shining through the slits of her eyes.

'How was the journey, Didi?' Sushi asked.

'Well, the voyage should ordinarily have taken three days and three nights, but the turbulence in the sea during this season stretched our journey to five days,' Kanchana said.

'Once our ship set sail, I wasn't even sure we would reach Rangoon. We heaved a huge sigh of relief at seeing the rice mills near the dockyard and the massive timber depots, their broken reflections dancing wildly on the restless breakers. We literally escaped the jaws of death.'

Kanchana began rehearsals with her fellow artistes. The circus girls gathered inside the eighty-feet-long practice tent. To get their blood running and bodies warm, they began the drill with light exercises.

As Sushi stood fanning herself vigorously, something in a corner caught her attention, and her eyes popped out with fear. She rushed towards it. She lifted the bouquet of dry, tiny red bamboo flowers as she would a decomposed rat, let out a screech and flung it far away. She then threw Kanchana a scandalised look and asked, 'Tell me, Didi, how did those filthy flowers land here? Where did you get them?'

'Sushi, why are you so frightened? What is it?'

'You tell me first, where did you find these horrid, skull-splitting bamboo flowers?'

'Will you just tell me what your problem is, Sushi?'

'These inauspicious flowers bloom only once in seventy to eighty years, and whichever earth they bloom in, they bring it to ruin. They bring either terrible famine, or the total devastation of the entire region, or the death of the king.'

'Is it so horrible?'

'It's far worse! Didi, my village is quite close to Mandalay. My grandfather used to tell us kids that there was one such bloom during his youth—forests upon forests of bamboo got covered in these wretched red flowers. And what do you think happened next? Within two months, our Mandalay was up against its worst crisis in living memory.'

'What crisis was that?'

'The British deposed our revered king Thibwa. They treated him like a common criminal, put him on a boat and exiled him to India, incarcerating him in a rundown manor in Ratnagiri. The people of Burma just pined away for him, while he lived the rest of his life like a poor, helpless mouse in abject penury. Our king never saw his beloved Mandalay again.'

'How could I have known this wretched story? A village boy sat in the street selling them. Why is such an inauspicious thing sold so openly here?'

'Oh, it is in demand here. Malicious people buy these flowers at inflated prices for voodoo and black magic.'

Sushi picked up that bunch of flowers and arranged for it to be dumped a good half mile away from the camp.

Within two days the circus was up and running. Just as Nirmal Roy had described it, Rangoon had flourished in the past few years, and now ranked among the pleasure spots of the world. Its electric energy, its bustling trade, the swarms of foreign tourists, plush hotels like The Strand, the increasing footfall of European and American officials, all these things together had caused splendour to spread thick and fast all across the metropolis.

In the afternoon, the guard posted at the circus gate came running to Kanchana's tent. 'Didi,' he said, panting, 'a madam is headed this way, escorted by armed soldiers. Could she be the wife of the Latsahib here?'

Kanchana wondered who it was. She quickly changed out of her silk dressing gown into a shalwar-kurta. She gave her hair a quick brush and got ready to meet the visitor. Meanwhile the 1000-feet perimetre of the circus ground had been traversed, and the doorman announced that the big-shot madam had arrived. Two accompanying police officers brought in the message that madam wanted to meet Ms Kanchana, the owner of the circus.

This was Marilyn Richardson, the wife of the deputy commissioner of Rangoon. She was in her fifties. She beamed exuberantly as she shook hands with Kanchana and immediately informed her that she was not interested in being entertained over a cup of tea; she wanted to have a look at the circus tent and, more importantly, the menagerie.

'I've heard so much about the great Indian circuses, about the way you love your animals—elephants, lions, tigers. I want to see them all.'

Nirmal Roy, who had been informed of the celebrity's arrival, came rushing to pay his obeisance. He bowed low and joined his hands together, as if approaching a queen. The British deputy commissioner was considered the equivalent of the king of Rangoon, and Roy was completely overawed by the occasion of the big man's wife suddenly turning up merely to take a round of the circus. They went all over the camp: Marilyn Richardson, Kanchana and Raghav, with manager Paranjape running in front with an end of his dhoti clasped in his fist. Marilyn's light brown eyes widened at the sight of the roof of the vast circus tent erected on six massive poles and the beautiful cloth panels decorated with fine filigree and appliqué work.

As they made their way towards the menagerie, Marilyn asked Kanchana, 'This circus was here in Rangoon some sixteen years ago, right?'

Kanchana was surprised. 'How do you know, madam?'

'I came to see your circus then. Not once, but twice. My husband was the sub-collector of Mandalay district then.'

The menagerie seemed to have hypnotised Marilyn altogether. When the hippopotamus Mustafa noticed people gathered around his trough, he lifted his half submerged head out of the water and looked around. Marilyn placed her hand over its soft, wet head and asked, 'How do you people beguile these jungle and water animals into your trap of affection?'

When Mustafa's beady eyes rested upon Kanchana, he let out a combination of grunts and gurgles—his preferred way of expressing delight—and opened his cavernous mouth wide.

Kanchana handed over two big cauliflowers to Marilyn, who tossed them towards the hippopotamus. Mustafa deftly caught them in his mouth and swallowed them in a jiffy.

Marilyn was particularly pleased with the hygiene the circus maintained in and around the cages of the animals.

'Kanchana, I am quite impressed.'

'Thank you, ma'am.'

As Marilyn neared the stable, she noticed, even from a distance, the beautiful rippling backs and muscular flanks of the horses. Their coats were buffed to a velvety finish. She immediately complimented Kanchana, 'You won't find such horses even in the cavalry regiments of the British Indian Army.'

When Kanchana noticed Raghav standing unobtrusively behind, she took him by the hand and pulled him forward. 'Ma'am,' she said with visible pride, 'please meet my dear husband Raghav.' The two of them together related to this inquisitive White woman the history and the administrative aspects of the circus world. When this was over, Marilyn took a deep breath and said, 'I am very proud, Kanchana, to have met a woman like you. Millions of women in India today live the life of pickles in a bottle. Your religion and your conventions do pickle women, they say. Against such a background of outdated thinking and the absence of education, when a determined, spirited young girl like you runs such a massive circus, takes over the responsibility of running this enterprise and travels across the countries of Asia, I can refer to it only as a miracle.'

'Thank you, ma'am,' Kanchana responded with humility. 'Please let your blessings stay with us, always.'

'Absolutely! Any time you or your people need me, or you have any trouble, you can knock at my door even in the middle of the night.'

It was a particularly fortuitous day for Kanchana. Even before she could utter a word of invitation, Marilyn announced,

'I am coming tonight to watch your performance along with my husband.'

The prestige of the show that evening was assured. As if to add sugar to milk, Mr Sinha of the Zeyawaddy Sugar Works too arrived with his family. Kanchana had kept up a correspondence with him, even if rather tenuous, from India. With some of the most important dignitaries of Rangoon occupying the ringside seats, the performers that evening were at their inspired best. Raghav presented his regular act where he hopped from the back of one horse to the other as they ran in tandem. That was followed by Kanchana and Raghav climbing up to the trapeze frame eighty feet above the ground and putting up a spectacular performance on the Roman rings. Marilyn, her husband and the other European guests gave the artistes a standing ovation. The icing on the cake was Raghav's item with the bouncing ropes. When he jumped five feet off those flying ropes and began doing multiple somersaults in the air, the audience turned delirious with excitement.

This was the moment when Kanchana missed Lakshmi the most. If only she had been present, their cavorting around the ring, their hair-raising act, would have taken everyone's breath away, mesmerised the audience. But succumbing to circumstances wasn't something Kanchana did. In spite of all the travails of bringing the circus to Burma, she had found the time to prepare a brand new act with Rajmangala. Now was the moment to put its attraction to the test. She lay down in the ring and planks of wood were placed on her prone body. When the spectators saw the 3,000-kilo elephant step on the planks, they froze in horror.

After the show was over, Marilyn introduced Kanchana to her husband, and he blurted, 'Oh my god! I had shut my eyes tight with fear. I was absolutely certain that what they would scrape out from under those planks was a squashed and mutilated body.'

'Oh, no, sir, she is my Rajmangala, my life breath.'

A completely enthralled Mr Sinha was the next person to go up to her. Introducing Kanchana to his wife, he said, 'This girl's father Sarang Shinde was a lion among men. He was a very close friend to me. The last time Kanchana visited Zeyawaddy was with her father. A chit of a girl she was then, and now look at her—tall as a tree. And this young man is your husband, right? Your performance was absolutely marvellous. Always remember that you have an uncle here in Zeyawaddy. If you need any sort of help, just reach out to me. It's your right.'

That night, Kanchana chuckled softly as she lay next to Raghav. Punching him on the forearm, she said, 'What if we hadn't come to Burma at this time?'

'It would have been an awfully stupid thing to do.'

29

Rangoon hadn't experienced such enthused Christmas crowds for a few years now.

The entire city was immersed in a celebratory mood

It was barely nine in the morning and there was already a huge crowd outside the circus gate. The excitement that they carried on their faces—the lungi-clad Burmese men and women—it had to be seen to be believed. Of particular note were the stripes of *tankha*—dabs of yellow made by the wet application of the juice of a vegetable similar to turmeric—that little girls wore on their cheeks, making them look particularly attractive. The excitement the circus had generated was such that at least half the city would have watched the night show, gone home and woken up at the crack of dawn to return for the morning show. After a quick bath they had wrapped colourful lungis round their waist to cover their legs. The women had woven garlands of flowers into their hair and decorated their necks with gold. That done, they had all made a beeline for the circus ground.

Parked at the main gate, Nirmal Roy was swinging from side to side like a happy elephant. Of the four shows held the previous day, three had run to full houses, and all the shows scheduled for today were sold out. The women from timber merchants' households with gold belts dangling below their pot bellies, rich rice traders in their coats and muslin dhotis,

Christian men and women on a holiday to Rangoon, they were all surging towards the circus like a river in spate.

Nirmal Roy had placed four big cardboard banners at strategic places with a notice that read: 'Sorry, all shows are house-full. Except for a few seats, all the rest have been sold out for the next three days.' Roy would cast a satisfied glance at the banners every few minutes, give his giant body a heave and let out a booming laughter. Even as he congratulated himself, he did not forget to hang a big coloured picture of Goddess Kali, her foot-long tongue hanging out of her mouth, her eyes red with wrath, a garland of freshly severed heads round her neck and dripping blood, her foot planted on the chest of a writhing demon, and holding aloft a particularly vicious looking trident. Roy had not forgotten to place half a dozen big garlands of different kinds of flowers round the image of this fierce goddess.

Catching sight of Paranjape's face, Roy said, 'Hey Paranjape, all shows are sold out. 'Ma,' he begged Goddess Kali, 'don't let this "All tickets sold" board come down for at least a month.'

Determined to get the maximum fun out of their Christmas holidays, the Burmese, young and old, as also children of foreign races located in Rangoon, had come surging into the circus ground. The children had brought their guardians tagging along.

'My head spins with joy at the sight of this cascading crowd,' said Raghav. I've performed right up to the border of Afghanistan, but never seen children descend upon a circus in these numbers.'

'Son, where else will these crowds go?' said Nirmal Roy. 'All the schools across Burma have been shut for the last ten days on account of the Japanese bomb scare.'

The fact was that Rangoon was on tenterhooks. Fifteen days ago, the Japanese had mounted a devastating attack on the U.S. Naval base at Pearl Harbour in Honolulu. Over fifty bomber aircrafts had flown together in a wave and blown the island to smithereens. For the two nights following the event, Rangoon had been in a state of turmoil. Rumours flew thick and strong that a Japanese army assault was now imminent. As a precautionary measure, schools had been ordered shut for an indefinite period. As a result of these enforced holidays, the Great Kanchana Circus had become an unintended beneficiary.

It was 23 December 1941. Christmas was two days away. Shops selling sweets and Christmas cakes were packed with children and decorated with flowers. Radio Tokyo had lately begun issuing threats of gifting a very special Christmas cake to the residents of Rangoon, hence the city administration had taken adequate steps to ensure the safety of its citizens. L-shaped trenches had been dug up in the gardens of a number of bungalows, deep enough for a person to stand in. Arrangements had been made for people to get into these trenches in the event of an air raid.

The sight of the jam-packed circus tent brought a smile to Kanchana's lips. She had slipped on a white gown over her circus outfit to come and stand by the ticket window. She had rolled her thick hair into a top-knot. Nirmal Roy went to her and said, 'Kanchana, get busy writing to your real estate agents in Bombay and Pune. Tell them to identify some plush property there.'

'Why?'

'I am guaranteeing you this: you will have a big bungalow each in those two cities before this season is over.'

There was no doubt at all that the Christmas season would bear abundant fruit for all in its best possible sense. The tent of Karlekar Circus stood in the adjacent ground, and Paranjape found out that it was attracting huge crowds too. It seemed to be a particularly satisfying time for circuses all across Burma.

It was around half past nine when Kanchana stood chatting with Nirmal Roy close to the ticket counter. Suddenly the sky burst open, and the deafening, grating sound of air-raid sirens rent the air. This was immediately followed by loud, panic-stricken cries of 'Run! Run! The Japs have attacked!' The sirens kept blaring while a stampede began everywhere on the ground—in the streets, in shops and temples. Since the show had not begun yet, the audience inside the tent instantly sprang to their feet. Ten thousand people gushing out of that limited tent space was nothing short of a flooded river bursting its dam. Raghav had anticipated the potential danger of such crowds wanting to rush out and had placed men with scissors along the wall partitions, with instructions to use them in an emergency. He had also left some gaps between the panels for making exit easy. This helped the crowd find its way comfortably out of the coop.

After fifteen minutes, the sirens went silent. People who had taken shelter in street corners and houses and shops came out and began laughing out of sheer relief and abusing the Royal Air Force for its cowardly scare-mongering. Twenty minutes passed, and the streets filled up again. The queues were back again in front of shops selling sweets, kites and Christmas cakes.

The circus tent too filled up again. Scorn was freely expressed against the White sahibs who paraded themselves as world conquerors. The circus rang its long bell. Charlie began playing a lively lilt that he had composed with the festival and the cosmopolitan audience in mind.

The clock struck ten. The tent began resonating with wolf-whistles and loud claps. Eleven midget clowns came dancing into the ring to the tune of Charlie's band, their loose, striped trousers flapping with their wriggles and minces and convoluted dancing steps. The children in the audience were beside themselves with joy. They guffawed, jumped and clapped. Some climbed on to their dads' shoulders and roared and cheered. Rajmangala made her entry swaying in her brocaded caparison, chaperoned by her caretaker Sulaiman. The splendidly decked out elephant garlanded a huge statue of Lord Shiva. After him rode in twenty-five girls, whistling, singing and clapping even as they pedalled on their bikes. Many elephants were lined up in the rear wing, getting ready to march in for the overture. The circus girls were climbing on to the elephants' backs. They would enter and ride around the central ring. In the menagerie, the stage managers and the cage boys were bringing the other animals out of their cages and organising them for the parade with which the show began.

That was when a strange wrooming sound echoed across the sky—quite like a whale filling up its mighty bladder with sea water for squirting it out again. Another sound ran parallel to it—as if the blade of a sword were leaping through the air with a long, extended swish. This time, however, the crowds in the streets and markets decided to ignore them as the panic-stricken responses of the administration. They sounded quite like the mock drills the British army indulged in every now and then. A few people were alert enough to lift their eyes to the sky. What they saw made their eyes pop out in disbelief and fear. An entire horde of them—at one go, one behind the other, some flying a little low and the others a little higher—not one or two but at least a couple of dozen Japanese aircraft were rushing towards them like a swarm of bees gone mad. The aircraft reached a high point in the sky where they described a sharp downward arc and came swooping upon the city. They once again turned their noses upward and climbed high into the sky. All over again, they turned around like enraged snakes with their hoods extended and began their fast, fearful descent towards the earth.

During this second descent, however, one could see sharp shafts of flame shooting out of the aircraft's bellies. It began to rain sparks. The aircraft took careful aim and came plunging down in fury towards the centre of the city. The bombs they had released before their descent came shrieking and screaming down and exploded with deafening booms as they hit the earth. Some of the aircraft pushed out barrels from their wings and began spraying volleys upon volleys of bullets with sharp rat-tat-tats of machine-gun fire. The harsh, ear-splitting sounds of sirens combined with the sounds of exploding bombs and the machine-gun fire made the heavens shudder violently.

Raghav's driver had just turned his jeep around to return to the circus ground after a visit to the Central Church. Kanchana had sent him to the church in the morning in order to get the blessings of Christ for her circus. That was when he heard the sharp whistles in the sky, the detonation of the bombs as they hit the earth, the rapid-fire crackle of machine-guns and the raucous wailing of the sirens. He saw with unbelieving eyes the aircraft come snarling, howling down like birds whose tails had been chopped off.

When the driver saw the blood-curdling scene being enacted in the sky, he broke into a shiver and lost control of the steering. Fortunately the jeep swerved drunkenly into a railing and jolted to a halt, its fender bent inwards from the impact. Raghav roughly pushed the driver aside and took charge of the vehicle.

Maneuvering the jeep with any speed through the pell-mell was impossible. Human bodies lay scattered everywhere, some dead, some dying, some crying for death. Abdomens ripped apart with machine-gun fire, entrails hanging out of their torn bellies, men screamed in pain as they held their intestines inside, running not knowing where. There were seriously injured heads everywhere—torn apart by free-flying shrapnel, split open by stones falling from disintegrating buildings. What were fancy buildings only a little while ago now stood with their stomachs disemboweled and thrown across the streets. Their wood and steel balconies swung precariously on a strand or two, ready to come crashing down with the first gust of wind.

Raghav managed to worm his way through the smoke and rubble of the town and reached the front of the circus camp. He could see in front of him fires raging everywhere. As he watched, the two company trucks standing on the other side caught fire; their fuel tanks exploded, releasing two massive balls of fire in the air that consumed the vehicles as if they were camphor pellets, leaving behind their bare steel skeletons.

Raghav's gaze turned towards the tent. People were scampering out of the tears in the cloth walls screaming and shouting, dashing into whichever direction looked open. The ensuing stampede had suddenly assumed a more menacing shape than the bombs falling out of the sky; a large number of children were getting trampled underfoot. A heavy, ominous whistling sound made Raghav look up at the sky. What he saw numbed his mind with fear. Two balls of fire the size of bullock-cart wheels were descending on the street right outside the circus ground. As he shut his eyes tight, they landed with a prodigious explosion that seemed to have blown holes in his eardrums. The next moment, he was showered by a thunderstorm of grains of cement, earth and sand. When he recovered his senses, he shook the grit out of his hair, blew it out of his nose and carefully cleared the area around his eyes before he cautiously opened them. There, right in front of him on the road were two well-sized pits that hadn't existed before, still billowing out dust.

It was sheer luck that he had brought the jeep under control and taken it to a side before this happened. The two bombs had caused considerable destruction to life and property. A couple of dozen people lay scattered about, badly roasted. The more fortunate ones had instantly been turned into coal and gained the stillness of death. A few, however, had still not given up, their ghost—they lay there twisting and turning and rubbing their heels in the earth. What made the scene more stomach-churning was their screams and groans that sprang out of inconceivable agony.

Among the dead, Raghav and his associates recognised a few forms. The three girls from Kerala along with their two Burmese caretakers were charred almost beyond recognition. The heads of two of them had been crushed to smithereens, as if a cow had stepped upon a couple of watermelons. Shrapnel had obviously penetrated inside and blown their skulls away.

When Kanchana saw the macabre graffiti of the body parts of her colleagues trickling down the wall, she felt a horrible churn in her stomach. The jolt made her head go dizzy and her knees go limp. She leaned against the wall, lowered herself slowly and sat gazing blankly at the shattered pieces of the circus called life.

30

An entire squadron of Japanese bomber planes had visited Rangoon, tossed down its machines of death and destruction and disappeared, and all that the British guns had to show in the form of retaliation was one solitary aircraft. And now nobody was sure when the invading Japanese army would come storming into the city. A dark and dreary future now stood before the six hundred thousand Indian residents in Rangoon. How could anyone continue to live here anymore? How was one to survive? They were frightened out of their wits. It had taken them decades of hard work to bring up their bungalows, their manors, their shops and warehouses that now lay so vulnerably exposed to the aggressor. The bombers could arrive literally any minute and raze to the ground what had taken them a lifetime of effort to erect. Even if by some miracle they escaped the wrath of the Japanese, how could they protect themselves from the viciousness of the gangs of Burmese extremists out on their racist agenda?

Very soon, another piece of gossip began doing the rounds of the city, as stomach-churning as the bombings: the remnants of the British army, people said, were packing their bags and abandoning Rangoon altogether. The mere thought of the consequences hit the Indians like a gust of chilling wind. Who would then take over as the new master? Would their fate finally be handed over to the whims of the fanatical Burmese rabble?

The Great Kanchana Circus had taken a merciless hammering. While its six-pole skeleton was still standing, its cloth and tarpaulin walls had been blown to shreds. The 3,500 steel chairs that had been laid out for the spectators lay strewn everywhere, tangled and twisted out of shape. Even the sturdy steel galleries had not been able to withstand the violence of the bombings, and they hung bent and broken in many places.

The facility of reaching out to someone for succor and sympathy had disappeared. Almost a dozen of the company people had been seriously injured: twisted limbs, broken bones and open, bleeding wounds. But where could one take them? Which hospital? It wasn't as if Raghav and the others didn't try, but the entity called civic administration had simply vanished. The administrative staff had abandoned their offices and the policemen their stations, searching for their houses in the rubble that the city had become. They had hurried home to their children so that they could give them a hug and a kiss of relief, assure their parents that they were still alive.

The Municipal General Hospital had built a formidable reputation for itself over decades for top-class healthcare services. Its reputation was being put to the severest test ever, and it was coming out a loser. Thousands of grievously injured people—interspersed with a large number of corpses—lay scattered around the campus like leaves on an autumn lawn. A good many of the injured still had shrapnel or bullets buried in their flesh, not allowing them to staunch the blood from their wounds. The searing pain that had travelled deep into their bones kept the unfortunates writhing and twisting where they stood or lay. They screamed for the doctors till they frothed at the mouth, wondering where they had gone. The doctors on duty were either in the examination rooms or in the hospital corridors, completely besieged by the injured multitudes, left with hardly any space to move around. They examined the patients nearest them, prised out embedded metal where they could, bandaged them and even infused blood where possible. But this was like baling water out of a flooded ship with a teaspoon.

The crowds kept on swelling, groaning, screaming, dying. The doctors themselves had arrived at a point where they could collapse with exhaustion. Medicines were already on the point of running out. The persistent cry for water had turned throats hoarse; thousands of patients accompanied by their anxious, terrified relatives had created a drinking water crisis too.

As for Nirmal Roy, the earth had been pulled out from under his giant six-foot-and-a-half body. The dark future that loomed ahead of him was close to unhinging his mind. The matter of continuing with the circus shows had been completely taken out of his hands and resolved. All his investment in the venture had been wiped out with one stroke. But over and above that, what was he going to do with this huge circus company he had invited from a faraway country? How was he going to handle them? Worries such as these were sucking the life-blood out of Roy more effectively than a bunch of leeches could.

Kanchana was finding it difficult to find her voice. A thick mucus of fear and grief had choked not only her arteries, but also her throat. She coughed and sputtered and finally spoke, 'Uncle, my circus has been wiped out, it's dead. What do I do with my 400 colleagues who accompanied me to this foreign land to earn their livelihood? What do I do with the 200 animals that are more valuable to me than all of us put together?'

The bird cages that had been hanging by the poles in the tent had fallen off in the stampede and snapped open. The extravagantly expensive birds in them—the beautiful kakatua and other parrots imported from foreign lands, the nightingale, the mynah and many other exotic feathered creatures—had taken to their wings and vanished. The booms of the bombs and the acrid smoke and dust would certainly have disoriented them enough to fly off in whichever direction they found the sky relatively clear. The two murderous words 'anarchy' and 'annihilation' had bonded this day, and the outcome of this demonic marriage was being felt every passing moment.

The circus staff had been sitting by the wayside for a while now. Suddenly they noticed a wave of men and women come rolling down from the direction of the Rangoon dockyard. They were caked in dust from head to foot, their faces dark with soot. Some had broken heads; some others carried the marks of bullet wounds. Blood dripped off their shirts even as they ran.

The circus staff stopped a few of them. They were informed that the dockyard was littered with close to 900 corpses. Most of the dead belonged to the fisherman community from the Arakan–Chittagong region. The landmark building called Sailors' Home had been burnt to ashes.

The long, dark shadows of twilight turned gloomier. Raghav had instructed his kitchen staff to cook whatever they could lay hands on. Out there, the town had turned dark even before night had arrived. Shops closed, cooking oil exhausted, no petrol pumps open for taking the jeep around; no post offices open either for sending a telegram to India to inform them of the jaws of death they had walked into.

Someone had circulated a scary rumour that the Japanese were likely to return at night for another round of bombing. Kanchana was furious, but then she realised that this rumour had been picked up from the hundreds of terrified citizens who had been running up and down the street screaming, 'There'll be an air raid tonight. Stay alert!'

The kitchen staff came out with plates full of rice and lentils. Kanchana took this opportunity to warn them, 'Fate has risen upon us like an incensed snake. Times are turning from bad to worse. Gobble up whatever has come into your plate today. There's no saying when you will see food next.'

The fear-stricken staff finished the meal in a hurry. It was December, one needed all the warmth that food provided. Kanchana and Raghav had not touched their plates. Their eyes were turned towards the menagerie; they were waiting for a message from that direction.

Four cage boys finally arrived with long, worried faces. One of them began in a mournful tone, 'Didi, our animals have just about been drinking water—they seem half-dead.'

'No meat? No fodder? They're not eating at all?'

'That's right, Didi, they haven't touched any of it. They've had such a fright after the bombing that even passing footsteps send them into a tizzy.'

Kanchana and Raghav stood up and went to the menagerie. Twelve elephants occupied the outer space, some seated, some standing. A single sight was enough to reveal their depressed state. Physically they were big—mountainous and powerful, but at heart they were extremely tender creatures. Kanchana had never seen Rajmangala look so woebegone. She still had on her back the caparison of the last show's parade. Nobody had had the time or the presence of mind to take it off her.

When she saw her master and mistress approaching, she stretched out her trunk and dragged them towards herself. She frothed a little bit and let out a strange, nervous cough. The other elephants also turned their beady eyes on them, wanting to be patted and reassured. Untouched fodder lay before their feet. Hoping that they could be persuaded to eat off their beloved owners' hands, the mahouts handed over bundles of fresh grass to Kanchana and Raghav. The elephants stretched out their trunks and sniffed at the grass, and then put some in their mouth, but they appeared to be doing so only as a mark of courtesy. Their heart was not in it.

When Raghav and Kanchana went close to the cages of the carnivores, their feet turned to lead. The animals that could have set the jungles trembling and the skies aflame with their roar and thunder—why were they standing now like frightened deer?

When the tinkle of Kanchana's anklets reached the tank where the hippopotamus Mustafa was housed, Mustafa organised his massive body, sprang out of water, rushed towards her, and began rubbing himself against her. He accepted the two cauliflowers that Kanchana offered and chomped on them for a little while, but he soon spat them out coated in all the saliva he had gurgled up. The hippo was breathing heavily as he went on rubbing himself against his mistress. Deep inside, perhaps, he was feeling like wailing out loud as human beings did, but he didn't know how to; all that he could manage was to let out a few whines and groans through his nostrils.

Such a long stay out of the water was beginning to dry and shrink Mustafa's skin, but the animal was refusing to get back into the tank. Finally, Kanchana put her arm as much around its bulky neck as possible and slowly led him towards the water. She had to lower herself into the tank to tempt Mustafa back in, which she ultimately managed to do.

As Kanchana and Raghav were taking their round of the menagerie, Paranjape came over to them and said pleadingly, 'Listen, Didi, you two had better get something inside you too.'

'No, I have completely lost my appetite,' Kanchana said softly.

'Raghav,' she said hoarsely, 'how do we pacify these mute darlings of mine? No temple nearby if you want to visit one. No town that is not going up in flames. We may not find commercial trucks because there is no petrol available, but I shall pull my troupe out alive and kicking, not merely out of the heaths and jungles of this foreign land, but also out of the jaws of this calamity that has descended upon us.'

Raghav took Kanchana's hand in his and gave it a tight squeeze. He looked over her shoulder at the ring-master and the assembled cage boys and said, 'All right, you people, go to your animals and bring them round to eating something one way or the other. You have been their trainers, don't forget.' The men dispersed to do his bidding.

As the two were stepping out, the clouds burst again, as if trying to rend the sky apart. This was immediately followed by the strident sound of sirens. The bombing could well begin in the next few minutes. Even the intrepid lions and tigers were thrown off balance and began casting fearful glances all around. The horses in the stables began to hop from one foot to the other. Fortunately, nothing untoward followed and the sirens dissolved in the night air. Everybody heaved a sigh of relief.

The likelihood of the circus's total annihilation had pierced Kanchana's bones. She woke up with a start in the dead of night and threw a flustered question at Raghav, 'What's happened to my bones? Even if a distant siren-like sound hits my ears, a chill goes straight to my bones. I don't mind if this storm crashes round my head, but I don't want my bones to fall prey to this instinct of fear. I hate fear.'

'That's what I've been trying to explain to you, Kanchana,' Raghav reassured her. 'We still have many huge mountains of calamities to confront, you and I.'

'I beg of you, Raghav, promise that you will never leave me again. If you do, life will become impossible for me.'

A sudden change came over Kanchana. She stepped out of the tent and looked at the dark clouds in the sky and said with determination, 'No matter what, I'll take my company back home. I have Daaji's blood flowing through my veins. I swear by his memory that the way I brought these 500 men, women and animals to this land, I will safely take them back to our motherland the same way.'

31

In more peaceful times, the big top of the circus would begin to glitter with the light of uncountable electric bulbs at seven every evening without fail. This evening, the area outside the tent walls was under the complete sway of a disconcerting darkness. The petromax lanterns that had been lit were required by government order to be used at minimum luminosity. The authorities feared that any brightness visible from the sky could invite air raids. Strict blackout instructions had been issued, which mandated that the upper three-fourths of the lantern should be covered with black paper, which left just the lower one-fourth band open to emit whatever light it could. The human shadows that this inadequate light created made them look like ghosts.

They were sitting scattered in little groups under the tattered tent roof—artistes, labourers, animal trainers, market boys, helpers, the rest of the troupe. Deep lines of worry creasing their faces, they sat sucking on pinches of tobacco tucked in their jaws or pulling on cheap, green Burmese beedis and cheroots in an effort to numb the hunger pangs in their stomachs and the anxieties in their heads. Their voices were low, their tone uncertain. From the menagerie on the other side came floating in the sounds of animals grunting, growling, lowing, rattling the iron bars of their cages, as if they could sense the predators of the unrealised future sneaking in and spreading themselves around.

The ornamented curtains at the entrance to the tent had been taken off, leaving the passage clear. An unplanned meeting was in progress to sort out administrative matters. Kanchana tried to keep the spirits up as she said, 'It's a good thing that we have our thirty-two trucks standing out there. We can get the women, kids and animals out quickly.'

'But taai, the bombing this afternoon reduced three of them to cinders,' someone squeaked from the darkness.

'Well, okay, don't lose heart. We still have twenty-nine, haven't we? Let's keep our vehicles close. We'll move out at the first opportunity. Till then, please cover them up with tarpaulin, branches and such things. Keep guards posted too.'

'Kanchana, a minimum of three people stay up at night keeping an eye on a couple of trucks each. There's no saying what the Burmese anarchists might do,' Raghav said.

'The Japanese army can possibly give the British a bloody mouth and barge in like wild buffaloes,' said Paranjape. 'Didi sahib, they have bombarded the airports at Myitkyina and Tavoy and a few other places too. If they continue with their assault and the British decide to tuck their tails and run, we will surely die.'

'Why?'

'The Japanese will be easier to handle,' chipped in Nana. 'The natives here are far more dangerous. They have not been able to stomach the predominance of Indians here. Look at the timber and rubber businesses and other professions too, look at the education sector too, it's Indians at the forefront everywhere.'

'That's the big worry, Nana,' said Paranjape, wiping the sweat off his brow. 'I was out a little while ago, with my ears cocked. The people here are certain that once the British move out, there'll be wide-scale looting and arson.'

They were all trapped in this vice-like grip of anxiety—Kanchana and the entire management. Time was slipping away while fate stood knocking furiously at the front door. Kanchana did some quick thinking and said, 'Damle!'

'Yes, Didi?'

'Your assistants should go running to the dockyard before five this morning. Buy all the boat tickets available, never mind if you have to pay double the price. If some of us senior people get stuck here, it won't matter, but I want my children in India.'

Till just the previous day, Rangoon had been so safe, so warm, not just for the foreigners, but for the natives too. Gold and rubies were being sold openly under the shades of trees along the streets as if they were wild berries. But in a matter of hours everything had changed. The bombing and the threat of a Japanese invasion had converted the colourful city into a frightening graveyard.

Kanchana was distraught. 'What's the use of having so many trucks in hand if we have no petrol to run them?' she groaned.

'But, Didi,' Damle broke in, 'who could have anticipated that the sky would crash upon our shoulders in this manner?'

'Damle, keep your people on the lookout all the time. I don't care whether the market is black or white. If there is no fuel, even our brains will come to a grinding halt.'

The secretariat at Rangoon was the seat of the government there. Its impressive red-brick building had, till just the previous day, stood as a visible symbol of iron-handed authority and power. Next to it was the Law College, and further down was the famous General Hospital that had earned an enviable reputation for itself for decades of excellent service. The state to which these emblems of authority and efficiency had been reduced now was painful to see. The steps leading to the secretariat building lay littered with corpses that had now begun to bloat and spread an unbearably putrid stench everywhere. Panicky pleas had been sent to the municipal administration for the removal of those bodies, but the municipal administration had collapsed too. The heavy bombing had created huge craters in the middle of roads. The water-supply lines had been blown open, causing flooding all around. The water lines that were still working had no workforce to turn them on or off. The plumbers, rag-pickers and sanitation workers were sitting at home, offering whatever protection they could to their own families.

Anarchy and chaos ran riot in the city of Rangoon. Administrative buildings were collapsing, banks were getting looted, people were scurrying everywhere, mayhem had taken over. The British regime that had prided itself on its discipline and had never tired of boasting of its steely army and unbending administration lay with its spine broken.

Dawn had begun to break. Everybody had quickly downed grams and puffed rice and other leftover eatables and washed them down with water. They were tired to their bones, their heads were heavy with sleep, but this sleep didn't dare to slide down into their eyes. Just then the sound of a siren floated in from some distance, causing everybody to shudder and turn their gaze upwards at the pitch-dark sky. In a little while it became clear that the sound hadn't been the screech of any aircraft but the siren of a vehicle and the squeal of tyres against tar.

A jeep screeched to a halt right in front of the circus gate, its windscreen covered with a protective cowl of net. The siren on its head turned silent. Two officials in red headgear and khaki shorts disembarked, accompanied by two armed guards. They came stomping their heavy boots and marched straight past Kanchana's flabbergasted group, ignoring them altogether.

The driver came running in with a can full of glue. On instructions from the officers, he went to the boards at the gate that had posters and pictures of the circus and painted them thick with glue. When this was done, the officers marched up to the boards, unrolled some poster-like sheet of paper and stuck it over the glue. They ensured that the paper was nicely stuck, turned around, and without so much as a glance at the bemused assembly, got back into their jeep and sped off with their sirens blaring.

Kanchana ran into her tent for a torch, ran back out and shone its beam on the newly pasted poster. She knew enough English and Burmese to manage small talk but could not read the Burmese script at all. But there were some in the management team who could, and they got about reading and understanding the notice pasted there. Certain kinds of poison, when consumed, begin by being just unsavoury, but as they slip down the alimentary canal, they begin devouring everything they touch. When the words of the notice began eating into Kanchana and Raghav, they felt that their bones were turning to pulp and feared that they would crumple to the floor.

NOTICE

Keeping wild and ferocious animals like tigers, lions, elephants and such other creatures in the city during times of war poses extreme danger to the security and well-being of its citizens. The circus is hereby ordered to dispatch all its animals outside the city limits of Rangoon forthwith at its own risk and expense within eighteen hours of receipt of this notice. This order shall be followed meticulously. If any negligence in the implementation of this order is observed by the authorities, an armed squad of soldiers shall take immediate possession of the premises and shoot the animals dead. Urgent cognizance must be taken by the circus administration of this order.

District Police Superintendant, Rangoon.
(As per the orders of the esteemed Commander of the British Army)

32

The scorching language of the notice and its implications fell into the ears and eyes like molten lead. Raghav quickly pulled up a wooden chair and carefully lowered Kanchana into it.

If the animals were not shifted out of town within eighteen hours, the inconceivable would happen. The circus girls took a particularly hard hit at the thought of their beloved animals being slaughtered. Some had stood on the trunks of elephants for doing the overture round at the beginning of their shows, while others had used their massive necks as thrones to sit on. Yet others had hung from the tassels of their caparisons and performed tricks to the beat of the band. This magical world where athletes and artistes of the highest order held the audience in a state of hypnosis! What kind of a demon was it that had set out to annihilate their world of joy and merriment?

The jittery young girls gathered around Kanchana. 'Didi, that White madam who had come to our show the other day, please meet her and ask for help.'

'This notice hasn't come from the police. It has come from the army,' informed one of the men.

'Whether it's the police or the army, they are branches of the same tree, the British government. I can say with certainty that the White madam can find a remedy to our problem.'

The meeting in the office tent and the questions before the assembly refused to dissolve. There was desperation in

Kanchana's voice as she pleaded with Nirmal Roy, 'Uncle, please do something! Read this notice—if they bomb my animals out of existence, I will die too.'

Nirmal Roy deftly gathered the chewed up paan in his mouth, spat it out and then carefully wiped the red spittle that had stuck to his lips. He lifted the reading glasses that had been hanging on his chest, placed them on the bridge of his nose and again began scrutinising the notice. Looking at the grave expression on his face, Kanchana said, 'Look, uncle, I have no intention of putting you through unnecessary hardships. Fortunately, I still have twenty-nine trucks in which I can load my animals and the company girls and take them to safety.'

'Oh, really? What's the hurdle, then?'

'Help me get out of this town along with my girls and animals. Do whatever you can, but please arrange petrol for my trucks.'

Nirmal Roy ran his palm over his substantial belly and turned around. Before stepping out, he took his hand to his throat, as if taking an oath, and said, 'All right. I have two or three friends who are timber merchants. In fact, one of them owns an oil depot. If necessary, I'll go fall at his feet. May I take leave now?'

'Well, okay, but just get me the fuel immediately, uncle. The rest of the mountain I am quite ready to carry on my head.'

'Good.'

Nirmal Roy gathered his staff of five and strode out. Despite Roy's assurance, Raghav knew no peace. He looked tense. Holding him by the wrist, Kanchana asked, 'Why do you look so uneasy? What's preying on your mind?'

'Look, Kanchu, if we want petrol, I think it is necessary to search in a few other places. I can't quite trust your uncle.'

'Why do you doubt him? He is a businessman to his fingertips.'

'That's exactly why. These ultra-clever businessmen are ants sticking to a lump of profit. They don't care a damn for a person when the chips are down.'

Fuel was such a grave necessity that it was important to tap as many sources as possible. 'If we don't get fuel, our animals will not be the only loss we will sustain,' Kanchana said. 'How can we even think of dumping all these lorries that have cost us lakhs and lakhs of rupees and clear out?'

'How about we send some of our men to Zeyawaddy? It's about thirty miles ahead, and Sinha Sahib has great influence. His properties are spread out everywhere.'

Kanchana sat down immediately and wrote a letter addressed to Sinha Sahib in Hindi. It read, 'The circus and my people have got trapped in this apocalyptic war. Please, uncle, do what you can, but arrange for fuel for our trucks. Don't think of me as your friend's daughter, I am your daughter too, a daughter whom fate has transformed into the mother of these hundreds of animals.'

A four-member group left for Zeyawaddy with Damle as the head. The instructions to Damle were: use whatever transport you get—train, bullock carts, bicycles—and take whichever route you have to, but reach Zeyawaddy quickly and come back victorious. Not content with this, Kanchana called over her local agents and pleaded, 'Go to the harbour and look for owners of private ships and boats; even pirates will do. Take their help and arrange for a ship.'

These pirate-brokers shot the one question that mattered most to them, 'What about the payment?' Kanchana caught the drift of their conversation and said, 'Yes, I know the banks are not functioning, and our cash is all locked up there. But I have a few kilos of gold to see us through these bad times. I also have Burmese gems. Payment will be no problem.'

After the pirate-brokers had left, Raghav reminded Kanchana, 'Bombs fall on water in the same way as they fall on land.'

'What?'

'Just go to the harbour and you will hear shocking stories of the ships that Japanese submarines have sunk.'

'Well, all that is true, but show me a place that hasn't been completely taken over by this grisly, demonic spell of time. What's the point in going numb and letting this fiend take us hostage without a battle? We have to do all that we possibly can to send our girls and our animals back to India through whichever route shows promise.'

Kanchana and Raghav drove in their jeep to the bungalow of the deputy commissioner which, they found, was placed under heavy security. The gravity of the atmosphere there shook them. The road leading to the bungalow was blocked. The fear that under-girded the strict vigil was quite evident. Richardson's personal assistant had placed his chair right next to the security officer sitting in the cabin outside, from where he monitored the entire situation. Kanchana's jeep was stopped well before they could reach the cabin. As she surveyed the scene, two things became clear to her: the master had not returned to the bungalow since the bomb attack the previous day; and a big meeting had been in progress since then at the governor's house. Every important military and civil official was present. The issues under discussion were how to stop the Japanese invasion and, more importantly, how to save their families from the destruction being let loose by the violent bombings.

Marilyn had reached the famous European Club of Rangoon very early in the morning. There too an important meeting had been underway in the presence of the wife of His Excellency, Governor Dorman Smith. The wives of senior officials of the city, Anglo-Indian ladies, the lady members of the French Friends' Club and the wives of the ambassadors from various countries had been sitting there since morning with long, worried faces, meals forgotten. They had seen the entire day through on the hot water that passed for coffee. The first two days of bombings had knocked the stuffing out of the British Army of Burma. Not merely the man on the street, but important newspapers like *The Rangoon Gazetteer* and *Eastern Dawn* had declared that the Japanese invasion was imminent and the British forces would not be able to stand up to it. This news had spread a pall of gloom over the deputy commissioner's bungalow too.

Kanchana made her way to the security cabin and began pleading with the personal assistant, 'Sir, please let me meet madam and the sahib just for the littlest while.'

'Sorry, ma'am, the orders are: no visitors.'

'Sir, my circus, in fact my life, is at stake here. Read this notice, if you don't believe me.'

'What a strange woman you are! When the entire state of Burma belonging to Her Highness Queen Victoria is being crushed under the steamroller of those Japanese rascals, you want to come here and talk about the fate of your rotten two-penny circus?'

Sentiment stood no chance against stark facts. Nothing could be done except to stand aside and wait. The entire day slipped away and it turned dark. With blackout orders being observed stringently, the windows of the bungalow had been covered either with black paper or dark curtains. The lamps too had been covered with black paper, making them look like the half open eyes of an ailing bird. It was now almost eleven and the continuous standing had stiffened the legs of both Kanchana and Raghav. But what was the point in returning to the circus ?

Just as it turned eleven, the guard on duty blew on his whistle. The Sahib's car passed by them, escorted by a number of army vehicles both in front and behind. As soon as they had zipped past, the massive outer gate was closed again and refused to open for a long time. Kanchana got into an argument with the personal assistant. 'Let me go in for a few minutes, and if you can't do that, carry a small note for me inside.' All her entreaties, however, fell on deaf ears.

Just then, the sharp, brassy sound of whistles rent the air and the giant gate was swung open. Beams of torches criss-crossed the dark air. With Security Officer David in the lead, two armed guards in front and two behind, some important personage was emerging from inside. When this group came close enough, Kanchana shot a glance at it. There she was! A folded shawl wrapped round her shoulder over a sports costume. Tall and impressive, she was striding out surrounded by six big, leonine dogs and two trainers. It was the royal retinue out for its evening air.

The moment Kanchana recognised her, she leapt forward and screamed out, 'Madam! Please save my animals!'

'Hello, why so distraught?'

'If your army officials actually decide to execute the threat and kill all my animals, how will I live?'

Marilyn stopped and signalled to her to come close to the security cabin. In a voice of authority, she instructed the officer, 'David, tell the guards to open the gate. I have forgotten something precious inside.' With that, she walked back inside with firm, decisive steps.

The night was deepening. Every moment that Kanchana stood near the cabin seemed to her like an eternity. It was after a full twenty minutes that Marilyn finally emerged, took Kanchana by the arm and began to talk as she walked out with her. The expression on her face reflected the agony in the pit of her stomach as she tried to find the right words in which to communicate. 'Kanchana, dear,' she began carefully, 'the time, this period that we are passing through is something unprecedented. You know that there is a very high-quality Scottish school here in Rangoon. That's why I brought over three of my sister's children to study here along with my own two. Now, however, my anxiety about my children's future is giving me sleepless nights. Ragoon today is sitting on the mouth of a volcano.'

'But, ma'am, my animals?'

'Yes, I had a big argument with my husband when I was inside, but what he told me also made eminent sense.'

'What did he say, ma'am?'

'He told me that there was a heated discussion over this issue in the high-level meeting held yesterday. In these war-like circumstances, the army refuses to listen to anybody on the matter of dangerous animals currently housed in the city. Your circus, at least, is privately owned; in contrast to that is the huge government zoo run by the municipal corporation. It has been served the same notice; if they don't move their animals out of the city limits within the given time, all their animals will be slaughtered on the spot.'

Kanchana's face lost all colour. Marilyn took her hand, patted it sympathetically and said, 'Take care, my girl.'

33

This luxurious neighbourhood of Rangoon had lately started being recognised as the Army Cantonment area. The entire area was dotted with huge white bungalows belonging to the European owners of tea gardens and rubber plantations, rich Burmese traders of gems and rubies, British agents and senior white officials. It was in these aristocratic environs that Nirmal Roy had his own palatial bungalow, complete with a sprawling garden and a swimming pool.

The unrelenting tension of the past few days had resulted in Mr Roy's large, rotund body running a low-grade fever that refused to go away. It was only since last evening, when he had taken his first sip of some high-quality scotch, that he had started feeling better. The people who hovered around him in Rangoon masqueraded as members of his staff during the day and carried appropriately stony expressions on their faces to suit the role. When evening arrived and the bungalow was adequately lit up, these same stony faces of daytime would transform themselves into glittering stars of the night sky. They claimed their places by right in Roy's drawing room as intimate friends and old-time buddies and raised glasses to each other's health and happiness.

Despite the tense times, Roy's manager had succeeded in procuring two Burmese masseuses for him. They were rather thin and lean, but were doing an honest job of rubbing his skin down. As massages went, Roy really had no complaint, but what was upsetting him was that they didn't look good enough for anything beyond that.

It wasn't as if Roy's men were so naïve as to not understand their boss's needs. Without Roy having specifically instructed them, his devoted men were busy searching through the night, looking for nubile girls who could meet their master's needs. As of now, he was pulling on a cheroot of green Burmese tobacco. He cocked his left eyebrow and bellowed at his minions, 'What have you done about the main thing, asses?'

Night was slipping away. Roy's restless eyes would often shoot across towards the garden in the darkness outside.

Nirmal Roy's face turned grave. He cast an eye on his drawing hall and looked at the litter of empty liquor bottles and his staff spread-eagled wherever they had tumbled. In spite of his inebriated state, he carefully walked over to his cupboard and pulled out a leather bag stuffed with currency. One of his favourite errand boys appeared with a smile on his face. 'Come along, huzoor,' he called out from the door. 'All is set.'

The two of them stepped out together. The boy had spent a sum big enough to buy five pagodas in order to arrange for the horse-carriage that stood outside. As the carriage picked up speed, Roy placed a hand upon the boy's shoulder and asked, 'Where to?'

'To Zareena, sir, who lives in the pink bungalow along the Irrawaddy river.'

'Oh, wonderful! She's a fairy from the skies. Big colonels, police officers, rubber planters—she flies high! The bitch refuses to spread her legs for native crows. How did you manage to persuade her?'

'I simply told her to be practical. If a Japanese bomb were to take her out tomorrow, not a dog would be left to cast another glance at her pink palace.'

'Waah waah!'

'She just smiled and agreed.'

Roy's face lit up with delight. In the ecstasy of imminent pleasure, he planted a kiss on his minion's face. 'Son,' he beamed, 'you have moved a mountain.'

34

25 December 1941. All the joy and excitement around Christmas Day celebrations had been bombed out of Rangoon. Nobody had ever witnessed Christmas under such dark, dreary, frightening circumstances. Heaps upon heaps of Christmas cakes lay stacked on shop shelves. The market was a far cry, even the road leading to the graveyard had never been as desolate as it was today. The citizens and their animals had no sleep in their eyes. There were only drooping, blood-red eyes everywhere. The churches, however, were full to overflowing. People were on their knees, pleading with, begging Christ, beseeching his aid in rowing their boats out of these tempestuous waters.

The minute hand kept moving forward, causing the hearts of the circus people to leap with consternation at every tick. Just a few hours to go before the deadline of the notice would arrive. Raghav and Kanchana were worried sick. It was Roy Sahib on whose assurance they had arrived in this foreign land, and now he seemed to have disappeared without a trace.

Why hadn't the team dispatched to Zeyawaddy returned yet? The sounds drifting in from the menagerie—moans, sighs and roars—sounded strange and unfamiliar. A weird, intuitive image had gripped the imagination—a wicked, slimy fate sat crouched inside there somewhere, tapping its nails, waiting for the moment in which it would take its murderous leap.

Paranjape came hurrying in from the other side. He thrust under Kanchana's tired eyes pieces of paper with scribbled appeals in Burmese and English and said, 'We are requesting the administration to give us a two-three-hour extension.'

'Okay, Paranjape. But if the extension isn't granted, I'll simply walk into the jaws of death.'

Circumstances were worsening fast. A disconcerting whisper had been going on in Rangoon since daybreak. It was Christmas day today. The black-hearted Japanese were surely going to serve Rangoon the black cake they had promised it earlier; it was inescapable. Today, the soldiers from the land of the rising sun were certainly going to drown the Rangoon sun in the adjacent bay. Rangoon was going to be bombed out of the map altogether.

To add to the misery, the sirens had been blaring away their cacophonous music since dawn. Their hideous reverberation kept up a constant terror in the hearts of the animals in the menagerie. Kanchana's legs knew no rest. Over and over again, she went rushing to the main gate. She was waiting for the fuel to arrive from Zeyawaddy. Out there on the road sat the twenty-nine drivers in their twenty nine trucks, ready to drive off at a moment's notice. Life in their limbs and fuel in their tanks was all they needed. They would fill up their tanks, load their cargo of girls and animals and race out. The next halt would be Zeyawaddy.

The transport boys who had gone to the harbour returned. The news they brought back was disheartening. After having sat there through the night, all they could report was, 'Didi, these people have decided not to issue tickets to any Indian.'

'What? Why?'

'Their first priority is the White sahibs, their families and their employees.'

'Oh dear lord! Not even a single seat?'

'Didi, we offered to pay them five times the price for just five seats, but it didn't work. All these big and small ships and boats are under the control of the British.'

The soft early morning rays began playing upon Rangoon, and what they threw light upon wasn't a pleasant sight: a face charred a frightening black with all the conflagration of the past few days. The golden dome of the Shwedagon Pagoda that was visible on the scorched horizon also looked like it had been covered by a dark veil of soot and smoke. It wasn't air that the sunlight met, but a putrid, malodorous substance that corroded the linings of the nostrils. Inside the circus camp, the stench that came from the direction of the menagerie through the tear in the cloth walls was so fetid that it defeated the tolerance of the strongest guts. The stomachs were less than half full, making it difficult for the sufferers to release full-blown vomits, but even the dry retches were enough to choke the life out of them.

The sanitation workers of the company went to find the source of this poisonous exudation and discovered the decomposed bodies of two adolescent boys concealed in the lower folds of the cloth walls. They were clearly victims of the stampede from two nights ago. It was altogether conceivable that the parents of these boys were among the 5,000 and more corpses that lay rotting on the streets of Rangoon. Who had the time to take a tally of the living and the dead? The sanitation boys took the decaying corpes away and tossed them wherever they could.

The hands of the clock moved on inexorably. Each forward movement pierced the heart and drew blood. If the gods themselves had lost credibility, where would men and animals go for refuge? People who were princes until a couple of days ago had suddenly become paupers. These were people who owned twenty-five rice mills each, who had diamonds and rubies lying in piles in their shops; but now, when they wanted to make a quick exit out of Rangoon, they had no petrol to start their fancy cars. They now stood in the street, falling at the feet of bullock-cart owners to help smuggle them out.

This time when Kanchana's eyes travelled towards the main gate, she spied two of the boys who had gone to Zeyawaddy in search of petrol. When she saw their faces beaming with victorious smiles, she suddenly felt recharged. 'The petrol tanker is on its way,' the boys shouted, 'it should roll in any minute.' 'Damle Sahib is himself seated in the front cabin of the tanker and sent the two of us ahead with the news.'

'Any trouble on the way?'

'None at all, Didi. Damle Sahib cannot be more than an hour or an hour-and-a-half away. The roads going to Mandalay are very crowded. Everyone, young and old alike, is packed in bullock-carts, buggies and horses moving in that direction.'

'Arey waah!' Raghav shouted in joy. But then thinking of another issue, he barked in anger, 'And what's happened to our Roy Sahib? Where has he gone and drowned himself?'

'Our boys are just back from his bungalow. Roy Sahib and his people have disappeared.'

Kanchana threw a look at the ash-grey sky and spoke in a grateful voice, 'Mother, Kalamma, you did run to your child's aid! Just let the fuel come, and I will have conquered the world, just watch!' She quickly ran her hand over her fevered brow and turned to the cook. 'Have you sent food to the truck drivers as I told you to? We can see another ten days through without food and water, but make sure the stomachs of our drivers are full. No stopping right up to Mandalay now, even if it is raining bombs.'

There were just three quarters of an hour left before the notice period ran out. For all their agitated mopping, Kanchana and Raghav couldn't staunch the stream of perspiration dripping off their brow. Just then, loud, frightening sounds of *zooom wrooom* were heard racing in from a distance. There was a big flash of fire in the sky, immediately followed by big red balls suddenly gaining body in an exponential hurry and exploding. These were immediately followed by the rat-tat-tat of machine gun fire. The same stupefying fear that had entered Kanchana's bones and sinews and buried itself deep inside the living cells of her animals only a couple of days ago! It was a repeat of the same nightmare. The ear-splitting noise was followed by an eerie, mind-blowing silence.

The entire town then began to echo with the sound of exploding bombs and disintegrating buildings. These were immediately joined by the swish and crackle of raging fires zipping through the city streets and lanes like snakes gone mad. Measured against these, the piteous cries of human beings sounded feeble and sickly. Even while the light-and-sound show out in the city continued, another couple of colossal explosions were heard very close by. Right on the other side of the main gate, the flames that shot up in the sky looked like oil wells catching fire, among which could be seen the burning skeletons of trucks doing a slow somersault up in the air. A veritable mountain of smoke leapt into the sky. Kanchana suddenly felt a painful cramp in the pit of her stomach. She shut her eyes tight and wiped the sweat pouring down her face and neck. Raghav, fearing that she could collapse any time, rushed to prop her up.

The tiniest fraction of time would have passed since that massive explosion, the time it takes the smoke from the barrel of a rifle to dissipate. The sounds of the retreating aircraft in the sky overlapped with the loud wroom of two jeeps accompanied by the blare of their roof-top sirens stopping right in front of the gate and was followed by the footfall of heavy boots stamping the earth.

The Japanese bombers left the sky after their incendiary exploits.

The British arrived within half a minute of the mayhem.

The same boorishness, the same apathy. The same indifference, the same absence of conscience. Kanchana watched the British and Burmese soldiers march in with their dead-pan faces, setting right their vile helmets, their eyes dry, empty, bereft of any emotion. Their faces were colourless. They had seen so many houses crumbling by the minute, so many fires dancing their naked dance of destruction, so many human beings in the throes of death that they had been washed clean of all human emotions. They neither celebrated the living nor sympathised with the dead. They came marching in like soulless automatons.

Paranjape stood nervously, the appeals in Burmese and English for a two-hour reprieve quivering in his fevered fingers. The display of the rifles unnerved Paranjape. Kanchana somehow managed to get the better of the fear in her belly. She lowed like a humble cow, 'Sir, sir, please wait for three, no, just two hours, or at least for one hour. My petrol tanker should be reaching any time now. Just allow me some more time, sir.'

Paranjape managed to muster the courage to step forward and stood in the way of the advancing soldiers. The squad leader wanted no challenge to his authority. His pupils danced. Two of his soldiers moved forward and simply lifted the man and deposited him out of the way of the advancing squad.

As Kanchana shot forward, Raghav held her forearm to restrain her. But she shook him away and cried out in a voice loud enough to reach the gods in their heaven, 'Please pardon us, sir!' At that, the squad leader stepped forward and simply pushed her aside.

The sound of gunfire followed, this time from the menagerie. The thump of heavy army boots and the agonised screeches, howls and bellows from the animals assaulted Kanchana's ears and she raced towards the menagerie shouting, 'What are you doing ... how can you ... oh, my babies, my babies!' Such huge elephants, but once the bullets penetrated their thick skin, they came down on their knees and keeled over to one side like torpedo-hit ships. Warm, red blood gushed out of the numerous punctures and began to form a pool around where they lay. Fearsome animals such as lions and tigers whined and keened and dashed against the railings of their cages as bullets pierced their skins. Even the court of Yama, the God of death, couldn't have witnessed a more gruesome display of barbarity.

It took merely minutes for the riflemen to see the massacre through. What had been healthy, spirited, ferocious, playful living beings until a few moments ago were transformed into carcasses drowning in a pool of their own blood. An entire world of joy and merriment had been wiped out of existence.

35

Life is nothing more than paper flowers—no sap, no fragrance.

Call it the black sleep of death or a doomsday nightmare, Kanchana had woken up from that delusional state. She sat staring with dry, dead eyes at her menagerie that had been so mercilessly obliterated.

The corpses of twelve elephants lay sprawled out, one next to the other. Those massive heaps of flesh and blood, those ghastly cadavers with bits and pieces shredded out, those sooty spots of burnt skin where the bullets had penetrated their bodies. When Kanchana turned her gaze towards the cages of the carnivores, she felt as if she was being rolled on a sharp bed of porcupine quills. The bars and sheets of the cages were caked with dark, congealed blood. Looking at the manner in which it was splashed all over, it wasn't difficult to imagine how the animals would have dashed themselves against the bars, how they would have lost their minds in an effort to escape the raining bullets.

The barrage of gunshots had frightened poor Mustafa out of his tank. He had somehow managed to pull himself out of the water, hoping to create some distance between himself and those murderous gun-toters, but he never stood a chance. The fusillade of bullets had chased him and brought him down in no time at all. When Bankat Singh had mounted his raid on the Islampura camp, the tools used for manufacturing guns had been hidden in Mustafa's tank. Bankat Singh had turned every inch of the camp upside down, but his eyes had missed the tank.

Kanchana and Raghav walked past this macabre scene. As her eyes fell on the stable that had been flattened out, and as the unnatural silence there penetrated her senses, Kanchana turned to her husband and said, 'Raghav, all I see here is droppings and hoof marks. Could those demons have shot down my beautiful horses too?'

'No, the British are thieves. Dirty bastards, they saw an opportunity and took as many animals out of here as they could.'

'Well, at least, they didn't kill them. But what about the rest?'

'When the Japanese bombs exploded outside, a few of our horses too got blown up along with seven or eight of our trucks. Five or six of them at least. A number of them were stolen away by the Burmese goons.'

'*Arey deva deva!* So we have none left now?'

'We still have sixteen or seventeen left. Our grooms and ring-boys managed to move them to a safe place.'

'Where?'

'Well ... a secure place.'

'How can they be secure when the sky above them is exploding?'

'Kanchu, don't give up hope. God is watching over us.'

'And what happened to Damle?'

'Neither he nor any member of his team has arrived yet. But he is a resilient man. If they are still alive, they are going to come back, you can be sure of that.'

They walked up to the main gate. The stillness there was pregnant with diabolical possibilities. The city was burning and a thick pall of smoke hung in the air. The tender rays of the early morning sun, the soft warmth, the free-flowing breeze had all been gobbled up by a vengeful providence. The

Shwedagon Pagoda and the high minarets of Sule Pagoda that shone on the Rangoon horizon—all their glitter had been consumed by the smoke too.

For how long can a distraught mind be duped with false cheer? For how long can a tormented heart be hoodwinked by sheer posturing of spunk and grit? Kanchana went into Raghav's arms, clasped him tight to her chest and let out a mighty bawl, 'O mother Kalamma! What have you gained by reducing my life to this state? My menagerie was my place of worship, didn't you know? What diabolical pleasure could you have derived by blowing it to pieces?'

'Easy, Kanchu, easy. Get a hold on yourself. God hasn't abandoned us, he still ...'

'Don't lie to me, Raghav,' she screamed, 'Why have the Japanese decided to destroy me? Why my trucks—'

'It's not like that at all, Kanchu! Just on the other side, there, at the corner of Thompson Road, there were some 400 trucks lined up. It's an important depot for American vehicles. Hundreds of trucks are parked there, ready to carry goods from the harbour to China along Burma Road. The Japanese blew that depot to smithereens today. There are no trucks and jeeps left now in Rangoon.'

Kanchana looked towards the other side. Barely four or five of her trucks had survived the morning bombing. The rest of them had turned to cinders. She could see the burnt-out skeleton of one, with the ghoulish figure of its driver leaning on the steering wheel. In a voice filled with distress, she asked, 'Are all our drivers dead?'

'No. Most of them had seen the bomber aircraft before they had offloaded their bombs and taken shelter under their vehicles. For all their alertness, eleven of them did get blown up.'

'Their last rites ...'

'The entire city has turned into an enormous cremation chamber. How many bodies do you think you can consign to the flames?'

36

Kanchana took a handkerchief from one of the ringboys and wiped the sweat off her face. She noticed the black, sooty blotch that the wiping had left on her handkerchief. Just to make sure, she again rubbed a clean corner of the handkerchief against the face, and what she saw gave her a proper scare. Every wall, every leaf, every piece of cloth, the air itself had coated itself black with soot. She asked Raghav in a meek voice, 'Is it really true that all my girls are safe?'

Raghav gave her a reassuring look and pressed her hand. Her girls were all safe and secure. The gunfire outside, however, had nowhere near halted. The tension in the air had not abated. 'Let's clear out of here immediately,' Kanchana said.

'Don't worry, Kanchu. Our company people have found a secret haven.'

'Where'

'About five miles away, in a nook alongside a small river.'

'So, why are we waiting? Let's get out of this horrible city as fast as we can!'

'Once we move out of the city into a suburb, the situation here has become so dire that it would be very difficult to return to it.'

'Why would we want to return?'

'We will have to return. If we have to send somebody to India for making advance arrangements, both the port and the airport are here in Rangoon.'

'Yes, of course. But we cannot stay here in the open, under this tattered tent. Just one bomb, and the game will be over for us.'

'Don't worry, I have made some temporary arrangement. Come on, come with me.'

The Padang maidan was a huge ground. It belonged to the Municipality and had been taken on rent for the circus. There was another month to go before the contract expired. Since it was a playground, frequent sporting events, big and small, were organised here and underground bunkers had been constructed for the players to keep their things and also for keeping gardening tools. Kanchana and her associates went to have a look at the arrangements, and decided that it was a place that eminently met their needs—it offered security in the event of air-raids.

Under the circumstances, it was a veritable heaven into which they shifted. The main six-pole circus tent still continued to stand, but its cloth walls and cloth roof had been blown to tatters and would create their own music when fluttering in the cold night wind.

In the dark of night, Kanchana spoke, as if in a dream, 'Three faces keep floating in my vision.'

'Faces?'

'Yes, the faces of our goddess Kalamma, my tigress Lakshmi … and—Marilyn ma'am—not sure why I see her face.'

'Kanchu, there are just two ways of escaping this conflagration—either by water or by air, and there is no way of accessing them except through Marilyn ma'am.'

The company jeep went crawling through the darkness of night in the direction of the deputy commissioner's bungalow. There was no question of switching on the headlights. Even the municipal lights along the streets hadn't been lit. One had to keep one's eyes open as wide as a jungle cat and grope one's way forward. The jeep moved carefully to make sure it didn't run over a living human being. Avoiding the craters burnt into the ground by the bombs was by itself a miracle.

The situation around Richardson's bungalow was quite intriguing. The heavy presence of the army that they had noticed during the earlier visit was missing. The semblance of authority seemed to have faded away. The security outside had gone lax. Inside the bungalow, there was the hurry and scurry of packing up things. Everybody was throwing anxious glances in all directions. Despite the darkness everywhere, David immediately recognised Kanchana and instructed two constables to accompany her inside.

'I have a feeling that ma'am is waiting for you,' he said. 'She had given me standing instructions to let you in as soon as you arrived.'

'How did she know I would come?'

'Ma'am knows about the unfortunate slaughter of your animals. But even before the rifles arrived at your camp, they went visiting the big government zoo with twice the number of animals you had.'

Marilyn Richardson sat in her drawing room looking bewildered. Five or six high-society women sat around her, looking uncertain and anxious. It was clear that they wanted to get out of the hell-hole called Rangoon at the earliest. When Marilyn saw Kanchana, she murmured, her voice thick with emotion, 'I am deeply sorry for what happened to your animals, Kanchana.'

'Let's forget that, ma'am. What has happened was written in my fate.'

'What will you do now?'

'I'm at my wit's end, ma'am. You tell me where a deranged mother who just lost 200 children should go.'

'Kanchana, we hardly have any time to talk. Look at my European friends gathered here—mute lambs en route to the slaughter house ... Whether our dominion here stays or ends, our prime obligation now is to ensure the security of our children. We have to do whatever we can to escape from here.'

'Ma'am, I fall at your feet, please help me. Do what you have to, but help me procure ship tickets for my staff.'

'That's impossible. Not sensible either.'

'You can do anything ma'am once you set your heart to it.'

'Those days are gone, my dear girl. Look at that woman sitting in that corner. She is the wife of the assistant commissioner of police. Even she hasn't managed tickets for her family yet.'

Kanchana's hopes came crashing to the ground. Marilyn said, 'Time's running out for all of us. In the first place, I don't think the air service to India will resume for the next two days. This evening, the Japanese dropped a bomb very close to the runway at the Mingaladon airport.'

The unrelenting sledge-hammer of misfortune seemed to have crushed Kanchana's future to a pulp. Marilyn understood the hapless woman's state of mind. Determined to help Kanchana, she left the hall. Snatches of the conversation that took place in the corridor outside between Marilyn and her husband drifted up to her ears. 'My love, it's only on your insistence, and for your sake only ... we may get two spare tickets.'

Marilyn hurried inside to convey this news to Kanchana: two tickets could be made available for an early morning flight the next day. There was no saying whether another aircraft would take off after that. The presence of Japanese surveillance aircraft over the Indian Ocean and submarines under it had intensified. She also said that David had been given the responsibility of escorting the passengers right up to the door of the aircraft.

When Kanchana turned to leave, Marilyn handed over to her two revolvers of French make and said, 'One is for you and the other for your husband. Bad times come unannounced. May God take care of you.' Kanchana was overwhelmed. As she looked at her benefactor through teary eyes, she thought of her mother who had died in Ambala and whom she had never seen.

Debates went on for a long time in the dark, dungeon-like bunker in the Padang maidan. Who should be sent to India by the morning flight?

The road journey to India was extremely long. One could go from Rangoon through Chittagong to Calcutta and then move southwards. Or one could take the Myitkyina route, then cross the dangerous river Dafa, enter Assam and travel southwards from there. This second route was far more dangerous. The terrain was impossibly trecherous, fraught with unimaginable perils. It would take a long time to cross it on foot—a minimum of six months. That was why it was important to immediately dispatch someone towards Kaagwad–Miraj. The circus owned a sixty-acre farmland there and a big bungalow on the Miraj–Mhaisal road. There were a few other things to get under control.

Mahaling and Hirabai said, 'We think Kanchana and Raghav should leave on the flight.'

'We?' Kanchana flared up at the very thought.

'Yes. You could reach India and send help. You may even be able to hire a ship to evacuate us from here.'

'Those days are gone. The ships are all under the control of the British authorities, while the Japanese are surveilling the sea,' Raghav said.

'You are suggesting we leave the company and our people behind in this inferno? Save our own skins? What are we without our people? So much better for all of us to die together,' Kanchana said firmly.

Raghav tried to explain to Kanchana why it was important for her to go, but she said, 'Raghav, what am I going to do when I reach India? I am nothing without my circus. Why talk of India? Even here in Burma, I can't spend a single night away from my people and animals.'

Kanchana refused to leave on the morning flight. After some more discussion, it was finally decided that Raghav and trapeze Champa would fly out. The two would be able to perform the twin tasks of setting things in order at Kaagwad and making arrangements to receive the main circus troupe after it entered India and facilitate its journey southwards.

The wind was flitting in and out of the torn sheets of the tent walls. It wasn't yet light enough when the rumbling sound of a motorcycle was heard. It was David. The last flight out to Calcutta was at eight in the morning, and it was critical to reach the Mingladon airport before the Japanese conducted another air raid. Raghav and Champa gathered some bags in the dark and were moving towards the motorcycle when David shouted, 'Have you lost your mind? You think you are going for a marriage party? Throw away the bags, just take the bare essentials.' The bags were quietly dumped in the tent.

Raghav sat behind David and Champa sat behind Raghav. As they set off, Raghav did not turn around to look at Kanchana one last time.

The motorcycle reached the airport in quick time. David was known to everyone there, and he received salutes and nods and open gates all the way up to the waiting room at the airport. Except for Champa and Raghav and a timber merchant with his obese wife, there were no other Indians travellers there. All the others were European officers with their slim, beautiful wives and their blonde children.

The Dakota was ready to take off. The passengers walked past the army security barriers and started climbing up a small flight of stairs into the aircraft. Raghav was somewhere in the middle of the queue when his face contorted and he stepped aside. He experienced a severe stomach cramp. With a beseeching look, he ran towards the toilet. David was furious at this behaviour. He took Champa and stood aside waiting for him to return.

Within a moment the sky was ripped apart. The siren was heard. Even before people could register what was happening, two flaming Mitsubishi-30s shot out of the early morning rays with a deafening roar. The sign of the rising sun was clearly visible on their noses. The two aircraft dived so low that their propellers raised windstorms on the tarmac. The next moment they began spitting out bullets with a frightening rat-tat-tat. Half a second later, the petrol tank of the Dakota standing there caught fire. There was a deafening sound and the Dakota exploded where it stood, its pieces flying in all directions.

When Raghav emerged from the toilet, David threw a smile at him and, without wasting a second, he held him by the wrist and pulled him out. While the airport was going up in flames, David was speeding away with Raghav and Champa behind him. 'You two are lucky, really lucky,' he screamed and laughed, without slackening his speed. He was taking them to the dockyard. He was determined to fulfill his mistress's command.

The road to the dockyard was littered with unclaimed bodies. The older ones had started to decompose, while the ones from the previous day's firing were relatively fresh. Heaps of rubble from collapsed buildings stretched across the middle of the streets already dotted with the burnt-out skeletons of vehicles.

The dockyard had been a picturesque place until four days ago. Its present state of disintegration made David's bile rise. The wooden planks on the waterside lay there half-burnt, but the scene that made one wretch was on the surface of the water only a few feet away. Just as a poisonous weed kills fish and causes their carcasses to come floating up to the surface in their hundreds, human bodies were bobbing on the waves, everywhere. Nobody had had the chance to take cognizance of the floating dead.

When they reached the dock, a boat was on the point of sailing off. The news of the airport's bombing had triggered panic here too. A boat stood ready to pull anchor and depart for Madras. David shook hands with a number of naval officers and began pushing his case for a couple of seats. But seats there were none. Besides, the people seated inside were either army big-wigs or other senior officers with their wives and children, none of whom could be persuaded to relinquish their seats. David got on to the deck where he noticed a friend, whom he finally persuaded to disembark with his luggage.

He rushed back to Raghav and said, 'There's just one seat available.'

'We'll wait and catch the next boat,' was Raghav's answer.

'Are you crazy?' screamed David. 'How long are you going to wait and for whom? You are the backbone of your company. Set off alone. Don't let this god-sent opportunity pass by.'

Raghav called Champa who had been standing at a distance. Climbing up a small staircase, he took her to the gangway.

Seeing that she was the only person going, Champa was flustered. In a piteous voice, she said, 'Raghav dada, how will I survive so far away from the company?'

'Don't worry, Champa. God will show you the way.'

The siren of the boat sounded. Raghav quickly removed the expensive, gold-strapped watch from his wrist and a thick gold chain from his neck and handed them both to Champa. Then he scampered off the boat. As he walked away, he looked back and shouted, 'All right, Champa, take care. Don't be scared.'

The boat moved away from the shore to the sound of its motor and the raucous calls of sea birds. David drove Raghav back to the circus camp.

When Kanchana saw Raghav's figure coming down the dark steps of the store room, she was stunned. Her eyes clouded with tears of anger. She couldn't stomach the idea of Raghav withdrawing in this manner. 'Why did you do this?' she snapped. 'How could you allow yourself to get lured back by your love for me?'

'Who can say, Kanchana? If God has destined that I should die with my head in your lap in one of the mountains here, who I am to fight that?'

These words fell upon Kanchana's ears like a blizzard descending on a broken branch. He sat down close beside her. 'Kanchu, death barely missed me this morning at the airport, rubbing against my shirt as it whizzed past.'

She whispered, 'There's little we can do except watch how often death crosses paths with us in this foreign land and in how many disguises.'

37

The bunkers in the maidan weren't entirely safe. When a bomb exploded outside, one of its red-hot shards came flying inside and lodged itself in the thigh of a horse. The horse let out a frightful cry and began hopping on its three good legs, going round and round in circles, snorting and neighing in agony. The groom Gyanchand told Kanchana, 'It's unbearable to see the poor thing in this state. It's not going to survive.'

'What's the remedy, then?'

'Putting it out of its misery. We'll have to shoot him.'

'This cycle of killing has gone on far too long. If you want to carry on with this trend of violence like the English and the Japanese, go do it somewhere else. From here on, I'd rather die than see another animal spilling its blood before me.'

The groom managed to pull the tortured horse away with the greatest difficulty. It no longer made sense to stay in the maidan. The circus staff began packing up whatever belongings they were left with. Four bullock carts were arranged for the earliest possible departure.

It was as if Rangoon had been afflicted with diarrhoea. The symptoms were getting repeated over and over again. The skies burst in flames, murderous aircraft rained their bombs, buildings collapsed, balconies got twisted out of shape, there was a mad stampede on the roads, people waded through rivers of blood—these things went on chasing one another in an unrelenting, irrepressible cycle.

Their bullock carts were full, no more space was left. Raghav and Kanchana stood by the roadside dejected and confused, wondering how to proceed. That was when a driverless four-horse carriage came careening towards them from the front. There were marks of fresh blood on its driver's seat. Raghav instinctively leapt into the carriage, found the reins and tugged at them. Finding the opportunity, Kanchana also leapt in by his side. Raghav managed to slow the horses down. The two noticed some sticky liquid on the seat and realised it was fresh blood.

Raghav pulled the horses to a halt. He got down and lowered the bodies of a British couple that lay in the carriage and of their butler to the street. Sushi and some of the company people climbed into the carriage and Raghav began driving in the direction that Sushi pointed to.

Evening had set in and darkness had descended on the trees. The blackout had ensured that there was no artificial light anywhere. There was no saying when the carriage would run into a half-crumbled wall or a collapsed tree.

As they drove, Kanchana turned to Pandu Nana and said, 'Eleven of our drivers died on the spot. It was a horrible thing to have happened, and yet I regret that we could not save even four or five of our trucks.'

'Pori, there were two houses that had collapsed in front, blocking the road altogether. Any number of trucks had burnt to cinders in the middle, and the rear end too was blocked with fallen trees. Even if there had been a truck worth retrieving in there, it would have taken us four days to clear a passage for bringing it out. Let go, Kanchana, what's gone has simply turned to dust. Stop thinking about it.'

As Kanchana sat mourning the drivers, Raghav said, 'Four of our midgets have simply disappeared. There's no news of our Batuknath and Sulaiman the mahaut since the slaughter in the menagerie.'

'So what you are saying is that twelve of our people have died, and an equal number have gone missing, or have left, yes? What could have happened to them?'

'If they did truly run out of luck, they could be under the debris of a ...'

Raghav couldn't speak further. A chill ran down Kanchana's spine. Somehow sensing their way through the dark, the horses came by a bamboo cluster. The sound of flowing water could be heard. A grove of peepul trees grew alongside a farmland stretching across seven or eight acres. There was a low-built house with tiled roofs, its front elevation made of wood in the Burmese tradition. Some well-used wooden furniture lay in front.

Kanchana got down from the carriage. She hadn't slept a wink for three straight nights, and all the fatigue of those impossible hours now came cascading down upon her. She sat on a stone parapet wall next to a paraffin torch bellowing out smoke. The company girls gathered around her. She looked at them, smiled wanly and let out an involuntary shiver. The ache in her body and the overpowering heaviness of her head made it impossible for her eyes to stay open. She gave in, tumbled on the stone parapet and sank into complete oblivion.

At least four or five hours would have gone by. In her slumber, Kanchana became conscious of a warm touch. It was Lakshmi, licking her. 'O mother, O divine mount of Goddess Durga, you had been trying to warn me, give me signs—by falling ill, by crying and growling unexpectedly—that I shouldn't cross the seas, but I didn't pay heed. Now look at the bind I am in.'

Some more time passed by. Lakshmi was licking away, sniffing Kanchana all over. But what was this snorting so uncatlike? And why had her tongue turned so long? She reached out for the nostrils of the creature and found it velvety and long instead of bristly and snub. She woke up with a start and what she saw in the dim light of the torch made her squeal with delight. She pulled the muzzle close to her, rubbed her cheek against it and shouted, 'Phakkadrao! Phakkadrao, my little boy! Where had you disappeared? I knew, I knew, I knew you would not desert me. I knew you would come back!'

Kanchana was wide awake now. Nevertheless, she pinched herself hard to confirm that she was not hallucinating. What she saw around her was straight out of a dream. A good fifteen or so horses of the company were gathered around her. After having got himself amply petted, Phakkadrao stood close to her, loath to create any more distance than necessary between himself and his mistress.

38

The latest headcount showed that the dreadful bombing had killed sixteen of them instantly, while thirty-five of them had gone missing. Nobody had any inkling of their whereabouts. The missing included the midget Batuknath and the mahaut Sulaiman.

A chilling truth dawned upon everybody. They had been abandoned by God and all other powers—natural and supernatural. If they ever managed to escape alive from the jaws of this destructive war, it would be only on account of their own efforts. Every inflamed breath, every frantic heartbeat had just one message to deliver: get ready, in heart, mind and body, to walk, walk and walk, for over 1,500 miles, walk till your legs fall off. The Arakan mountains, the Naga mountains, the mountains of the eastern Himalayas, high enough to graze the skies, all of these will have to be covered on foot. Steel yourself to scale high peaks, negotiate deep, treacherous gorges and impassable ravines; cross wild, fast-flowing rivers, dense forests and poisonous jungle tracks.

Travelling over this killer route could take three months, or it could take nine months—nobody had the knowledge to work out a definite timeline.

There was no saying who would be lucky enough to reach India in one piece, kiss the earth of their village, sit among their own people, pat the backs of their own animals.

There was a stream that ran along Sushi's farms; it wasn't a fast one and the banks were open and widespread. Mahaling would get into the water with his fifteen horses in the company of the trainers and ring-boys. The mission was to get battle-ready for the ordeal ahead.

Mahaling gathered the circus troupe around him and asked, 'All right, then, if our tigers and lions ever slip out of their cages and sneak out into the open, they don't ever go very far from the camp and sneak back in. What could be the reason for this behaviour?'

'Simple!' laughed the boys. 'They are, after all, tamed animals. They are used to moving around on the soft, pliant soil of the ring. Their claws and soft paws are not ready for the thorns and brambles and stones of the jungle track. '

Then began a concerted effort to re-acclimatise the animals on the banks of the stream. They were made to walk through the thorny slush, the stones, the mires and bogs that caused their hooves to sink into the earth. This drill wounded the horses' hooves and legs, but there wasn't much choice. The long, arduous journey ahead required them to be accustomed to what was to come.

When Sarang Daaji had toured Burma some fifteen years ago, he had appointed Sushi's father as his purchase manager. Daaji had been so impressed with the man's honesty and sincerity that he had stuffed fistfuls of expensive jewellery into his trouser pocket as a parting gift. This farm had been bought out of that largesse. It was out of gratitude that Sushi was now sheltering the company.

The troupe had to find a way out of there and they sat poring over maps till late into the night—handmade maps, British maps, sketches made by adventurers who had hacked their way through the Burmese jungles. Kanchana and Raghav had made plenty of enquiries too. They had managed to locate a couple of retired soldiers of the British army and hired them to help find the best route back to India. Gnarled, tanned fingers travelled up and down the maps as the midnight oil burnt on.

'This sea route, going up the Rangoon harbour to Akyab, Arakan and Chittagong is entirely blocked now. While this old route through Prom, this one moves along the Irrawaddy; it means a few weeks of travelling on boats and big launches. But then, it also includes trekking through densely forested hills. It isn't as easy as it appears.' Thousands of displaced people were travelling up this Irrawaddy route, making this option unsafe.

The fingers on the map moved away from the coast into the inland areas. 'Look, this road circles around Pegu and moves towards north Burma along the Yoma mountains. The real artery of Burma: along this is the Burma Road that takes you to the north. Travel 350 miles along this road and you will reach Mandalay. Go slightly at an angle, cross the river Sittang, travel from from there to Tamu, then across the Naga mountains and you are in the Indian towns of Pallel and Imphal in Manipur. Looks so easy on the map, but it is 2,200 miles of travel through terribly inhospitable terrain. How many days and how many months it will take depends upon the strength of your legs, your destiny and, of course, the forces of nature.'

'Instead of that, we can travel 500 miles straight ahead from Mandalay and reach Myitkyina.'

'Yes, yes,' broke in Kanchana, 'it won't take the Japanese army much time to reach this Rangoon–Pegu belt, but it will take them time to keep moving up, conquering these areas right up to Myitkyina. The airport at Myitkyina may continue to stay functional for a good time, they say. Let's gather our courage and reach there.'

'But what do we do up there after reaching in such a hurry?'

'Fly off to India! My girls and men would require two cargo aircraft at the most. Once they are safely transported to India, my problems are over.'

It was impossible for any one of them to sit on their hands doing nothing. Dagdu had his little furnace going at all times of the day. Large quantities of coal would be fed into it and set crackling and sparking. He would then place steel bars into it, bring them to white heat and hammer them into shapes of spear-heads. Taranath would be busy with his saws and awls and planers to make utility items of wood. Jaanrao Matang would collect vines and grasses from the nearby vegetation and turn them into ropes and strings of various sizes.

Dagdu dispatched the grooms and ring-boys to the nearby villages with instructions to collect as many steel bars as they could find. He would bring them to red and white heat and work with his sledge hammer to turn out horseshoes and sharp-tipped nails. Fortunately, the shrubbery surrounding both banks of the stream was quite dense, giving them sufficient privacy to continue working without piquing the idle curiosity of the world outside.

The day had dawned. Kaachana woke up with a start. From the other side of the house came floating the melodious notes of a flute. Somebody out there was playing the evergreen Bhairavi, the queen of all ragas, and was beautifully channeling all the pain and pathos that rested in the insides of that piece of bamboo.

Kanchana couldn't hold herself back and she walked rapidly in the direction of the sound. On a low branch of a peepul tree sat a person with his back towards her, his face partly concealed by the leaves, playing with the abandon of a cowherd. It was Charlie, completely lost in creating music, his eyes half closed. The poignant music betrayed his state of mind.

The situation was worsening by the day. In faraway Europe, Hitler's Germany and Mussolini's Italy had deflated England

and France. But even so, such total indifference to East Asia was not what one had expected from the rulers. Rangoon had been reduced to the state of an abandoned courtesan. This Paris of the East had been receiving the bitterest lessons of its life from Dame Misfortune and the rampaging Japanese army.

Among all the professionals in the world, the class of professionals called the baniyas or traders is the shrewdest. Whatever the trade be, gems or flesh, their single-point agenda is to jump into the business and mint money. From fish, jute, flowers to human skulls, wherever they can make profits, these adventurers are sure to go there scrambling.

Raghav knew such smart operators in Rangoon. They had travelled the harbours of the world; they knew the strengths and weaknesses of all humankind. They had the confidence to swing any kind of racket in any country, with any army of the world. These hard-boiled baniyas had their fingers firmly planted on the pulse of the world. The soldiers of all armies of the world had their young and innocent recruits who could go hungry, but they absolutely needed their daily fix of alcohol and cigarettes and the occasional whore, and these clever operators would be there to exploit these weaknesses. Raghav had forged links with these baniyas because the reputation of the Japanese was not of the best kind. They could cross all limits of inhuman torture, it was said. No support could be expected from the psychologically beaten British. And in four months' time would start the monstrous, demoniacal, destructive rains that were known to deluge the mountains.

A baniya suggested to Raghav, 'Do what you have to, but get to Myitkyina 900 miles north of Rangoon. Once you are there, whether the aircraft standing on the runways are the British Dakotas or the Japanese Mitsubishi-30 bombers, getting you on board those planes and depositing you in India will be our responsibility.'

'Well, all right. Once the work is done, how would you like to be paid? In currency carrying the Queen's head or the pagodas?'

'Are you joking? The only currency we deal in is deep-red Burmese rubies or yellow, sparkling gold.'

The fond hope that the Japanese bombings would stop after some time proved illusory. On the contrary, the Japanese infantry began to make rapid advances through Singapore and Malaya. The Rangoon bombings were quickly followed by the roasting of the airports at Memio and Tavoy. Hanging on in the vicinity of Rangoon was nothing short of inviting death.

It was decided that they would move out of their secret hideout in Rangoon the next day. They needed seven or eight bullock carts to move out. Enquiries in the neighbouring hamlets revealed that there were bullock carts available for hire, but the cart-men couldn't be induced to step out of their houses for any price. Even when a few were finally persuaded, their women and children refused to let them go.

'So, what do we do now?' Raghav asked Kanchana.

'Well, we can buy the carts and the bullocks and mules, and consider it a long-term investment.'

'But who will drive the carts?'

'Our circus artistes are basically children of farmers. They don't need to be trained separately for driving a bullock cart.'

Raghav went to the nearest market and immediately purchased eight pairs of bullocks and carts and mules.

Whatever could have been loaded on the backs of the company's fifteen horses was put in the carts. The heavy trunks and other unnecessary items were left behind in Sushi's house. The horses, including Phakkadrao, were made ready before dawn. Kanchana gave them a once over and said in a worried tone, 'Our horses are so handsome-looking and of the best breed. These beautiful animals with their broad backs and lion-like manes could attract the envy of the British—as also the Japanese.'

'Well?'

'I suggest that our grooms and ring-boys start with them in the dark, and stop journeying as soon as the sun rises and it's light. They can rest in some nook or corner of the hills and resume the journey after sunset.'

An hour before they were to depart, the company barber Tuka was invited in. Kanchana instructed him to cut off the long tresses of the circus girls. He used a pair of scissors for most of them, but with some, he used the trimming machine to give them a grass-cut. Many of the girls broke into lamentations. They prided themselves on the beauty of their hair. Lovely tendrils and curls would snake down their foreheads and play on their cheeks and neck. A few cruel snips, and the garden they had tended with such care turned into an ugly heath. The girls were heart-broken. Some of them tried to sneak away to save their hair, but Kanchana brooked no resistance.

Kanchana also sat herself down before Tuka. 'All right, now, dada, snip off my hair too. Staying alive is way more important than flouncing our hair.'

Kanchana could well understand the pain she was causing to the young girls. She gathered some of them in her arms, kissed them on their cheeks and said, 'Girls, I understand your disappointment. But we all know what it means for young girls to be travelling through jungles, particularly during these times of strife. When assaults are mounted or when wars are won, the first things that hungry wolves jump upon are the flesh of women; land and wealth come next.'

The girls were silent. Thick cloth was cut into strips and tied around the girls' chests to flatten them. Then they were given loose shirts to wear. What had earlier been a bevy of girls would now easily pass for a bunch of boys belonging to some monastery.

39

A local peasant of Sushi's acquaintance hurried into the camp in the evening and informed Raghav, 'There's a village called Surangi on the other side of the river. You may be able to get two trucks there.'

'What kind? For buying or hiring?' Raghav asked.

'Whatever it is,' Kanchana butted in on overhearing the conversation. 'Even if it's double or triple the price, snap it up.'

'What about fuel?'

'Both their tanks are full.'

'We have 300 mouths to feed—fetching grains, as well as clothes and other things of daily use, will become so much easier with these trucks.'

'Send a boy over immediately.'

'I'll go myself. Can't risk missing these trucks. They are no less than gold mines for us, Kanchana.'

Raghav set off with a group of forteen boys, their hopes riding high. About two kilometres into the journey they came upon a small but wide river. Darkness had descended on the water by the time they reached there. The four Burmese youth who had brought the proposal were waiting at the bank. They told Raghav, 'Only three of you can come with us.'

'What does that mean?'

'Two drivers and one other person.'

'Why?' Raghav asked in a loud voice.

'We can't let a crowd tag along and bring disaster upon ourselves. A number of secret squads of the Japanese army have infiltrated into these jungles. If you run into them, you will surely meet your end.'

'But we're getting the trucks, aren't we?'

'Don't doubt that. We will be true to our word.'

Mahaling and Taranath exchanged glances. It was decided that Raghav would go for the deal, take the trucks in his charge and return. He would have two drivers and Akaram Jogta for company. They waded through the knee-deep water in the darkness and reached the other side. After some distance, their dot-like forms dissolved in the darkness. Raghav had assured them that he would be back with the trucks in two hours' time.

As the rest of the group waited for them to return, it turned darker. The hours kept slipping away. The jungle surrounding them looked frightening. A good five or six hours had gone by. It was midnight now, but there was no sign of Raghav. The men were in a fix. What should they do? As they were knocking their heads together, a loud explosion was heard from the direction of the village. This was immediately followed by flames shooting into the dark sky. The vegetation around them suddenly lit up and could be seen shimmering in the glare of the flames.

Mahaling and Taranath were at their wit's end. What could have happened? And where were they—Raghav and his escorts? Why had they not returned? Could their lives be in danger? The night was slipping away; the fire in the bushes in front had also burnt out. What were they to do now? Kanchana would be waiting in the camp with their luggage all packed and ready. What if Raghav didn't return? What would they tell her? How would they face her?

The morning light grew strong. Kanchana spotted the team returning to the camp. When they had come close enough, Kanchana's heart leapt to her mouth. Where was Raghav?

When the news of Raghav's disappearance spread in the camp, a wave of worry washed over it. The troupe had seen and heard the explosion of the night before. Had Raghav been caught in the conflagration? Something really serious had happened. Nothing else could have kept a valiant man like Raghav from returning. If he had to, he would bore his way through a mountain and return to the camp.

All through the day Kanchana was distraught. It was as if an eighty-foot tent pole had collapsed on her head. Time ticked on and the day disappeared. Darkness began to spread slowly like a crab pushing out its limbs. The pressure began to mount. How long would they have to wait for Raghav's return? For how many days? As Kanchana's head whirled in a hurricane of worries, the circumstances were changing rapidly. The news that fell on their ears was not heartening. A huge Japanese contingent was moving upwards towards Rangoon from Pegu. Also, the chicken-livered British had abandoned Rangoon and were all scampering towards northern Burma.

There was no news of Raghav and moving forward was imperative, but Kanchana was in a bind, unable to arrive at any decision. The entire company sat with its eyes glued to her tent. As darkness spread and the night advanced, Kanchana's breath began to catch. She would not be able to bear a second separation from him and would much rather die. Her feet had turned to ice. She was finding it impossible to move on without Raghav.

She could imagine nothing but the worst. Had he been brought down by a wild animal? Had he run into one of the renegade Chinese soldiers on the loose in the jungle? Or had Japanese troops taken him into custody? When she saw Hirabai come in, Kanchana's dam burst. She hugged her and began to bawl, '*Aatya*, you people will have to carry on without me. It's going to be impossible for me to leave Raghav behind.

I'd rather die searching for him in these jungles than abandon him here.'

'Does running away suit Sarang Bhavoji's daughter at all?'

'So, what do I do, Aatya?'

'*Aga*, your father worked so hard to build this company. Look, I don't understand anything but this, and that too because I've heard this from your father some time or the other. The boys who take sheep out for grazing are simply called herders, but a shepherd is one who is willing to snatch a lamb out of a tiger's jaws, who leaps into a burning sheep pen and takes the little ones out of the fire's reach. He doesn't mind getting roasted to death in the bargain. How can you forget all this?'

'But, Aatya, what can I do in this situation?'

'Whether the kunku on your brow stays or not, for the sake of saving your flock, you will have to keep on marching with this fire upon your shoulder, pori.'

Kanchana sat, silently turning things over in her head. Then she sprang to her feet and embraced Hirabai. She wiped the tears from her cheeks and tied her stole tight round her waist. She set aside her mountain of sorrow, and ordered for the march to begin. They would trudge through the dense jungles leading towards Mandalay.

The memories that Kanchana had of her earlier visit to Mandalay were still fresh. Mandalay had been, in fact, the capital of Burma during the Middle Ages. Its wide, well laid out roads, its beautiful, extensive gardens, its magnificent pagodas spread across acres of land, the pagoda entrances guarded by huge Chindas—creatures of Burmese folklore, half tiger and half lion—sculpted in stone. The Hindu temples covered with three layers of colourful, decorated roofing curling upwards; the magnificent palace of King Thibwa, surrounded by moats with fresh, deep-blue water, with red and white lotuses nodding their heads over it; the fruit and flower market called the Zega Bazaar teeming with busy customers—these magical scenes of a city of dreams had stayed in Kanchana's memory across the years.

Alongside Mandalay flowed the Irrawaddy. On one side of its vast plains was this prosperous city. Right behind the Thibwa Palace were the tall Mandalay Hills, capped with magnificent Buddhist temples.

At a quick pace of 30 miles a day, the 350-mile journey from Rangoon to Mandalay should have taken twelve or thirteen days. The travel, however, was frequently interrupted by the bombers flying overhead, or actual bombings on many occasions, necessitating a quick scampering into the woods nearby, adjacent to a stream, and waiting out the danger. They would have to repack all over again once the peril had passed. Consequently, it took them eighteen days to reach the outskirts of Mandalay.

The company's girls, Shanta, Babita, Kamal, Suman and the others, were travelling in men's clothing, as mandated. Womanly vanity, however, was hard to vanquish altogether. They would carry palm-sized mirrors in their purses into which they would peer whenever possible and tidy their short hair.

As if in solidarity with the girls, Kanchana too had cut her hair short, but she travelled in women's clothing. However, the strain of constant uncertainty had wiped all beauty and softness off her face. Worry lines had deepened on her brow. After the disappearance of Raghav, the very anchor of her life, she could just about stay on this side of sanity.

The travails of the journey made every muscle in her body ache. She would wake up with a start in the middle of the night. She would hear the rustle of the leaves in the jungles, the burble of the river, and along with these, she heard the sound of footsteps, as if somebody was moving in the vicinity. The memory of Raghav would leave her distraught. If he was somewhere close by, why was he not meeting her? If he was not meeting her, was he alive at all? This last thought would make her shudder.

When the hills behind the city of Mandalay first came into view, when the Buddhist stupas atop them had been identified, when the red tiled buildings of the headquarters of Burma Rifles began to take shape in the distance, the wearied travellers experienced a sense of thrill and their feet involuntarily picked up speed. But as the distance closed enough to give them a glimpse of the piteous state of the city, their hearts sank.

It was after many, many years that Kanchana was returning to Mandalay with images of a celestial, Kashmir-like place in her mind, but when she landed there, she felt like she had been delivered a punch in the midriff. The entire city looked like a once beautiful mirror shattered into a thousand shards.

Kanchana turned towards Mahaling and asked, 'Uncle, what's happened to this city?'

They looked around with unbelieving eyes. The recent Japanese bombings had set the whole place on fire, destroyed beautiful buildings and created an apocalyptic hovel of dust, smoke and rubble. Mandalay now gave the impression of a rose garden that had been visited by a herd of wild asses. The flower shrubs had been stamped out; all that was left behind was the droppings.

The blight brought by the war had triggered a health crisis. Cholera had broken out in the city, further confounding the misery of the citizens. Six to seven hundred corpses were being added every day to the mounds of carcasses that lay scattered across the city. The municipal administration had become as defunct as it had in Rangoon; thousands of dead bodies lay decomposing on the streets, releasing a noxious miasma that made breathing impossible for miles around. Mandalay had now become a breeding ground for maggots.

Experience brings wisdom and discretion. No getting into the city. Find a secluded spot in the surrounding forest and keep your head down. India was a distant dream. Hundreds of miles needed to be traversed before that dream could be realised; and that would require men and animals to stay in good health.

The circus troupe located a densely wooded area near the Irrawaddy and set up camp there. The tent-pitchers quickly cleared up some space and planted their poles behind the screens of the bushes. They soon had about twenty tents standing. The first to be accommodated were the girls, their ayahs and the elderly. The young men needed nothing more than a stone slab under their heads for passing out, but arranging for the girls at every stop had acquired more sacred observances than any religious ritual. The expanse of the Irrawaddy was immense, big enough to accommodate ten rivers the size of the Krishna. There was thus no shortage of water for the troupe and its animals.

The huge reservoir of the Irrawaddy was very close to where they had pitched camp, and beyond that, spanning the awesome spread of the river was the spectacular Ava Bridge. It was three-quarters of a mile long and it rested on eleven trusses. Calling it a bridge was an understatement—it could easily pass off as the sporting track of the sea gods. It was so strong and wide that it carried two pairs of rail tracks—back and forth—for the trains that ran north. On either side of these tracks were roads for vehicular traffic.

This bridge was considered vitally important because it formed a segment of the majestic Burma Road that had been built for carrying American goods from the Rangoon harbour to China. When evening fell and the shadows lengthened, the prodigious shadow of this bridge would fall upon the

Irrawaddy. The ripple of the water would make it appear like a humongous monster turning this way and that on its side. At twilight it would turn dark and look like a colossal, frightful python lying suspended on the horizon.

It was barely two days since the circus company had settled there when somebody brought in the astounding news, 'The gigantic bridge up there may be blown up any day now.'

'What? Why would anyone want to do such a thing?'

'The stupid Japanese, who else?'

If she could have helped it, Kanchana would not have spent any more than a night in Mandalay. The faster she could cross the mountains and valleys and reach India, the better it would be. However, the British had posted armed guards at the mouth of the Ava Bridge, with instructions that not an ant should be allowed to pass over it. For a month, therefore, not a single displaced person had crossed the Irrawaddy.

As a result, Mandalay was choked with thousands upon thousands of terrified people, way beyond its capacity. They had come fleeing with their lives from Rangoon, from Pegu and Maymyo, with the single intention of crossing over to India, and were now stuck on this side of the bridge. These large multitudes had been reduced to a state of utter wretchedness. The Japanese bombings and the outbreak of cholera had pulverised all healthcare facilities out of existence.

Kanchana's instructions were clear. Nobody was to go anywhere close to Mandalay. If ever an emergency compelled them, no horses should be used. No point in inviting people's attention towards themselves. The girls had altogether forgotten about dressing up or adorning themselves. They had enjoyed the early days moving around in their rough manly dresses and using abusive, masculine language with each other. By now, the novelty had been lost and habit had set in.

There were a few philandering eyes along the journey, numerous enough to worry Kanchana, whom all this concealment could not altogether fool. Passing strangers would let their lecherous eyes linger a little longer, a guard or two would show traces of incipient lust; clearly, despite all the camouflage, there was enough that showed to rouse passion. Kanchana never tired of warning them, 'Girls, stay on the alert!'

Some of the circus boys were out for a round of the Mandalay Hill pagodas. They saw a crowd gathered by the side of the Su Taung Pyae Pagoda. A Japanese aircraft had just flown by, creating a hubbub there. Right below the high railing where they stood was a sliced-off piece of hillock; beyond that was a path going to the other side. Suddenly one of the boys looked closely at the path and cried, '*Aho,* Taranath bhau, look down there!'

'What's it?'

'Bhau, look at that cow-elephant there, with that bell round her neck. Look at the earthy colour of her skin.'

'What's there to see?'

'*Aho,* why don't you look at the animal? Do you see that dome on her head? Doesn't she look familiar?'

'What are you saying?'

'That's our Rajmangala!'

'Yes, she is a complete replica of Rajmangala! The same loop in the trunk, the same curve in her tusks.'

As they stared open-mouthed at the animal, the elephant disappeared in the milling crowd around her. Taranath broke into a sweat, his throat went dry. He took some water and splashed it on his head. 'I swear by my mother,' he said in a spooked voice, 'it was Rajmangala's ghost, for sure.'

'I am sure of that too. I also noticed the mahaut sitting on her neck. He was the exact image of our Sulaiman. The same loose trousers, the same long shirt and the same flat, crumpled cap that he used to wear for his namaaz!'

'But are they really ghosts?'

'What else would you call them? Didn't we see those White butchers slaughter the entire herd of our elephants? We saw them lying before our eyes as heaped up flesh. How could Rajmangala have escaped that? And even if we grant that she escaped, how could she travel in one piece and arrive here 350 miles away?'

'Well, even if we take your version to be true, ghosts are known to move around in the darkness of the night. Why the devil would this elephant want to go haunting the markets in the light of the day?'

'Tara bhau, times have changed now. They have no choice but to come out during the day. The Japanese bombers rule the night these days, don't they? The ghosts would have worked that out too.'

The incident put such a fear into them that they began to avoid the Mandalay bazaar too.

The fear of the dark had settled deep in the hearts of many. To make matters worse, the army administrators had ordered a strict blackout. Nobody dared to light a cigarette. The dismal scene of the slaughter of the animals in Rangoon had left a permanent scar on the minds of the circus staff, and it was the most recurrent subject of their dreams, particularly that of the girls. The mountain of dead bodies, the corpses of their sixteen elephants haunted them. They jabbered in their sleep, got up with a start and held each other tight.

Mahaling was out astride Phakkadrao's back on some chore in the vicinity of the Mahamuni Pagoda. Suddenly Phakkadrao became edgy and fidgety as animals do when they smell a predator in the jungle. He began neighing and shaking his muzzle and his footing became uncertain. Mahaling found this behaviour very strange. Phakkadrao refused to respond to the reins to the point that his nostrils began to bleed. It was with the greatest difficulty that Mahaling somehow managed to drag the horse away.

When the company people returned to the camp, Kanchana got to hear of Phakkadrao's strange behaviour and was perplexed. It had started tailing Kanchana these days. If there was one being that was as upset as Kanchana at Raghav's disappearance, it would have to be Phakkadrao. Kanchana, at least, could talk about her feelings to others, but this facility was not available to a dumb horse. He had lost interest in food. His pupils were surrounded by a big band of white. He stayed as close to Kanchana as possible. Even when she went to sleep, Phakkadrao sat barely a few feet away from her. If she ever woke up in the middle of the night, she would find the horse standing guard. Kanchana had begun to wonder whether the spirit of her father had entered this beloved animal.

In any case, since the trip to the Mahamuni Pagoda, Phakkadrao had become completely distracted. He appeared to be afflicted by some illness or by some evil spirit. He became indifferent even to the best oats served to him. Kanchana was at her wit's end.

Precious days were slipping away as the enforced confinement along the river stretched on. The crowd of asylum seekers increased with every passing day. Kanchana would sit staring at the massive structure of the Ava Bridge. The police guarding the entrance showed no sign of withdrawing. Meanwhile, the Japanese bombers would return every two or three days for a cursory round of bombing and fly away. The heat, the sultriness kept mounting; dust clouds kept rising; the stock of grains in the market had begun to sink alarmingly; cholera kept taking its toll of 600–700 people every day. Everywhere around the old palace of King Mindon Min, in the Zego market, alongside the Pyagme Pagoda, lay the corpses of cholera victims. There was no mechanism for clearing them away. Flies gathered over them so that they could carry the contagion among the living.

The headquarters of Burma Rifles at the foot of the Mandalay Hills had lost all resemblance to an army base. It had now morphed into a camp for the homeless and the displaced. One day a bomb fell on the Upper Burma Club of the British and reduced it to rubble. Kanchana had begun to abhor this ugly, lustreless Mandalay. Wherever she looked, she saw uprooted trees, bent telephone poles with wires hanging like gallows, bombed-out, soot-laden buildings and rotting bodies. She couldn't bear these sights anymore.

It was now almost a month since they had arrived in Mandalay. She gathered seven or eight of her people and mounted an assault on the Ava Bridge checkpost. She deliberately threw a tantrum at the guards stationed there. 'Who are you to stop us here? Can you imagine what will happen to us once the rains arrive in these parts? There are already over a hundred thousand refugees crowding every corner of Mandalay. Why are you here, you English people? To save us or to kill us all?'

'Madam, where's the point in arguing with us? Please go meet His Excellency, the Governor Dorman Smith at the Governor's Lodge.'

Kanchana did not tarry long at the bridge, but went marching to the Governor's Lodge. When she was not allowed to cross the Lodge gates, she made her way back to the bridge checkpost in a fury. Looking at her incensed state, the officer on duty at the checkpost chose not to get into any argument with her.

Kanchana again began agitating. Casting a worried look at two fluffs of cloud in the distance, she shouted, 'What has God installed on top of your shoulder there, a head or a block of wood? Don't you understand that the bigger the crowd you assemble here in Mandalay, the longer you detain them, the worse it's going to become? Those jungle tracks on the other side are still dry, please let us cross them now.'

'Sorry, madam, we follow the orders of the Divisional Commander.'

'What cheap bounders you British are! And all this talk of being diligent and conscientious! People are dying like ants by the thousands on the streets of Mandalay, but it makes no difference to you!'

Phakkadrao had not been able to regain his composure. In fact, his state of agitation had steadily increased. He had lost weight and refused to eat anything. He had now stopped visiting Kanchana. He would try to chew off the tether that held him to the stake.

A reasonable sized stockade had been erected under the trees to house the animals. Its bamboo-frame barricade would be shut during the night to provide security to all the horses and dogs herded inside. Phakkadrao had been tied to a stake inside the stockade for the last two nights, but he knew no peace. He neighed and pulled at his reins and stamped his feet and made the life of the other animals miserable.

Looking at his state, Kanchana instructed that he be left free inside the stockade. The groom removed the shackles and left. When a ring-boy returned early the next morning to feed the animals, the horse was gone. It appeared as if he had leapt over the barricade and disappeared into the night.

Kanchana was disconsolate at hearing the news. Raghav's intimacy with the horse was public knowledge. It was through the occasion of breaking the horse that Raghav and Kanchana had come to know each other. Phakkadrao was not merely the initiator of Raghav's love for Kanchana, but an active participant in their story. The disappearance of this mascot was an unbearable blow to everybody.

Kanchana spent the entire day wallowing in grief.

The Japanese planes had not paid their visit that day. The gloom around the Irrawaddy was a little more in evidence that evening. The darkening shadows thrown by the setting sun were lingering for longer than usual. Having nothing else to do, the boys had taken off the clothes on their back and were washing them on the river bank and splashing about in the water. Some had brought metal plates along with them to gather small fish and crabs. It was after a long time that Charlie had found himself a branch on the umber tree and was playing on his clarinet instead of the usual flute sitting atop it.

Suddenly, a clamour rose from the lower end of the sand dune beyond the river. The boys began shouting and laughing and banging their metal plates in excitement as they ran up the dune. When Charlie and his friends heard the bustle, they jumped off their branches and ran down to see what the hullabaloo was about.

The commotion reached Hirabai's and Kanchana's ears and they too rushed out of the tent and craned their necks. The first to emerge were the boys banging on their plates. Right behind them were Charlie and his friends. It was quite like a wedding procession led by a band of musicians. Kanchana raised herself on her toes to see what was beyond, and what she saw thrilled her heart. It was Phakkadrao, dancing as he danced to the tune of circus music.

Everybody stood staring goggle-eyed at the retinue that was marching towards them. As they peered through streaming eyes, they couldn't be sure whether it wasn't a dream, after all. There, right in front of them, was Rajmangala rocking and swaying as she closed the distance between them. On her neck sat Sulaiman, and on her massive back sat Batuknath and his four midget friends.

Rajmangala spotted Kanchana from a distance and she lifted her trunk and trumpeted. She picked up pace and halted in front of Kanchana. She lifted her trunk all over again as she would for garlanding the idol of Lord Shiva. There was no stopping Kanchana's tears. It was impossible to understand how Phakkadrao's mind had worked, how he had smelt Rajmangala out in that crowded market, how he had turned jumpy and jittery in his desire to reconnect with her, how he had finally found her and finally escorted her back to their camp.

40

The return of Rajmangala was a much needed relief to Kanchana in an otherwise dismal situation. Kanchana couldn't wait to get the details. Looking at Sulaiman with unconcealed admiration, she asked, 'Uncle, I still cannot believe my eyes. How did you manage this magic? How did you whisk Rajmangala away from that massacre and bring her all this distance away?'

'Pori, I didn't have to do much, it was Rajmangala's feet that did the magic. When those demons began to fire, Rajmangala was standing outside the menagerie. The gunfire rattled her so much that she ran out and hit the road. I just tailed her, and tailing me came Batuknath and his bunch.'

'But there was butchery going on all around the city! How did you manage to save Rajmangala?'

'I drove her into a mango grove. We spent the day there in hiding. Staying on in Rangoon meant giving an open invitation to death, so we snuck out of the city at nighttime. I had heard of Mandalay as a city on the way to India, so it made sense to move in that direction. We would rest in the woods on the way during the day and travel during the night.'

Rajmangala was nothing less than a gift of God to them. Her return to the circus could well mean that Providence had punished them enough and was ready to smile at them again.

How Raghav acquired Rajmangala was a delightful story by itself. There is a hamlet of shepherds in the Udgiri jungles just above Malkapur on way to Konkan. They had a cattle-pen right next to the temple of the Goddess Kalamma where they kept a couple of dozen cows.

As soon as it was light, the cattle herder would release the cows for grazing in the forest around the temple. Once the cows were out of the pen, he would collect the fresh dung to carry away. He was surprised one day to see that along with the cow dung, there was another kind of faeces that couldn't possibly be of his cows. After noticing the faeces over a few nights, the cow-herd decided to stay behind, atop a nearby tree for the night and investigate. And sure enough, he noticed a very young elephant calf enter the pen at midnight. It spent those few hours with the cows and left at the crack of dawn.

The boy had caught the calf and sold it to Raghav. Rajmangala had grown up and, along with Phakkadrao, become the light of his life.

Kanchana didn't stop at just feeling happy about the elephant's return. She took her to the ancient Shiva temple close by, where thanksgiving prayers were offered for the return of the men and beast, and sweets distributed. That was when their attention went to the other side. A number of corpses lay by the side of the road—the victims of the bombing from a couple of days ago. Among them was a group of Hindu mendicants, young men in their mid-thirties with their long hair tied in a top knot, dressed in orange-coloured shirts and lungis. Next to them lay their effects, bows, arrows and brass pots for carrying holy water. The sight was enough to stun Kanchana and the rest of the troupe. The game of life and death was being played out ruthlessly here. Then came all kinds of disturbing news on the radio: the Japanese had set off with their armoured vehicles and their artillery, and a huge army contingent was rapidly moving north. Enemy infiltrators had also begun penetrating through the jungles of the Shan province and from the direction of Maymyo. There was no point, therefore, in trying to hammer sense into the undependable, uncomprehending, cowardly British. Whatever had to be done now, they would have to do it on their own.

'There is one way out,' Mahaling suggested to Kanchana, 'there are some big fishermen here who can provide us with large rafts.'

'How will that help?'

'Don't you see? They will take us to the other side of the Irrawaddy in no time, within an hour perhaps.'

'And then what? The road from there is through impossibly dense forests. And the distance up to Myitkyina, it's 375 miles. Is that mere chicken-feed?'

Whatever the situation, one thing was clear—it would be much better to risk their lives on a journey than hanging on there and dying.

It was decided by common consent that they would raft their way across the river in the next two days.

They swallowed whatever little was served and went to sleep. In a little while, the world around them suddenly exploded. The blast was more dreadful and strident than the sound of the bombings. Everybody was up and staring at the strange, phantasmagorical happenings at the other end of the dark sky. The bridge at the other end was going up in flames, releasing mighty clouds of dust and smoke. The red lights were dancing their surrealistic dance on the dark waters of the Irrawaddy.

The very same night, the fishermen brought Kanchana an unnerving piece of information: a steel stanchion at the other end of the bridge had been dynamited, thus blowing up the lifeline across the river. And who could have done this foolish deed? The Japanese? No, it was the British, who thought that when the Japanese arrived at Mandalay through air and across land, they should not be allowed to cross into Myitkyina and the northern parts of Burma.

Two days later, a hopeful piece of news reached Kanchana. 'A train is going to set off towards Myitkyina either tomorrow or early morning the day after. There's a thirty-two wagon train standing at the other bank that arrived from Myitkyina, and now it is getting ready to make the return journey.'

Kanchana's eyes lit up with anticipation. 'Let's try and slip out on top of that train.'

Mahaling told Kanchana, 'Do you see how much they care for their soldiers? They have trains ready to ferry them out in spite of such brutal bombings.'

'What do you know about the happenings behind the scene, kaka?'

'What happenings?'

'The Governeor of Burma, His Excellency Dorman Smith is stuck here, isn't he? It's only to help him escape that this entire drama has been arranged.'

This train had to be boarded at any cost. Failure to do so would mean that the book of their lives would almost certainly end in the jungles of Burma under Japanese shellings. Mahaling, Pandu Nana and Sushi rode up to the railway station to meet the officials at two in the afternoon. They took with them Shanta and Suman dressed in men's clothes. What they saw stunned them. The entire place was in ruins. The bombings had reduced the buildings to debris and the fire had burnt everything to ashes. A few half-shattered walls stood here and there to totter with the wind. With the roofs blown away, dry bamboo roofing had been put up to create some shelter from the sun.

The senior official spoke: 'We have to flee from here before the Japanese forces arrive. So, yes, how many tickets?'

'We will need a minimum of three compartments.'

'What?' asked the astounded official. 'Are you carrying a marriage party in the middle of this war?'

'It's not a marriage party, sir. It's our circus company, the Great Kanchana Circus.'

'Oh! I've been to your circus once, back in Calcutta.'

'Sir, some of our artistes are unwell. They—'

'Oh my god! Cholera?'

'No, no, sir. It's nothing as serious as that. Don't be scared. But we want at least three bogies.'

'Impossible! If you want to travel in our Army Special, you need a proper sanction. You have to show at least a recommendation from some dignitary.'

Sushi immediately pulled out the special letter that Deputy Commissioner Richardson had given to Kanchana and handed it over to her.

The official seemed satisfied. 'I can provide sufficient room,' he said, 'but don't hold on to such absurd expectations as three entire coaches.'

After a lot of haggling, he agreed to provide one full coach. The under-the-table settlement would not be in Burmese or Indian currencies; it would be exclusively in gold coins. What the official demanded and received from the impoverished circus company was at least five times the legitimate charge for a coach, but Kanchana had no choice but to acquiesce.

As he stood up, Taranath once again beseeched, 'Give us at least one open wagon for our animals.'

'Animals? What animals?'

'An elephant and fourteen horses.'

'What rot is this, now? Carrying animals on the train is no different from jumping into a pit,' barked the official. 'For one, there is a ban on carrying animals on trains during these times. For another, you have no idea of the practical difficulties involved here. The army units that are setting off on the train have been living on starvation diet for many days. These chaps won't think twice before chopping up one of your horses and roasting their flesh in our engine furnace. So think about it.'

As they were ready to leave the half-devastated railway station, one of the Burmese railway officials called out to

Kanchana. As she began walking towards him, he pointed towards Shanta and Suman, he said, 'Not you, madam, send those two boys of yours here.'

Furious, Kanchana marched up to the official and said with asperity, 'What do you want?'

'Why do you get angry, madam? All I was saying was that instead of you yourself taking the trouble of coming here, you should send those young boys.'

The two girls stood flustered, in their men's dress. The two sergeants standing next to the official were, however, leering at the girls and pressing each other's hands.

When they returned to the camp, Kanchana burst out at the girls, 'What was the need for you two girls to come with us?'

'Why? What happened?'

'Didn't you see the officers and their men ogling at you so suggestively?'

'Didi, we are sorry.'

'Keep this in mind: the sly, vulgar looks of some men can even singe young plants. And you are girls!'

The packing began in the dark of the night. Girls, artistes and all the others were easy to arrange for, but how were they to carry all these animals safely to Myitkyina? The animal trainers and the ringmasters sat biting their nails over it. Everybody was in a state of high anxiety. The train was due to depart from the base of the Ava Bridge on the other side of the river. The bustle, therefore, would have to begin at the crack of dawn. The river would be crossed on rafts so as to reach the station on the other side. The troupe shook off the lassitude of the past few days and got busy as they always did when transferring from one camp to another.

For those who were assigned the task of walking the animals to the river bank, there was no night's rest. They were required to reach the other side by half past three and get the animals walking to the station. Whenever on the move, they would cover as much distance as possible before the sun became hot. A raft had therefore been lined up at midnight to take the animals across; the light of its lamps was visible from afar. While Kanchana was busy winding up things in her own tent, Rajmangala and the fourteen horses began their climb down the sandbanks.

The animals walked across the shallow water and climbed on to the raft. When Rajmangala, weighing 2200 kilos, stepped in, the raft tilted to one side, but the rowers had had plenty of experience carrying heavy logs of teak and they knew how to do the balancing act. When Kanchana came and stood on the bank, Phakkadrao refused to move forward towards the raft. She rubbed her cheek against his muzzle, ruffled his mane and finally persuaded the horse to move with the grooms.

Dawn had just begun to break, and the silhouettes of the pagodas on the Mandalay Hill as well as the town had started separating from the sky. Around that time, some six or seven of the circus girls came up to Kanchana with the complaint that the ayah was not allowing them to go to the river for a bath. Kanchana flared up at them. 'Why do you need baths every day? Are you going into the ring to perform?'

Hirabai stepped forward. She roared at all the girls, including Shanta and Babita, 'Haven't you got an iota of sense? Go, finish up whatever is left of your packing. There's no saying when this train will reach its destination.'

'That's just what we are saying, Didi. With the long travel ahead of us, there's no telling when we'll get to bathe next. Our bodies will begin to stink'

'Silly girls, it's already turning light. Get the helpers to fetch you a few buckets and quickly finish your baths.'

'No, Didi, it's still dark enough to allow us some privacy. We'll just run to the river, take a few dips, and be back in no time.'

'Arrey, hold on! Where are you off to?'

'We'll be back before you know it,' they shouted as they ran away into the darkness.

A little more light, and Mandalay began to emerge with greater visibility. The Ava Bridge python too began to frolic on the waves of the Irrawaddy. The helper boys and the labourers pulled out the tent stakes, tied them up in neat bundles and took them to the bank, ready for loading. Within very little time, all the luggage had reached the bank, and people stood waiting for the arrival of the rafts.

Kanchana was breaking her head over how much more gold jewellery she would have to palm off during the journey when three ayahs rushed in with terror-stricken faces. One look at them, and Kanchana feared the worst. The small trunk she had picked up slipped out of her grip. The fear in their eyes had something to do with the girls. She held one of the ayahs by her shoulders and shrieked, 'Where are they? Where are my girls?'

It was as if lightning had struck the camp. There was panic everywhere. Everyone began shouting the names that came to mind. 'Shanta! Babita! Shaalan, Maalan! Where are you girls?'

Hell broke loose. Helper boys, labourers, performers, everyone made a dash for the bank and scanned the vast stretch of the river. There wasn't a soul in sight. All that one saw to the north was the Ava Bridge python playing upon the waves. As the search became more intense, the mystery thickened. What could have happened? They couldn't all have drowned at the same time. Where had they disappeared?

After they had covered a fair distance, they found the shirts and trousers of the girls wound up in a bundle, completely dry. Clearly, they had been way too enticed by the clear water to hold themselves back. Moreover, the soft morning breeze would have made staying away impossible. They would have peeled the grimy men's clothes off their backs and jumped into the river naked, like fish slipping into water. There was no way of knowing what happened after that.

Desperate, the search party pressed on downstream. Suddenly, someone noticed at a distance the markings on the soft silt of what looked like human footprints. When they were close enough, it was evident that they were the prints of army boots moving up to the river, and from there across the grass over a dune they dipped into the depression on the other side. As soon as the boys in the lead reached up to the top and looked at the other side, they shrieked in horror and turned their faces away. Kanchana and the ayahs who were right behind hurried up and let out blood-chilling screams as they ran down the incline into the depression. There, in the slime lay the stark naked, violated bodies of the girls they had been searching for. The army wolves had been hungry and merciless. Predators like hyenas and vultures would have hung their heads in shame at this sight.

Kanchana's mind went numb. Her throat choked, her bulging eyes refused to return to their sockets. The tragedy unhinged her. It was one of those miserable days that didn't even give her the luxury of grieving, allowed her no time to mourn and cry. The ayahs brought some saris and covered the naked bodies. It was only then that the boys came down.

Hirabai lost her mind. She lay down next to the bodies and twisted and turned and writhed in agony as the pieces of an earthworm do when crushed by the hoof of an animal. She threw sand on her face, gathered the slime and poured it into her hair. She wanted to bawl, but all she could get out of her throat was a sharp, grating keen. Mahaling, her husband, didn't know how to console his distraught wife. The sight of the ravaged bodies of his two daughters had shattered him too.

The sun had risen. Time was slipping away. The train was due to leave for Myitkyina at noon, and this would almost certainly be the last train. There was luggage to be loaded on to the raft.

Fate was giving them new lessons in how to respond to the direst of circumstances. Some men ran to the camp and brought back crowbars and pickaxes that they always carried during their journey through the jungles. The bodies could not be abandoned for dogs and wolves to feed on. The men quickly dug up a pit deep and wide enough to accommodate the corpses and lowered the bodies into it. One of the women brought over seven new saris and seven coconuts from the camp trunk. The dead girls were covered with a sari each and the coconuts were deposited into the makeshift grave. Earth and sand were then quickly pushed into the hole.

41

The old railroad was built two feet above the boggy ground. The sleepers were made of Burmese teak. The stones around the rails were quite infirmly set, causing the train to shake violently as it ran. It had earlier been announced that the train would carry only the army units, but as it happened, there were a number of others who were desperate to flee.

The journey on that train was extraordinarily strange. Quite like a tired old woman leaning heavily on her stick as she makes her way to her daughter's house, the train chugged along the rails gasping and wheezing past jungles, mountains and rice fields. It was pulled by a steam engine using coal as fuel. The entire area around the tracks was misted over with thick, acrid smoke, which had the peculiar peaty smell of burning grasslands, with liberal quantities of coal dust and particulates. Even the tiniest climb uphill set the engine groaning and panting like a beaten beast of burden.

The engine would keep running out of coal or water and it would cough and sputter to a halt. It would generally be stopped over a small rivulet and made to stand like a child, while the engine men pulled up the water with buckets tied to ropes. The soldiers were also roped into the task. There were plenty of old timber depots scattered along the railroad, which were denuded of all leftover logs and splints.

The train's occupants were sapped of energy and frightened out of their wits. The fear of death had taken a firm grip on their minds. They had no way of knowing when it would come and where it would come from; whether it would fall from the sky or explode from the earth below. Some mischievous soldier would purse his lips and imitate the harsh drone of a Mitsubishi fighter aircraft, which would jolt the sleepy-heads out of their drowsy state, and their terrified screams would trigger a bout of laughter all around.

It was the strangest train to ever have run on rails. It followed no time-table, observed no rules, it stopped when it wanted to—or was compelled to; it ran as fast as its tired lungs allowed it to. It was in as much of a hurry as its passengers to save its life. The bogies were stuffed tight with 150 passengers each, tamped down like flour in a can. There was no fan; there was no water either. The summer sun heated up the roof in no time, particularly if it was stationary. The cry of the thirsty children, the unbearable heat and stuffiness of the coaches and the tension of the circumstances through which they were passing had beaten all the spirit out of the hapless travellers.

Governor Dorman Smith travelled in a special coach along with his rather heavily built wife, children and an ADC. He too had to arrange for a flight at Myitkyina that would take him to India. When the train had started, a number of British Army officials and soldiers had occupied the spare seats in the Governor's coach. But a few hours later, when the train stopped to get its breath back, the Governor got the army captain accompanying him to have all the rest thrown out. In their place he brought in his personal staff of water-carriers, cooks, helpers, masseurs and the like, all dark-faced Indians. These Tamil natives all wore huge turbans and loose, flaring shirts. The Governor had lately realised that except for their dark complexion, these poor people had no other shortcomings. They were always willing to pull water, do every kind of job, even lay their lives for their White Latsahib master if the occasion demanded.

Close to the Governor's coach was an open rake meant for carrying four-wheeler vehicles, and there, ensconced on its own, in solitary grandeur, sat the Governor's frightfully expensive Rolls Royce. It had been firmly secured to the floor of the wagon with chains and bolts. It seemed to have no concern at all with the maddening storm of war. Alongside it, on a plank of wood sat its chauffeur and two mechanics, shivering in the cold wind. If they were to fall ill—or even die—from being exposed to the strong wind, it wouldn't really matter; fresh slaves could be bought by the heap. But this queen among cars had been brought over from London to Rangoon by a special boat, and its safety and security surely had to rank above that of dispensable human beings.

The sky would suddenly resound with the arrival of bomber aircraft and the train would rattle to a halt, under whatever camouflage was available—a dip in the valley, the shelter of crags, a small wooded patch somewhere. The travellers, fearing that the train itself would be targeted, would scramble out, scatter across the rice fields or whatever empty spaces were around, and conceal themselves as well as they could. Once the rumble in the air had faded away, the engine would blow its sharp whistle and begin crawling forward. The refugees and the army men would bunny hop out of their holes and climb on to the moving train.

The rail road to Myitkyina and the road for vehicles ran together all the way—through mountain passes, across valleys and along river banks—in a straight line, mostly, but occasionally the roadway would pass from under the rails and come out on the other side, and re-cross all over again.

As the evening rays of the sun turned golden, Kanchana looked out of the window to the other side and suddenly noticed Rajmangala trundling merrily along the road along with the fourteen horses, the ten bullock carts and her fifty odd circus staff. A number of them carried what looked like long bamboos with red flags fluttering at the top. What exactly they could be was difficult to guess.

The train moved a little distance and stopped at the river in front. The engine had heated up and was letting out big white sighs. Buckets were lowered down the bridge into the river and the work of pulling water up began. The caravan of Rajmangala and the horses was now catching up up with the train. Kanchana looked at the procession with great curiosity. Midget Batuknath was sitting bare-chested on Rajmangala's neck with his tasseled cap worn backwards, an ochre lungi wrapped round his waist. Sulaiman walked with a jaunty step alongside the animal, dressed up like a Hindu sanyasi in a loose ochre robe. The horsemen too were dressed up in identical bright, orange clothes. A number of the walkers carried in their hands brass metal pots usually carried by ascetics, while some others carried bows and arrows. Kanchana was utterly bewildered. Had she seen these clothing somewhere?

Taranath looked at her and laughed. Do you recognise the costumes our boys are wearing?' he asked.

'I have a feeling I've seen them somewhere.'

'Do you remember we had gone to Lord Shankar's temple the other day? After Rajmangala came back to us? There was this bunch of corpses of ascetic *gosavis* lying all over the place.'

Kanchana slapped her forehead in disbelief and laughed as she said, 'So, our idiots stole clothes from the corpses?'

Everyone burst out laughing. 'Yes, they are born artists, our people. Wherever they find themselves, they put up a show and make a living.'

The advance of the cavalcade was suddenly blocked by British policemen manning the outpost there. The entire congregation of holy ascetics broke into loud cries of 'Jai jai Baba Vishwanath! Take us with you to Amarnath!'

Sulaiman was playing Baba Vishwanath, while all the others were his acolytes. The constable at the post, however, was in no mood to budge. He had placed his baton across Sulaiman's chest. Old Sulaiman, however, was high on a few healthy drags of marijuana. He let his fingers run down his long, tapering beard and let out a loud cry, '*Jai Ali, Sankari gali, Jamuna chali, dekho dekho ud chali*,' and other such mumbo-jumbo. Batuknath, sitting on the elephant's mane, responded, 'Yes, Maharaj. Please keep the honour of our faith!' Saying this, he pulled out five eggs from somewhere and tossed them towards Sulaiman.

Sulaiman deftly caught them and then started throwing them in the air one after another. This juggling of eggs in the air had hypnotised many a circus goer before, and accompanied by Sulaiman's chanting of '*Ai mere Ali! Jaa bhaag dushman ki gali! Kar uski khopdi khaali!*', it left the constables there completely befuddled. What floored them completely was when the eggs dancing in the air suddenly sprouted wings and turned into pigeons. Two of them went and settled on the shoulders of the constables. The policemen were completely flabbergasted. These were clearly Hindu yogis who were capable of performing impossible feats. They dropped their batons and reverently allowed the entire company to cross over to the other side.

The train rattled on, past stations that had been razed to the ground. Buildings no longer stood in their places, the platforms were pockmarked by huge pits everywhere. The burnt out, ashen structures in the vicinity looked like cremation grounds.

There was a crowd of railway employees and villagers on a platform on the way that brought the train to a halt. 'Don't move beyond this point,' screamed a few of them. 'Japanese soldiers have descended on the jungles ahead. We have seen them with our own eyes!'

The Governor's staff was nonplussed; they went running to their master to seek his instructions. The shadows in the forests turned darker and the fear of an assault sent cold winds buffeting across the thirty-two coaches. The ADC emerged after a long time and announced, 'His Excellency the Governor says that turning back would be a serious loss, while moving forward is full of danger. We should keep moving ahead as best as we can.'

It had turned completely dark by now. With the perpetual fear of bombings lodged in the head, the blackout rules were followed meticulously. The steam engine did not flash its bright headlight to see its way forward through the night, but settled for a much dimmer version. The passengers inside sat frozen, less because of the cold winds and more out of sheer fear. They just didn't know what route death would take to reach them: bombs from overhead or the train slipping off the rails into the gorge below.

It was around midnight that people saw the bombs exploding in the night sky, followed immediately by the rat-tat-tat of machine gun ire. The train creaked to a halt and switched off its headlight altogether. The dance of death kept on being played out in the sky, while the passengers below sat listening to the thumping of their hearts and the chattering of their teeth. Not wanting to be trapped inside if the train caught fire, a number of them leapt out of their bogies.

Kanchana and the entire circus retinue leapt out and landed safely along the track, with their feet touching soft, gooey matter that felt like cattle-dung, and their legs got coated with the matter almost up to their knees. The kind of stink that pervaded the air was enough to bring the bile up, and to singe the hair in the nostrils. Everyone of them vomited out whatever little food their stomachs had, but the retching barely subsided even after they had walked out of the slime.

The bombers did not take long to disperse. Although the train had got away unharmed, the engine refused to start. It had been pulling the train for close to thirty hours without stopping, and the engine driver had spent himself staring out intensely for all that time. The stoppage on account of the bombing had given him the opportunity to close his eyes, and he had simply rested his head in front and passed out. Nobody had either the courage or the callousness to shake him out of his deep slumber.

Dawn arrived and darkness began disappearing, but the fetid smell that had stuck to their legs refused to dissipate. Only when it got sufficiently bright did some people go towards the railway line and resolved the mystery of the stench. It was a field of corpses that had been sown a few days back with the merciless gunning down of a trainload of passengers. It was on these corpses that the passengers had jumped down; pieces of putrid flesh and skin could still be seen sticking to their legs. Barely managing to hold their retching, they made a dash for a stream that ran close by. Fortunately, the water was clear, and the soft loamy earth and fine sand on the bank gave them the opportunity to scrub themselves clean.

After the circus troupe had given themselves a good, cleansing bath and the motorman had caught a refreshing, reviving nap, it was bright enough to get moving. The train let out a sharp whistle and began to slowly roll forward along the jungle track. Kanchana and her people ran and scrambled into their compartment. Their hopes of soon hitting Myitkyina and then escaping to India on the first available flight rose again.

42

Myitkyina (pronounced Michina) is one of the oldest posts of northern Burma. It was the capital city of the ancient Shan kingdom. It was also an important station for army movements in the Far East. A few days of march brought you up to the Chinese border. To the west, you first crossed the Kumaon range of mountains, then negotiated a large number of fast-flowing mountain rivers hurrying to meet the Chindwin and then trudged past the mountains of the Eastern Himalayas—thus covering a distance of almost 400 miles—to reach Assam in India.

Around 920 miles from Rangoon and 488 miles from Mandalay, Myitkyina was predominantly populated by the Kachin tribe. In the Burmese language, Myitkyina means a village on the bank of a river. The major trading item of Burma—teak—would be logged in the upper reaches of the Irrawaddy and sent down the river stream for various towns along the bank. There was a famous riverside harbour for this activity during those times. The other two important conveniences that the city boasted of were an old railway station and an airport nestled on a shoulder of the forest. The town had been visited by American Baptist missionaries some forty years ago, leading to the promotion of the Christian faith.

There were plenty of bamboo and thatch huts on the other bank of the Irrawaddy, but the crowds that had assembled in the town now bore no proportion to the number of huts. People had poured in from all across Burma—Mandalay, Maymyo, Rangoon and the Shan ravines—and pitched tents wherever they had found space. Indians and White Europeans formed the largest contingents of these refugees. A good number of them were the wives and children of British army and civil officials along with their dependent elderly.

The circus troupe hoped and prayed that on reaching Mytkyina, they would get into an aircraft and fly straight to India. If that didn't materialise, god forbid, they would be left with no alternative but to escape through the mountain route before the rains arrived. Kanchana had come to believe that although it was time-intensive, it would probably be the only realistic option available and she needed to prepare for it. But here too, as in Mandalay, the policies created by inscrutable British minds came in their way. The civil and military officials had got it into their heads that the irrepressible crowds assembled in Myitkyina would make the movement of their officials impossible; therefore, the jungle tracks, particularly those going towards the Hukawng valley, had been blocked.

As soon as Kanchana arrived at Myitkyina, she got into a confrontation with the civil and army officials and screamed over and over again into their ears, 'Please, please let us go!' She knew from experience that all that yelling and pleading would come to nothing. But Kanchana was not the kind to give up. She made periodic dashes to the airport, hoping to cadge a few seats, but there were just not enough aircraft plying.

One morning the circus people saw huge billows of smoke rising from the quarters where the administrative offices of Myitkyina were located. Some of the helper boys ran to Kanchana and shouted, 'Didi, look, a Japanese bomber has crashed there!'

A few local agents who arrived later to meet Kanchana had a different story to tell. 'No aircraft crashing there, madam; it's our own Deputy Commissioner of Myitkyina and the British Collector here who have set fire to government offices.'

'Oh my god! Why would they do that?'

'The Collector now strongly believes that the Japanese will be here in the next four or five days, so he is ensuring that no maps or important administrative documents fall into enemy hands.'

'What are you saying?'

'The Deputy Commissioner's staff is not only tearing the maps off the walls of the government offices, but off school walls too.'

Half of April had gone by and there was now a strongly noticeable change in the air in Myitkyina, with clouds gathering in the morning sky. Dakota aircraft would not get a clear enough view of the runways. They would circle the air till as long as they could and drift away like barren clouds.

Even before the Japanese invasion, nature had rendered the Myitkyina airport useless. Then came the communication from Ledo and Dibrugarh in Assam that their refugee camps were overflowing, and that they could take no more. Hope, however, continued to feed the delusion that aircraft service could resume some day.

Kanchana's obsessed mind would forever be making the rounds of the Myitkyina airport, and every two days, she would do so in person and meet her travel agent. 'I want two, just two loads of a cargo plane. Once my girls and their old ayahs reach India, I'll be free to die.'

'Kanchana,' asked Taranath, 'why do you have to be so desperate?'

'You men will be able to fight your way through somehow; but these young circus girls, they are like delicate glassware—'

'Yes, Kanchana, but where are the aircraft?'

'Look, the world lives on hope.'

'You do worry far too much.'

'The terrible tragedy that struck us at the river bank in Mandalay, I cannot get the horror of that out of my heart. My faith in humankind has vanished altogether. The devil seems to reside in everyone's blood. There is no saying when it will break human constraints and attack.'

Taranath was agitated. 'Kanchana, how long can we stay here to indulge the whims of these White sahibs? Let's keep moving forward till there is strength in our limbs.'

'It's not in my nature either to sit around rotting, waiting for someone's orders.'

'Well, then?'

'We are carrying the responsibility of a lot of lives on our shoulders. If it had been two or three dozen instead of the huge number that we actually have, I would have set fire to the wind and reached India long ago.'

The rumour market was turning hotter by the minute. The latest news was that for the past four months, Japanese squads had begun infiltrating the dense forests around Rangoon and Mandalay. They had imprisoned citizens and dragged them away like animals. These prisoners were being subjected to unimaginable torture in those jungle hideouts. They were being thrashed like bullocks and dumped into cages. When Kanchana heard of these persecutions, she went numb. Had Raghav been taken prisoner by the Japanese?

About a hundred thousand Indians were trying to escape via the Akyab–Chittagong route, but they had suffered severe calamities half-way. There were no boats sailing to Akyab, and the pestilence-ridden valleys along the jungle tracks were bringing people down by the thousands. Then there were those 30,000 who had crossed the Chindwan to hit the route to Imphal in Manipur. Among them were soldiers of the British Indian Army and the British Army from Burma. Traversing across those punishing trails that went past impossible ravines and gorges had ripped their uniforms to shreds.

The white clouds in the Myitkyina sky had melted, allowing a few Dakotas to make landings and compelling Kanchana to make innumerable rounds of the airport. She, however, was merely a solitary circus owner among the melee of hundreds of wives and children of the British sahibs. Many of these White women often had a suitcase in hand, some had merely a purse, with which they had fled to Myitkyina. There were others who hadn't had the time to change, and arrived at the airport in high-heeled sandals and long night-dresses. Their calculations, obviously, were fast-track ones: reach Myitkyina, catch the flight to Calcutta, Delhi, Madras, wherever. Within two to three hours they would be in India.

This was how the journey to safety began for the very senior officials, including Dorman Smith. The next batch of people was the seriously wounded soldiers. Kanchana had entered the ring with the firm determination of having her circus girls flown away. She had declared her intention of paying whatever price was asked for the seats. She had also handed over to the agents enough money to take care of any advance on-the-spot payments. But as the days went by, her patience began to run thin.

The journey across the dense, bramble-ridden, stone-littered mountain paths had now begun to haunt Kanchana's dreams. She got in touch with a local shoemaker and placed an order for special walking boots to be delivered within two days. Its sole would be leather and the uppers would be made of canvas. Everybody's foot measurement was taken and the entire amount was paid out in advance. The next evening the shoes were ready, and she had wanted to carry them straightaway on horseback, but the shoemaker offered to treat the leather with some kind of Burmese oil to soften it and make it rain-resistant. The delivery, therefore, would happen the next morning.

There was a school next to the refugee camp, that's where they sat down to plan their journey. Under the dim yellow light of the wick torch, the faces of the local agents and advisor friends were lined with worry. 'Madam,' said one, 'there's a biggish village called Pakaku a few miles away. We've heard that armed Japanese soldiers are roaming around freely there.'

'This has to be true,' said another informant. 'The Deputy Commissioner and the Superintendent of Police had a joint meeting today. The Brits were openly saying that the 215th Regiment of the Japanese army has quietly descended on the Irrawaddy bank a few miles from here. They have started shooting all the stray dogs so that they don't reveal the movement of the army through their barking. Looks like the invasion may happen any time now.'

'Oh god! So then, will they blow up the Myitkyina airport?'

Another night passed. Somebody was listening to the radio quite early in the morning. One of the performers of the company was listening apprehensively to the impassioned speech of the American General Joseph Stilwell, who had been put in charge of the China–Burma theatre of war and who had recently led his men out from another part of Burma to Assam on foot. 'I claim,' he was saying, 'we got a hell of a beating. We got run out of Burma and it is humiliating as hell. I think we ought to find out what caused it, go back and retake it.'

The sky that day was amazingly clear and blue. The sun shone its bright rays over the British families scattered across the Myitkyina airport, some in make-shift travelling tents, others under the open sky. If the weather held, they still carried hopes of being flown across to the safety of India just a few hours away. The sunshine had therefore given their expectations a fresh fillip and brought energy back to their limbs. They also heard the faint hum of an aircraft approaching from a distance.

Kanchana jumped astride Phakkadrao and set off with Mahaling and Taranath. The clear-blue sky had sprouted some hopes in their hearts too. There would definitely be a flight or two taking off today, and by any means, they would put into it as many of their girls as could be managed. The drone of the aircraft had become clearer as they pushed their heels into their horses' rumps and galloped off.

There were two aircraft up there, and they took three circles each before aligning themselves with the airstrip at the other end of the airport. When the crowds gathered in the open spaces saw the planes on the point of touching down, they completely ignored the guards on duty, went into overdrive and tried to position themselves as advantageously as they could. Some had tickets, most didn't; they thought they would somehow elbow their way into the aircraft and pay ten times the penalty. But this way they would be out of this incendiary theatre of war; that was the only thing that mattered.

A few on the ground noticed some movement behind the panes of the aircraft. Suddenly they saw panels open up and the barrels of machine guns slide out on either side like the claws of a crab poking out from under its shell. That was also when they noticed, hidden amid the cluttered pictures of flowers and leaves, the deep yellow emblem of the rising sun on the noses of the planes. There was no time for reaction when the guns opened up a fusillade of bullets that simply mowed down the hordes of people that had come swarming round the air strip with such hope and energy. Bags, suitcases, sandals went flying in all directions as people started falling as they ran, or just keeled over where they stood bleeding from the holes that had suddenly erupted all over their bodies. Both sides of the Myitkyina airstrip were suddenly littered with bodies writhing and kicking and thrashing as life-blood drained out of them onto the tarmac.

Kanchana and her team stood some distance away from the airfield, watching the scene with horror. They saw the fire that strafed out of those Japanese bombers all along the runway.

They heard the last screams of pain when the bullets found their mark and brought human beings down like sugarcane stalks being scythed down. But for all these disorienting events happening before her eyes, Kanchana had enough of her father's training in her system to not lose sight of practical matters.

She turned around and raced Phakkadrao into the Myitkyina bazaar. Along with the airport, the marketplace had been bombed too. While the shattered buildings stood mute and charred, people were screaming and running frantically in all directions. Avoiding the craters and the smoking embers, Kanchana wended her way to the shoemakers' lane, and what she saw there made her feel that a bomb had fallen straight on her. The line of shops lay razed to the ground; the flames emanating from the debris were even now devouring the shoes that had been especially made for her entourage.

There was nothing Kanchana could do but to wipe the warm tears flowing down her cheeks, roll up her sleeves and get on with the next thing on the agenda. She slapped the rump of her horse and rode back to the bank of the Irrawaddy. The news of the bombing at the airfield had spread all over, and now there was no point in waiting for anybody's permission. The circus people began to roll up their belongings and get moving. The horses were loaded up with whatever their backs could carry. Rajmangala had been turning her beady eyes behind as if looking for someone. When she saw her mistress come riding in on their horses, she trumpeted loudly. The message to men and animals was clear: no more hanging around in this city of darkness.

43

The road from Myitkyina to Assam across the Kumaon range and the Hukawng valley stretches for about 400 miles, and is counted among the remotest and toughest mountain trails in the world. A British team had shown the exemplary courage of trying to survey the stretch a few years back. They had hired porters from the local forest tribes of the Nagas and Kachins, gathered teams of elephants, horses and mules, and set to work with great intrepidity, but the wildness of the land had finally got the better of them.

The contraband runners of these mountains, for whom the smuggling gems and precious stones from Burma to China was a proper livelihood, had managed to get a far better understanding of the nearly interminable sequence of ravines and gorges that marked the area.

There were other factors too that made the journey across these mountains dangerous and daunting. Cholera, diarrhoea, elephantiasis and black fever were only a few of the diseases that the traveller was wont to contract.

An equally fearsome aspect of travelling through this region was the head hunters. Some among the Naga communities indulged in this macabre sport. They would bring people down with poisoned arrows, decapitate them and carry their heads away as trophies. They would make garlands of these heads and hang them in their temples and huts as decorative pieces:

on walls and from the bamboo rafters of their roofs. They obviously valued them as war trophies and showed them off as a mark of social status. These were the regions, the forest trails through which the evacuees had to hack their way forward, never knowing when a poison-tipped arrow would swish out of a bush with their name written on it. The story going round was that during the last couple of years the violent Nagas had collected over 200 heads as trophies.

Kanchana woke at dawn on the day they were to bid goodbye to Myitkyina. Two or three girls arrived to help her. Suddenly, they found Hirabai standing in the doorway. Kanchana was surprised, because life seemed to have lost all meaning for Hirabai since the time Shanta and Babita had died. She would just potter around like a mute gleaner picking a grain here and a grain there. All the enthusiasm and music seemed to have drained out of her life. Nobody remembered seeing her talking to anyone since that tragedy. Kanchana had got after her, trying to provoke her to speak a number of times. 'Hira-aatya, say something!' she would nudge her.

'What do I say, Kanchu? I just want to die.'

'How can you say that, Aatya? You remember, you were the one who would inspire me to carry the fire on my shoulder and keep walking. If you give up like this, where will we go?'

'Kanchu, by taking away Shanta and Babita, God has plucked out both my eyes. But I continue to live somehow because I know that if I die, Mahaling will not survive me by an hour. Which is why I suffer the punishment of living; there's nothing else left.'

The first 110 miles on the road were mainly through the plains, brambly in patches, sandy in some regions, passing through fields sometimes, the kind of road that the lorries were willing to negotiate. After that came the Kumaon range, and a little further ahead was the Daru mountain pass, located at a height of 5,200 feet. Past that, another seventy miles ahead lay the hill town of Mei Kangawn, and beyond it—the dreadful, notorious Hukawng, valley of death, uninhabited to the point of showing not a single settlement for forty miles at a stretch, not so much as a tiny hut.

When the circus company had hit the punishing route, they could hear the booms and barrage of bombs and gunfire a good distance across the Myitkyina region; but this time, it hadn't sounded like a one-way discharge, it was more like volleys being exchanged.

Keeping in mind the military significance of Myitkyina, the Japanese Air Force as well as the Japanese infantry advancing through the jungles were making strenuous efforts to get it under their control. On the other side, however, the remnants of the British and American forces were also finally showing some determination to fight back. It was an effort at not only defending an important army station, but also protecting the Burma Road, the critical artery that kept supplies between Burma and China flowing.

The Myitkyina that was retreating behind them was already up in flames. Big pillars of smoke were leaping into the sky from many different parts of the town.

The trail through the jungles was steadily filling up with more and more refugees in frantic movement towards India. Bullock carts and horse carriages loaded with Indians were making as rapid a progress as circumstances allowed. Men, women and children, all carried wicker baskets, the kind used in tea-gardens, on their backs and in front, stacked to the brim with whatever was considered absolutely necessary to carry away. A number of them carried supple bamboo poles on their shoulders, either end swinging with bags and bundles of assorted sizes. Some carried heavy metal trunks on their shoulders, others balanced rolls on their heads. A rare few had horses and mules to carry their luggage, emaciated animals that wobbled along on half-full stomachs. There was a fair smattering of Brits among those making the exodus.

Added to all the perils of a trek through the Burma wilderness was the menace of the deserters of Chiang Kai-shek's nationalist army. Tired of the rigours of prolonged warfare and finding survival difficult in a fast-changing power scenario, these renegade soldiers had taken refuge in the thickness of the Kachin jungles. They now roamed free as wild dogs and wolves, preying off the unfortunates that were fleeing through the forests. Whether it was their innate character or whether circumstances had brutalised them, stories of the savagery they were letting loose on women, young and old, were enough to make the flesh crawl.

The White soldiers had already begun to disintegrate, both physically and mentally, when finally, on 4 May 1942, the Allied Command announced the withdrawal of British and American forces from Burma. Well over 30,000 refugees had already been consumed by starvation, by the travails of the road and by the dread diseases they were encountering on their nightmarish journey. Those who dragged on did so nursing maggots in their suppurating wounds and cholera germs in their guts.

So many days of incessant flight, starvation and the disorderly state of the army had impacted the health of the soldiers too. Their unwashed, tattered, grime-covered uniforms still hung over their bodies; they still wore their leather belts and caps, but starvation had taken the flesh off their bones, giving them the appearance of scare-crows walking on stilts.

The army officers' wives trudged on like zombies. A large number of them had been so sure of catching a flight at Myitkyina, or they had had to leave their homes in such a hurry that they hadn't even changed out of their high-heeled footwear. Not in their wildest dreams could they have imagined the kinds of roads that they were now being made to walk. Within a mile the footwear had become utterly useless and had to be tossed away, and their feet and those of their children treaded on live embers, blistering and tearing and bleeding on the jungle floor.

As the refugees advanced into the journey, they were met by sights they had not encountered before. Countless lorries had run out of fuel and been abandoned by the road; some had tumbled into ditches, some others lay with their axles broken, with nobody making any effort at retrieving them.

A few miles further down, the circus people noticed a car they recognised from a distance. It was Mahaling who first caught sight of the deep greenish-black Rolls Royce of the Governor Sahib, the most expensive car in the world, that had been brought over from London to Rangoon with such tender care. Its big staff was nowhere around it . It lay under inches of dust, all its tyres flat, its glasses smashed.

Kanchana had been trying to hold him back, but Mahaling's curiosity got the better of him and he went up to the fallen car. When he peeped in through the broken window of the driver's seat, he recoiled in horror, withdrew a few steps and threw up. There, in the driver's seat, sat an apparition in what had been a white uniform, the skull leaning forward towards the steering, all in readiness to drive away. In the passenger seat lay his driver's badge and his colourful headgear.

'Why would this poor chap have stayed back alone?' queried Kanchana.

'The mechanics and the others would have moved ahead, but this honest Dravidian Indian must have hung back out of loyalty to the vehicle, waiting for the help he had been promised.'

A few more miles ahead and the road was littered with corpses on both sides: Indians, British, master, servant, rich, poor. Death, the ultimate monarch, had marked this patch of land for complete suzerainty, literally exposing to the bone the vulnerability of life. Miles upon gruesome miles were littered with cadavers in various stages of decay, baking in the sun like fish left out to dry after a good harvest. As the travellers moved on, they now met small settlements of about a hundred or so houses that belonged to the Kachin tribe. The entries and exits of these hamlets were almost invariably marked by heaps of corpses. Not very long ago they were travellers who had finally succumbed to the unequal battle with hunger and exhaustion. The stench of putrid flesh that lay thick in the air made breathing impossible for the circus troupe as it went past those fields of death.

The caravan of Rajmangala and the fourteen horses moved on at decent pace, preceded and followed by the 300 odd members of the circus company. While the horses carried rice flour, the girls took turns riding on Rajmangala's back, often allowing her to do some distance without any human burden at all. They knew quite well the strain of travelling down the treacherous route, for animals as well as for humans.

The five ayahs in charge of the younger girls had all been artistes in the company in their youth. They were pushing their seventies now, and the journey had begun taking its toll. The company had covered barely fifteen miles on the first day. On the second day, they had halted beside a stream, and the cook had circulated a dozen or so bowls filled with hot water that passed for tea. The ayahs went and held Kanchana's feet and cried, 'Look, Kanchu, we've had enough of this grind. We don't want to stir an inch ahead from here.'

'What are you saying? You have been our source of courage. How can you speak such defeatist language?'

'Listen, Kanchu, sitting in one spot and grinding corn by the sacks is one thing, but walking through this miasmic jungle at the pace of a horse is quite another.'

'Now you listen to me, my aunties, this kind of despondent talk won't do at all. I haven't brought the company this far in order to abandon you in the middle of a jungle.'

'But we are clearly slowing down your march, aren't we? We want you to snap your bonds with us and move ahead with the others.'

Kanchana transferred the loads of four horses onto other animals and got the ayahs to ride on their backs. Hirabai was junior to the others by fifteen years, but the tragedy that had befallen her girls had aged her well beyond her years, so much so that even riding the back of a horse had become a task for her. Mahaling would hold on to the reins and walk with her horse.

The Japanese plunderers still hadn't made their appearance, but the local hoodlums of Burma had gone on a rampage. The nationalist soldiers of Burma had united under the leadership of Dr Ba Maw to campaign against the British and create disruption in support of the Japanese. But the free-booting renegades of the dismantled army of Chiang Kai-shek had a single-point agenda—uninhibited, unrestrained and even-handed plunder. Whites, Blacks, locals, all who had stuff to loot were grist to their mill.

Kanchana would gather her troupe-mates every now and then and tell them, 'I don't want to lose even a single one of my girls from here on. That's why we have to stay alert and stay together all the time.'

The footwear of the company people had given up their ghosts within three days of the jungle march. Marching under the hot sun all day had drained the girls of their last drop of energy. They called a halt at night outside a village temple. They were so tired that they had no appetite, but the cook managed to rustle up some rice broth and passed it around to everyone.

Kanchana called everyone over and made a sign for the cobbler Gana to come forward. Gana brought two horses forward and off-loaded the two sacks they had on their backs. Two helper boys stepped forward, opened up the sacks and started emptying out the contents piece by piece. They were shoes of assorted shapes and sizes, and one look at their condition was enough to know where they could have come from. A number of them were stained with congealed blood. Their soles had thick layers of hardened earth on them. Some shoes, in fact, had tatters of blood-caked socks tucked away at the heel end.

The young boys in the troupe had been put to this task. Traversing the mountain trail winding through the Hukawng valley was worse than walking over red-hot coal. Footwear was the first thing it shredded and consumed. Then came the heat, fevers and lashing rains, which reduced the poor traveller to a mumbling clod ready to fall by the wayside at the tiniest push and die.

That was why, if rapid progress had to be made, in fact, if any progress had to be made at all, the feet needed to be protected and kept in good shape, and that could be done only with a sturdy pair of footwear. With the specially ordered shoes having gone up in flames at Myitkyina, Kanchana was left with just one choice. She had instructed the boys to remove the boots of dead soldiers along the way and collect them in sacks. What lay stretched out before them was the result of this effort.

When the girls dithered over wearing the used shoes, Kanchana took them to task. 'You see those 8,000-feet-high mountains there? We have miles upon miles of these mountains and gorges to cross, and they will tear your soles to ribbons if you haven't got proper shoes on. Understand?'

'But these men-sized shoes—'

'I know, they won't fit you, but I've found the remedy for it. We have Gana here, who will rip these shoes up, cut them according to your sizes and sew them up again.'

'But for that, we will need to take a four-day halt somewhere.'

'Forget four days, we are not taking a single hour's break. We'll have these cobbler boys work through the night on the shoes; take turns sleeping, if required, but we have to reach our destination before the torrential rains really catch us, haven't we?'

The harrowing route had begun to drive plenty of the travellers to despair and made a mockery of all their time-tables. They would gather all their belongings and be on the road by seven in the morning. Sulaiman, however, had to start off at five because it was necessary to have Rajmangala keep pace with them. The rest of the troupe would overtake them, move forward and wait at the destination for an hour or so before the elephant and her mahaut arrived. This was the routine Sulaiman and Rajmangala followed every day.

Everybody in the forest knew how precious a commodity an elephant was, and the company people were not unaware of it either. The probability was strong that some miscreants could lie in wait in the jungle, kill the animal and divest it of its expensive tusks. Hence a team of ten able-bodied guards travelled with Rajmangala from the very first day. They were armed with swords and spears and had clear instructions to use them if the need arose.

Men and animals were being driven as fast as they could, uncaring of their empty bellies and the roughness of the terrain. The fast pace and the humidity would often wet their clothes with perspiration, but there would be no halting to get their breath back. The clothes would dry on their backs. The few who understood the song of the jungle moved with their ears cocked. There were some bird songs they were alert for, for they would be the harbingers of rain.

44

A Military Police barricade stood at the turn of the brambly road. The path towards the left was open to traffic, but the one that went straight ahead was blocked by the soldiers. As they pushed away any refugee trying to move past the barricade, Kanchana stood with her elephant Rajmangala, her horses and the 300 odd circus staff, watching the disdain with which the miserable travellers were being turned away.

As she watched, her temper began to rise till something inside her snapped. 'All right, friends,' she said, with a dangerous edge to her voice, 'follow me.'

The policemen on duty noticed this huge throng moving menacingly forward. Whistles were blown and arms were raised. The captain of the squad came rapidly forward and shouted, 'Hey, you, madam, where do you think you're going?'

'To my country! My India!'

'Go, then, by all means go. But that's the route you take.'

'Why not this one?'

'Madam, this is called the Milestone 102 Gate, and this route has been kept reserved exclusively for the use of White soldiers.'

Kanchana let her tongue loose. 'You bastards! Don't you have any shame saying this to me?'

There was no holding her back. 'Is your conscience entirely dead? Have your eyes gone so blind as not to see the hardship of these poor refugees? They've dragged themselves across a 1,000 miles and more. Running like hunted animals, dodging Japanese bombers, fighting disease and death at every step.'

'Why're you getting so het up, woman? Who's stopping you from taking this other road?'

'Why not this Fort Hertz one, I ask?'

'I've told you. This route is reserved strictly for the Whites.'

'You wretched fools! Cowards! Is that White empress of yours leaving her throne in England to come over with a gun and fight for us?'

'Watch what you are saying, madam!'

'When it comes to spilling blood on the frontiers of your empire, or to getting crushed under armoured vehicles, when it comes to getting blown to pieces on torpedoed ships, you have us Indian soldiers to do it for you, but when it comes to finding safe routes out, they're reserved for your filthy White soldiers, are they?'

An ordinary Indian woman lashing out at him in this manner, that too in the presence of his subordinates, was more than the officer was willing to take. He pointed the barrel of his sten-gun at her and barked, 'Madam, if you don't immediately get a hold of yourself, I will shoot you!'

'Oh, you will, will you?' Kanchana snarled back. 'Well, all right, go ahead and shoot, then!'

Taranath and Mahaling tried to pull Kanchana away. She had turned red with anger. She protested, 'I've had enough of these arrogant White pigs' nonsense, I can't take it anymore. If they hadn't blocked us back in Mandalay and then at Myitkyina and wasted over two precious months, we would have reached our motherland long ago.'

'Didi, these numbskulls have done exactly the same thing elsewhere too, we hear. Down there through the valleys of the Chindwin and the Salween rivers, along the road past Tamu to

Pallel and Imphal, they've got these same segregation of White roads and Black roads.'

'Come what may, I'm now determined to take my people through this route that lies in front.'

The senior members of the company surrounded Kanchana and pleaded, 'Kanchana, please, please try to understand. In this fit of anger you may shoot down a couple of soldiers, but the hundred bullets that will come racing back in return will destroy our people.'

'I don't care!' she roared.

'All right! You may not care for your own life, but this journey has already consumed fifty of us. Of the 300 that remain, 70 are women. Whether we like it or not, Kanchu, all that is left in our hands is to handle these ugly circumstances with as cool a head as possible.'

'Yes,' she snorted, 'yes, patience, tolerance, courage, resilience, it's for explaining to us the meaning of these words that this trail is running this school for us in these jungles.'

Once in a while, in their movement forward they would come across groups of three or four soldiers belonging to the British army—starving and despairing. They could barely manage to put one foot before the other and trudge on. Down the dusty road was a small hillock and a soldier dressed in tatters went round for easing his bladder. For some reason he lost his balance and went rolling down the slope like an empty drum.

While his friends watched from above, a few formidable, vulture-like jungle birds flew out of the neighbouring trees and swooped towards the fallen man like a swarm of locusts. They opened their six-inch long beaks and let out shrill caucous cries as they descended upon him. Strong, hooked beaks and razor-sharp talons immediately began tearing the hapless man apart and within minutes his writhing body had turned still. The birds were now ready to fight among themselves for as much of a share as they could snatch for their dinner.

The caravan crawled on. The road seemed to have taken charge of teaching the travellers all the different aspects of life: smiles and tears, life and death, victory and defeat.

45

Keep walking. Keep walking. Walking without a break had become the very purpose of life. As she walked, Kanchana's toes ached excruciatingly. The bones of her legs and her calves would turn warm like an overworked machine.

Once night fell, there would be lentil soup or watery thin Burmese peyheen for dinner. Then she would rest her back against the ground and close her eyes. After barely an hour's restless sleep, she would again be awake. When she got up, her ankles would throb painfully. She would often experience a catch around her waist. But she didn't have the luxury of tending to her aches and pains. The future of over 300 troupe members compelled her to keep moving forward.

In the hope of finding some relief, she would tie a nylon rope tightly round her waist and keep walking in step with the rest of the company across heaths, streams and jungle tracks with uncompromising determination.

It was pitch dark everywhere. The company had stretched out on the grass meadows alongside the jungle trail.

Kanchana would not even have slept for three hours when she got up. She picked up the spear that lay by her side and set off for a round of patrolling. Two big dogs joined her.

Kanchana surveyed the circus paraphernalia that lay scattered on the grass. Eleven boys had been appointed for patrol duty round the clock, but the incessant walking had drained them out and they had fallen asleep on duty.

This was the fourth night that she had been doing these rounds. She just couldn't go to sleep. Some of the company seniors had woken up too and they looked at her with worry. This could bring grievous harm to her, despite Marilyn's revolver that was tucked in her waist. Taranath got up and rushed towards her. He shouted as he neared her. 'You want to die, do you? Why have we appointed night-guards then?'

'My duties are quite different, kaka,' Kanchana responded in a thick voice. 'You see these grasslands, don't you? Wherever there's such thick grass, there are bound to be deer; and where there are deer in such numbers, there'll be tigers too.'

'Huh?'

'How can you not see? Our girls sleeping out in the open on these grasslands are exposed to carnivores—like me, any mother will be on guard.'

The trail stretched on endlessly, mile after crushing mile. A number of people would collapse under the shade of trees and watch with envy and despair the sturdier ones going by.

A bunch of five or six dog-tired men had gathered their legs in their arms and sat under a stunted tree. With their torn, dirty, ill-fitting clothes and faces shrunk with constant starvation, they looked like they had reached the end of their desire to strive on.

Suddenly, a thin, piping call reached Kanchana's ears, '*Aga ye* Kanchana …'

Kanchana stopped in her track and turned around to look at the group under the tree. There, in the midst of the corpses of a few dead refugees and soldiers, she saw a painfully thin man who was alive. His eyes looked yellow as cream gone bad. Seeing the flustered look on Kanchana's face, the old man introduced himself.

He was Yasmin Inamdar, a horse-groom from Budhgaon. He had gone to Burma with the Karlekar Grand Circus, where the circus had suffered the same fate as Kanchana's company. A couple of months back he had been separated from his company.

Kanchana had her men served the remnants of their food to Yasmin and his four associates. Only two or three of them had the strength left to swallow the food. They sat there with their heads nodding like spring dolls.

Yasmin managed to down three or four morsels. He looked at Kanchana and said, 'It seems that you haven't really recognised me. In our youth, your father Sarang and I spent some time together in Parshuram's circus. But you turned out to be turncoats.'

'Why do you say that, kaka?'

'I got to hear that you were married off in the style of a king's daughter. Your father also chose a good match for you in that circus boy Raghav, but you didn't bother to send an invitation to this uncle of yours.' As Kanchana was racking her brains for making suitable excuses, the man said, 'Don't worry, I was joking. But here is something that is far more important: I saw your husband barely a month and a half ago. I recognised him because I had known him even before he became your husband.'

Yasmin's words sent an electric current through all who heard him, and they rushed to stand around him. Kanchana went limp in the legs and sat down. Holding Yasmin's wrist, she pleaded in a hoarse voice, 'Kaka, swear by Allah. Tell me that you are not making fun of me.'

'How can I joke in such a matter, girl? I swear by Allah that I saw him, in the forest just outside Mytkyina.'

While Kanchana was too overcome to talk, the other elders kept the conversation going. 'He is alive a hundred per cent,' said the old man, 'but it was clear that he was not a free individual.'

'Why do you say that, kaka?'

'He was in the company of a few ragged men who were being made to scrub themselves in a jungle stream. There were five or six of these men who were being watched over by some slit-eyed, flat-nosed soldiers.'

'But you could have been mistaken too,' Kanchana wondered.

'Well, I could have been, but his eyes fell on me, I could see that he recognised me too. It was an event that almost cost us our lives!'

'Why? What happened?' Mahaling asked in a worried voice.

'When my companions here and I suddenly came out from behind the trees, one of the gun-toting men pointed his gun at us and made us kneel down. I couldn't understand his language, of course, but they frisked us. We had nothing, of course, except these rags covering our bodies. A soldier who was perhaps their senior barked something which suggested that he wanted us shot down. But some exchange took place; perhaps they did not want us scare-crows as prisoners and they also didn't want to waste their ammunition on us. Finally, after we had rolled at their feet for sufficiently long, they just kicked us out of there and we were happy to scamper off at our fastest.'

'But you did see Raghav?' Kanchana queried again.

'Of course I did, pori, barely seven or eight steps away from me. And he recognized me. I could see from his eyes that he was terrified that I would announce my recognition of him. Obviously, in that circumstance, that would have endangered my life too.'

'Kaka, how did he look? Was he all right?'

'Well, his limbs were intact and he didn't seem to suffer from any physical disability, but he looked emaciated. His hair had grown long and his beard too.'

'Tell me more, kaka, tell me more,' Kanchana pleaded.

'What's there to tell, pori? We just met for those tense few minutes and managed to escape with our lives. It's plain luck that I met you here, so I could tell you he is alive. He is alive, you can be sure of that, but only Allah can tell when you will meet him, if ever.'

'Don't say that, kaka, don't say that. Goddess Kalamma has kept him alive, she will find a way to bring him back to us.'

Yasmin's news brought hope surging back into Kanchana's heart. 'Kaka,' she insisted, 'You can join us on the journey back.' But Yasmin was beyond caring about life and death. He smiled wanly and said, 'Pori, what can you do if Allah has marked me out for death on this unknown road? We all have to die, some here, some there. But can you do something for me?'

'Do what, kaka?'

'When you reach home, please go to the shrine at Kelshi near Dapoli and place a *chaadar* of devotion on the grave of Yakoot Baba Kalandar on my behalf.'

Kanchana stood up and placed her head at Yasmin's feet. She looked at his sorrowful face and gave into his hands some jaggery and a small packet of dates.

Then she turned around and began walking away with her company mates. Very soon the spot under the tree turned dim.

Chaper 46

Christina Kennedy was travelling through the dense, impenetrable forest along with nine girls. They were clad in identical brick-brown school uniforms that flared up at the waist. A couple of them were Burmese, a few others looked Mongolian, but the majority of the girls were White and had thick blonde hair. Four of them seemed to be at the cusp of adolescence, while the others were younger, puppy fat still showing on their innocent faces.

The girls moved along the thick grass, cutting through the slush underneath. When she saw Kanchana, she called out, 'Hey, circus lady!'

Kanchana was stunned. Who was this tall White woman, properly middle-aged, who now stood in front of her?

'Kanchana madam, right? Hello! Imagine meeting you here!'

As Kanchana stared at her thoroughly perplexed, the woman announced, 'I am Christina, teacher at the Rose Baptist Convent and the rector of the residential unit.'

'Oh, how wonderful!'

'Well, you can't possibly know me! We had come to Rangoon for the Christmas holidays and had seen your sensational circus.'

A soft smile played on Kanchana's lips. She looked at Christina, full of admiration. Here was a school teacher who had dared to challenge these jungles and mountains in an effort to save her young wards.

Looking at the young girls plodding through the slush, Kanchana asked Christina in a worried voice, 'How did you land up here? Did someone cheat you?'

'Well, it was a deception of sorts. The indifference of our White rulers.'

'Where are the parents of these girls?'

'A couple of them are senior officers in the big oil companies in Rangoon; some others work in the jute industry in Calcutta. The fathers of more than half these girls have gone to fight on the Anglo-French battle-front in Europe. When Mandalay began to burn in the bombing, I had to run from pillar to post to ensure the safety of my little birds. The school administration placed that responsibility on my shoulders.'

'But why would you abandon the security of cities like Rangoon and Mandalay and come into these jungles up north?'

'What choice was I left with? We were deceived.' Her breath caught and she stopped to regain her voice. Continuing in her despairing tone, she said, 'When we left Mandalay, we had been told to somehow reach the Myitkyina airport along with our girls. We managed that with great difficulty, but the Military Command did not honour their word.'

Christina looked haggard. She sat down on a wet rock and spoke in an aggrieved voice, 'What happened at the Myitkyina airport that day has settled like shrapnel deep inside me.'

'Well, we were also short-changed at the same airport.'

'How hopeful we were as I stood with my little girls at the fringe of the runway. Had the airplane taken off, these children would have reached their warm nests within just two hours.'

'Why didn't they?'

'The bureaucracy stabbed us in the back. My girls were pushed aside and the governor of Burma, Dorman Smith, his wife and his colleagues rushed into the Dakota aircraft right in front of me.'

'Ago bai!'

'I ran to him and pleaded with him, to have mercy on these innocent girls and arrange for their evacuation. Begged him to at least let a few of them leave. But he was in no mood to relent ... And now, there's nobody left to care for these children. They are trapped in the vortex of this war.'

It began to rain. They could not sit on a stone slab and talk. Christina, Kanchana, the little girls, the unfortunate artistes of the dismantled circus—all of them were running.

As they ran together, Christina filled Kanchana in on a lot of other things. Kanchana asked her, 'Are yours the only set of students to have been hit by misfortune this way.'

'Oh, no, not at all. There have been other schools too that have been hit hard. While I was at the Myitkyina airport with my girls, in the crowds I noticed the children of St. Mathew's School at Moulmein and St. Michael's School at Maymyo. What fate has dispensed to them is no different from what has fallen to our lot. For all we know, they may also be slogging up a similar jungle track at this moment.'

'Madame, I admire your fighting spirit.'

'Kanchana, these girls have braved bombs as if they were Diwali and Christmas crackers. Their young eyes have seen human beings roasted alive as if they were animals on spits.'

'How many students did you have with you in all?'

'Thirty girls. The ones who were really small—seven to eight-year-olds—we left them behind in a village called Labana on the way. The priest at the church and his wife have promised to look after them until we return to take them away.'

'But I see only nine with you.'

'Six of them contracted cholera. They became so weak that it was impossible to bring them along. We found a Naga chief in a village who took them under his care. I've left my younger sister Rose behind to watch over them.'

The travel through the wilderness was cruel on the delicate young girls. Their shoes had turned ragged, some had no shoes at all; their toes were swollen, their nails chipped and bled as they limped and plodded on through the rain. Kanchana was very disturbed looking at them. Only if she had more horses!

The girls were either soaking wet with rain or sticky with perspiration. Just a few of them had another flimsy frock they could change into. A few thin, frayed blankets that they had procured from some church were wrapped in wax paper so that they didn't get wet; for all one knew, these rags too could have cholera and other lethal germs hiding inside them.

As it was turning dark, they came across a small settlement of low-built bamboo huts. Hardly huts, they were more like skeletons made of rotten, black, termite-infested bamboo. The doors were wide open, and the whole place looked deserted. The owners could have abandoned their houses out of the fear of contracting dreaded diseases like cholera, diarrhoea or elephantiasis from the refugees. That would wipe out their entire settlement. They would have thought it wiser to clear out of the way till normalcy arrived.

The travellers took over the huts and spread out as well as they could. For the first time since they had started, Kanchana did not sleep with her own company girls, but shifted to Christina's hut. In front of her lay the nine little girls snuggled into Christina. They had lit up a fire in the hearth there and spread around it in a semi-circle.

Christina would break into violent bouts of coughing. Some girl would break into incoherent babbling, another would break into a sob as she slept. Two of the girls began to shiver uncontrollably, upon which Kanchana added a log or two to the fire and woke Christina; they both held the girls close to their chests to give them whatever warmth they could.

After the girls' bodies had turned sufficiently warm, Kanchana tried to feed them with some leftover broth; but the poor girls were so deadbeat that they didn't even have the strength to part their chapped lips. It was past midnight now.

Little by little, the girls stopped shivering, and the women too went to sleep.

It was their second wet stop on the journey. Kanchana and Christina had gathered the girls in the middle and gone to sleep on either side of them. After a day's travel, sleep had claimed them by an inalienable right.

Darkness began melting by slow degrees and light began to insinuate itself in the denseness of the vegetation-choked jungle. The trudge of every single day, the unrelenting forward movement over the edge of a blade, the unwavering alertness of feet, eyes and ears to the hazards that the fearful wilderness was prone to spring upon them—the mind and the body had begun to pay an appalling price for this constant vigilance.

Bisons, lions and tigers in the dense bushes and carnivorous birds of prey in the cloud-laden sky; the fear of renegade Chinese deserters and a parallel dread of violent Japanese soldiers made night-long patrolling a compulsory exercise.

No peace during the day and no rest in the dark hours. Battling against leeches and the buzzing swarms of mosquitoes in the evenings had become routine for the hapless travellers.

Much as the mind wanted to jump out of bed and get busy, the tired bones would refuse to answer back with the same enthusiasm. Why should the morning have arrived in such a hurry? Rose and Dolly, however, could not disregard the call of nature any further and they stepped out of the thatch into the pre-dawn wind. There was a faint drizzle in the air, but relieving their bladder was a matter of greater urgency. They went behind the hut and moved a few steps forward through the slime into the thick vegetation ahead. Taranath's voice rang out just then from the next thatch, 'Come on, everybody, we have no time lose. Get up now and start folding things up.' They never tarried.

Kanchana was sleeping in the makeshift tent somehow fashioned out of pieces of tarpaulin. She suddenly felt something very cold touching her stomach. Her heart missed a beat. Could it be a snake? She sprang up and threw a log into the fire. In the dim yellow light of the flame that leapt up, she saw that it was one of Christina's girls that had gone cold. The thorny jungle, the starvation and the trauma of war had claimed another victim.

The journey, however, had to take precedence over everything. Men and animals set off yet again on the unrelenting trail.

47

'With the skies pouring down in this fashion, are the rest of the girls going to last?' Kanchana asked, worried.

Christina easily got out of breath when she talked. She said, 'I have been sending lots of messages, right from Mandalay and Myitkyina, to the camps in Ledo, Dibrugarh and Lekhapani in Assam, begging them to do something to save my girls. I believe that my efforts are not all going to go waste.'

As they sat that night round a bonfire, Kanchana said, 'I can tell you a good way of protecting oneself against the rains and the cold winds that we've been facing here.'

'What is that?' Christina asked.

'We have forested areas like Shahuwadi and Shirala in the Sahyadri range in our part of the country. The rain falls in sheets in those jungles. For four months at a stretch, it just pours. But in spite of that kind of downpour, our people keep working right through the day in all that slush and storm, and they do so only on account of the *irali*.'

'What is this irali?'

'Describing it will not help. I'll show it tomorrow,' Taranath replied.

The next day, when they came into a bamboo patch, Taranath hacked out a few slim bamboo shoots and split them into strips lengthwise from end to end. He then wove the strips warp and woof so as to prepare a frame with a cavity that would cover the head at the top end and go right down covering the back up to the calves. Immediately after, fortuitously they came upon trees with broad leaves, which were tacked over the frame, taking care that the lower end of the upper leaf lapped over the top end of the lower leaf. When the contraption was ready, it made a long, inflexible, hollow sheath that covered a person all the way down the back from head to calf, shoulders and arms included.

The girls took full advantage of the shelter that irali offered.

When the rains subsided, the sturdier among the circus men, like Dagdoba and Taranath, would carry them either on their shoulders or in their arms and walk for miles. It was only when it was raining heavily that carrying them became difficult.

The rains had arrived in the Hukaung valley—as also in the rest of northern Burma—a good five weeks earlier than normal. A month had already passed since then. There was thick, tall grass everywhere, the entire jungle was submerged deep in slime and the trees were covered with moss. It seemed that a series of calamities had covered the spirit of the intrepid travellers with a coating of fungus. The White girls travelling with Christina had become family by now. However, their aches and pains and their delicate constitutions made it difficult for the company to carry them forward with at least relative safety.

The stoppages on the way had increased. The worry that bugged them at each stop was the fear that the mountain rivers would get into flood. Once that happened, it would take a good two to three months for the floods to subside. Camping on this side of the floods wasn't an option either. Even at a fistful per head per day, where would food come from for feeding over 300 people? The option was just one—suffering all the agonies and moving ceaselessly forward.

Christina's health began to rapidly deteriorate. Her state suggested that she wouldn't be able to survive this assault on her system for too long. However painful the separation would be, it had become crucial to find a safe haven for her little wards. And *voila,* as if in answer to their prayers, it seemed that the gods had rushed to their help. They came to a small village on the bank of a raging stream, and springing out of all the vegetation they saw a cross atop a structure made of bamboos, elephant grass and whatever other building material the forest could provide. The relentless rains had given the church walls and roof a thick coating of moss.

Some members of the company immediately accompanied Christina to see whether the church could be persuaded to extend some help. The pastor of the church Father D'Costa was an experienced old man. The reddish-blond beard on his chubby cheeks made him look particularly friendly. He had been working for his church among the Karen, Kachin and Naga tribes for many years in this faraway nook of the jungle. He peered through his thick glasses and locked Kanchana and Christina in his gaze as they sat speaking to him in the parlour.

Father D'Costa called the eight little girls close to him and touched their cheeks affectionately. After having given them his blessings, he suddenly flared up and shouted, 'I don't understand your stupidity. If you were so possessed with the mad notion of travelling through these jungles, why couldn't you have started much earlier?'

'How could we have done that, Father?'

'What do you mean how could you have done that?'

'Your confused British administration and your dim-witted military bosses were playing games. It was on account of their yes-no-maybe tendencies and their utter inability to take decisions that thousands fell prey to the Japanese bombings. The survivors were mopped up in the jungles by leeches and dysentery and cholera.'

Father D'Costa's big round pupils flickered. He looked upwards at the church ceiling made of bamboo slats. Voice thick with anxiety and agitation, he said, 'You have no choice but to go ahead. But please do exercise the greatest care. This vast, dense jungle is not safe at all. Something like 5,000 Chinese renegades have let themselves loose in these jungles. They are animals, all of them, dangerous as wild bisons. Barbarians!'

'Oh dear god!'

'And you have these little ones travelling with you! I can see that you have sixty or seventy women with you too. Never forget that they pounce on female flesh like hungry dogs. They have no pity, no compassion.'

As they sat talking to Father D'Costa, the dark, sinister shadows of recent tragedies were gnawing at their insides. Christina's steadily worsening bouts of cough were an added worry. If only this priest could take charge of the British girls, it would be a big load off their chests. When Kanchana ventured this suggestion, Father D'Costa assumed his most sermonising voice and declaimed grandly, 'Service to mankind is the greatest of all gospels. I can't imagine a better way of serving God than being of service to these delicate little flowers. But you know well enough how awfully expensive it is to run a mission in this faraway wilderness. But again, how can I say no to such a saintly assignment?'

The priest stayed silent for a while and then let out a deep sigh. 'I am fully aware,' he said, 'of the financial status of Indian circuses. You people earn a lot of money. You are, perhaps, the richest people in the land.'

'It's not quite like that, Father,' said Kanchana.

'How is it not? An ordinary person would find it difficult to rear a cock, and here you are, the owners of lions and tigers and elephants!'

'Almost our entire menagerie was slaughtered, Father. Time has reduced us to penury.'

'Yes, but the richest cannot turn into paupers overnight, can they?'

Father D'Costa's words confounded his audience. When he saw hopelessness creeping into their faces, the priest said, 'After all, these girls will remain with me in the forest. Keeping them sufficiently nourished won't be an easy task. You will have to bear the expenses of their upkeep. You may deposit some money in the church accounts.'

'But we don't have any money!' Kanchana said.

'Look, I'm not saying I want cash. In fact, I'd prefer gold. It's generally jewels, ruby and gold, that one finds among the traders at the harbour, the opium merchants and you circus people.'

After a lot of debate and yes and no, it was finally decided that the girls would be left in the care of Father D'Costa the following day. As they were returning to their dilapidated huts in the jungles, the girls looked perturbed. When they slept that night, they clung to Kanchana and Christina like new-born pups stick to their mothers.

It was quite late in the night when Kanchana heard a whisper from Christina, 'Are you still awake?'

'How can I go to sleep? I just can't bring myself to leave these children behind.'

After lying silent for a long while, Christina said in a choked voice, 'Kanchana, what am I, after all, but an ordinary school teacher? A weakling! That's the reason why I am always so unwell. That's why Jesus Christ arranged for me to meet a strong woman like you. I am convinced that my girls will be safer with you than they will be with any priest or nun.'

Despite the circumstances, Kanchana chuckled and said, 'You do appear upset with that priest.'

'What kind of a priest is that? Concealed inside that cassock is a proper businessman. Talks of gold and rubies for providing protection to my girls.'

If the rains didn't wind up operations in good time, seeing the next two and a half months through would be arduous. How would they satisfy their hunger pangs in these leech-ridden, soaking wet mountains? Once their stock of grains ran out, how would they be able to combat the cold, wet winds on a diet of grass and leaves? Whether their minds were in agreement or not, whether their bodies were willing to put their muscles into it or not, they had no choice but to swallow hard and keep marching.

The next day, the travellers struck a strange kind of track, weak and crumbly, with the packing of the earth so loose that Rajmangala's legs would suddenly sink in more than a foot deep in the slime. As she tried to swing the other way to retrieve balance, the girls atop her back would break into loud cries of panic. As they moved on, they hit upon endless acres of slush and mire. Elephant, horses and even men feared falling flat on their faces. At one place, Rajmangala's front foot landed into a hole below the slime and she lost her balance. If she had fallen, the girls sitting on her back could well have fallen and got squashed under her weight. It was fortunate, however, that she was a trained circus animal. She brought her strong trunk into play and recovered her balance before disaster could strike.

The winds at their next stop were wet and biting. The day-long walk had tired Christina out considerably. Kanchana did not miss the darkish hue that had filled in the lines on Christina's face. As the night deepened, her state worsened. Her breath stuck in her throat with a strange rattle. Kanchana placed her palm upon hers and asked, 'Teacher, are you in some kind of pain? Is there some tablet in your kit that you want?'

'No, nothing. I'm all right.'

'Shall I make some black coffee for you?'

'No. Kanchana, the parents of these kids living in faraway lands had thrust a responsibility upon me, and I fought beyond my strength and means to meet them. What prior experience did I have of these days and nights of struggle across such desperate, dangerous forest paths? There's no saying what awaits me tomorrow.'

'How will it do to lose heart like this?'

'If I don't survive this journey, please do all you can to save my girls.'

The next day dawned. Kanchana put some coffee on the hearth for Christina, but before it could be served, Christina had breathed her last. Kanchana called out to her troupe members through the pouring rain. Everybody took a last look at the dead woman. They had neither the time nor the stamina left for much mourning. Besides, the little girls Christina had left behind had to be consoled and cared for.

They were in a hurry to leave. They had to cover as much distance as they could before the clouds churning in the sky released their moisture upon an already soaked earth. They didn't even have the time to give her a proper burial. The earth was soggy too. They took the instant decision of placing her body in a groove next to a big tree that had fallen earlier. They covered the body with big and small branches so as to prevent predatory birds from tearing into her

The girls, very young though they were, had learnt enough lessons in the ruthless school of adversity. They lined up next to where their teacher was interred, said a silent prayer and resumed their walk.

Little Dolly riding astride Mahaling's shoulder suddenly pointed towards her left. Turning back towards Kanchana and the others, she screamed, 'Mother, look there!'

The entire company halted and looked in the direction where Dolly was pointing and froze. Stretched out across the wet grass in a neat row were eleven corpses. The company had become quite used to seeing corpses in all forms: bloated, decomposed, wet, burnt, crushed; but this scenario of the corpses laid out in a proper row was entirely new. For one, the blood that lay pooled next to each corpse looked fresh. Not more than ten or twelve hours would have passed since their slaughter. For another, their heads had been separated from their bodies by one single stroke of a sharp blade. It was evident that before being beheaded, they had been blindfolded and made to go on their knees with their hands tied behind their backs. The moment their eyes fell on the corpes, the circus men broke into an involuntary murmer, 'Japs—it's these Japanese bastards!'

Along with the malevolence of the Chinese renegades, stories of Japanese atrocities had also been doing the rounds. If ever an enemy agent or soldier fell into their hands, tradition demanded that he be dispatched to heaven by a single swish of the blade.

The row of corpses was an announcement to this theatre of war, 'We, the Japanese Bushido, have arrived!'

48

It was one of those rare nights when the rains let up. Kanchana was deep in sleep, as if snuggled in the warm comfort of dry grass. Somebody was shaking her by the hand. Through the dim, yellow light of the warm hearth, she saw that two of her circus girls were staring at her with terrified eyes. 'Didi, get up please,' they were pleading in a thick whisper. 'Someone has attacked the girls in the hut behind there!'

Kanchana shot up like a spring. She quickly heard out the girls. Around twenty-five girls had gone to sleep in the bigger hut on the other side after the long day's trek. Taking advantage of the darkness, some eight or nine soldiers had sneaked into the tent.

'Who are these people? What do they look like? What kind of clothes are they wearing? Which country?'

'Didi, going by their small eyes and their jet-black hair, they look like Chinese soldiers. We managed to punch a hole in the straw wall and sneak out of the hut to come to you.'

'Let's go quickly, let's not have a graveyard here as we had on the bank of the Irrawaddy.'

Kanchana stepped out and looked at the hut some distance away. Screams had begun to reach her ears across the dark night. The men sleeping in the hut behind them had got up too. They were all rushing to the hut, including Mahaling, Taranath and little Batuknath. Before they could create a ruckus to alert the soldiers inside, Kanchana signalled to them urgently to stay quiet. 'There's no point in alerting them. They are armed,' she whispered.

She called two girls over and told them, 'I want you two to go back into that hut, do you hear me?'

'Didi, no!'

'Don't be scared, be brave! I want you to become devious sirens. Weave a net around them. You are *my* circus girls. I want you to destroy those Chinese monkeys by weaving a web around them.'

'But, Didi—'

'Don't worry! Just be brave. Hold their attention for a little while.'

These soldiers had been absconding from their army for a few months now; whatever they could find in these unforgiving jungles—food, medicines, weapons, even an occasional woman of the Naga tribe—they had made it their law to pounce on them like hungry wolves and consume them instantly. When they had seen the circus girls gathered under a single roof with nothing to prevent them from indulging their animal impulses, they had been delighted. They were warming up now to get busy with their merriment in the middle of the jungle.

Just then the thatch door of the hut opened and two girls walked in. When the soldiers saw their inviting faces, they were besides themselves with excitement. They put their guns to one side and advanced towards the young girls.

Within a minute, a sharp whistle was heard outside, on hearing which the two girls shouted, 'Come on, girls, run,' and they themselves dashed towards the door. At the same time, one entire wall made of grass and leaves caved in. The bewildered soldiers saw outside a big group of well-built circus men standing with flaming torches in one hand and stout sticks in the other. Before they could so much as blink, the torches came flying through the air and landed in the grass at their feet, immediately setting the entire hut on fire.

Those of the soldiers who could gather their wits and run out had no time to pick up their weapons and take aim. They were set upon by a flurry of stick-swinging men who aimed for their heads and legs. The circus men had also spread nylon ropes around the exit, which they raised and pulled taut, causing the fleers to trip and fall flat on their faces and get flailed as they lay on the ground. They were then lifted bodily and tossed into the fire that was raging inside. Three of the Chinese, however, did release a volley of gunfire before they were overpowered by Mahaling and the others and flung to their death in the inferno.

The rest of the night was spent in the neighbouring woods leaning against the trees and dozing. When the morning breeze began to blow strongly, it was all they heard. Whenever it slackened, the sound of water burbling in the stream beyond the woods reached them. Suddenly there would be the screech of a bird. Even while dozing, Kanchana had kept her ears cocked. The big leaves of the tree nearby fell down with the wind.

'Come, girls,' she whispered. Let's clear out of here.'

Just then, Sulaiman walked in with a worried face. Tensing up, Kanchana asked, 'Yes, kaka?'

'Everything is in order, Kanchana, but where's our Phakkadrao?'

Kanchana's voice caught in the throat at this fearful question.

49

Light had just begun to creep in. The darkness that had engulfed the mountains in the Kumaon valley had begun to melt and the dense green of the vegetation had started reclaiming its space. The dew drops on the leaves would still take a long time to depart. However, the secret surveillance team had been up and about much before the forest had woken up from its sleep. The gun-carrying soldiers manning their posts were short and sturdily built, with a peculiar yellow tinge to their complexion. This Japanese unit had set up its camp on the top of this sloping hill that stuck out like an ugly nose between two deep valleys.

There, among the bushes, sat a heavily built Japanese General. He had in his hands the latest model of a pair of high-resolution binoculars with which he was scanning the surrounding landscape. His name was Shojiro Lida. He was in his fifties. He had lately decimated the British army and taken charge of Rangoon. He was now touring these mountains night and day so that he could study the topography extending from the Kumaon valley to the border of China in order to mount a new assault. In the hierarchy, he was one among the top five generals of the Japanese army.

During the period preceding the War, a number of international training programmes had been organised in places like London and Paris on International Relations and Cooperation. During times of peace, groups had been created with senior army officers of various countries and these groups were sent for four-month-long training programmes at the international level. General Lida had represented Japan in three such training programmes in European cities. As a result, he had gained passing competence in English and had also created a network of European friends. His vast international experience was evident from the manner in which he carried himself.

His heavy army uniform was specially designed to meet the needs of tough assignments. The flat Japanese cap on his head, the jacket that sported the gallantry medals and ribbons of participation in many theatres of war, the thick belt round his waist that carried a revolver and a kukri-like blade—his presence proclaimed authority. Five officers of the rank of captain would always be standing behind him hanging on to every word he uttered. Their main job was to immediately implement whatever orders were issued.

The day had turned quite bright now. The binoculars now clearly showed the valleys on either side, a few miles of the small rivers and streams that passed through them, and the jungles all around. The general was paying sharp attention to the small paths and jungle tracks that wound their way through the trees. At some distance was a mountain range that he examined with particular interest. The road that climbed up the shoulder of the mountain in front descended on the other side and took the traveller to the river Dafa. This was the road that took one to India.

Despite the sharp resolution of the binoculars, the mountain road looked unclear and dim.

Lida noticed his deputy Yanagida approaching with urgent steps. He carried a pad in his hands on which something had been scribbled in a hurried hand. Yanagida gave his boss a crisp salute and stood in attention. Lida's brown eyes closely examined his deputy and noticed two or three deep wrinkles on his forehead.

Cocking his eyebrows, he asked in an authoritarian voice, 'Any disclosures?'

'No, sir.'

'So, those prisoners are still not out with their confession?'

'Not a single word, sir, unfortunately.'

The General's proud face turned tense. He began to see the prisoners' refusal to cooperate as a personal insult. As he walked down the small slope, his shoes creaked.

Small cannons had been mounted on all sides. Right in front were some sixty or seventy mules contentedly chewing on fodder. A mule has the quick-footedness of a horse and the resilience of a donkey. The Japanese forces were exploiting the ability of these beasts to carry heavy loads, using them to drag heavy artillery across to such inaccessible places. It was these mules that had saved the prestige of the Japanese army on numerous occasions.

As he walked down, he growled, 'Yanagida, I won't give these cunning secret agents any more time. This day shall be the last day of their life.'

'Yes, sir,' Yanagida said with a slight bow, 'but I don't think there is any reason for worry. The British authorities have already declared their surrender on the radio and announced the withdrawal of their forces two months ago. I don't see any more danger lurking anywhere around.'

'Yanagida, you don't know anything. I have definite information.'

'Sir?'

'It's always good to remember that those smart-alecs on the bank of the Thames will never retreat permanently from Burma.'

'Yes, sir.'

'They were brought to their knees only because their supplies were cut off. But they are certainly busy preparing to mount a counter-assault on Burma, of this I have definite information.'

'How's that to be done, sir?'

'They have selected twenty-two of their shrewdest, bravest soldiers from the British and the Indian armies and turned them into secret agents who have infiltrated the jungles here.'

'Oh, I see.'

'The men we caught are without a doubt agents from the enemy forces.'

They had descended to a slope with plenty of twists and turns. A temporary but large prison made from bamboo and wood came into view. The prisoners inside looked filthy; they could as well have been wild beasts for all the care that was taken of them. They carried many months of beard on their faces. For bath, they were just given dousings with a bucket of water thrown on them from outside the wooden barracks once a fortnight or so. The clothes on their backs they had been wearing for months, giving them the appearance of cave-dwelling primitives.

Two of these prisoners were Raghav and Akaram Jogta. When they heard the sounds of heavy boots approaching them, Raghav stood up and Akaram began wailing as if a calamity had descended upon him. The clothes they had originally worn had been discarded as rags long ago on the Rangoon road. A small Japanese unit had caught them near Rangoon. Just two months ago, they had been presented before General Lida at Pakaku, a village near Myitkyina.

For the first two or three days, the general had not allowed them to speak. His suspicion of them had risen with each passing day. Here was this fellow Raghav who displayed an immense capacity to tolerate pain. He had to be an agent of the British Indian Army, else he would not have survived the merciless thrashing he was subjected to. The other fellow Akaram Jogta would begin to wail like a woman at the sight of a whip and hop like a dancer in the temple of some Indian goddess. He would howl and cry and mouth curses incessantly. This mismatched pair had confused the Japanese officials.

As soon as he heard the sound of the boots, Raghav got up and went to a corner of the bamboo barrack. The chains and rod tied to his body jangled. He had now become accustomed to these ornaments. They gave him company even when he went to sleep.

When the two were presented before the General, the big man cast a pitiful glance at them. The clothes on their back had become so awfully muck-ridden that they could as well have been dipped in slime and dried out. The hair on their faces made them look like gorillas.

This time, the General made use of his interpreter Chocho. He looked in such fearful temper that the junior officers surrounding him had turned tense. He looked at Raghav with great ferocity and then turned to look at the vulture that sat high on a neighbouring tree. A sneer playing on his lips, he told Raghav through Chocho, 'Look, you Indian shit, look at the vulture sitting on that tree. It simply waits for people to reach the verge of death. Your time has also come. So, it will be better if you confess.'

'Confess to what, sir?'

'Just tell me this much—which unit of the British army do you belong to? What's your rank? Where are the other twenty people who slipped into the Burmese jungles with you? What is the exact nature of your espionage activities? Where has your secret communication system been installed?'

'Sir, your people have been beating me black and blue since the very first day. There isn't a joint in my body that they have not tested, they've stretched my skin tighter than a drum. And I'm telling you clearly again—'

'Yes, speak up.'

'Even if you break my teeth, tear out my cheeks or pull my tongue out of my throat, my answer will remain the same: I am nobody's secret agent. I'm an artiste, an acrobat and nothing else.'

General Lida's face turned red as he turned to Yanagida and said, 'Does he take Japanese generals for complete fools? In the British army you Indians simply lick their boots! You have forgotten your glorious past and have no backbone left. All right, Yanagida, get the firing squad ready—'

Ten soldiers marched in with their guns. Five of them went on their knees while the other five stood behind them, waiting for the command to fire.

Just then, the loud neighing of a horse was heard. Raghav was electrified at the sound. He didn't know whether to laugh or cry. He let out an unsure but loud yell, 'Phakkadrao! Phakkad, I am here! I'm here!'

He was utterly stunned when he next heard Kanchana's call cutting across the dense jungle in response, 'Raghav? Is that Raghav?' The call echoed again and again from all directions.

'Here, Kanchana! Here! I'm still alive. But please, for god's sake, don't try to come here. This place is a trap of death! Please!'

Before the troupe members could make sense of what was happening, Kanchana leapt out of the bushes and sped like an arrow towards Raghav. She rushed to him and held him in a tight embrace.

When Raghav saw Phakkadrao, he understood how Kanchana and the others had managed to trace him in the impossible forest. The horse had begun to lick at Raghav vigorously. Behind Phakkadrao had come the remaining five or six horses of the company and following them were the other male members of the company. It was only the girls who had continued to hide in the bushes for fear of harm.

General Lida was watching the unfolding scenario with bewilderment. With a sign he had conveyed to his men that they should not interrupt the coming together. The prisoner whom he had considered a dangerous agent and this woman who had shot out of the bushes like a deer—their hugging and clinging to each other, the warmth of their love for each other had left the General gawping in astonishment.

Lida's eyes then drifted towards Taranath, Mahadev, Gunga Dobari, Charlie and the rest. Each one of them was carrying a little British girl on their shoulders. What were these European girls doing on the shoulders of these brown men? The confusion was turning knottier by the minute. But of one thing he was now sure: the young man he had all along suspected was no cunning spy, but a regular fellow.

The General's mood softened. He signalled to Yanagida and both Raghav and Akaram were released from their ropes. Kanchana rushed forward and began to massage Raghav's limbs vigorously to bring blood back into them.

She finally turned towards Lida and pleaded, 'Sir, we have nothing at all to do with your war. We are circus artistes. It looks like my poor husband has been taken prisoner on account of some misunderstanding.'

Interpreter Chocho gave the General a flawless translation of Kanchana's words. She then went on to give details of the riots in Rangoon, the massacre of her menagerie, the deadly 2,000-mile journey, and the circumstances in which the British girls had arrived into their camp.

General Lida looked at the ragged band of men assembled around him. He could tell that the concern in Kanchana's voice was genuine. One would need to be particularly stupid not to believe that what the woman had said was most likely true, and Lida prided himself on being an intelligent man. But what about those British girls?

'Hmm,' he finally responded, 'it does appear that we were wrong in thinking of these men as spies. How could a pair of spies have such a retinue of men and animals rooting for them? And a woman who clearly seems to love this man here.'

'Sir,' Kanchana went on, greatly encouraged, 'we are all circus artistes, acrobats. We are members of a circus company that's made a name for itself in the country and internationally too.'

Lida got into consultation with Yanagida and his captains. While the junior officers displayed suppressed excitement, Yanagida was positively cooing at his boss, smiling from ear to ear and rubbing his hands in glee. Lida laughed at the thrill he had generated in his men, nodded vigorously and turned to Kanchana.

'Look here, lady,' he said, 'we are quite inclined to believe your word. But if you are circus artistes, as you claim, could you demonstrate some of your skills for us to judge you by?'

'Of course we can, sir,' she said and whirled around and looked at Raghav, eyes flashing. Raghav read the message, shrugged off the stiffness of so many days and called out to Phakkadrao standing close by, 'Come, son, out in the ring!' He followed that with a whistle that had Phakkadrao trembling all over.

The horse instantly raised its forelegs high, gave its magnificent tail a vigorous shake and trotted up in front. It then began galloping in a circle. Raghav cried out, 'Jai Bhawani! Jai Kalamma!', ran alongside the horse, leapt in his stride and landed on the galloping horse's back. The horse was skillfully trotting in a circle in the available space, while Raghav was now dancing on the animal's back. The spectators were stunned. They watched in awe and broke into applause.

Raghav then began somersaulting as he stood on the horse's back. That done, he jumped off the horse to the earth, and in the next leap went back on the animal without losing his balance or footing. The Japs were awestruck. Could he be the reincarnation of one of their Hindu gods? The popular monkey-god, Hanuman? The thrilling show of horsemanship had even General Lida spellbound. He had involuntarily sprung up from his seat and stood gazing at the miracle, clapping.

When Raghav finally hopped off the horse, Charlie and his band cooled off. Kanchana immediately signalled to him to resume and again teased Phakkadrao back into action. 'Come on, my water sprite,' she shouted, 'show us your colourful dance!' Charlie got his band to pick up a lively tune and brought his flute to his lips. A trumpet, two clarinets and a small drum made of iguana skin got into the beat to create a foot-tapping, energetic number. It was after months of dismal times that such a sparkling piece of music was being heard, and Phakkadrao had come completely under its sway. He shook himself and broke into a vigorous dance. The other four horses also got pulled into the spirit, threw their tails into the wind and joined in. The Japanese were so mesmerised by their show that they all but broke into a jig.

General Lida stood transfixed. What he saw before him was the unprecedented sight of men dancing in a frenzy and horses gamboling as if under a magic spell. His own body, taut and well-maintained with all the karate and judo that he had done, was itching to join the man-and-horse wizardry that was being played out before him. Watching these acrobats in action brought vigour back into the soldiers; it uplifted their spirits.

Fired up by the mission of getting her beloved back, Kanchana strode up to the General and said, 'Sir, are you now convinced? Please believe us. All of us artistes are from the land of your Buddha and of Gandhiji.'

'Oh, Gandi?' With that, he handed over his burning cigar to his orderly, pulled out his wallet, took out a small photograph and thrust it at Kanchana. 'Do you recognise this person?'

'Where's the question of not recognising, sir? I have personally met Gandhiji twice. When I was a kid, he had come to attend a congress in Madras, and next I had met him in the colony of sweepers in Delhi. My father had taken me with him both these times.'

The General smiled a little and pulled out another small photograph. He was turning chattier by the minute. When Kanchana saw the picture, her face lit up with a mix of joy and reverence. That stiffly ironed Gandhi cap, that young, handsome face below it, those earnest eyes, and that sweet, familiar smile playing on his lips—Kanchana broke out in a joyous voice, 'Sir, this is our Subhas Babu! Subhas Chandra Bose! I saw him in Madras once in the company of Jawaharlal Nehru. Besides, I had also run into him on the road near Satara.'

'Yes, we Japanese call him Chandra Bose. Right now, this gentleman is in Germany. Our prime minister, General Tojo, and our other senior officers are going to take an extremely important decision soon. The plan is to call your Chandra Bose here from Europe and to help him all we can in his fight against the British.'

General Lida had lost all his stiffness. He again got into an animated discussion with his officers. But since the conversation was in Japanese, the circus artistes could only guess by the expressions on their faces that things were going well for them.

Finally, looking at Kanchana, General Lido said, 'The show you put up for us army people in this wilderness was amazing. My men and I are thrilled.'

'Thank you, sir.'

'I'll let you go free. But tell me, these girls that you are taking with you, are they British?'

'Yes, sir, they are,' Kanchana said, her voice somewhat wary.

'How did you come upon them?'

'Sir, their school teacher was chaperoning them across this route to the safety of the Indian border. She died on the way, handing over their responsibility to us.'

'In which case, considering that they are British, I will have to ask you to hand them over to us.'

'How can I do that?' Kanchana retorted with some asperity.

'Since they are British, and I'm a general of the Japanese Imperial army, these girls are the progeny of our enemies to us.'

Kanchana hit upon the best argument that she thought would work with this Japanese general. 'Sir, how can I explain their situation to you?' she pleaded. 'If there had been a few women in your unit, I would have handed them over without a thought.'

'We are not so ruthless, young lady,' Lida smiled and said.

'I believe that, sir. Army men like you may provide the shelter a father provides, but who will give them a mother's love and warmth? Without these needs being met, these girls won't survive two days in this murderous jungle.'

General Lida smiled in agreement. The furrows on his brow vanished. He declared that Kanchana could leave with the girls.

Just as Kanchana was about to thank him and depart with her troupe and the girls, the General called over his quartermaster and instructed that they be given as many cans of tinned food, biscuits, pickles and condensed milk as they could carry. The circus crowd grabbed this opportunity and collected enough eatables to last them for the next four or five days.

Holding Kanchana's hand tight, Raghav said, 'What a strange day! In the morning I was staring at a firing squad. Akaram and I were sure of being blown to pieces. But look at fate now, I get to see your beautiful face!'

50

Everyone had, of course, been delighted with the way they had outmaneuvered the Chinese rebels and later escaped the bear hug of the Japanese army. But the wound it had left behind on one of them was causing great consternation. A Chinese rebel's bullet had hit Mahaling's thigh, bringing down a person the size of a tree, and made everyone sick with worry.

'Kaka,' Kanchana would comfort him, 'the pain will subside soon.'

'Pori, this pain has bored a hole through my head. I can't bear it any more. Please shoot me and free me of this agony.'

Hirabai had come to breaking point at the sight of her husband's state. She would stuff an end of her sari in her mouth and try to stifle the sound of her wails. 'The gods first plucked out both my eyes. At least you get better. Otherwise I'll have to bang my head against a tree and finish myself off.'

Mahaling beckoned his wife closer and swept his rough hands over her head. She then placed his head in her lap, which finally brought some sleep to his wearied body.

Mahaling's health worsened with every passing day. It had become impossible for the poor man to even go limping through the torrential rains. They had to make a stretcher for him by pulling a sheet across two bamboo poles so that four persons, one at each end, could carry him across all the mud and slime. The thought of resting on the way was beyond imagination. The rains were expected to intensify and it was important to cross the river Dafa before that. Once this dangerous mountain river got into its stride, it would make crossing impossible for even an army for the next few months.

The food they had brought over from the Japanese was close to running out. As a result, they had to cut down on their consumption and supplement their intake with whatever vegetables they could find in the jungles. Those unwell were served whatever broth could be readily prepared. The British girls had been brought up on bread and butter, and the jungle vegetables often upset their stomach, bringing them down with loose motions. One major relief for everybody was that they had moved out of the cholera-infested region without having suffered.

However, Mahaling developed very high fever and a shooting pain in his abdomen one night. He had turned very weak, and his state had further intensified his wife Hirabai's melancholia. The deep, painful wound left by the atrocities visited upon her daughters Shanta and Babita was nowhere close to healing, and now the Chinese deserters had crippled her husband so badly. 'Raghu dada,' he groaned, 'things are not right with me. These jungles want to claim me after my daughters.'

'No, no, don't say such things.'

'I don't think I'm going to survive this,' Mahaling spoke in a mournful voice. 'Please take care of my Hira after I am gone.'

It was early in the morning and everyone was moving as fast as possible through the slime covered terrain, moving into a leviathan of a mountain looming over them from a height of 6,000 feet or more. Negotiating it in this blinding rain was a task that even the gods would have found difficult to perform, but waiting the rains out was not an option either. Hence they moved, without stopping, without tiring. That very narrow track along which they moved sometimes looked like a worm crawling in the slime, or it suddenly shot up so straight and high that it looked like a greenish vine snake travelling up a tree trunk.

It didn't take much time for such jungles to break into a rash of moss and slush everywhere; four or five days of good rainfall were generally enough. This year, the rains had begun in the second half of May. All jungle paths, mountain trails and defiles had turned dense green already. The circus troupe would occasionally travel past water-filled rice fields, where the path winding over the embankments would often be nothing more than mud and slime. By and large, walking across the flat lands did not create much trouble, but sometimes a human or an animal foot would suddenly sink into an invisible hole below, and pulling it out of that suction would often test the mettle of both man and animal.

Merely four of their horses had survived, not counting Phakkadrao. The load that they carried had also gone on reducing steadily. In order to increase their speed, Kanchana had abandoned a number of heavy goods, things like silver boxes, trunks and wooden cases, which were expensive but inessential. Even so, whatever little was left had become a burden for the poor, emaciated animals to carry on their backs. They often tumbled on their faces when their forelegs suddenly sank into the sludgy earth. When the loads on their backs were heavy, the nylon rope for keeping the loads secure on their backs would be tied rather tight. The undulations of the track would often cause the luggage to shift forward or backward, making the ropes bite into their skins and create wounds and abrasions. That would bring the jungle flies buzzing in, causing the abrasions to suppurate. Some of their injuries would not even respond to the application of jungle herbs.

Sometimes the vegetation on both sides of the trail was too dense for Rajmangala to muscle her way through. On such occasions, a team of men would go up with their machetes, chop off the obstruction and clear the way for the elephant to pass. When they ran into patches that were terribly uneven, pocked with holes and debris, another team would rush forward and smoothen the way ahead.

It was a strange, unpleasant day for Rajmangala. For the past two days she had been suffering from diarrhoea, discharging watery excreta with disturbing frequency. In the previous two stops the troupe had made, jungle flies and mosquitoes had been making life miserable for her.

The next morning was relatively better—the intensity of the rains had reduced. The road, however, was still slippery and difficult and it was uphill all the way. They would see the top of a hill and buck themselves up to reach it at a good clip; but once there, the top of another hill would come into view, and yet another one beyond, everyone of them promising an arduous, dangerous climb. How high did one have to go on climbing? How many more hills? How many twists and turns? Did the road actually have an end at all?

They had decided to make a small halt in the afternoon and eat some of the food in their stock. But just then, a brand new problem suddenly stood looming right in front of them. The very sight of it made their heart jump into their mouth. A colossal twenty-five foot rock stood bang in the middle of their path like a black djinn. Going round it was impossible because the slopes on both sides plunged sharply. Trying to negotiate those slopes was a sure invitation to being hurled hundreds of feet into the canyons below.

It didn't take much time, however, for the initial fear to dissipate considerably. They all had the blood of circus artistes coursing through their arteries. The rock was a challenge for them to shake off their idleness of so many days and finally flex their muscles. The sight of the rock excited them and made their hearts beat faster. They fished out from their luggage the strong, durable ropes they used in their shows. They chopped up bamboos for rungs and soon had a rope ladder ready for use.

The first thing they did was to secure Mahaling tightly to his stretcher. Holding the stretcher straight up, eight strong men got in front and below and rapidly climbed the ladder, carrying the stretcher up to the top. The next set of circus men tied deep, three-cornered Naga baskets to their backs, similar to the kinds used in tea gardens, seated the British girls inside the baskets and made their way up. The journey was so thrilling for the girls that they clapped their hands in glee all the way up.

When it was time for the seventy odd circus girls to climb up, the very sight of the rope ladder made their eyes shine with excitement. It had been an everyday routine for them to go tripping up such ladders to reach their trapeze swings under the circus roof. The walk across the jungles on thorny, stony tracks had caused the soles of their feet to break into blisters; now, with the opportunity of doing their favourite walk up a rope-ladder literally swinging before them under the 1,000-pole roof of the sky, they were thrilled. They went waltzing up rapidly, laughing and screaming in delight all the way. Once they were up there, the men carried the older ayahs on their shoulders and scaled the rock.

From the top, they looked down at the deep gorges and ravines below them, with their streams and waterfalls, the velvet green of the vegetation spreading across for miles. The sight filled them with awe. But when their eyes turned towards the foot of the rock, they saw the five horses, including Phakkadrao, and the 3,000-kilo Rajmangala, and their spirits plummeted. The thought of bringing up that mountain-sized weight made their limbs go cold. Their throats went dry and lumps developed in the pit of their stomach.

When Kanchana saw their crestfallen faces, she immediately got after them. 'Why are you standing there with such long faces? The water sloshing inside you is the water of the Krishna, the Koyna and the Varna. Let's show the water of these lands of China and Burma the stuff that our water is made of. There is no stopping us.'

The circus men immediately got busy. Having anticipated their needs for this journey across the wilderness, they had kept sufficient packing cloth and ropes with them. Raghav and Kanchana had also placed upon them the burden of carrying ten six-foot long poles made of steel. The helpers stepped forward and bolted two poles together to give them five twelve-foot poles. They placed them parallel to each other, tied bamboos across them and assembled a raft strong enough to carry the weight of an elephant.

There was enough man-power available, and it didn't take them long to tie ropes that would pull the raft up. The plan was to carry one animal at a time. They would be tightly secured to the raft with ropes. The horses were blindfolded with strips to cloth to ensure that they didn't get disoriented and confused with the ground dipping rapidly below them. This was how the five horses were lifted up one after the other.

Once on top, the blindfold was taken off Phakkadrao's eyes. The horse peered down to see Rajmangala standing at the foot of the rock. It was for the first time since he had known her that she looked scared. Phakkadrao neighed in delight and communicated to her through the flash in his eyes, 'No reason to worry, my friend, the trek is not as difficult as it looks.' This was exactly how he had neighed delightfully when he had spotted her in the bazaar at Mandalay after she had broken away from the company.

Hauling up the elephant to the top of a twenty-five foot high rock, however, was a different challenge altogether. Kanchana herself went down to help Rajmangala board the raft. As

Rajmangala was being secured to the raft by ropes, she patted the elephant on the back as a gesture of reassurance. Dagdoba was a smart person. Kanchana had been yelling at him all these days to discard heavy stuff like steel chains, but he had steadily been ignoring her. It was now those very chains that were being used to secure Rajmangala to the raft. Kanchana took this opportunity to express her gratitude for Dagdoba's foresight. 'Dagdu dada, if it hadn't been for you, we would have been left with no choice but to leave my darling Rajmangala behind in these jungles.'

Meanwhile, serious discussions were underway on top of the rock. The air was wet, the rock was wet and covered with a layer of moss, but choices there were none. Strategy and determination were required to bring Rajmangala up safe and sound. Raghav patted Phakkadrao's back with confidence. Stout harnesses were placed on Phakkadrao and two other horses. Strong ropes were attached to the harness which the horses would have to pull up together, in the manner in which bullocks draw water up a well in leathern bags over a pulley. Everybody else would be pulling the ropes tied to the other edges of the raft that would bring the elephant up.

Down below, at the foot of the rock, once Kanchana was sure that Rajmangala had been securely tied to the raft, she climbed up the rope ladder to the top. The process of pulling that giant load up a straight 90° drop began. It was not impossible for the rope to develop a twist or to get caught or even snap somewhere, hence it was important for a human to be with the elephant on the raft, and Sulaiman volunteered to do this. A wide-blade knife in one hand and a goad in the other, he took his position alongside Rajmangala.

Everybody held their breath. There was tense silence everywhere. Suddenly one of the crowd let out a battle cry: *'Pundlik, Harivarade Shri Gyaneshwar Tukaram Maharaj ki Jai!'*, and everybody responded with a resounding 'Jai!'. Rajmangala's head had been secured to the raft. She sat looking indifferent to all the activity around her. As the raft slowly began to move upwards, the spectators' hopes rose with it. The hands that were pulling the ropes had got into a strong rhythm. Everybody cheered the pullers on: 'Pull … dear friends … pull hard! One … two … up! One … two … up!'

One set of ropes had been tied to the harnesses of the horses. Care had been taken to ensure that it did not suddenly give way; one end of it was tied to the trunk of a robust tree. Within a short time, the raft had risen quite close to the upper ledge. The girls too joined in: 'Pull … friends … pull hard! One … two … up!' Rajmangala too felt the sense of victory and glee, and joined in with her own joyous trumpet. The air suddenly began to throb with the thrill of the adventure.

Just then, a tormented, tortured shriek assailed everyone's ears. It was Phakkadrao neighing in unendurable agony. One of his hoofs had lost its grip on the wet surface of the rock, and in an effort to gain some kind of a grip, he had tried to get some purchase on the moss with his hoofs. They went scraping across the rough surface and left a trail of blood all over. Phakkadrao got tangled in the rope that he had been pulling with two other horses and he slipped over the edge in an effort to somehow break his skid. The other two horses that had been yoked to the same rope fell as they lost their own balance. It was very difficult for anyone to really understand the sequence of events from the top or foot of the rock, but what they did see was blood gushing out from under the two horses.

Kanchana rushed to the edge and peeped down, only to be struck by a bolt of lightning. She collapsed where she stood, unable to coax a sound out of her gaping mouth. Phakkadrao had been thrown over the ledge, and the nylon rope tied to the leather harness round his neck had suddenly twisted itself to form a noose in which the horse was now choking. He was frantically thrashing his legs in the air as he swung by the rope.

His bloodshot eyes appeared to be ready to fall out of their sockets. There was froth bubbling out of his nose and mouth.

By sheer force of will, Kanchana found her voice, gained some control over herself and shrieked, 'Raghav! He's getting strangled! Our Phakkadrao is hanging by a noose! Cut that rope! Snap it from the top here! Cut it!'

'Yes, I'm coming!' Raghav yelled out, his voice echoing back from all sides.

'Don't waste time! Cut it now! Cut the rope now! Or Phakkadrao will surely die!'

'Just hang on for a bit!' The hills and the valleys sent the cry resounding in multiple echoes.

'What are you waiting for, you idiot,' she screamed hoarsely.

'All right!' Raghav shouted back in annoyance. 'I'll cut it right now. But keep in mind that the raft has just arrived at the brink of the ledge. If the rope is snapped now, it will just go hurtling down the way it climbed, Rajmangala, Sulaiman and all the rest of them!'

Kanchana lost her mind. A shiver ran through her and she ran towards the wet tree in front. She began banging her head against the trunk and cried, 'Why this, Mother Kalamma? How much more do you want to test us? My people, my animals?'

51

The agonies of survival and dying, the calls, the grunts, they all took strange colourings in the wilderness here.

The sky turned rapidly dim late in the afternoon and darkness began to descend into the gorges and ravines in an unseemly hurry. The circus team had managed somehow to do the impossible and bring the raft over the ledge, with Rajmangala in it. But once the tension was off the ropes on the raft side, some of their ends had turned loose on the other side, which caused them to go racing down with Phakkadrao choking at the other end. The poor horse crashed on the rock below with such force that he would certainly have broken his back. His head lay at an unnatural angle to his body. It wasn't clear what was bubbling out of his mouth—froth or blood. Although the skin hadn't broken anywhere, there were big swellings in many places, suggesting that ribs and bones had smashed and the blood released under the skin was collecting in pockets inside.

A twitch or two, and Phakkadrao turned still. His soul had fled. Raghav had been holding his grief in check for a long time. Once the twitching stopped, his dam burst with a loud, heart-rending cry. When the seniors of the company signalled an immediate departure, he addressed them and Kanchana with folded hands and said, 'Wait, wait please! Give me a little more time. Let me run my hand once over my darling Phakkad's face before leaving!'

'How's that possible, Raghav?' Kanchana protested, 'Even if you decide to lower yourself down there, it'll be a few hours of work. This death-dealing road has snatched away happiness from every one of us. Get a grip of yourself. We must move on.'

It was with the greatest difficulty that Raghav was made to see reason.

The darkness gathered on the mountains peaks had begun rolling downwards. Everybody had frozen stiff with the shock of the accident. The uppermost thought in everybody's mind was to clear out of that doomed place and move to the security of a plateau somewhere.

Rajmangala's face had turned dark with anguish. The two horses that remained were refusing to stir an inch. Phakkadrao's death rattle had bored deep holes into their consciousness. They would stretch their necks involuntarily to peep over the ledge beyond which their leader lay dead and withdraw in horror. Their strength and stamina had drained out of them, but it was not in Kanchana's blood to forsake her men or animals. If the saving of the remaining lives required her to carry her burden of sorrow and plod on, then that was exactly what she would do. She took two fistfuls of some cooked food and fed one each to the two terrified horses. Then she held their heads close to her chest and ran her fingers through their manes.

Then she went down on her knees and held the animals by their legs. Standing up after this, she began to walk. The poor, beaten, emaciated animals turned towards her with their mournful eyes and stepped forward.

Soon all of them were striding rapidly out of that dark valley, making their way upwards.

52

The cycle of misfortunes kept turning interminably. The perpetual assault of adversities, however, had still not drained Kanchana of mental and physical strength. There was the joy of having managed the impossible of saving Rajmangala, but the loss of Phakkadrao had almost amputated her hands.

The bullet embedded in Mahaling's thigh had turned his leg gangrenous. He came down with a raging fever in the night, and on the third morning he took his last breath. Hirabai sat on her heels and watched blankly as her husband was consigned to the earth. The jolt of losing him turned her into a block of wood. She just sat there with a vacant face—no tears, no weeping or beating of breast.

Raghav and Kanchana could sense that fear, distrust and dissension had begun showing in the company and were threatening to weaken its foundation. A few of them had begun to resent the presence of the British girls and the drain of resources required for their upkeep. Some others thought their presence was slowing down their pace. Dagdoba dada had never been the kind to get into disputations of any kind, but here he was now, scratching his dense beard and saying in a peevish tone, 'May I say a few words?'

Some other disgruntled souls saw the opportunity and gathered under a tree for an impromptu meeting. Taranath began, 'We hear that the river Dafa is no more than a few days' march from here. Cross that, and we are in India. But it seems that we have deliberately slowed down our movement. We are crawling, when we should be running.'

'Kanchana, pori, can't we move a little faster than this?' said Dagdoba.

'How is it possible, kaka? You see Rajmangala's state? And then we have those British girls too. Delicate as butterflies. They'd die if pushed too hard.'

'See, Raghav dada? You see now?' a few voices piped up from behind. 'See what fancy our Didi has taken to those girls with white skin? What we cannot understand is how her heart can go out to the brats of those White bastards whose guns so totally exterminated our circus.'

'Look, I don't care for boundaries of countries. I don't see people's colour, caste and creed either. If my mad heart gets entangled in the love of humans and animals the world over, what do I do?'

'But they're Christian! British—'

'What's all this, Raghav? I fought for them with that Japanese general. When a baby slips out of the mother's womb, there is no god standing there with stamp and ink-pad to mark it as White or Black, Hindu or Christian, German or Japanese.'

That left everyone speechless. But sure enough, in a while floated a grouse from behind, 'So then we'll find our relief only in death, yes?'

'Why should you die? Think about this: with the kind of resources and connections in the administration I had in Rangoon, would it have been difficult for me to manage two air tickets or two seats in a boat sailing to India? Raghav and I could easily have slipped out and saved our own lives. That's not what we would ever do. Circumstances have taken such a peculiar turn. Here stands Rajmangala teetering on the edge of death, there sits Hirabai who lost her entire family on this journey and neither of them has the strength to take two steps forward. So then, tell me, what do you think I should do?'

The assembly was again reduced to silence, with no solution in sight for the problem that had been simmering. Kanchana scanned all the anxious faces surrounding her and said, 'Look, I have an excellent way out. It makes no sense to give in to sentiments and remain stuck here with upwards of 300 stomachs to feed. It can only mean starvation; we are already living through it. So, please, will you listen to what I have to say?'

'What's that?' Dagdoba asked.

'I will stay behind with Rajmangala, Hira-aatya and these little girls. If Hira-aatya and Rajmangala's health improves, I shall set off immediately behind you; if not, I will just hang back for a few months and take life as it comes.'

'But what about the rest of the company?'

'Raghav will travel with you as the owner of the company.'

53

A soaking wet morning. There was no time to lose by thinking too much. A quick decision was absolutely imperative.

A malevolent spirit seemed to be hovering over the company, hungrily looking for opportunities to consume it, piece-meal or in one single gulp. In the sky above too, steadily darkening clouds had been patrolling for a few days now, eyes bulging, itching to come thundering down any time.

It hardly mattered where the assault arrived from—whether from the earth or from the sky—defence was almost impossible. The demons of the wilderness wanted more and more human flesh and blood to feed on.

The burden that Kanchana would be required to carry alone was that of the weak and ailing—a very heavy weight, and very fragile too. There lay Hirabai, rolled up like a bundle of rags, cooking in her own fever. The British and Burmese girls were not in any better state either. A few of them had been suffering from runny bowels; cholera again, quite likely. Carrying these delicate wards safely through rain and slush across those thorny tracks for another three days was an intimidating task.

Rajmangala lay on the other side of the slushy path, her trunk listless. There was some serious mess inside her stomach. The grating sound in her throat had worsened. Her breath and her grunts sounded like a metal floor being swept out by a thorny bamboo broom. Could she have sensed the disaster that time had wrought upon the company? She needed two or three days of absolute rest. Without that, even her pillar-sized legs would crumple on the way like dry grass.

The decision was finally taken in the afternoon. One set of people began gathering together the remnants of their belongings that could be carried, while the hardier set pulled out their axes and machetes and got into the bamboo bushes. They hacked out stout bamboo poles and sturdy branches, dressed them, and in quick time they had erected a hut that would provide warmth and shelter. The walls were made by weaving tree stems and supple bamboo shoots tightly together. For roofing they used a single sheet of tarpaulin that the Japanese had given them. This was a piece of good fortune, because the usual thatch roof and thatch walls would have become home to all kinds of disease-carrying worms and insects and leeches and made settling down difficult.

The company crossed the stream later in the afternoon, with Raghav in the lead. Even as Kanchana stood and watched, the caravan had gone and climbed the dense green hillock yonder. Suddenly she noticed that they had all halted. They had stopped to catch their breath, perhaps. They were taking a last, lingering look at where she was stationed, perhaps, capturing images for future memories. Then they moved on and disappeared from sight. The hillock suddenly turned desolate.

Kanchana now had Hirabai, the young girls and Rajmangala with her. Also with her were two strapping young boys named Bheemu and Apparao, who had been forced upon her, despite her protestations. That made it a party of eleven people and one cow-elephant.

As the sky darkened, the entire ambience suddenly took on a forbidding appearance. As the evening deepened, the gloom swallowed up the bobbing mountain tops and the rustling streams and springs, leaving the roaring winds in solitary command.

Kanchana lit up the hearth. She gathered whatever wild vegetables were at hand, crushed some garlic pods and got some Burmese peyheen soup ready. There was no salt in it, but the garlic had compensated by bringing a pleasurable tang into the steaming drink. The girls slurped it up greedily. A completely exhausted Hirabai had lowered herself near the warm hearth and passed out. When repeated efforts to wake her up failed, Kanchana sat down and took her head upon her lap. She forced open the Hirabai's fevered lips and poured a few spoons of the soup into her mouth. That over, Hirabai again rolled over and slipped back into her swoon.

The night wind was blowing at a steady pace. Suddenly there was a sound of feet walking across the slush outside the door of the hut. Two of the girls got up in fright and moved closer to Kanchana. Making a reassuring sign to them, Kanchana called out from where she was, 'There's no latch inside. Just open the door and come in.' The thatch door opened and in walked Raghav, soaked to the bone. He gave the impression of having crossed several rivers to reach here.

Raghav gave his body a vigorous shake, dried himself with a piece of cloth as well as he could and came and sat near the hearth. The faces of the half-awake girls lit up at the sight of Raghav.

'*Aho*, you should at least have escorted them up to the bank of that river!' Kanchana said in mock reprimand.

'Our company girls came down on me like a ton of bricks,' Raghav offered by way of explanation. 'They were furious. How could I have abandoned their Didi in the middle of the jungle! Didi is their friend, their benefactor, their mother-figure ... They absolutely refused to allow anybody a word in between.'

'Well, all right. Then?'

'What could I do, then? Handed over to Taranath and Dagdoba some money for expenses on the way and some gold, and turned round instantly.'

Kanchana laughed softly to herself. Reading her mind, Raghav asked in a mischievous tone, 'Why, Kanchana, didn't you like my coming back to you?'

'How can you say this, Raghav? Who can be happier than I am right now? Don't you know that the wounds of a life time, all my aches and pains now respond to your salves alone?'

54

For two nights running it was just consuming peyeen gruel-rice and sleeping. On the morning that followed, Raghav showed some bustle. He took Bheema and Apparao with him, chopped some stout tree branches and bamboos growing along the stream and added an extension to the hut. Rajmangala now had her own private bedroom.

As Raghav sat downing his gruel in the afternoon, he observed Rajmangala carefully as she sat chewing at the wet fodder that Apparao had served to her. The weather being damp and cold as it was, this wet food would simply not do for the elephant, and he was racking his brains on what could be done. He got up after a little while, called over the boys and the three of them went into the jungle again with their axes and machetes. Kanchana heard Raghav's delighted call much before dusk. She dashed out of the hut to see the three of them carrying big loads of green banyan branches on their heads, grinning from ear to ear. The sight of all those leaves cheered her up too. Rajmangala suddenly caught the heavenly whiff and shot up like a spring toy. For a pachyderm like her, leaves of the banyan tree were no less than a seven-course dinner for humans. That evening, Rajmangala had a grand dinner and slept with a smile on her lips.

On the morning of the third day, they were all lazily stretched out on pieces of cloth. It had been after months that their worn-down legs had known of two continuous days of rest. The knots in the limbs had released. Suddenly a loud, harsh cawing of jungle birds broke out. It could well mean the oriental rat-snake or a python, or some other predatory creature. But to the trained ears of the hut dwellers, it sounded different. To them, the commotion of the feathered heralds suggested a bigger movement happening down the trail yonder.

Curiosity brought them all rushing out and the hut fell empty. They ran up to a mound on the side and began peering into the distant trail where it emerged from the slushy, rotting undergrowth. What met their eyes was an unprecedented sight. There were about twenty rifle-carrying soldiers of the British Indian Army in the lead, and it seemed that there were as many bringing up the rear. In the middle was a raft-like structure made of stout bamboos and to that structure was secured a commodious chair, and sitting on the chair like a cobra with its hood spread wide was a big-built, blonde-haired phenomenon. This Bada Sahib's thick head of hair was pulled back in the fashion of the times and on his face he sported thick, big whiskers under a bushy pair of eyebrows. There he sat pulling on a cheroot as some fifteen or so palanquin bearers carried him with dispatch on their shoulders over the miserable road.

The bearers belonged to the local Naga community and had evidently been chosen with the greatest care for their strong, well-built, muscular bodies. Being natives, they knew how to handle the track best, and would have been hired at exorbitant prices. There were two other similarly secured chairs on rafts, but they were smaller in size. One of them was occupied by a high-class British memsahib. The entire retinue would have counted eighty to ninety persons, and they were speeding with a substantial supply of food and other necessary provisions.

As Kanchana peered at their faces, she suddenly remembered where she had seen this gentleman before. It was while she was climbing up and down the stairs of the British administrative buildings at Myitkyina that she had seen this face, even if from a distance. She suddenly shouted, 'The DC, the DC! He's the Deputy Commissioner of Myitkyina!'

The hubbub of the march had brought the girls too running up to the mound. Not in their wildest dreams could they have visualised the passing of such an entourage through this godforsaken land. They were White men, Kanchana thought, the same class as the girls; they might be willing to take their responsibility, she began to hope wildly. The contingent suddenly climbed up the incline and was now straight in front of them. This was a rare opportunity to be grabbed with both hands. If they didn't step forward and sing out their grievances now, this opportunity would slip away. The retinue was now barely ten feet away from them.

Kanchana, Raghav and the two boys quickly lifted the British girls closest to them and stood right in front of the passing cavalcade. 'Sir, sir!' they began yelling to attract the attention of the big man, 'please stop, sir!' The sudden clamour brought the palanquin bearers instinctively to a halt. The big man rested his light eyes on Kanchana and Raghav for a moment. Taking advantage of this, Kanchana called out in an importunate voice, 'Honourable sir, sir, these are your kids! British kids! Just take them along with you, sir, we don't want anything for ourselves. Please save them! Please offer your protection to these flowers of god, sir! Please, sir! Please wait, sir! Listen to us! Please don't be so ruthless, sir!'

Kanchana petitioned and implored and went on her knees, but she couldn't penetrate the calluses that had grown round the administrator's unfeeling heart. All that he emitted was a puff of cheroot smoke from his swollen lips. He lifted his left hand and brought it down smartly on the arm of his chair, which, translated into words, told his bearers, 'How dare you stop! Keep moving, you rascals!'

The cavalcade resumed its uncaring, remorseless way forward. Kanchana squeezed the child in her arm tight against her chest and sank to her knees in despair. The beautiful woman who sat on the chair behind the DC's cast a curious look at the girls clinging to the dirty shirts of those dark Indians. But that was only for a second. She turned her face away quite quickly in the other direction, as if she had never seen the kids. The DC, however, had put on display the highest degree of administrative skill in ensuring that he, his family and his flunkeys didn't get trapped in the wishy-washy notions of responsibility and accountability.

That evening, Kanchana and Raghav gathered the children tight in their arms and lavished all their affection on them. Raghav let out a deep sigh and said, 'It's amazing, isn't it, that human beings can develop such stony, unfeeling hearts? They've gone and done just that, these British administrators. Wicked and inhuman! There are tens of thousands of children from the schools and orphanages of Mandalay and Rangoon tramping down this unforgiving trail right now. Countless among them have been trampled into the jungle floor like blades of grass, and yet the DC can sit pulling on his cheroot and stride on.'

'Forget it, Raghavrao! Let's be thankful for not being like them. We've spent an entire lifetime holding mute animals to our chest as if they were born of our own womb. These girls are human children, after all. The colour of their skin may be different, but their laughter and cries are the same as ours, aren't they?'

55

They had now travelled almost 1,300 miles since leaving Rangoon. Mountains of calamities had collapsed on their heads, rivers of sorrow had overflowed the banks along the way, but the kind of loneliness that descended upon them now was something they had never experienced before. The soul-destroying depression of this desolate, wet mountainous land began to cut deep into both Kanchana and Raghav.

The British girls had names like Dolly, Rosanna, Anne, Lilian and suchlike. Just for the fun of it, Kanchana rechristened them as Jai, Jui, Shevanti, Phulvanti, Mogri, Sadaphuli and Champakali. This brought them somewhat closer to Kanchana's heart. They were also easier for her to pronounce. But she would keep forgetting who had been named what, and then she would simply address them as *beti*, daughter. They, in turn, would address her as Mother, and Raghav as Papa. These girls would burrow into her like bees getting into their hives. They often took the gloom away from the dark, dreary nights of the jungles.

It was natural for Rajmangala and the girls to take a liking to each other. The elephant spent her entire time in close proximity with Raghav, Kanchana and the girls.

The wilderness, the untamed winds and the unfolding circumstances had sharpened their senses. The slightest unusual sound would make them prick their ears. One night it seemed that there was someone out there in the swamps, shivering in the biting, merciless breeze, trying to shrink into a ball and roll himself into a warm place like a wild animal. Kanchana, however, did not want to take any chances. She picked up the kukari, a sharp Nepali blade, and softly but swiftly opened the door. But for the skin on him, the man standing outside could have been a bare skeleton rattling in the wind. He had on a tattered army uniform and the hair on his head and face had matted up with grime. He gave the impression of a wild fox that had reached the last stages of starvation.

The man was very likely a soldier of the British Indian army who had lost his way. He was shivering violently, desperate to find some source of warmth. When he saw a half-burnt hearth inside the room, he didn't bother with courtesies and hobbled straight up to it. Once there, he just went limp and crashed to the floor. In a minute, he had fallen fast asleep. He didn't seem to pose any danger. The poor, emaciated man was fighting for his own life.

In a little while, a strange reek spread across the hut, to the extent that some began to sneeze and cough. Kanchana fished out some carom seeds and tossed them into the embers. The strong smell of the carom slowly began to overcome the malodour.

When she got up in the morning, she saw their filthy guest sleeping on his stomach. Kanchana could see signs that the man had got up, half-roasted a bunch of slim bamboo stems and chewed them up before going back to sleep.

The sun had finally appeared outside and the rains had withdrawn. Everybody was served with a round of peyheen. The two boys had found a few hands of wild bananas, which helped settle the hunger pangs a little bit.

Another hour, and the soldier sprang up from his sleep like a wraith. His name was Gyan Singh, he said, and he was from Punjab. He had two brothers, a pair of twins, who were, like him, serving in the British Indian Army, and could right now be wandering around in some jungle somewhere. Gyan Singh had somehow drifted into a trail that would lead him to Milestone 102, and had been moving along rapidly for upwards of forty days, and had now finished off in this hut. His two brothers, however, were still missing. Before they had drifted apart, they had decided to return to their motherland together. A few months back, they were on the verge of getting married together under the same roof on the same day; but a telegram had suddenly arrived that had sucked them into the jaws of the World War.

The demoniacal route had reduced the three brothers to wretchedness. Gyan Singh said, 'There's a river two and a half days' walk away from here— the Dafa. I waited for a full month on its banks for my brothers.'

'Really? So, what was the point in coming back all the way here?'

'There's not a soul left there. Not so much as a worm crawling. The slopes have all disappeared. In fact, the river has swallowed up the valleys on either side.'

'One full month on the bank of a mountain river? How did you manage it?'

'Well, actually I met a holy man there. A perfect saint of a man. He owns some twelve or fifteen elephants, and has a team of mahauts taking care of them. He uses these elephants to carry across the river as many displaced people and runaway soldiers as he can manage. People on the other side—in Imphal, Assam—and the Nagas on this side affectionately refer to him as "Elephant Uncle".'

'Interesting! Who could this person be?'

'His name is Robert Dickens. He works as a manager of a big tea estate in Assam. A native of Scotland. He loves elephant breeding. This last month alone he helped thousands cross over to the other side on elephant-back.'

'Amazing!' broke in Kanchana. 'Where will we find them, your Robert Dickens and his elephants?'

'On the other side. But, ma'am, the Dafa river has taken on such a wild form that it can wash away mountains if they dare obstruct it.'

Kanchana gave Gyan Singh one of Raghav's lungis and a kerchief. He went to the stream flowing on the other side, and returned with a clean body and a washed set of clothes.

When he saw Kanchana in a downcast mood, he asked, 'You look very worried, ma'am. Is anything bothering you?'

'It's now been five days since my company of about 300 people headed in the direction of the river. I don't know whether they managed to cross it, or are stuck on this side.'

Dinner that night consisted of wild bananas cooked into a dish accompanied by some rice. The girls went to sleep soon enough, but Kanchana knew no rest. The bug that had got into her head refused to relent. Had her company people managed to cross the river or not?

She went over to where Rajmangala stood. She ran a loving hand over her rough trunk and said, 'See what's happening, my darling? My little girls have shrunk so much from starvation, and fear. They can't be weighing any more than a sheaf of grass.'

Rajmangala gave every sign of hearing and understanding. She flapped her ears—large as winnowing baskets—and looked as if a successful exchange of information was taking place. Whether it's man or animal, it so often happens that the best remedy for many an ailment is words of affection. As Kanchana's monologue went on, Rajmangala showed distinct signs of wellness.

Raghav too had decided to give the river a serious shot. A unanimous decision was made before they went to sleep: they would set off at the earliest and reach the river bank. They were up at the crack of dawn the next day, packing all their belongings. Hirabai and the seven kids were asked to sit inside the baskets resting on Rajmangala's back. There were other things too. Raghav, Kanchana and the two boys decided to carry the load of the sacks and bags on their heads, shoulders and arms. They now had Gyan Singh with them. He would show them the best route to their destination.

They made two halts on the way. It couldn't be called a way at all, actually, because no feet seemed to have crossed it. There was no settlement close by either, hence no weekly market to which people could have been coming and going. It was thick bamboo jungles all the way, occasionally replaced by dense shrubbery. The five adults carried heavy blades with which they cleared the way for Rajmangala to pass through. The rain fell, heavy and incessant.

Sometimes they would hit wide stretches of grasslands laden thick with growth. There was danger of suddenly falling into invisible pits that were aplenty in the ground. Some of them were deep enough to reach up to a man's chest. The remedy was to keep poking at the earth with long bamboo sticks. More than the humans, if Rajmangala were to fall into one of those traps, bringing her out of it would be next to impossible. They no longer had any bullocks at their disposal for this purpose.

They managed as much speed as they could and reached the bank of the Dafa on the third day. They were immediately rewarded with the sight of biscuit wrappers and empty food tins floating in the slime. It looked like they had been only lately tossed away. When Raghav noticed the stamp of the British Indian Army and the picture of the Queen of England on them, he cried out in glee, 'If the DC's convoy has crossed the river, as it seems, then our company would certainly have crossed a couple of days earlier!'

But for all these positive signs, neither Raghav nor Kaachana were fully satisfied. Seeing them anxious, Gyan Singh handed Kanchana a sort of black pipe. It was a telescope. Gyan Singh laughed at her surprise, scratched his beard and said, 'In all this running around through the wilderness, there are just three things that I have held on to: my life, my pistol and my telescope.'

The bank was densely covered with vegetation. In front, towards the right, a deepish stream went and met the river. The men logged some wood and erected a makeshift hut at the spot. Rajmangala too went for a stroll in either direction of the hut. They now had to wait for the water current to subside. Gyan Singh had ample experience of these parts. 'This is the sole spot from where you can cross the Dafa from Burma into Assam,' he said. 'That makes it a strategic place for controlling movements and action in all directions.'

The rains would stop for barely an hour or two in a day. The water refused to show any sign of slackening. The noise that it created through the night made it appear like a thousand alligators and crocodiles had begun to lament in mournful voices. The first night was so scary that the little girls could get no sleep at all. But strangely, Hirabai, who seemed to have sewn up her lips till now, suddenly piped up in excitement. She clapped her hands in joy at these mournful sounds and laughed loudly at the clamour of the water. All was clearly not well with her.

One day they noticed through the pouring rain the movement of dark hairy animals on the other side. Their first guess was that they could be rather large sheep. But once the rains had subsided, the scene cleared. They were bisons of the Burmese jungles, the *pyaung*. They were known to be dangerous and it would pay to be cautious. Instead of humps on their shoulders, these bisons had a large mass of muscles that indicated their enormous strength. They looked aggressive and mean, and possessed particularly sharp horns.

It rained cats and dogs for four days in a row and then stopped entirely for the next two days. The night sounds were punctuated by what sounded like Dakotas crossing the sky with considerable frequency.

A little on this side of daybreak. The morning air was whistling away with abandon. Kanchana, who had been lying with her body curled up tight, suddenly opened her eyes and sprang to a sitting position. She peered through a hole in the grass wall and saw a few flames drifting on the other side. She sensed the sound of a crowd of people approaching. She shook Raghav awake; Gyan Singh and the others woke up too. They ran outside to an elevated spot behind the hut and squinted deep into the dark. Very soon they saw countless deep yellow flames of torches that soon began to show the silhouettes of those carrying them.

Well over forty soldiers were scrambling down the slope, and they were hurrying towards the river bank in visible excitement. But how could they possibly cross the black, raging waters? Then, suddenly, the bubbly sound of heavy objects being immersed in water reached them, and Gyan Singh recognised it instantly. As the darkness dissolved and the fog evaporated, the lumbering forms on the other bank could now be identified. Eight elephants were trying to get into the water at the same time. Gyan Singh didn't have much investigation to do.

The bank on the Indian side was astir with mahauts and Naga men looking for spots for lowering their beasts into the water. At little distances, the elephants were being persuaded to step in and test the depth and strength of the flow. Meanwhile, the ragged, haggard soldiers on the nearer bank found themselves perches on the rocks and tree stumps and waited with unconcealed fervour for the elephants on the other side to cross over to their side and take them across to India.

Gyan Singh understood that this was a bunch of lost soldiers and the Army Base at Assam would have got information of them. It appeared that the army had then made this adventurous plan of getting these soldiers across the river as soon as circumstances allowed.

Kanchana, Raghav, Bheema and Apparao involuntarily turned towards each other, and exchanged looks of irrepressible ardour. Again, as if maneuvered by an unknown force, they looked towards Rajmangala. Raghav broke the spell by shouting out, 'You see it, Kanchana, don't you? The elephants on the other side will cross over soon and carry these soldiers back to India! Our India! So, why should we hang around rotting here?'

'I too am eager to leap across to the other side, but how do we cross this mountain of water in the middle?'

'On our Rajmangala's back!'

'But think, Raghav, she is still recovering from an incapacitating illness. Besides, the current in the river is so awfully strong. Don't you see danger there?'

'No way! I am absolutely confident that once Rajmangala gets into the water with us on her back, she will take us to the other side, come what may!'

Uncertainty continued to reign on the Indian side. Elephant Uncle, skilled mahauts, Naga boatmen and the jungle tribes of fishermen were gesticulating at each other and arguing vociferously. What seemed to have been decided was the necessity of transferring the soldiers from this side to that at the earliest. But they could not assure themselves of a safe entry into the screaming waters. It needed the most careful crossing over. If they got trapped in the vortex of the killer water, there would be no saving them.

Raghav and Kanchana got busy preparing for the earliest departure possible. The thought of crossing the river on elephant-back was exciting for the girls too.

The weather had suddenly turned. Sunlight had lit up the surface of the river. Jungle birds and water-birds were cawing and quacking and chirruping and whistling on either side of the water. This gave Kanchana the confidence that this was a god-sent opportunity. If not exploited, the next one could take months to arrive. Hirabai, strangely, had fallen in spirit again. She looked depressed and melancholic.

It was now around 11 o'clock. The sky was clear as mercury.

On the other bank, two old expert fishermen were walking about with a few others. They walked in the upstream direction for about 500 metres. It seemed from the way they were patting their chests that they were talking with a good deal of confidence. But Elephant Uncle appeared skeptical. A decision was finally reached and the elephants were lined up on the Indian bank trunk to tail. The Naga men let out a loud rallying cry, remembered their gods and herded the elephants into the water.

The line of elephants began moving steadily forward, cutting the fast flowing water as it moved. They would have got in almost 200 feet when two of them turned nervous and fidgety and refused to put their next foot forward. The mahauts sitting on their necks tried all they could to make them move, but the elephants refused to budge. They then turned right around, lifted their tiny tails and scampered out through the slime on the bank and disappeared.

But the six big elephants plodded on, uncaring of the waves that were hammering them. Crossing raging rivers appeared to have been a challenging sport for them, and they were determined to test their mettle. It appeared that the waves too knew them. Their button-like, excited eyes were rolling in their sockets in a wild frenzy. Robert, the boatmen, the helpers and the Naga villagers were egging them on loudly, each in their own language, bucking the water-girdled animals to move on.

The charged-up mahauts used prods and loud verbal persuasions and finally got the elephantss to go for one last-ditch, live-or-die effort. Another ten minutes, and the second half of the river had been crossed too.

The soldiers waiting on the Burmese side broke into a wild dance. The mahauts made the elephants lower themselves on the bank to let them get their breaths back. They dipped into the sacks on the elephants' backs and brought out big wheat cakes and sugarcane sticks to feed them. Their rest would have lasted about forty minutes. During this period, Gyan Singh had virtually become one of the group. He and the mahauts were friends and knew each other by name. He introduced Raghav and Kanchana to them and conveyed their desire to cross the river in their company. The mahauts could see no reason to turn down their request.

Suddenly somebody blew a sharp, army kind of whistle from the other bank. There was Uncle Robert, frantically waving his hat and trying to communicate the presence of grave danger in the west. Every head turned in that direction to see dark black clouds descending over the shoulder of the mountain there.

The mahauts then turned their gaze towards the surface of the river and noticed that the colour of the water had turned distinctly darker and muddier. The meaning was quite clear: the upper reaches of the Hukawng valley had experienced heavy rains some time during daybreak. That was why the water level in the river had also begun to rise. It spelt big danger. Whistles were blown across the river and the mahauts quickly began rushing their elephants back into the water. A worried Raghav turned to Gyan Singh and told him, 'Look, our

Rajmangala is not well; please request them to place her in the middle.'

'All right, then, move on! Don't waste your time talking. Push her forward.'

'Thank you, brother. We'll proceed immediately!'

The river began changing its appearance with every passing moment. The bright sunshine of a while ago had disappeared altogether; to add to the anxiety, the water had increased its pace too, hammering the elephants with its powerful current. Raghav cleverly managed to place Rajmangala in the middle of the bunch, making support available for her from the front as well as behind. In no time, the wind joined in the assault too.

The elephants that had crossed over to the Burmese side with great pride less than an hour ago now looked scared. Robert on the Indian bank looked particularly agitated. He was frantically signaling his mahauts. Raghav and Kanchana could not understand his language, but they were not required to either. The desperate man on the other side was telling them that he wouldn't mind their waiting on the Burmese bank for the next two days if needed. But the mahauts were muttering to themselves that those two days could so easily stretch to two months. Robert's concern was his priceless animals, while the mahauts were more focused on returning quickly to their wives and children on the Indian side.

A final decision was taken: the mahauts raised their sharp prods and brought them down with purpose on the backs of the mute animals. The elephants let out a loud shriek and raised their trunks in rebellion. But the agony of the spearing was so excruciating that to escape the punishment the poor dumb creatures were left with no choice but to take on the waters, eyes shut.

Rajmangala kept moving forward in the middle of this crowd. Huge, dark rollers were racing down upon them from upstream. The riders holding on to their bamboo seats on the elephant's back were taking a drenching of their lives. Unbelievably, half of the river was crossed in a while, but the force of the water had gained such muscle that it had virtually begun to heave the legs of the elephants upwards.

Rajmangala's instinct told her that the peril had reached its zenith, as any elephant on the warfront would know when a flaming cannon shot landed at its feet. She lifted her trunk against the black clouds and turned back. When Raghav realised that his beloved elephant was turning tail, he was livid. He began belabouring her on the head and neck with the point of his prod. Rajmangala began to bawl and howl in pain.

The girls in the baskets began wailing loudly and shut their eyes in terror. Kanchana too lost her head at this maltreatment of her pet and screamed, 'What are you trying to do to my precious darling?' When she found Raghav unresponsive, she struck Raghav heavily on the back. Raghav turned his head round to see a horrendous sight. The six other elephants accompanying them had all turned upside downlike like paperboats.

The utterly appalled Raghav then looked up in front. The double shock spooked him. The mountain of water on this side too had swollen to terrifying proportions. It had now become impossible to withdraw out of the eddies swirling in all directions. Suddenly Rajmangala's feet lost contact with the river bed. She began floating like a piece of wood and started to thrash about. She took a few tumbles, but suddenly a spirit of desperate valour and agility took possession of her, as that of a snake slithering out of an inferno.

The people sitting atop her shut their eyes waiting for the inevitable to happen; but Rajmangala had not surrendered yet. As she gathered all her strength and spirit and pushed forward, she felt something solid and woody just in front of her. It was a kinjal tree that had toppled from the bank into the river, and it was large enough for the branches to extend far into the water. Rajmangala lashed her trunk at the branch and began to trumpet loudly.

Raghav saw Gyan Singh on his knees on the bank, frantically waving and trying to direct his attention towards something. Raghav couldn't understand him, but Kanchana did. 'Up, up!' she shouted. 'Take the girls and walk over Rajmangala's trunk to the branch, and then across that to the bank.' Kaachana tied three of the girls to her body and scampered across the trunk to the branch, and from there in one jump, she landed into the deep slush back on the Burmese bank. Raghav held Hirabai and Bheemu and Apparao took charge of the remaining girls, and they took the same route to the bank as Kanchana had.

Every last ounce of energy had drained out of them. They lay like logs in the mud and slush by the bank. Even breathing had become an effort. The dark, roiling surface of the angry river presented a menacing sight. The monstrous flow had carried away every trace of the other six elephants, along with those who had been riding upon them, on its unforgiving current. Rajmangala lay on the bank, half her trunk submerged in the turbid water. The muddy water was receiving sharp, thick squirts of red each time she exhaled.

When Kanchana noticed this, she forgot her own exhaustion and dashed to her. 'Look, look Raghav! See what our poor baby has done to herself!'

'Oh my god! Where is this blood coming from?'

'That's just what I'm wondering. She obviously hit her trunk so hard against something that she's badly injured it.'

'Why is there so much blood in the water?'

'In an effort to first secure herself so that she could throw us out of the water, she hit her trunk against the sharp end of the broken tree trunk. It got impaled, thus creating a ramp for us to cross over. That's how she saved us.'

The blood trail was thickening on the bank. Rajmangala's skin lay torn open, smeared with blood and assailed by flies.

Gyan Singh hugged Raghav and Kanchana. He couldn't prevent tears of joy from streaming down his cheeks. 'Where did you get this kind of luck from?' he exclaimed. 'All the other elephants got washed away. You escaped by the skin of your teeth.'

The bank had turned dark. The trauma suffered by everyone was so severe that nobody had the desire to so much as move from where they sat. The force of the water had increased, causing Rajmangala's lifeless body to float up and rock where it lay.

Kanchana and Raghav could not stop the flow of tears. They would look towards Rajmangala's corpse and join their hands together over and over again as a mark of gratitude. She had been a gift from Kalamma Devi of Udgiri in the faraway mountain range of the Sahyadris. The goddess had dispatched her own mount to this distant land for their safety and security.

56

Forty days of torrential rainfall had turned the river banks soft and boggy. The entire wilderness in these parts was under the spell of some maverick spirits. The numerous stories, imaginings, songs and elegies haunting these dark, dense forests—it was as if a phantom opera was playing out, forever on the point of climaxing. Sometimes there would be no rains; sometimes the wind would be soft and mild. Then, suddenly, the galloping river would start clamouring. The demoniacal battle between the crocodiles and the alligators would resume with all their accompanying shrieks and blood-curdling battle-cries.

A fortnight had passed since the terrible mishap. The morning was rain-free and there was a light wind blowing. The sound of the roaring river and the sounds of waterfalls and springs from the mountains nearby could be heard with reasonable clarity. It was on such a morning that the trumpeting of a cow-elephant reached their ears. It wasn't a shriek, it was a call for someone. It sounded so much like Rajmangala's call that both Raghav and Kanchana leapt out of their beds and ran out to investigate.

The wound of the recent tragedy was so raw that even the sight of the spot where Rajmangala had died caused it to bleed afresh. Hence they had built another hut a good 500 meters away on slightly higher ground. When they rushed out this morning, the first direction their eyes turned towards was the dreaded spot. Could it be Rajmangala's ghost that was calling out to them? Or some other supernatural form that she had acquired? The darkness melted away as they watched, and all that they could see was the fast-flowing river, nothing else.

In the fortnight that followed, the same cry was heard at least twice, if not more. Having spent their entire lifetime in menageries, in close contact with not just the animals but also their urine and excreta, both Raghav and Kanchana could recognise every nuance of every mood, every look, every gesture, every sound and smell that emanated from them. They knew, therefore, that this call was not coming from the nearer bank but from the farther one, and it belonged to a female calling for her mate. There was an animal in heat on the other side, and it certainly had nothing to do with Rajmangala. They possessed nothing that could make life tolerable. Danger and distress lurked at every step; the rains were so heavy and incessant that humans were never less soggy than the trees of the jungles. The battle against sogginess required that they should never let the fire in the heart and the cinders in the hearth die out; managing that was a conquest in itself. Gyan Singh had plenty of experience of these parts, and he assured them that the intensity of rainfall would suddenly drop well before the month ended.

Roots and tubers were altogether missing from these jungles. What they did get was jungle bananas and slim bamboo shoots, and that combined with crabs and fish and boiled grasses kept the stomachs decently full. If it turned out to be a really bright day, the men would go into the jungles, loaf around, cross streams and suddenly come upon patches of wild mushrooms growing in the grass. On a lucky day they would also land multiple hands of fully ripe jungle bananas hanging on the rock edge. The feast thus gathered would thrill the girls.

An amazing sight greeted Raghav one morning. When he stepped out of the hut, a few steps away he saw three greenish-black droppings, each the size and shape of an upturned bucket. He immediately called everyone outside, and the circus-trained eyes recognised them without a blink. 'These are fresh elephant droppings. There is an animal roaming free close by.'

'But how can that be?' Kanchana asked. 'We haven't seen any herd of wild elephants in these parts.''An elephant it certainly is, but whether wild or domesticated we don't know.'

The sky that day was sparklingly clear. Black clouds had vanished like school children gone truant. Well before it had turned dark, Kanchana brought out some fish curry from an earthen pot and everyone sat to wolf it down while it was hot. As she lifted her eyes and looked out of the open hut door, she was stunned at the sight of a huge cow-elephant standing on the other bank of the river, staring wistfully across the water.

That lonesome animal became the topic of serious discussion that night. Its behaviour over the last forty days was discussed threadbare. Why should she be roaming around the jungle and haunting the river bank? Day after day after day? Kanchana voiced a thought that sprang in her head, 'The stray elephant that has been doing the rounds of our hut here, could it be that the cow on the other side has some bond with him?' Everybody's eyes lit up.

Another couple of days rolled by. As Raghav was passing by the stream, he encountered a whiff of a pleasant fragrance in the air. He went into the bushes from where this smell was most likely emanating and soon enough he came upon a huge banyan tree, its branches laden with reddish-pink fruit. Overjoyed, he quickly climbed up the tree and buried the blade of his axe in the wet trunk. As he picked the fruits off the branches, he imagined the delighted faces of the girls at seeing this treat.

Just then, he felt he saw some movement in the dense shrubbery below him. He looked down and saw a sight that tickled the cockles of his heart. While he had been plucking the fruits, leaves and tiny stems had been falling to the ground in a shower, and there, feasting on the delicacies was a broad-backed elephant. Raghav instantly pulled out the axe he had buried in the trunk and began to lop off all the thin branches within reach. These he kept tossing to the greedy animal below, who never seemed to complain that they were too many. The poor, hungry creature collected as many as it could in the sweep of its trunk, tucked them into its mouth and went for the next sweep, chewing on them with great relish. Raghav exchanged looks with Bheemu and Apparao who were sitting on the neighbouring trees and the three pairs of eyes scrutinised the animal with great care. It was a Burmese elephant and obviously belonged to someone. There were clear signs on its back as well as on its legs to indicate the use of chains.

The beast had not had enough food for many days, and it took full advantage of the feast that was raining down at him from the heaven above. Raghav softly whistled at the boys and a few signals were exchanged. The decision was made that they would surprise the animal and capture it.

They timed themselves through signals for a synchronised jump from the trees and leapt together shouting, 'Let's catch it!' The elephant, however, turned out to be smarter than they had thought, and for all its bulk, it sprang like a leopard and disappeared into the tall, dense bushes without a trace.

On Raghav's instructions, Bheemu and Apparao collected as many leafy stems of the banyan as they could and carried the load on their heads to the hut. They laid it all out at a little distance from the hut and waited for night to fall. The boys hid close by to keep a sharp watch during the night.

The two watchmen managed to stay awake till very late in the night, but just before dawn, when the wind had turned cooler, they fell into a snooze. The sun was shining brightly when Raghav stepped out of the hut and kicked the boys awake with a laugh. The three then examined the heap of banyan stems and saw that while the boys were collecting their forty winks, the elephant had quietly sneaked in and cleaned out as many of the leaves as he could, leaving the hardier stems behind.

57

The night was spooky and intimidating. The wind was howling and snarling. Suddenly, a loud, rattled cry hit Kanchana's ears. There was some tussle in the darkness of the hut and then a scream. A succubus seemed to have climbed on Raghav's chest and was choking him as she shouted, 'Get up, my man! Look, my daughters are running into the jungles! Hey, Shantey, stop! Stop, please Babitey! Get up, my dear husband! How can you be sleeping like a log at a time like this, you Mahalingya?'

Kanchana jumped up, rushed to the hearth and rekindled a dying piece of wood. In its light she could see Hirabai sitting astride Raghav's chest and squeezing his throat with both hands. Raghav was trying to pull her hands away and kicking his heels. Kanchana pushed Hirabai with great force, causing her to topple over and regain her senses somewhat.

Lunch was just over and Kanchana was playing some games with the girls. Raghav sat chatting with the boys, and Gyan Singh sat with his nose buried in what looked like an old map. Suddenly, they heard the loud trumpet of an elephant, and their trained ears knew that it was a cry of great distress. Could the animal be in heat? Could it for some reason have gone mad? Could it be trundling up in a passion to bring the hut down?

Worry was writ large on every face. The men picked up stout sticks and nylon ropes and stepped out cautiously.

Just then, the dark, hulking object materialised right in front of the hut. It arrived and almost immediately, let its forelegs fold up—and collapsed. Everybody's attention was drawn towards the rear part of the sole of its left foreleg. It had a wound as large as a human palm, caused perhaps by a sharp stump of wood or a jagged piece of stone. The wound seemed to be ringed by pus. Jungle-flies were buzzing all around the wound, making even a moment of peace impossible for the poor beast.

When formidable animals like these get wounded to the point of helplessness, they are on their way to death. The predatory or scavenging birds of the jungle get wind of this helplessness and begin gathering around it in swarms. They begin feasting off it even as it lives, tearing off the skin and flesh while all that the once powerful creature can do is to flail and shriek in unimaginable pain. Some eight or ten such birds had already started hovering over this unfortunate creature and begun to get a foretaste of it. The small rips on its back stood as evidence of the assault. It would take no time at all for ten to become a hundred, and the elephant knew it. That explained why this king of the forest had come seeking shelter and protection at a human door.

Raghav, Kanchana and the others rushed out with their sticks and swung them at the nearest birds, shooeing them away. The animal trainer in Raghav suddenly came alive and he immediately began to pat the injured elephant lovingly and reassuringly.

Kanchana ran inside, heated some water and brought it out. She began carefully pouring the hot water into the wound, which not only made the flies scamper away instantly, but also brought maggots wriggling out in large numbers.

Bheemu extracted oil from bamboo shoots and Apparao crushed its leaves to squeeze juice out of it. They extracted some juice out of the joints and their poultice was ready. Meanwhile, Kanchana had washed the wound, scraping the pus out as best as she could.

Raghav was sitting with the prone elephant's head in his lap. He would make cooing sounds to distract it, scratch its head and play with its flapping ears.

The relief from the pain that the worms and flies had been causing to the animal for hours was enormous. It had also been given a decent feed. A wave of drowsiness overcame it and the poor creature fell asleep.

Within no time, that black mountain of an elephant became an inseparable member of the family. Its nails had grown big and had been biting into its flesh, so Raghav promptly brought out a file and pulled them out. Its physical and emotional wounds began to heal.

Two days had gone by when Kanchana and Raghav were woken up at dawn by the trumpeting of elephants. The call went across the water to crash into the valley on the other side. As the darkness over the wide span of the river lifted, it revealed a sight that made jaws drop. There on the other side was the cow-elephant, calling out to her mate full-throatedly, and the mate on this side was so ecstatic that it had lifted up its trunk and was waving it like a flag.

These calls and counter-calls were deeply passionate, redolent of the pain of separation and soaked with the desire to be with each other. The water of the river seemed to be swimming in their eyes. How could they meet? How quickly? This was the ferment, the anxiety that saturated their plaintive exchanges.

Gyan Singh pulled out his monocular and inspected the other bank. Lowering the instrument, he said, 'I'm sure both these animals belong to Uncle Robert's stable. The day we had failed to cross over, if you remember, a number of alarmed elephants had turned their backs and scurried away on the other bank. The elephant on the other side could be one of them.'

'So, who is this prodigy that sits right in front of our eyes here?'

'It is quite clear to me. Of the six elephants that got washed away along with those forty odd soldiers, this could be the lucky one that somehow survived somewhere on this side. The river has since then not given it any opportunity to cross back. Otherwise, the presence of a domesticated animal on this side doesn't make any sense.'

The new elephant was immediately christened Sarja.

Days were drifting by. As each day passed, the ardour in the calls of both Sarja and his friend on the other side—Rani—gained a deeper resonance. Every single pair of eyes was looking at the mighty river, praying fervently for its spate to subside. Gyan Singh too joined in the craving for the other bank. 'I don't want to stay here even for a minute more.' he exclaimed. 'I want to get into India right now.'

'But you still haven't got any information on your brothers.' Raghav said.

'Two days of travel from the other bank takes you to a post called Lido. They have set up huge camps there for the displaced people and injured soldiers. My brothers could likely be searching for me in the rows of the corpses kept there.'

There was just one thought topmost on everyone's mind: when would the water subside?

58

The rains were simply refusing to let up. The clouds were crying their eyes out on the dense green mountains. The thirteen people living in that hut had turned sick of the moisture all around. Fate had more or less snatched the tongues out of those hapless English girls. They would either cling to Kanchana and try to burrow themselves deep into her or they would lie staring vacantly at the roof made of dry twigs and coconut fronds. Where could their parents be? Would they even have survived the devastating war?

The one person who was indifferent to her circumstances was Hirabai. In stark contrast, Kanchana's heart and mind knew no rest. Nearly two months had passed since her company had set off towards India, leaving her and the rest behind. Had they managed to reach home?

The rains lashed the bank of the Dafa with a vengeance. The cold they brought along was merciless. The elephant, Sarja, would sit with its trunk curled up and keep its long ears pricked, as if focusing on the sounds outside, but it never heard the intensity of the rains faltering. For four or five days in succession now, the downpour had not so much as allowed the door of the hut to be opened. The hearth was continually fed with damp logs that filled the hut with smoke. Everybody sat around soaking up its warmth or stretched out on bamboo mats with their knees folded tight into their stomachs. They had made little cups out of the knotted parts of thick bamboos in which they drank black coffee, but it didn't help much in driving the cold out of the young girls' bones.

For two days in a row, they couldn't go out to respond to the call of nature, because stepping out for a minute meant nothing less than going out for a bath in the rain. The cold would really come into its own during the night. With salt having disappeared long ago from their diet, the ability of the body to withstand this kind of cold had taken a bad hit. However deep they tucked themselves into Kanchana's body, the chattering of their teeth would not stop.

Kanchana sat with them one night and explained in her broken English, 'Look, little babies, the body needs salt. Without it we cannot last.'

'But where do we get it from?'

'We can recycle the salt that oozes out of our bodies.'

'How do you mean?'

'Wherever there's sweat stuck to your bodies or to your friends' bodies there's salt. Lick it all up and you get it back into your body.'

It was mind numbing, this cold, that had gone and clung to their bones faster than any leech could. The girls took Kanchana's advice and began licking themselves and each other vigorously, often giving Kanchana a healthy lick too. It made them feel better. It was good entertainment anyway. Seeing them enjoying the game, Raghav, lying at one end, chipped in. 'This is nothing new, girls,' he said. 'I've heard the experiences of many people during my travels. Russian convicts thrown into prison or exiled to Siberia, even the prisoners in Malaya here, have survived by not merely licking sweat, but also by consuming each other's urine. The important thing here is to survive.'

One night the rain relented for an hour. Raghav took this opportunity and stepped into the river along with Bheemu and

Apparao. They got lucky and managed to catch two slithery, four-foot-long creatures—either eel or some kind of snake, but who cared? They were something that could bring some heat back into their bodies.

Raghav chopped their heads off with his knife and threw them away, just to ensure that the girls didn't get a fright. Then he cut them into little pieces and took the meat inside for cooking. After it was nicely cooked, Raghav drank up a mugful of the broth to test it for any trace of poison. When twenty minutes went by and he felt no adverse effects, the meat was served for all to consume. Everyone slept well that night.

For the next few days, there came spells of no rain. That made stepping out of the hut possible. One day Kanchana took the girls out to a relatively calm part of the river. Bheemu and Apparao had cut lengths of wet banana trunks and kept them ready for this occasion. Raghav and Kanchana tied these trunks to the stomachs of the girls and let them into the water. Bheemu, who didn't know how to swim, tied one to his stomach too. They spent a long time floating on the water and splashing around.

The next ten days it again rained incessantly, creating the old problem of procuring food. For how long could they go on feeding on crabs, river shrimps and jungle leaves? Soon enough, the stomachs of four of the seven girls became upset. Their runny bowels drained them of all energy. To satisfy their hunger they would eat some half-cooked food and irritate their bowels all over again.

Then they ran into a day for which they had no precedent. A clear day dawned and remained clear, although the leaves on the trees continued to drip. Sick to the gills because of so many days of incarceration, the four men took this opportunity to venture out into the jungle with their knives and axes. They were itching to go far out and bring back something worthwhile and their legs were equally eager to run with their hearts. But despite plodding on for hours, they did not run into any food.

Suddenly something sharp pierced Bheemu's foot and he let out a scream. All of them gathered at the spot and looked closely to find that it was the sharp protrusion of an object that lay buried in the soft earth. When they dislodged it from the earth and cleared the muck, what they saw took their breaths away. It was a broken piece of the blade of an aircraft propeller. Everybody's faces suddenly lit up and hopes rose high. The piece almost certainly belonged to a Dakota, and it could well have been carrying supplies for the army.

The four men immediately scattered in four directions and began an intensive search of the land around. They went down trenches, hacked across thick vegetation, crossed streams and climbed hillocks; a few more steps—and there lay the wreckage of a Dakota in a pit. As it had crashed, it had mown down a few trees and now lay covered under their branches.

At a call from Raghav, they all gathered and closed in on the fallen plane. They saw the completely burnt skeleton of the pilot still held to the seat by the metal wirings of what was once a seat-belt. From the disintegrated state of the skeleton and the growth of moss and vegetation around the craft, the accident would have been at least a couple of months old.

Keeping the burnt-out aircraft at the centre, the four men fanned out in an expanding circle, searching for food tins, cigarette packets or anything else that could be of use. After a long search, they suddenly came upon a fifty-kilo sack of rice carrying the stamp of the British Indian Army. It had been so well sealed in plastic wraps that it had survived the violence of the rains.

The feasting that followed, however, lasted only for five or six days. Once the sack was brought out of its plastic sealing, it began soaking the wet, cold air and disintegrating into mildewy powder.

Raghav came by a deserted hut. While rummaging through it, he looked up and found tucked in the roof a piece of leather which seemed to ring a bell in his head. He brought it down and sniffed at it. He later put a small piece in water and boiled it. Yes, it was almost certainly deer skin. In places with such wet climate, where food becomes difficult to procure, the people salt deer skin and sun-dry it during the warm season. It becomes their sustenance during long rainy spells. It became the sustenance for Raghav and Kanchana's family in the hut.

In the next few days, the winds changed and the rains lost intensity. Trees began to sway and birds began to chirp. The hope in Gyan Singh's eyes sprouted new leaves, and this became infectious. They all began to see a ray of light at the end of the long, dismal tunnel they were stuck in.

Water-laden clouds still continued to patrol the sky. Everybody was asleep one night when Kanchana woke up to a sound. A loud whiplash of a sound. She instantly sat up as a knot developed in her stomach. From where she sat, she could see the surface of the river below the stars. Sarja had knocked the grass wall down with the second whiplash of his trunk, thus bringing the river into the line of sight.

Raghav too woke up. '*Arey*, up, everyone!' he screamed as he ran out. 'Start getting ready!' Up in the sky, the clouds surrounding the mountains had melted away and the sky was twinkling with a million stars.

Raghav swept his eyes over the river bank and saw that a big slope had developed. The sand on the riverbed had begun to glisten at a number of places. The little pools that had formed in the middle of these sand patches reflected the moon in all its glory. The entire ambience was enchanting, with the stars so inviting that one could drink them all up in a few giant gulps.

As he stood watching, a mountainous form walked from across the other bank. It had already crossed half the span of the river. As he scrutinised the moving object more carefully,

Raghav realised that it was the elephant from the other side—Rani. She was braving the waters in order to be united with Sarja. She was waving her trunk as she rolled along, as if admonishing everybody, 'Up, you morons! How can you be sleeping right now? The river has split! This is your opportunity to escape. Miss this, and you may very well die on your bank.'

The people in the hut broke into frenzied activity. Without being told, Sarja went down the slope and reached the bank. Kanchana lifted the English girls one by one and placed them in bamboo baskets. The baskets were then placed on the elephant's spacious back. Raghav ensconced himself comfortably on its broad neck. Clothing, sheets, coverlets and whatever else would be needed for the rest of the journey were rolled up into a bundle and placed at the rear. The smaller pieces of nylon ropes were knotted together again for securing the bundles. Right in front sat Raghav, behind him the bundles; right next to the bundles was Kanchana, with the baskets in which sat the seven girls. Also loaded on the back was a sackful of coconuts and as many hands of bananas that could be gathered. Right at the tail was seated Hirabai. Bheemu and Apparao had secured her with ropes as tightly as they could.

Sarja now began walking over the wet sand with gusto. Rani, who had crossed more than half the span of the river, had raised his pitch of excitement. Raghav signalled to Bheemu and Apparao to jump on to Rani's back, but the boys were enjoying plodding through the water. 'Raghav dada, we've met God. We'd prefer to walk beside Sarja.'

'But why risk your lives?'

'There's no danger here. In case the elephant turns unruly, it will be good to have free movement.'

Sarja was halfway through the river. There he met up with his lady love. The riverbed here had risen, splitting the flow and creating an island of sand. The water on the other bank still looked insurmountable. Sarja lifted his trunk and slapped it lovingly against Rani's. They were meeting after months of separation, and the joy of reunion was palpable. They entwined their trunks and rubbed their backs against each other. But even as they were doing so, they were registering the speed of the water flowing by them, its changing rhythm and all the danger that it signified. They twitched their ears. Raghav too turned apprehensive. He couldn't help commenting, 'God! The water looks rather deep on this side. This mad Rani took quite a chance.'

'Dangerous it most certainly is, Raghav. Looking at the current, there are more chances of dying than of surviving here.'

'So, now you decide what we should do.'

'Are we left with any other choice? Let's pray for Daaji's blessings and hope for fate to play itself out. We'll take it as it comes.'

Kanchana let out a deep sigh and hugged the girls. Wiping her eyes, she said, 'Don't be scared. Close your eyes, and don't open them even if you fall into the water. Who knows, a path may spring up even in the water.' Then she turned to Raghav and Gyan Singh and tried to buck them up. 'Only one of two things can happen—either the joy of dying or the celebration of life.'

The elephants had no time for instructions. As both of them entered the water, circus-men Bheema and Apparao leapt and landed straight on Rani's back. Gyan Singh held on tight to the nylon ropes on Sarja's back. Both the elephants began giving it their all as they waded through the fearsome current. When the depth of the water increased, their heads and their backs sank into the water and with them went the passengers on their backs. Then they lost contact with the river floor and began floating on the water like massive logs of wood.

There is an end to misfortune too. Under the water, there was a sharp turn, and that had caused a layer of sand to collect in a pile on the other side. As soon as the elephants noticed that, they put their entire weight on their feet, supported each other and ploughed into the wet sand. The river went past them on their right and the two found the other bank on their left.

Crossing the ten or twelve feet wide sand bank, the elephants began ascending the slope. The adventure with the undercurrent had hit them so hard that they had no stamina left for celebrations. As they were struggling up the slope, Raghav's eyes went to the rear. The little ones, Kanchana and Gyan Singh were still clinging to their seats, but the slot on Sarja's tail was empty. 'Where's Hira-aatya gone?' he yelled.

Everybody was thunderstruck. Has she been taken away by the current. Raghav checked the ropes, they were not broken anywhere. Quite the opposite, it appeared that the knots had been carefully opened and Hirabai had left of her own volition.

The darkness around the river had disappeared, the morning was clear, but the sun had not really risen. As a matter of fact, dark clouds were already gaining dominance over the mountain peaks. Nature could again take a turn and come pouring down any time soon. Kanchana was quite convinced that Hirabai had undone the rope herself and slipped out. Apparao and Gyan Singh were all ready to dive into the water and hunt for the lost woman. Kanchana, however, cast an eye at the frothing blue of the river, the green of the trees and the steadily darkening black of the clouds. She looked at the greenness of the bamboo groves on the other bank. Every bunch of green bamboos appeared to her like the green saree in which Hirabai was clad.

She then turned at the two who were ready to set off and said, 'Turn round. Your efforts in that direction are not going to fetch any results.'

As they began stepping out of the river bed, Raghav was finding it difficult to hold in his grief. He was finding it very difficult to leave Mahaling's and Babita-Shanta's Hirabai behind. Kanchana took Raghav's hand in hers and said, 'Let go, Raghav-ji. What would poor Hira-aatya have done after returning to her country? Her life, her deliverance, her pilgrimage spot are all buried deep in these mountains here. If she wishes to spend the rest of her life here, who are we to cause obstructions?'

The slope on this side was very slippery, with the earth being almost blood-red. Sarja was finding it very difficult to climb up this slimy surface. He could find neither any foothold nor any incline. Turning nervous, he let out a cry for help and immediately heard a response from the top edge of the slope. Rani had instinctively sensed that her partner was in distress and had been waiting for some time for his call to arrive. When it finally did, she was ready and waiting. She instantly stretched out her trunk to which Sarja hooked his own. One big heave with the lady's legs firmly anchored in the earth, one big effort from Sarja, and he was home.

The moment they were on Indian land, everyone, including the girls ensconced on Sarja's back, let out a loud cry of victory. They all climbed down the elephant's back and gave each other hard, long hugs for having escaped from the jaws of death.

59

It was as if Kaachana had been transferred from sleep in one life into a sleep of another life altogether. She heard somebody calling into her ears, 'Hello, ma'am, get up!' She felt that she was rocking on a mattress of clouds. When she regained consciousness, she realised that she was lying on a make-do stretcher made of bamboos. She could sense that two boys in shorts and white shirts were carrying her to some place with rapid steps.

Remembering the girls, she sat up, alert. Who were these men carrying her on the bamboo stretcher? She soon noticed that all the others who had crossed with her were being carried on similar bamboo stretchers. She shut her eyes and lost consciousness again. She was put into a van and driven somewhere. Then, suddenly, the strong odour of medicines assailed her nostrils.

Another few hours of sleep followed. When she came to, she realised that she had been admitted to a make-shift hospital erected temporarily in the war zone. It was completely made of bamboo.

A number of camps had been established in a town called Lido at one end of Assam. Kanchana and her colleagues were being treated in one of them. Their exhausted bodies refused to get up from their beds. The Assam Tea Planters' Association had opened up these camps with the help of the British government in order to take care of injured soldiers and refugees. There were braziers everywhere, heating water for people to take baths. The food supply was a little inadequate, but strong Assamese tea was being served in big mugs in unlimited quantities.

After groggily observing what had been happening around her for barely an hour, Kanchana again surrendered herself to sleep. Was it sleep at all, or total loss of consciousness? A near-death experience? She had no idea how many days had passed since she was first put on that iron bed. One day, however, after great effort, she forced her heavy eyelids open. She felt that she was floating like a corpse on the scum at the bottom of a well. Up there, at the mouth of the well, she noticed a number of people looking down at her with anxious eyes. Even before she could formulate a question, she recognised among the tense, troubled faces the features of three British girls who had undertaken the fateful journey with her. Did that mean that the other girls had arrived safe in the hospital too?

Among the crowd gathered around, their eyes nailed on Kanchana, exuding love, care and anxiety, the faces of the European parents of the girls could also be seen. This meant that these relatives had got into the jungle belt of Assam in search of their children much before Kanchana's caravan had reached Lido. They had been waiting at Lido for months, perhaps, hoping that one of the refugees emerging from the Hukawng valley would be their child.

Amidst the crowd up there, she also noticed Raghav staring down at her. Raghav had parked himself in the camp hospital, waiting for her to regain consciousness. As soon as he saw her emerging from her coma, his chest turned tight and his eyes turned moist.

Her lips spread into a contented smile and a dimple appeared on her left cheek. She heard the British girls scream out in joy, 'Mother! Oh mother!' Their guardians joined the others in spontaneous claps of joy. Holding Kanchana's hand in his, Raghav said, 'Look, Kanchu,' he said, 'look at the state we have all been in. Barely a few months ago, we were quenching the fire in our bellies by eating grass in the jungles; but here, in the comfort of the camp, I haven't been able to down even a few morsels of food for the past four or five days.'

'Why is that?'

'You were teetering between life and death for these past few days. The parents of these British girls were constantly at the church nearby, praying for your life. They consider you a messiah because you brought their kids to safety.'

For a moment Kanchana felt her old energy flooding back into her; but at the very next moment she was racked by an excruciating pain radiating through every muscle, every joint, every pore of her body. She smiled stoically at her state and pondered the emotions she had stirred in the people who stood surrounding her. Who were these people? From which lands? What connection did she have with their country, religion or culture? And yet, they held in their eyes an overwhelming affection for her. This faith, this gratitude, this outburst of tenderness. 'Bravo, girl!' they were acknowledging wordlessly, 'Thank you for herding our kids out of those murderous ravines and bringing them to safety.'

Suddenly, her eyes paused on a face that seemed strangely familiar, and she was startled. Where had she seen this person before? The longish face, the golden-brown head of tousled hair, those big, expressive, authoritative eyes … Just then, a team of doctors arrived and shooed the gathering away—'Please leave the room immediately. Let the patient get some rest.'

It took Kanchana a good four or five days to completely regain consciousness. She got to know that only five of her seven little girls had survived the ordeal of the journey from the Dafa bank to Lido. For two full days after crossing the river, they had had to continue with their journey on the merciless road before meeting the first relief workers. By the time they reached the camp, two of the girls had given up.

She saw near her pillow a few bouquets of roses and packets of chocolates along with small letters of gratitude. The fathers of some of the girls were senior officers serving either in the English army or working in the Rangoon oil refinery. A number of them had stayed on for many days, awaiting the return of their little darlings.

Later that afternoon, when she came out of her stupor, she saw Raghav standing by her bedside, a green coconut in hand. After she had finished drinking the coconut water, Kanchana asked, 'Raghav, who was that man standing to one side this morning? Fair, long-faced, blond hair?'

'Oh, yes, that man!' A mischievous smile flashed across his face. 'Why don't you jog your memory harder and try to remember him?'

'I've been trying, but I just can't place him.'

'Make a wild guess then.'

'Hmmm, I can't place him. But I feel it's someone I have seen recently. Seen him earlier too … but why, I don't remember.'

'This is how it has always been. When power goes to the head, when wearing the cloak of authority and influence, a person begins walking on the cloud of arrogance and conceit. However, when Fate deals them a hard blow and when the bricks of authority slip away from under their feet, they begins to see themselves for what they really are.'

'What are you saying?'

'Kanchana, he's the District Collector of Myitkyina. In the jungles, on the other side of the Dafa, we had beseeched him to stop for the sake of those young girls, the girls that belonged to his community. But this merciless man had not heeded our pleas.'

'So, what now? Why is he here in this faraway jungle?'

'The DC reached here and his only child, seven-year-old Elina, died in an epidemic. Despite the best medical facilities and the team of army doctors available to him, he could not save her life.'

'What a tragedy!'

'DC sahib has now been appointed the Refugee Commissioner of Assam Province. He was here on an inspection tour of the hospital. He was amazed to see you here. After finishing his round, he came back and sat by your bed for a long time. You were, of course, in a coma at the time. In a daze he sat holding your hand and sobbing. He said …'

'What did he say?'

'He said, "I lost my daughter. She was my whole world … This terrible disaster has brought me back to my senses. I have now decided to spend the rest of my life taking care of these young kids..Your cries of distress in that frightful jungle haunt me. You implored me to save the girls, but I was consumed by the power of my post. My heart had become numb. My ears had turned deaf to your entreaties. No amount of remorse is enough. If only I had stopped that day with my squad, those girls would have reached Lido earlier and the ones who died on the way would have survived. Perhaps then our Lord would have spared my daughter's life. Now, my heart simply bleeds for every child in distress."'

The knot in the pits of Raghav and Kanchana's stomachs had not dissolved. They had managed to reach this far, but they were still anxious about the fate of the rest of their troupe that had left earlier. With no news having reached them, both Kanchana and Raghav were worried.

The tormenting journey over the past many months had tested their bodies to the very limit and they had been advised compulsory rest for some time. In due course, they managed to establish contact with a few company workers who had arrived earlier. When they were informed that their troupe members had taken trains to the south a month and a half before they arrived in Lido, Kanchana and Raghav were hugely relieved.

Two or three days of rest worked magic on Kanchana's health. She began to go out for morning walks on which she often got into conversation with nurses from Assam. They were curious about her trudge across the Hukawng valley.

The toilets of this emergency hospital were outside the building, requiring the patients to walk some distance to relieve themselves. Raghav was returning one evening from the toilet. It had turned dark outside. Suddenly he noticed a short person in the crowd, who vanished before he could give him another look. There was something very familiar about him.

It was only when he reached Kanchana's bed that his brain made the connection. 'Oh my God! Saibu chachu?' he blurted out.

'What are you saying, Raghav?' Kanchana was surprised.

'Yes, Kanchu. I saw a person exactly like him.'

'What rubbish! Why would he come so far?'

'Why would he duck away on seeing me if he wasn't Saibu?'

Kanchana's face tensed up. She groaned as she told Raghav, 'Please do be careful, though. Like with the wind, you cannot tell what that wretched man might do, where he might turn up.'

Early the next morning, Raghav was feeling quite stiff. He didn't feel like leaving his bed, but a visit to the toilet was necessary. Looking at his state, Kanchana decided to escort him. There were two separate bamboo shacks in two directions, which functioned as toilets. Kanchana stood at the fork where the paths split. Raghav left for the men's section.

As Raghav stood inside the toilet, he heard somebody's foot slipping. He quickly turned around. There stood Saibu with a Rampuri knife in hand. He had been on the point of lunging at

Raghav when the wet ground caused him to lose his balance. At the very sight of him, Raghav yelled out, 'Police! Police!' Saibu shot forward like an arrow and lifted his knife in order to attack Raghav. Despite not being in the best of health, Raghav managed to get Saibu's wrist in a tight grip. Saibu, however, was so inflamed with hatred that he did manage to drive the tip of the knife into Raghav's back.

During the commotion that erupted, a couple of policemen arrived at the scene and overpowered Saibu. They made preliminary enquiries and took Saibu under arrest. The British police administration instituted a formal inquiry into the sordid episode. The investigation unearthed enough evidence to expose Saibu's murderous plans, with the result that the Provincial police immediately threw him into prison.

When Raghav and Kanchana were setting off for their journey to the Dimapur railway station in Nagaland from where they would catch the Calcutta Mail, the British DC, in his capacity as the Refugee Commissioner, arranged for a special Jeep for them. Kanchana and Raghav were moved by the tears flowing down his fair cheeks as he bid them goodbye.

Deboarding the train at the Miraj railway station, the group—Kanchana, Raghav, Bheemu and Apparao—loaded their luggage in bullock carts.. These carts travelled to the tinkle of the bells tied round the bullocks' necks and reached the outskirts of Kagwad by late afternoon. As they cast their gaze across the vast lands that stretched up to the horizon, they felt that they had travelled across eons of time.

Kanchana gave three months' leave to the members of her circus, after which she began rebuilding the company from scratch. She took lorries on hire, collected elephants and horses, animal by animal, and then set the company boys to publicise their return to the circus arena.

The market was the same. The circus art that had been evolving incrementally right from the time of the Mauryas was the same. The people's hearts were large and their temperament merry. The boys went about announcing their return to the field:

Hear, oh hear!
All you circus lovers, hear!
The World War arrived and departed after raining tons of bombs.
But like the Phoenix,
the Great Kanchana Circus has risen from its ashes.
Come! Come to see—exciting as ever, with new items,
the girl from your own soil,
the brave Kanchana Kagwadkar
who places her head in the maw of a tigress.
And Raghav Bhosale, the magician of the bouncing rope.
Come, come and see
the circus that has mermerised viewers for generations!
550 men and animals will perform acts of dare devilry never seen before!
Yes, we are the Great Kanchana Circus
We guarantee unlimited fun if you come,
regrets if you don't!

Afterword

Gladiators are a fascinating part of the history of both ancient Athens and ancient Rome. Known for their commitment to rigorous physical culture, phenomenal agility and disdain for life, the gladiators would step into the arena and battle with wild animals like lions, leopards, bears, bulls, elephants—even hippopotamus and crocodiles. They even fought one another to the death. These were, perhaps, the earliest circuses.

The roots of the Indian circus, too, extend as far back as the Maurya and Gupta eras. This was also the period when the king of the jungle—the elephant—was tamed and brought into human society. It found its niche in games, religious rituals and on the battlefield. The taming of the horse and its scientific training for various uses forms a history of its own.

Even after the Maurya and Gupta periods, numerous Indian sportsmen displayed their stunts with the big cats as a part of village entertainment. But it was only after a few German circuses arrived in Bombay (now Mumbai) 150 years ago that Vishnupant Chhatre of Sangli and Yashvant Morey of Wadgaon (Paanaache) were provoked into setting up their own circuses of the same standard. Inspired by Chhatre and Morey in Maharashtra, Keeleri Kunhikannan and his disciple Pariyali Kennan of Tellicheri (also known as Thalassery), laid the foundation of this profession in the Malabar region of Kerala. The establishment of the Indian circus opened up avenues for livelihood and stardom for the poor but adventurous young men and women of the countryside. Their skills and courage became their ticket to glory.

The moon in the sky is the darling of us earthlings. It is particularly dear to children across the world, but alas, it has always been beyond their grasp. However, during those happy days, when they saw the circus elephants go rocking past them, when they gawped at those fairy girls performing impossible acrobatics on the trapeze, when the jokers with their tomato-noses and multicoloured pajamas somersaulted before them and farted talcum powder at one another, the little ones were transported into a heaven of their own, their dear Chanda Mama almost there to give them company.

However, there are some people who claim to be friends of animals, a large number of whom are not only frauds, but also ignoramuses. Their jaundiced eye has brought this robust sport to its much lamented demise. This Indian art form that claimed kinship with Mauryan times has been senselessly obliterated through deliberate circulation of misinformation by these 'friends of animals' and a controversial interpretation of a few articles of the law.

While researching for my novel on Subhas Chandra Bose, *Mahanayak*, I was on a visit to Burma (now Myanmar) in 1997. Happenstance took me to a shop for old books in the tourist town of Bagan. There, I landed a report written by a British official, which sucked me into the amazing world of Kanchana and her circus.

On 23 November 1943, the Japanese Air Force began bombing Rangoon (now Yangon), the then capital of Burma, which was counted among the most flourishing trade centres of the East. A swarm of about 700,000 to 800,000 displaced Indians ran for their lives in an effort to somehow reach India. At a modest estimate, at least ten percent of them lost their lives to hunger, exhaustion, dysentery and myriad illnesses.

The Karlekar Grand Circus of Maharashtra and the Rakhumai Circus from the south were holding wildly successful shows in Rangoon at the time. Fearing that the wild animals would create havoc if they broke out into the city, the British administration, in a heartless knee-jerk reaction, had them shot to death. It did the same with the other violent animals in the public zoo.

During my visit to Burma in the nineties, the military junta had been occupying the seat of power. Newspapers and other media of mass communication had been gagged. It so happened that the day on which I was in Mandalay, rumour broke out that a Muslim boy had fallen in love with a Burmese girl. That very same night, I saw with my own eyes a mosque set on fire by miscreants into which seven citizens were tossed for good measure. During my two-day stay, not one line appeared in any media regarding the arson.

Travelling within the town was also prohibited during this time. Visitors were deposited at their hotels from the airport, taken to their permitted places of work and then brought back to the airport. Infringing this law could result in a few years of rigorous imprisonment. I, however, was a foolhardy young man then and took the risk of travelling across the length and breadth of the country. It was during this crisscrossing that Kanchana came to life on the CinemaScope screen of my mind. On a couple of occasions, the call with authorities got to be quite close, but, to my good fortune, I managed to wiggle out of it.

So as to familiarise myself with the landscape across which Kanchana made her frightful journey with her circus troupe, her animals and a few White schoolgirls, I undertook a dangerous expedition that took me across Mount Popa and Myitkyina and through utterly wild forests leading up to Lido Road in India. I have also walked the banks of the Dafa river, which figures in the climactic part of the novel.

Rudyard Kipling has located his two *Jungle Book* volumes in the forests of Central India. They enriched world literature by creating an enthralling relationship between human beings and wild animals. Little Mowgli and his jungle friends (as also his enemies) are etched so deep in the consciousness of the readers of the world that no jungle talk is ever complete without reference to them. I believe that in its own small way, *The Great Kanchana Circus* creates a symbiosis between man and animal, between civilisation and wilderness, through the bonding that one sees from close quarters among circus artistes and their wild wards.

Although this novel is a work of fiction, it is based on a strong foundation of facts. During my five-odd years of research, I met a large number of old circus owners, artistes and acrobats. These interactions brought me extraordinary remembrances and stories of the animals who were half responsible for the success and popularity of this art form. These were the animals that gave shape and spirit to the four-footed characters in this novel, Phakkadrao the horse, Gajaratna and Rajmangala the elephants, Lakshmi the tigress and Mustafa the hippopotamus. Most of the episodes that occur in the novel have actually happened somewhere at some time. The shooting of Gajaratna is a replay of the owner of Walawalkar's Royal Circus shooting his dear animal during their Singapore tour.

The circus as an art and profession came into being well over a hundred years ago in Maharashtra, Karnataka and Kerala. It gathered momentum largely because it provided wherewithal to the extremely poor physical exercise enthusiasts in the far-flung villages of these regions. During those difficult times, these provinces had neither big irrigation projects nor sugar mills as they do today. The rain-dependent farms could never be trusted to provide sufficient sustenance to the large peasant families. Thus, it happened that a cowherd boy of Tasgaon named Parshuram Mali and a daredevil peasant girl from

Khadaklat named Tarabai Shinde put together their separate circus troupes. They brought over from neighbouring Goa some modern Portuguese bands whose music could mesmerise not only the human ear, but also send tremors racing through the legs of four-footed creatures.

The Indian circuses of those times gained such a reputation that they soon had a dozen or so French and German couples as artistes on their payroll. A ringmaster and animal trainer named Damoo Dhotre from Pune earned a great name for himself in the famous American travelling circuses Ringling Brothers and Barnum & Bailey. Most of the big Indian circuses of those times made successful tours to South-east Asian countries, Europe and the Arab countries.

Lokmanya Bal Gangadhar Tilak was so impressed by the stunts of Parshuram Mali that he conferred upon him the title 'The Lion of the Indian Circus'. Mali's 'Parshuram Lion Circus' toured everywhere from Singapore to Japan to Germany, and left its mark there.

A large number of Indian women artistes gained recognition on account of their adventurous spirit and fearlessness. Tarabai Gulab Shinde with tigers. Others like Jamela and Chhabutai, also from Maharashtra, Revarki from Lahore and Biba from Karnataka, also became important crowd-pulling names.

Like a seed falling in the crevice of a rock and slowly growing into a banyan tree, this novel went on gathering shape and dimension in my head for a couple of dozen years.

About fifteen years ago, as I was observing the demolition of a shanty town in Mumbai, I heard an old labourer singing a song as he sat resting under a tree. The Burmese words of the song sent a shiver down my spine. I found out that he was a circus artiste who belonged to Rakhumabai's outfit. Even more amazingly, he was one among those who had trekked hundreds of miles across the forbidden Burmese jungles after their circus had been bombed out in Rangoon. He took me to Telangana, where a few more of his colleagues from the circus were still alive. From their mouths, I heard stories of the murderous journey they had made across that unforgiving Himalayan terrain. Like an explorer opens a rusty trunk in an old mansion and gets besotted by the scent of the silken fabrics inside it, this subject now held me by the scruff of my neck.

In Kaagwad, Karnataka, I ran into two brothers, Shantappa and Annappa Pujari, who once owned The Great Karnataka Circus. One of them was then eighty-five years old. He rode eight kilometres over a jungle trail on his old Hero bicycle to meet me. In the good old days, their circus had been a household name. The Pujari brothers sat with me for hours and told me thrilling stories of their times. Then, there was Salim Bhai, a descendant of the owners of the celebrated G. A. Circus, who often accompanied me on my tours of Miraj, Mhaisal and the townships of Karnataka.

I met Suman in Khandesh. She had spent sixty years of her professional life with almost all of the reputed circuses of her time. I also met Shaili, whose husband was phenomenally gifted circus performer, on whom the character of Raghav is modelled. She showed me photographs of every one of his somersaults and the cartwheels he performed on horseback. This prototype of Raghav is just one among the dozen artistes I met, who made the spectators' eyes pop out and jaws drop with disbelief.

At Sangli, I gathered notes from a gentleman named Vibhute who had been an animal trainer with circuses for many years. In the villages of the hilly regions around Satara, I met male midwives who, in their time, helped with the parturition of many tigresses and lionesses, which mostly delivered four cubs at a time. It saddened me to think that these animal trainers and male midwives, who had roamed around half the world, were today counting their last days in anonymity.

A hundred years ago, the circuses of Maharashtra, like the Deval Circus, the Morey Circus, the Tarabai Circus as also the Royal Circus and the G. A. Circus of Bombay, and those of Kerala, like Kamala, Jumbo, Gemini and Rajkamal, had scaled unimaginable heights in body-building, agility and acrobatics. The Kamala Circus of Tellicheri in Kerala was the first circus in Asia to play in three rings. This one single circus alone possessed 105 elephants. It is a matter of deep regret that this great Indian art should have met its demise on account of misinformation, often mischievously spread.

About thirty years ago, news broke of a few animals dying of starvation in a circus or two. The friends of animals went to court. Some others leveraged their closeness with political leaders and brought in a law that prohibited the use of animals in circuses. The tradition of elephant breeding by ascetics and temple organisations, their upbringing for public festivals in places like Mysore had been going on for centuries. Court orders were passed in a hurry, and all these activities were brought to a close. The breeding and nurture of these animals in the urban areas were stopped.

People like the late Prime Minister Lal Bahadur Shastri and the great nationalist leader Subhas Chandra Bose possessed knowledge of this field sport and held it in high regard. There are plenty of photographs that show Indira Gandhi with her two small children, Rajiv and Sanjay, enjoying circus shows in Delhi and the Trans-Yamuna open spaces. Tragically, people who understood and cherished this sport are no longer around.

Many great men, starting from Emperor Ashoka to Chhatrapati Shivaji, have bred elephants and horses, as have the sadhus and sanyasis. Elephants were used in warfare with the same devastating effect as the bombs of today. These immensely powerful animals dashed against fortresses and brought them down. But while they were put to use, they were also loved and looked after. In those ancient times, extensive scientific study and research were conducted on the husbanding, breeding, nurturing and training of animals like elephants, camels, horses and bullocks that were used for war and for peaceful purposes. In the third century AD, a sage named Matang wrote a treatise titled *Gaja-Shastra* that deals with the science of nurturing elephants. Another sage named Shalihotra Muni researched and wrote on the rearing and training of horses. Our modern friends of animals do not know about these stables and nurseries of old times. They also do not realise that modern circuses, along with providing high-quality entertainment, also served as breeding centres for the big cats and other wild animals.

When Lal Bahadur Shastri was on the point of setting off for a tour of Tashkent (then part of the U.S.S.R., now the capital of Uzbekistan), a few members of the Indian Circus Federation went and met him. Shastri told them that he was well aware of the awe-inspiring shows of the circus and about the contribution of the valiant and skillful acrobats who often staked their lives in the performance of their acts. He told them that he was soon going to take some landmark decisions for the progress of the circus industry and requested them to wait till his return from Tashkent. Unfortunately for the circus industry, Shastri never returned. He died a mysterious death in Tashkent.

A dozen or so animals died accidentally in a certain circus, and a ban was imposed upon the use of animals in Indian circuses. As many as 177,000 people die in road accidents every year, which makes 485 deaths every day. Should that mean that vehicular traffic should be stopped on Indian roads?

Those magical circus nights have vanished from our lives. However, after being smitten by the lost glory of this magical art form for decades, I have tried to recreate in this novel the thrill and wonder of the circus that my generation enjoyed during its salad days. Kanchana, the extraordinarily heroic protagonist of my story, may be seen as an authentic composite of those champions of old—both men and women—who took this spectacular medium of recreation to dizzying heights.

Much of this story unspools in the impossibly difficult jungles that lie on the border of India and Burma. Writing this story has been a cathartic experience, a joy that only rarely falls to the lot of a novelist. I have presented to the readers the thrills of this great, awe-inspiring field sport, which was created with the coming together of extraordinary men and animals and died because of misdirected altruism.

1 April 2026 Vishwas Patil

A Note on the Photographs

I received many remarkable photographs of the circus world during the course of my research, generously shared by owners and performers of various circus companies. I owe my sincere gratitude to Shantappa and Basappa Pujari of Kagvad, Saleem Bhai of G. A. Circus of Bombay, Bhagwantrao Morey, the heir of Morey Circus, Mr Agashe and Mrs Suman for their invaluable support.

I am equally grateful to a few Indian officers who served in the British Indian Army during the Second World War for providing rare and significant material that has enriched my work.

Also, my special thanks to Mr Raj Deshmukh for his constant help and support.

Circus-women like Tarabai Shinde, Revaraki of Lahore, Biba, Chhabutai and Rakhumabai were national celebrities. Mounting tigers and putting their heads in their jaws were their favourite acts.

The Globe of Death

No yawn could be mightier

On a roll

The circus pavilion was irresistible for both the young and old.

Friends are never a burden

The next bullet could come from anywhere!

Even elephants found the violence of the water difficult to withstand.

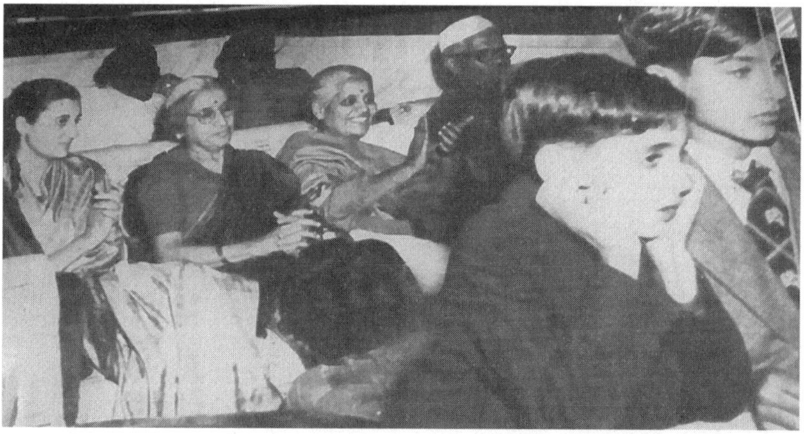

Indira Gandhi knew the educative and entertainment value of circuses. Seen here with her sons Rajiv Gandhi and Sanjay Gandhi.

Prime Minister Lal Bahadur Shastri with officials of the Circus Federation of India

Army unit preparing to cross the Dafa river

The jungles by the river were dark, dense and dangerous.

What jaws, those, to take the weight of a human body!

The weight of the plank alone would have flattened most people.

Performing acrobatics on a moving horse was a mind-boggling feat.

Agility? Skill? Dare-devilry? Or sheer madness?

Who is more supple,
the rope or the girl?

The pocket-sized hero

Butterflies on bikes

Indian circus owners